PRAISE FOR *Cookin*

"In *Cooking for Ghosts* Patricia V. Davis manages to combine an exuberant lust for the good things in life with an eerie sense of foreboding. This is an exceptional, uniquely gratifying novel. Make yourself something tasty to eat, put your feet up. You're going to be reading for a while.

—David Corbett, award-winning author of *The Mercy of the Night*

"Patricia V. Davis brings together four amazing women, on an equally amazing ship, and cooks up something magical and mystical, as well as something intrinsically human. *Cooking for Ghosts* is a reminder that all of us harbor secrets — friends, lovers, mothers — even iconic objects. Davis's characters entice us into their world, and the more we get to know them, the more we get to know ourselves. A delicious and perfectly spiced read."

—Vicki Larson, award-winning journalist and co-author of *The New I Do: Reshaping Marriage for Skeptics, Realists and Rebels.*

"*Sex and the City* meets *Julie and Julia* and *The Ghost and Mrs. Muir.* Very unique and fun read."

—Marsha Toy Engstrom, The Book Club Cheerleader

"Ghosts, romance, friendship, and food...what a great combination. From the very first page, I was drawn to the characters and their lives aboard the Queen. A bit of history, woven through a newly formed partnership, wrapped in mystery and intrigue. A wonderfully delightful story."

—Books or Books

"...Completely amazing."

—*RT Book Reviews*

"In this poignant yet joyful tale, Patricia V. Davis vibrantly illustrates the value of female friendships. Despite remarkably diverse backgrounds and experiences, the women of *Cooking for Ghosts* cultivate a deep and inspiring bond that serves to strengthen their lives."

—Shasta Nelson, author of *Frientimacy,* and founder of GirlFriendCircles.com

"...OMG — Patricia V. Davis is amazing! She brings painful, real-world issues to light through the words and actions of the women in her story. They become as real to us as the tragedies and triumphs of our own lives, cracking our hearts open to create our own internal transformation alongside them."

—Siobhan Neilland – Founder, OneMama.org & FightingForYourJoy.com

"...Complex, rich, and satisfying... Especially recommended for mystery enthusiasts looking for something different in the way of setting, feisty and strong female characters...and a story line brimming with revelations and intrigue that aren't easily predictable.

—*Midwest Book Review*

"Davis's patient hand at storytelling threads itself into a perfect and suspenseful character of its own in this wonderfully dark and moody tale brimming with beautiful juxtapositions: modern technology with old world tastes and scents, surface interactions with deep, ghostly otherworldliness, and the common narratives around women and friendships with the ethereal, the intuitive and the feminine."

—Amy Guth, President, Association for Women Journalists Chicago

"An exquisitely written story about four dynamic women who confront the ghosts from their past, with vivid imagery that shines a light on the majestic legacy of the RMS Queen Mary."

—Mary Rohrer, Executive Director, QMI Foundation

"Patricia V. Davis is a bright light in the San Francisco Bay Area literary scene, a person with talent and energy. An exciting voice in publishing, she is a writer to watch."

—Sam Barry, Author, contributing editor at the literary magazine *Zyzzyva*

COOKING FOR GHOSTS

THE SECRET SPICE CAFÉ

ISBN 13: 978-0-9899056-4-0

Published by HD Media Press Inc.

This is a work of fiction. Names, characters, places, dates, and incidents either are the product of the author's imagination or are used fictitiously. Any resemblance to actual persons, living or dead, business establishments, events, or locales is entirely coincidental.

PUBLISHER'S CATALOGING-IN-PUBLICATION DATA

Names: Davis, Patricia V. (Patricia Volonakis), 1956 – author. Title Cooking for ghosts by Patricia V. Davis. Description: New York : HD Media Press, [2016] | Series: The Secret Spice Café trilogy ; book I | Identifiers: ISBN: 978-0-9899056-4-0 (trade paperback) | 978-0-9899056-3-3 (hardback) | 978-0-9899056-5-7 (Kindle) | 978-0-9899056-6-4 (Nook) | 978-0-9899056-7-1 (iPad) Subjects: LCSH: Female friendship—Fiction. | Self-realization in women—Fiction. | Queen Mary (Steamship)—Fiction. | Ghosts—Fiction. | Restaurants—California—Long Beach—Fiction. | Cooking—Fiction. | Family secrets—Fiction. | Murder—Fiction. | Vendetta—Fiction. | Man-woman relationships—Fiction. | Redemption—Fiction. | LCGFT: Ghost stories. | Romance fiction. | Detective and mystery fiction. | BISAC: FICTION / Contemporary Women | FICTION / Visionary & Metaphysical | FICTION / Mystery & Detective / International Mystery & Crime Classification: LCC: PS3604.A97269 C66 2016 | DDC: 813/.6—dc23

Cover design and typeset by Tanya Quinlan
Interior design inspired by the *RMS Queen Mary*

Printed in the United States of America

COOKING FOR GHOSTS

BOOK ONE

THE SECRET SPICE CAFÉ

PATRICIA V. DAVIS

HD Media Press Inc.

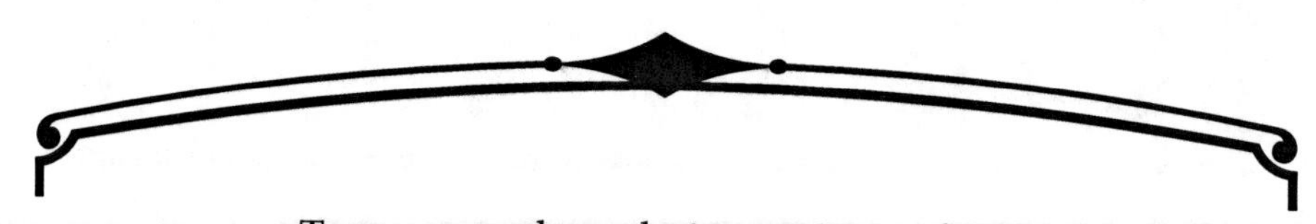

To every mother who's ever lost a child;
to all the children who never had the mother they deserved.

In memory of my beloved father-in-law, Jack,
who taught his sons to "Always do the right thing."

(Thank you for my husband, the only one of the four
who inherited your beautiful gray eyes.)

ACKNOWLEDGEMENTS

In order to get this book written, I had to ask a lot of questions. The questions were all over the board: "How does one obtain a concealed weapons permit?" "What lingo would a chef use to tell a line cook he's run out of shrimp?" "What type of wood are the decks on the *RMS Queen Mary*?" "How do you strangle someone?" To find the answers, I pestered a lot of people — food critics, historians, a judge, a six-foot-five martial arts master who works out at my gym. I also got to sit aboard the *Queen Mary*, drink wine in her fabulous Observation Bar, and chat with some charming ship aficionados. To those who shared their knowledge, sparked ideas, critiqued, or took the time to assist me in any way, I appreciate you so much, and want to thank you by name. With a list this long, I know someone will be left off inadvertently, either by me or by someone else in the editing process. If that happens, please tell me. There are two more books in this series, giving me two more chances to make it right.

Consultants: Mary Rohrer, James Brandmueller, David Allen, and other members of the QMI Foundation, Sam Barry, Eric C. Gladstone, Justin Oliver, Clark Marckwordt, Betty Tsamis, Nina Snyder, Joan Maragoudaki, Judge Rosemarie Montalbano, Bob "The King" Wubker, Captain Will Kane

Photographers, Filmmakers: Pyrat Wesly, Shaun Barnett, Lydia Selk, Nikos Volonakis, Parker Chittenden, Kenny Regan, Joe Bertoldo, the late Craig Anderson

All kinds of help and inspiration: Amber Burke, Maro Iacovou, Alexandra Roumbas Goldstein, Angela Parks, Audrey Kruger, Bruce Laker, Cynthia and Sarita Taylor (the real life ones!), Simona

Carini, Daryl Branson, Deborah Grabien, Johanna Felix and Rebecca Simmons at the *Queen Mary*, Doyneta Sillery, Kasey Corbit, Trish Clifford, Philip Ferris, Lee Goff, Lisa Vella, Douglass Christensen, Vin Zappacosta, Sharon Walling, My Awesome Work-in-Progress Readers, The Secret Spice Crew, Lynn Manizza, Sandra Collier, Kim Henry, Keishira Robison, James Robison, Vicki Larson, David Corbett, Siobhan Neilland, Amy Guth, Shasta Nelson, Jeff Rigby, Connie Breeze, Ava Boote, Aaron Selk, Peter Davis, Peter and Margaret Rollett, Maryann Maisano, Bill Russo, and *WindyCity Greek.*

Agent, Advisors and Publicity Team Rock Stars: Gordon Warnock, Jen Karsbaek, Laurie McLean at Fuse Literary, Kelly Preston, Jane Hunter

And a very special thank you to: The *Royal Mail Ship Queen Mary*

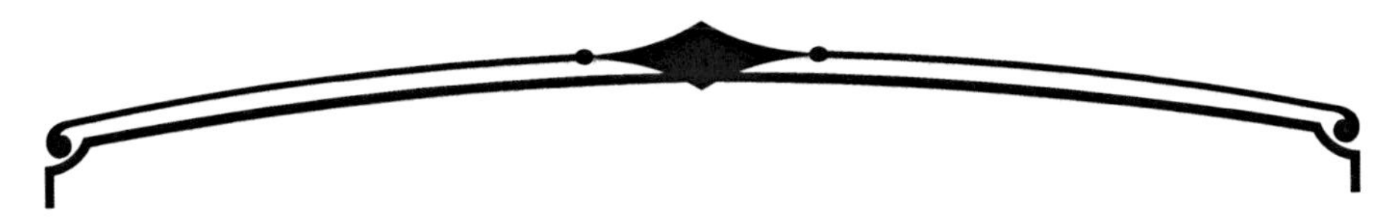

Perhaps if Death is kind, and there can be returning,
We will come back to earth some fragrant night...
We will come down at night to these resounding beaches
And the long gentle thunder of the sea...

— from "If Death is Kind" by Sara Teasdale

"She breathed. She had character... She was, above all else, the nearest ship ever to a living being."

— Captain John Treasure Jones, the last Captain of the *RMS Queen Mary*

PROLOGUE

Somewhere in the Atlantic, 1949

In an ocean as dark and still as death, the Queen floated. The scythe-shaped moon engulfed in mist gave off only a dank tinge of light. Waves skimmed lazily along the Queen's sides, like the careless caress of an indifferent lover. She was only fifteen years old, but she'd already witnessed so much misery: war, love lost to tragedy, and once, a vile murder that had left a stain on her no sea she traveled had ever washed away.

Now she was about to witness another. The killer's rage was silent and patient. And yet, she could feel it. In desperation, the Queen willed her fog horn to blow...

Under the cover of the dimly lit stairwell on the deserted sports deck, the sailor waited. He'd timed it well. The watch wouldn't make his rounds up here until after it was over.

Long before he could see his prey, he heard the click of her heels on the planked wood, echoing off the water as she approached. He pressed himself back further into the darkness as she came into view, her eyes focused on what he'd stolen to lure her, carefully placed so that it would be visible to her while he remained hidden. As she bent to pick it up, he stepped swiftly behind her and clamped his forearm around her throat, cutting off her scream and her breath as he pulled her into the shadows.

She felt her windpipe close up and the blood rush to her head. She couldn't twist around to face him, but — *oh, God* — she knew who he was. How ironic. In a life as mousy as the color of her hair, the one impetuous thing she'd dared do, would end her. As dreary as her life had been, she didn't want it to be over.

So she struggled. She dug her nails into Death's rigid forearm and clawed at the skin on his elbow. But he only swore at the blood she'd managed to draw and kept that arm hooked resolutely under her chin, dangling her legs up off the deck, pressing even tighter against her throat as she kicked. He shook her and she felt the cool night air hit the sole of her foot as one of her shoes fell off. The thump it made against the deck startled him. He lost his vice hold on her for an instant and she tried again to scream. He slammed his other hand across her nose and mouth. With a rush of stinging pain, the salty iron taste of blood filled her mouth, mingled with the smell of his familiar aftershave. Who'd have thought Death would come wearing Old Spice? He'd groomed himself as carefully for her murder as he once had for her seduction. She went queasy with the realization that his arms were not the only part of his body that felt rigid against her.

But mere seconds later, she was too lightheaded to feel disgust or even fear. She now lay in his arms, compliant, his hand still pressed against her bloodied mouth and nose. Her head was tipped back as he continued to suffocate her and she could see the night sky, a depthless backdrop for the stars that flickered through the gauzy veil of ocean fog. And the moon looked like a grin. Lovers walking the decks below must think it all so romantic. Dimly, she could hear the band playing in the ballroom. She was amazed she could even recognize the tune — a new one, just come out that year:

"Some enchanted evening, you may meet a stranger..."

Her final act was to pray that he wouldn't dump her before she was truly dead. As cruel as his arms were, at least they were warm. She didn't want the ice cold water to be the last thing she felt.

The crewman making his rounds looked at his watch. He was ten minutes early, and strangely enough, so was the ship's horn. He looked out over the water. Misty, but not too thick. Not because of fog, then. He made a mental note that the timer might have to be adjusted. No sooner did he have the thought than the whistle sounded again, low and long and...inconsolable, he thought fancifully. "*Mary*'s larynx," was built to emit a note so powerful she could be heard at least ten miles away. For a reason he couldn't fathom, a sound he heard repeatedly every day and every night was giving him the shivers. He sensed a movement to his left at the far end of the deck and turned. *Whoo-ee.* A couple was clenched together in what looked to be one steamy embrace. She was so wrapped up in him she'd lost one of her shoes. They were too shadowed for him to see their faces, but he could make out that the man was wearing the uniform of a fellow crewman. Uh-oh. Trouble there. It was against the rules to consort with guests.

But it was none of his business. He'd walk down on the other side and give them another ten minutes. If the crewman had any smarts, he'd be out of there with his dolly bird before then. The watchmanturned again, back the way he'd come.

The whistle sounded again.

Yep, that would definitely have to be checked.

The sailor remained motionless as the crew member on watch walked away. That had been too close. The lucky bastard. Good thing he'd decided to keep his nose out, or else he'd have found himself with a slit throat, and there'd be two bodies to get rid of. He needed to be quick, before the asshole came back. Looking down into the dead eyes of the women he held, he spoke gently to her, as though they were still lovers. "Now you know. Nobody walks away from me."

Moving closer to the rail, he took a swift look around, then flopped her over the side. She slipped under the water with scarcely a splash, and the churning of the ship's motors did the rest, pushing her almost immediately out of sight.

That should make the fish happy, he thought.

But her shoe was still on deck. He picked it up and was about to throw it after her when he thought he heard the watch return. *Fuck.* Unnerved again, he slipped back behind the steps where he'd hidden while waiting for his victim, and tossed the shoe into a vent unit. No one would find it there. But even if they did, he'd be long gone. The ship docked in the morning, and he planned to slip away before anyone could get nosy about the gouges on his arm. He stayed where he was, listening, forcing his breathing to slow.

False alarm. He came out from behind the steps and, with studied casualness, headed back to his quarters.

Not a moment too soon. The watchman had circled around a second time, and was relieved to see that his fellow crewman and the girl he'd been with were gone. Now he could call it a night. He frowned as an overhead lantern flickered on and off.

Then a second one.

Then a third.

What in hell was going on with the *Mary*? Probably a short. Walking up to investigate, he noticed that lying on the deck directly beneath those lanterns, one second in shadow, one second illuminated in a sphere of light, was a doll.

A Raggedy Ann doll.

He bent to retrieve it, then thought better of it. Whatever family it belonged to would probably remember where they'd been and come looking for it. He left it there.

The lights continued to flicker as he walked on.

PART I: THE WOMEN ARRIVE

A Chemist, a Cocktail Waitress, a Widow, and a Witch

CHAPTER ONE

Long Beach, California, Sunday, August 1, 2004

Of the four women traveling in the snappy red Porsche on Interstate 710 toward the *Queen Mary*, only one of them was openly skeptical, and that was Jane. The other two passengers, the ones reserving judgment, were Angela and Rohini. The fourth chatted vigorously as she drove too far above the speed limit for the comfort of the other three, and that was Cynthia.

"You will *love* it. I promise you," she was saying.

"Cynthia, are we driving a getaway car?" snapped Jane. The top on the car was down and there was so much wind blowing about that she had to raise her voice to be heard. Added to that irritation, she felt cramped in the tiny back seat, her knees forced nearly to her chest. Good lord. She'd been mad to agree to this — to open a restaurant, sight unseen — with one woman who she knew very well had some serious issues, and with two others who, up until an hour ago, she'd only ever communicated with over the internet.

She blamed Oprah. And that bloody *More* magazine that touted "actualization" to women over forty. And blogging on websites that "empowered women" and fuck all else she'd been hammering at like a neurotic woodpecker to keep herself from falling completely to pieces these past two years.

Seriously, what had she been thinking? She was *forty-six*. She should go back to England, back to Newcastle where she belonged, back to her lab at the university and her pupils. If she had any sense, her middle-aged spread would be the only thing she'd be working hard at now, preferably with M&Ms. Absolute stacks of M&Ms.

When Angela had told her what she was going to do and then suggested she join in, Jane thought she was taking the mickey. But as she listened to Angela talk with more excitement than she had since university, Jane found herself factoring in the excruciating wretchedness of her own life these past two years, and Angela's idea began to transform from something preposterous into a genuine possibility for a fresh start. The next the thing she knew, she was taking an extended leave and heading to New York to pick up Angela, who'd already sold her house and the bakery — everything, in fact, that she'd shared with Marco — and was waiting fretfully for Jane so they could hotfoot it to California.

Now here she was, sitting squashed against Rohini, one of the two she barely knew, in the minuscule back seat of a humiliating sports car belonging to the other woman she barely knew — Speed Racer in peri-menopause, apparently — who'd just finished telling them that they were way over budget. And who would pay for that, then?

They were out of their minds, the lot of them.

Rohini was the first to point out the conspicuous, albeit in the tranquil manner they were all coming to recognize was her usual way. "But Cynthia dear, that's fifty thousand dollars more than we'd agreed," she said as she struggled to keep her long black hair from blowing in both her own face and Jane's. "That's rather a lot of money."

Jane snorted. An underestimation if there ever was one.

Cynthia looked in the rear-view mirror at Rohini and waved a hand, airily. "I'm good for it. You know I am." Then she swore in Portuguese, as the little car swerved.

That was it. This ride, this conversation, was making Jane ill.

"Will you bloody well *please* keep both hands on the wheel and slow down?"

Angela glanced behind her from the passenger seat and exchanged an uneasy look with Rohini. This was not at all the propitious start to their partnership they'd been hoping for. "Um... let's go over this again," she said to Cynthia. "Exactly why did we need to spend the extra money, and how will this affect the payback schedule we'd agreed upon? Because I'm not sure we're willing to make any changes to our contracts at this point."

There. She'd gone for her best take-charge tone and thought it came across reasonably well, considering that she couldn't seem to prevent her right hand from making a grab for the dashboard every time Cynthia careened into a turn. And that in between she'd been biting her nails again, a habit she'd thought she had beat.

"Oh, no, no. No — this is my gift. Not to worry," Cynthia assured them with a smile. Of course, she kept it to herself that the money was not actually hers to give. But a successful businesswoman had a certain image to maintain. She'd pay it all back. Somehow.

They were almost to the docks when the argument was cut off by Rohini's exclamation as three massive, orange-red smokestacks with their distinctive black trim became visible in the distance.

"Look — there she is! Oh, she's beautiful!" She gazed at the *Mary* as though it were calling her name.

"Oh. My. God. Jane, can you believe it? We made it! We're here." Angela all but stood through the open roof to get a better view.

From the rearview mirror, Cynthia caught the expression on Jane's face at her first glimpse of the majestic ship, and allowed herself a tiny smile of satisfaction. Saved by the *Queen*.

Not quite. As eager as Jane was for her first in-the-flesh look at her new home, she was not to be deterred. "I am worried, Cynthia, actually," she continued where they left off, even as her eyes stayed fixed on the historical ship. It had been built in the late 1930s as "the world's most luxurious ocean liner," then converted into a warship during WWII, then back into a cruise ship again. But by the mid-sixties, she was considered past her prime, and was subsequently sold to Long Beach to be docked there permanently as a floating hotel and museum. Jane felt her chest constrict as she thought of how much Antoni and Gabriella would have loved to see it. She sucked in a breath as the car drew closer. Oh, how bittersweet it was to feel the moist, cool air of the ocean again.

Shaking that off, she went on resolutely, "We'd agreed to an equal ownership of twenty-five percent each. The fact that we've all borrowed that startup money from you does not mean that *you* can dictate these decisions unilaterally —"

"Would you have this restaurant without me?" Cynthia ripped through Jane's lecture as she used her card key pass to release the electronic gate and then pulled into the parking lot for the *Queen Mary*. "Could you have gotten that much money from a bank, with no credit rating and no collateral?"

Right after she'd spit that out, she regretted it. Now Rohini and Angela were wearing twin expressions of distress, and Jane looked so outraged that they'd be wiping pieces of her spleen off the leather upholstery any minute.

"As it happens, Cynthia," she huffed, "I *can* get the money from a bank, and it's not too late for me to do so!"

"Well, I can't," Rohini blurted, hoping to avert disaster. "I came to America with just my spices and some clothing. I even sold my wedding ring."

"Me neither," added Angela, biting her nails again. "They don't make widows' pensions like they used to."

There was silence in the car after Cynthia settled into a parking space and cut the engine. She wanted to cut her tongue out too. Shit, shit, shit. *When* would she learn to keep her mouth shut and just let Jane vent? Now, because she couldn't resist a cheap shot, she'd probably ruined everything.

Hoping to make amends, she took a deep breath and turned around to face Jane. "I'm sorry. You're right — we're equal partners. I overstepped, okay? As I was trying to tell you, the opportunity came up to get Tony Chi. I promise you, once it's out that he was involved, we'll make up whatever it cost and then some. Wait until you see how beautiful and functional our restaurant is. And I meant what I said — it's my gift. To us. To our dream." Her tone became even more cajoling as she looked at each of them. "Please. I know what I'm doing. I've been in this business for years. Trust me. Okay?"

Jane still looked mutinous.

Nossa! thought Cynthia. It's like she knows I'm lying. But how?

Rohini and Angela exchanged another anxious glance.

Then Jane said, "*Fine.* I won't say another word until we see what you've done. Now will you let us out? My legs have gone numb. When you said you'd pick us up at the airport you didn't say it would be in a clown car. 'Four-seater' — what absolute rubbish. That's all any of us needs is to get stroke from a blood clot."

No, not a propitious beginning at all.

But Cynthia's three business partners were soon appeased. Up close, the *Queen* was an even more stately and elegant masterpiece than she'd looked in the photos Cynthia had sent to each of them. And the redesign of the dated and dusty restaurant on her Promenade Deck was...

"Wow," said Rohini. She stopped so suddenly that Jane nearly ran into her back.

Angela put out a hand to steady herself. "Oh. My. God," she said again, her New York roots evident in that favored exclamation.

But Jane said nothing. She was too stunned. Cynthia, whom she'd begun to suspect was a bit of snake oil salesman, had created a small miracle.

The L-shaped space was completely transformed. While maintaining the art deco flair and the planked gleaming wood flooring that was characteristic of the ship's original motif, there was a contemporary airiness about the dining room and the layout now. The traditional and the innovative were harmonized by the woven-fabric seating and unique oiled-bronze lighting fixtures. The dark paneling had been removed and the fresh paint covering the walls looked like thick, rich cream. The soft color seemed dappled with hints of saffron where touched by the sunlight coming in from the wide, expansive row of windows. They offered a sweeping view of the Pacific Ocean from the dock where the *RMS Queen Mary* had remained moored since 1969.

Madness indeed, thought Jane once again, as she looked over the gloriousness of that insanity, right there in front of her, spelled out in persimmon-colored letters on the nostalgic, nouveau-style signs near the two entryways, one that led out to the deck and one leading out to the main lounge. She recalled how the four of them had deliberated over the name in endless, exuberant emails that had zigzagged from Newcastle to New York to Las Vegas to Mumbai. And now, all that planning, all those life changes for all of them, were over. And The Secret Spice Café was a reality. Hers to share with three other women who would from now on be a very big part of her world.

Jane intended to make the best of that, starting right then. They were watching her apprehensively. And why wouldn't they be? Her behavior had been piggish. Well, she'd made a mess of everything else in her life, but she'd be damned if she was going to muck this up as well.

"Marvelous," she pronounced. "Absolutely marvelous." She looked at Cynthia and said sincerely, "Well done."

Angela and Rohini breathed a joint sigh of relief, and Cynthia beamed at Jane the same way her first-year chemistry pupils did when she complimented them on their work. "Wait until you see our office. And our staterooms and the rest of the ship! Everything's been upgraded and it's all fantastic."

"And the kitchen? What about the kitchen?" asked Rohini, all but bouncing in her shoes. It was the first time the others had seen her so animated.

"Ah. Well, the galley has all been remodeled, but there's something going on with the back scullery. It's puzzling. We've been trying to remove an old freezer, but it's like the damn thing's been fused to the wall. The other day, one of the crew —"

As she was about to elaborate, a striking teenage girl walked into the dining room from the door to what might have been the office Cynthia had mentioned. "Ah, *filhinha,* there you are." Cynthia opened her arms and smiled.

"*Mamãe,* the concierge just phoned to say the bags have been delivered from the airport. I told them to send them on to the ladies' staterooms, like you said." She walked into Cynthia's arms and looked at Rohini, Angela and Jane with interest.

"Everyone, this is my daughter, Sarita. She's been looking forward to meeting you all. She's heard a lot about you, as you can imagine. And of course, you've all heard a lot about her."

Sarita laughed. "I'll just bet they have, *Mãe.* Let's hope at least some of it was good. Hello. Nice to meet you," she said, coolly composed despite her mother's blustering protest at her remark. When she smiled, her resemblance to Cynthia was unmistakable.

Jane hated herself for feeling a pang of envy. "Nice to meet you, Sarita. Your mum's had nothing but good things to say, I assure you. How are you finding California so far?"

"I like it a lot. It's been fun watching the progress on the restaurant. And it beats the weather in Vegas at this time of year."

"Lovely," smiled Jane and hated herself a second time for the stiffness she could feel in her face. Hoping to hell no one had noticed, she added, "Well, then, I shall head up to my room. I should like to get my things unpacked, maybe have a lie-down."

"Good idea," said Angela. "I can feel jet lag starting to hit, myself." She beamed at them all. "Besides, I can't wait to see if our cabins are as gorgeous as the rest of this place. This is just so exciting."

Rohini said, "I'm not at all sleepy, but I'll come along, just to check that my spices made it safely." She rubbed her palms together. "And then I want to get a look at that kitchen."

Sarita looked at her, her tone polite, but skeptical. "There are spices in the bags they just brought over?"

Studying her keenly, Rohini nodded. "Not in all of them, but in my bag, yes. I only brought the one."

"But, aren't you the one who flew in from India?" She glanced at her mother, then back to Rohini. "Um…I'm pretty sure those bags went through customs. I don't think they allow you to bring in food."

Rohini grinned impishly. She was already getting the sense that this was one unusual teenager. "Don't worry, darling. Spices aren't food. They're just…spices."

Before Sarita could reply to that, Cynthia asked her, "Where's the new bus boy?" She started shouting in Spanish. "Esteban? Esteban! Where are you? I need you to take the *señoras* upstairs!"

Sarita rolled her eyes. "His name's Emilio, *Mãe*."

At Cynthia's shout, a handsome, dark-haired boy in his teens came out. New as he might have been, he was already used to being called by someone else's name.

"Should I go with them?" Sarita looked at Cynthia hopefully.

Cynthia shook her head. "Esteban can manage on his own. You and I have some important things to finish up this afternoon. Come with me." She crooked her finger at her daughter, then teetered hastily toward the office on her four-inch heels. Looking disappointed, Sarita followed behind.

As the three other women tailed Emilio as he directed them up to a richly-carpeted corridor that smelled of beeswax and brass polish, Angela whispered to Jane, "I didn't know Cynthia could speak Spanish as well as Portuguese, did you?"

Jane sniffed her disapproval. "I'm more impressed that she can walk in those shoes."

Cynthia closed the door to the office and then put her ear to it to be sure that everyone had left the adjacent dining room. She turned to Sarita. "Okay, tell me."

"Tell you what?" Was it Cynthia's imagination, or did Sarita look just a little guilty?

"What do you think I'm talking about, *filhinha*? Did he call?"

"Oh! I'm sorry, *Mãe*. I was thinking about something else. Yes, he called. Well, someone from his office did." Sarita looked at her mother with sympathy. "He's coming. Just as you expected."

"Did they say anything about the money?"

"Come on, *Mãe*. Don't be silly. It was probably just his office manager or secretary. How would they know anything about it?"

Cynthia stared at her. "Did they at least tell you when he would get here?"

Sarita nodded. "Not until late October. He's still away on business and can't make it before then."

Cynthia sank into one of the new leather desk chairs. She said nothing as she absorbed this information.

At length, she spoke. "Well. We knew this was coming. But at least we still have a few months to make this whole thing work."

Silently, Sarita walked to her mother, leaned down and hugged her.

They'd had the option of renting living space in Long Beach, but the four were unanimous in their desire to experience staying aboard "the greatest ocean liner to have ever graced the seas." One look at their staterooms was all it took to know they'd made the right choice. A step into them was a step back in time, as luxurious as the rest of what they'd seen of the *Mary* so far.

Smooth, lustrous panels of inlaid wood in shades of oak and mahogany adorned the walls. In homage to the era of the ship's heyday, much of the framed hanging artwork was original Art Deco, as were the wardrobes and cabinetry which offered plenty of storage space along with their beauty. There were no right angles on the ship, it being bowed in the middle, so all the furniture for the cabins was custom-made from woods forested from different parts of the world and equally as sumptuous as what was on the walls. The counters, desk and table top made of black speckled marble were shined to a luster, as were the brass-rimmed and glass portholes which looked out to the periwinkle blue of the water.

A number of the old appointments were left intact for historical illustration, such as the cabin call boxes and the "saltwater" versus "freshwater" taps in the bath, there since the days when saltwater baths were considered therapeutic. But the old world was nicely balanced with modern amenities. There was a flat screen TV, a small fridge and icemaker, a wine cooler, a state-of-the-art microwave and coffee maker. The bed, with its goose down comforter and pillows, along with Egyptian cotton sheets, was the size of a lake.

For the moment, Jane barely glanced at any of it. In fact, she'd only just managed to get inside her door before she started to cry.

And that was going to be a problem. She knew from experience that once she got started doing that, it would take her a long time to quit. Her eyes, being so light, would go bloodshot, and with her fair English skin, that meant a red nose and splotches on her face for hours afterward. She did not want to go down to dinner — her first face-to-face meal with her new business partners — reddened and splotched. They'd know she'd been crying. Well, at least Angela would know. The others might assume she'd been drinking. Her people had that reputation abroad, unfortunately, and she most certainly did not want to do anything to perpetuate that myth. But whether they believed she was drunk or guessed she'd been crying, she'd be mortified either way.

She sat down on the bed and took a few deep breaths. She had to make herself stop. She couldn't think what might have set her off this time. Maybe it was that "Mr. Toad's Wild Ride," and the way she'd barked at Cynthia during it, when it was clear now that the poor woman was just as anxious as any of them about all this. Or maybe it was being blindsided by how much Sarita reminded her of Gabriella. Not in looks, but in manner.

Gabriella had been precocious for her age too. And quick to jump in with a cheeky comment in front of strangers, one that would embarrass her mother, just as Sarita had embarrassed Cynthia with her remark this afternoon. Gabriella had been that independent, even at seven years old. And when Jane had seen Sarita walk into that room today and speak to them all with such aplomb, instead of shuffling her toes or looking bored, as Jane would have done at that age, she couldn't prevent herself from thinking that this was how Gabriella would have been, had she lived.

She gulped back sobs. *Damn it to hell.* She'd promised herself she wouldn't do this again. She bit the inside of her cheek, pulled repeatedly at the blonde bangs of her pixie-cropped hair, hoping the irritations would distract her from her wretchedness. But all she managed to do was make her mouth sore and her forehead pinch. And the tears kept coming.

"Hello."

Jane yelped and jumped so high she nearly fell off the bed. She swung around. Standing behind her was a little girl, no more than five years old. She was barefoot and wearing a nightgown.

"Good heavens! Where did you come from?" Jane glanced toward the cabin door and saw that it was open. "I thought I'd closed that. You scared me to death." Jane was wiping at her eyes with one hand, while she held the other over her drumming heart. *God.*

Well, at least fright worked just as well to stop tears as it did hiccups, evidently.

"I'm looking for Missy Doll."

Well, listen to that. This one spoke the Queen's English as well as the Queen herself. Her hair was the color of strawberries in sunlight, and Jane caught a whiff of what might have been lavender shampoo.

Jane gave the room a cursory glance. "Sweetie, you won't find any dolls in here." She pulled a tissue from the box on the end table near the bed and blew her nose, swearing at herself under her breath when she noticed there was mascara on her fingertips. She'd have to repair her makeup as well. And now, on top of all else, there was this child to sort out. "You'd best get back to your family before you're missed."

The little girl didn't answer. She just stared at Jane. Then she asked, "Why were you crying?"

Well. This was getting uncomfortable. And as was usual when Jane felt uncomfortable, she resorted to snippiness. "That's my business, now, isn't it?" she said. "Shame on you for running around the halls in your nightie and barging into strangers' rooms. It's dangerous."

"I know. But I can't remember where I'm supposed to go."

Poor little mite sounded so dejected that Jane relented. "Well, all right, then — not to worry. I'll just make a call to the concierge and we'll find out. I'm sure your family is looking for you. What's your name?"

The little girl just kept looking intently at her. A rather peculiar child, evidently. "You sound like my Missy Doll," she finally said.

"Little one, what's your name?" asked Jane again, even more kindly this time. "I can't get you back to your family unless I know."

Just then, her cell phone began ringing from inside her handbag. She turned to reach for it and had to rummage around to find the phone while it shrilled. "Damn." Then, "Hello?"

"Jane, are you coming down?"

The line was filled with static. They'd been warned about that. The metal of the ship sometimes caused the service to be a bit dodgy, but she could make out that the voice on the other end was Angela's. They'd said two hours. Had that much time passed already? She hadn't even unpacked.

"I'll be down shortly. I've run into a spot of bother — oh!" She'd turned as she was speaking to look back at the little girl.

But she was gone. And the door to Jane's cabin was now closed. Jane hurried to it and pulled it open. The corridor was empty save for some soiled room service dishes and trays left on the carpet outside several of the stateroom doors. But she could still smell lavender.

"Jane — are you there? What's going on?" Angela's voice came through the phone again.

Jane sighed. "Nothing at all. I'll be down soon."

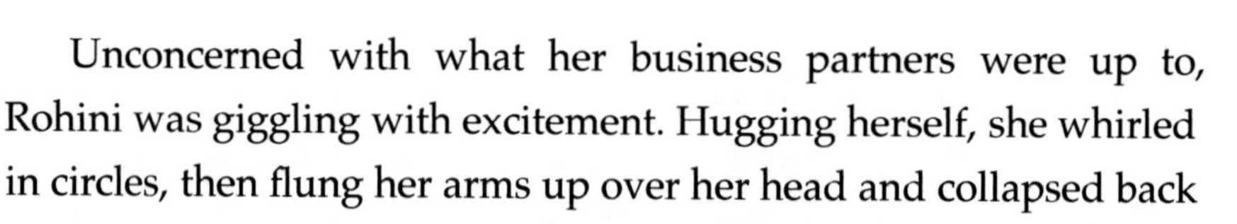

Unconcerned with what her business partners were up to, Rohini was giggling with excitement. Hugging herself, she whirled in circles, then flung her arms up over her head and collapsed back in dizzy elation onto the enormous bed in the glorious stateroom. *Everything* was glorious. She was here. This was her room. The Secret Spice was, in part, her restaurant.

Hers.

And when she'd first seen the *Queen* from the back seat of Cynthia's preposterous little car, she knew she was headed to exactly where she should be. She couldn't stop smiling, until, abruptly, a lump formed in her throat and her eyes misted with tears.

"I made it, Zahir," she whispered. "I made it."

She sobered as she thought of him, of all he'd done for her, and all that she might still need to do on her own.

But that wasn't for today. Today was for celebration and thankfulness. Getting up from the bed, she opened her case, pulled out all the little plastic sacks of spices and herbs she'd packed, and sighed with relief. Not a one had opened or torn. Even so, she could smell their pungent bouquet right through the protective wrappings. *Rauvolfia Serpentina, Jaiphal, Javitri, Khus Khus, Ashwagandha* and more — why did cinnamon always smell the strongest? There were dozens of varieties that she'd stuffed inside shirt sleeves and trouser legs and white cotton gym socks, just like a drug dealer might hide a stash. The TSA had missed them completely. They'd even affixed a sticker to the top of her bag: "Checked by Homeland Security."

Giggling again at that, Rohini placed all the smaller sacks into a large white bag she'd found in the wardrobe. The bag had a price list for various laundry services printed on it. With that mission accomplished, she took her treasures downstairs to the kitchen.

But she wasn't two steps in before she stopped stock still and remained right where she was, listening.

"Oh, my," she murmured to herself. "Oh, my, my, my."

Now she understood why she'd felt that the ship had summoned her.

To anyone else who might peek in, the kitchen appeared silent and empty. But not to Rohini. She could hear the walls sighing.

Gradually, she walked further inside, and the sighs turned to whispers. She stood still, breathing cautiously, waiting, watching.

In unison, the stainless steel cooking utensils dangling from the long, narrow cylinders that were screwed to the walls began to sway, soundlessly. The copper pots that hung from the ceiling over the two spanking-new ovens and eight burner stoves began to twirl, gracefully. Every inanimate object in the room that wasn't bolted down was waltzing eerily, on its own. To Rohini, the dance seemed sad rather than ghoulish.

Walking quietly, listening carefully, she followed the hushed sounds as they moved along the walls, leading her back to the scullery. As she approached, an ancient, enormous, floor-to-ceiling freezer blew out a puff of ice cold air as its door swung wide open as though it were greeting her, then gently clicked closed again.

Unafraid, Rohini observed it all. Still clinging to the laundry bag filled with her precious sacks of spice, she turned in a full circle, leisurely, so as not to miss any of it. After a while, she set the bag down on one of the gleaming stainless steel work tables. Bending into a full and formal curtsy, she spoke aloud.

"It is my great honor to meet you, Your Majesty."

CHAPTER TWO

Two Weeks Later

Angela had a splitting headache. Even the delicious coffee Rohini had brewed wasn't helping it, as it was caused by the endless bickering between Cynthia and Jane. Although they'd reached an accord over the more costly yet gorgeous restaurant design — Rohini had dubbed it their "dining room détente" — they continued to disagree about most everything else. This time it was over a potential employee.

"A *felon*? You want us to hire a felon?"

All four of them were at their desks in the spacious office. Though replicas in style, the desks were unique to each woman in every other way, testaments to who they were.

Rohini's desk was Spartan. A leafy, flowering plant in a bright green ceramic pot — green for hope and luck, she'd told them — was her only embellishment. She had a pen and a neat pile of pages set in front of her. One page listed the contact information of potential kitchen help, such as line cooks, busboys and dishwashers, and the second listed the names of wait staff whom Cynthia had already hired. A third held ideas for entrées she planned to suggest, and the fourth was the résumé of the man under discussion, a chef.

In contrast, Angela's desktop held haphazard piles of cookbooks and plastic accordion folders crammed with recipes she'd accumulated from when she'd owned the bakery: favorites she knew by heart, new ones she hoped to test, sugar-free ones for the diabetic or the weight-watcher, and whatever others she'd deemed essential to hoard. Strewn in front of her, on several sheets of waxed paper, were more than a dozen blocks of baking chocolate — samples sent by suppliers from which she was trying to choose. Near them, next to an open packet of Wrigley's spearmint gum, was a dog-eared paperback with the title, *Self Matters: Creating Your Life from the Inside Out*, by Dr. Phil McGraw. The book was open to the middle and splayed face down, much to the likely vexation of its spine, which, to add insult to injury, was now not only cracked, but stained with organic dark chocolate.

Jane and Cynthia's desks each held spreadsheets, an electric calculator, a computer, restaurant supply catalogues, and other items necessary for handling the minutiae of running the restaurant, a responsibility they shared. But while Cynthia's desk would be considered orderly, Jane's desktop organization was so rigorous with color-codes, labels, and alphabetizing, it looked menacing.

And to those with a discerning eye, it was intriguing that Cynthia was the only one of the four who had a photograph of a family member sitting on her desk. It was of Sarita, taken at a park when she was four years old, eating a vanilla ice cream cone and clutching the string of a yellow balloon.

Now Jane sat at that meticulous work station — or battle station, as it were — with her foot tapping and her arms crossed against her chest, while Cynthia stood behind her desk, leaning across it with her hands pressed palms down against the desktop.

Combat positions for both.

"Not 'hire' a felon, Jane. Let him have his job back. The chef who worked in the restaurant that was here before ours did a damn good job, by all accounts. We need a damn good chef. And he hasn't been a felon for ten years. He served his time a long time ago."

"Yes, for murder," shot back Jane.

"Manslaughter, Jane. There's a big difference."

"Oh, well, my mistake, Cynthia. I hope someone explained that to the corpse of the man he killed."

"Oh for godssakes, Jane. You're so unbelievably judgmental."

But even while Cynthia held steadfast in her crusade for the cook, there were gray shadows smudged under her eyes and she sounded as weary as Angela felt.

This was getting out of hand, Angela thought, before she cut in.

"Okay, you know what? Time out." She looked at Jane steadily. "Jane, didn't we all agree that Cynthia would be in charge of the hiring?"

Jane gaped at Angela. She hadn't expected her to take Cynthia's side on this. "But surely…I mean…a murderer, Angela? Truly?"

"He told me what happened when I interviewed him. People — even good people — commit crimes for many reasons," Cynthia argued, her frustration evident in every word. Angela knew what was eating Jane today, but something had been gnawing at Cynthia for several days now too. She'd always been energetic, but lately, she was a whirlwind.

Angela opened her mouth to say something again, just as Jane swung around and glared at Rohini. "You're the one who's going to be supervising him. Haven't you got anything to say about this?"

"In fact, I do." Serenely unaffected by the escalating tensions, Rohini put down the résumé she'd been reading while the other women argued. "Cynthia is quite right. The man has impressive credentials. And if he worked on the ship for three years without incident, I see no reason not to hire him."

Jane was floored. If they were honest, Cynthia and Angela were equally taken aback. Apart from one eccentric and wholly unyielding insistence that there be no further renovations to the scullery, Rohini had sidestepped any decisions concerning the running of the restaurant with a blithe, "Whatever you three want. I don't care."

Now here she was, marching straight into the fray on behalf of a chef she'd never met, who'd done time for allegedly beating a man to death.

Jane stood up furiously. With jaw clenched and shoulders ramrod stiff, she slammed shut the ledger she had open on her desk, and switched off her calculator. "I'm done in here for today. But I'll say this — if anything happens, it's on your heads." And with that, she stalked out.

Cynthia picked up her coffee cup and muttered something unintelligible and probably not very flattering in Portuguese. "What's got her panties in a twist today — can someone tell me?"

Angela wanted to ask Cynthia the same question, but once again, Rohini smoothly stepped in. "Well, as today is the two-year anniversary of her daughter's death, I would imagine that might have something to do with it."

Cynthia choked on her coffee, then spilled what was left of it all over her desk when she dropped her cup. "What? What did you just say?"

Angela looked at Rohini with surprise. "I can't believe she told you. She hates to talk about it."

Rohini's tone was evasive. "I only learned of it recently. I don't know the details."

"*Santa Maria!* Why didn't either one of you tell me this? Oh, no. That poor woman. And to think I've been such a bitch to her all morning. Oh, no, no, *no*. Oh, this is terrible. What *happened*?"

Rohini jumped up. "Cynthia, your blouse! What are you doing? It'll be ruined." As Cynthia peppered them with questions, she'd unbuttoned her pricey silk blouse, pulled it off, and was now using it to frantically blot up coffee from the papers on her desk. Rohini snatched some paper towels from the kitchenette setup against the far wall and brought them over to Cynthia.

Angela sighed. No avoiding it now. "Gabriella drowned when she was on a fishing trip in Italy with her father." She hesitated. "She was my niece. Jane is married to my brother."

"She's married? She never said. To your brother? You never said." Cynthia was almost in tears now, standing at her desk in her bra, her fist clenched to her heart, as Rohini helped her clean up the mess.

Angela bit her cuticle as she looked at the other two women. Who was she kidding? She hated talking about this just as much as Jane did. It always made people uncomfortable to hear about someone else's misfortune. Maybe it would help if she eased into it. "Jane and I met as roommates in college. In Rome. We were both there for one semester, in the spring."

Her eyes warmed for a moment, as she reminisced. "I haven't been very many places, but I'd bet that there just can't be any place in the world like Rome in the spring. It's just like in the movies."

"A Roman holiday?" Rohini smiled encouragingly, as she dumped coffee-soaked paper towels in the trash bin.

"You betcha." Angela laughed and reached for her coffee. "Anyway, Jane was studying medicine." She jerked her shoulder. "I was there because, you know" — she gestured to all the folders of recipes she had piled on her desk — "I wanted to be a pastry chef even then, and Rome was the place to learn. So my parents paid to let me study there, just for that semester, as a 'compromise,' they said. Because I was already engaged to someone they'd picked out for me, and I was going home to get married right after, in June."

"Your parents picked out your husband for you? I didn't know they did that in the States." Rohini was back at her desk, leaning on her elbows, her chin in her hands, listening attentively to Angela.

Angela made a face. "We don't usually. But my parents are from Italy. They're old-fashioned. They said it was 'up to me,' but the way they'd presented it, I knew it really wasn't. So I agreed to the marriage even though I didn't want it. And I went to Rome because I knew that if I didn't go then, I'd never get the chance again."

"Well, surely you could have?" Cynthia was sitting at her desk now, still in her lacy bra, the soggy papers forgotten, unconcerned that her impressive bosom was on display as she listened to things she was hearing for the first time. "I mean, you said your parents weren't forcing you —"

"Ha!" Rohini interjected. "You'd be surprised how easily some parents can coerce their children into doing what they wish, without physically forcing them." She sounded so uncharacteristically bitter that the other two both turned their faces toward her at once. Seeing that, Rohini waved a hand in the air. "Never mind. I'm sorry I interrupted. Go on, Angela."

"My brother had already graduated and was still figuring out what he wanted to do, so he told our parents he'd come with me, to keep an eye on me." Her laugh was cheerless. "He's such a smooth talker. He had no intention of doing anything of the kind. He wanted to have fun. He wanted *me* to have fun. In fact, he hoped the trip would make me change my mind about getting married so young. He thought it was a big mistake."

Rohini looked at Angela with unabashed envy. "Your older brother didn't want you to get married? Where I come from, that would be unimaginable."

Angela smirked. "Yeah. He didn't want me to get married. *I* didn't want me to get married. But as I'm sure you've both concluded by now —" she held up her right hand and wiggled her ring finger —"I did it anyway." She paused. "Although, I'll tell you, not before I'd had the time of my life in Rome. And it was all because of Jane."

"Jane?" Cynthia and Rohini exclaimed together.

Angela nodded. "Yep. Jane. She was nothing at all like she is now. She was so vibrant and alive. She got me out of my shell, got me seeing, going, doing."

"And men?" Cynthia would ask that, naturally.

"No, nothing like that. After all, I was engaged."

Cynthia smirked. "Too bad for you. The best thing about Rome is the men. They're like the cherry on the cake. Oh, no, wait — *you* were the cherry."

Rohini sniggered at that, again amazing the other two.

Angela went on. "At any rate, Jane and I were always together, when she wasn't studying, that is. Because — God bless her — she wasn't kidding about getting that degree. Coming from a working class family in northern England, her education was very important to her. She was the first in her family to go to college."

"Ah." Rohini tapped her finger in the air. "Northern England. That explains her accent, her phrases. As you know, in my country, we're flooded with Englishmen. That's why I speak it as well as I do. But the ones I've met so far don't sound quite like Jane."

"Yep. She gets that a lot. Just like I get a lot of remarks about my Brooklyn accent. We're kindred spirits in that way. Blue collar roots. Only she got the college degree, so you don't hear it as much, unless she gets worked up about something." Angela shrugged. "You know what they say. You can take the girl out of —"

"Sin City?" Cynthia toasted her with the empty coffee cup.

"Kolhapur?" Rohini added with a smile of solidarity.

Angela laughed, feeling more at ease. She was really getting to like these girls. "Sure. That's what I was going to say."

She went on with her story. "Anyway, about a month later my brother came back to Rome after backpacking through damn near the entire country. And the only reason he did was because of that promise to my parents. By then Jane and I were roommates, and I introduced them." She paused, cleared her throat, fought for control and lost. "He took one look at her. One. That was all he needed. And I knew right then what she would mean to him."

They waited, silently sympathetic, as Angela sniffled and pulled open all the drawers of her desk. "Where did I put those damn tissues?"

Cynthia shrugged, and held up her stained blouse. "What the hell. Here — blow your nose on this."

As intended, that got a watery chuckle out of Angela, but it still sounded dangerously close to a sob. Finding her tissues, she wiped her eyes and went on. "You should have seen them together. First of all, they were gorgeous. I mean, *gorgeous*. She had all that natural blonde hair and he was so dark. What a contrast. And they were always laughing."

"Oh, that's lovely." Rohini exhaled at the image. "I so enjoy a good romance. Even Bollywood hasn't managed to put me off of them."

Angela grimaced. "Yeah. Romantic love is always great in films, cheesy or otherwise. I can't say I believe in endless love and devotion myself. Not since my cousin Rocco broke his wife's neck, a woman he supposedly adored."

Looking back down at the tissue she was tearing to shreds, she didn't notice the look of astonishment the other two exchanged at that as she mused on. "But I can say that Jane and Antoni seemed happy together. Nobody I knew had a relationship like they did. Especially not me and Marco." She made another face. "Marco was the boy my parents chose. I realized not even a year after we got married what a horrible mistake I'd made."

Rohini *tsk-tsked* and Cynthia's face held disgust.

"But I stayed because we had a baby right away. My son, Vincenzo. Marco said we had to name him after his father."

Cynthia lifted a brow. "Well, you're a regular font of top secret information today, Angela. An unhappy marriage, a murderous cousin, a son named Vincenzo, after his grandfather. And how old is your boy?"

"He's twenty-four." *Dammit.* Now, why had she brought that up? She wasn't ready to go there. Acknowledging all this was bad enough.

Hoping to distract them, she got up for more coffee. "Getting back to Jane and Antoni. They not only fell in love with each other, they fell in love with Italy and decided to live there. I saw them at my wedding and about once a year after that, when they flew into New York to see my parents. Each and every time, they just seemed to glow, like —" she gestured with the coffee pot —"like gods. Jane and I stayed in touch in between their visits. She still encouraged and supported me. Always. She was the reason I finally got up the nerve to defy my husband and my parents by buying the bakery. I would never have had the guts to do that if it weren't for her. Thank God I did. That bakery got my son through college and helped me keep our house after Marco died. Jane made me feel like anything I wanted to do was possible." She looked at Cynthia sadly. "You'd never think that about her now, would you?"

Cynthia shook her head gently. "I guess I wouldn't. *Ay dios mio.* How some of us change."

Angela went back to her desk and set her steaming cup down. "For a long time it looked like they couldn't have children. That was their one unhappiness. But like with everything else, Jane refused to give up. Being a pharmacist, she knew a lot about medicine, and she was determined that it would happen. She was thirty-seven by the time they finally had Gabriella."

In the typical Sicilian expression of agony and joy, Angela clasped her hands together and beat them against her chest. "You should've seen that baby. Worth waiting for, I tell you. And as she grew — Oh. My. God. She was something — the darker skin like her father, the pretty green eyes and gold hair like her mother. Everybody loved her. And of course, Jane and Antoni adored her, though they had... different ideas about how to raise children." She paused and her eyes filled again as she wrestled with the admission. "Sometimes they argued about that."

"Huh. Different ideas that they argued about. *Quelle surprise,*" remarked Cynthia.

Angela looked at Cynthia sharply. "That was French. I've heard you speak Portuguese, Spanish and now French. Not to mention English. How many languages do you speak, Cynthia?"

Cynthia shrugged. "Knowing a few expressions in a language doesn't make me an expert. Go on with your story." But inside she thought, Careful, Cynthia, *careful.*

Angela didn't notice Cynthia's discomfort. She was too busy shoring herself up to tell the rest. "Antoni makes his living by renting out his fishing yachts. Sometimes he took Gabriella out with him on day long excursions. She loved the sea as much as he did. One day, they were with a party of tourists who wanted to drop anchor at a beach that Antoni wasn't that familiar with. There were tide pools. Gabriella was playing in one. She was right by the shore, the water not even up to her waist. She already knew how to swim so well."

Cynthia drew in a sharp breath and Rohini closed her eyes. They knew what was coming next.

Angela opened her mouth, shut it again. Two years later and it was still so, so hard. "None of that mattered because there was a hidden undertow. It sucked her down, right in front of my brother's eyes. She was gone within seconds. He jumped in after her, but she'd completely disappeared. He kept diving and screaming her name. When he realized she was gone for good, it took four of the men with him to pull him out of the water."

"*Nossa Senhora.*" Cynthia crossed herself.

"Poor Daddy. Poor little girl," murmured Rohini.

Angela didn't even bother to try to stop her tears now. "Everything fell apart after that. Jane blamed Antoni. She'd always felt he was too protective of Gabriella. She thought that Gabriella was starting to display her resentment by becoming disobedient."

"Do you think that was true?" Rohini studied her.

"Honestly? I can't say. A few times, in the year before Gabriella's death, Jane phoned me, complaining that my brother was trying to raise his daughter the way our parents had raised me. But if you asked him, *he'd* say that Jane was too lenient. I didn't see them often enough to know." More tears rolled down her face and fell to her lap as she looked at Rohini. "I just don't know."

Cynthia pulled her chair up to Angela's desk and patted her arm. "This is a senseless speculation, *menina.*" She spread her arms wide. "It was an *accident*. Okay — assume he was an overprotective parent, like yours were with you. Or assume that maybe Gabriella was *so* adored, that she was a little spoiled and just felt like being naughty that day."

Angela's eyes widened at that.

Cynthia held her hands up. "I'm not making any accusations. All I'm saying is that families have disagreements and people make mistakes and children disobey their parents and accidents happen." She lifted her shoulders. "That's the way life works. What's the sense of blame?"

"The point is that Jane thought Gabriella was defying him by deliberately going into water she couldn't handle just to prove he needn't baby her so much. She didn't believe the accident happened the way Antoni said it did. They fought about this after Gabriella's funeral. Jane told him to leave."

Cynthia looked stricken. "Oh, no. Please don't say she told him that."

"She did. The whole family was there. And for Jane — of all people — to carry on like that in public, it was like a horror show. None of us had ever heard her raise her voice to Antoni, not even once. But that day, she was screaming at him. It was like she hated herself for saying what she was saying, but she just couldn't stop the words. Antoni left that night."

"Oh, that makes it all the worse," said Rohini brokenly. "If they had each other, they could help each other heal."

"He sailed out on one of the yachts and has been gone ever since. *Two* years. After he left, Jane moved back to Newcastle. She lives in her parents' old house with her mother, and teaches at the university there. She hasn't been the same since. Nothing's been the same since." Angela was crying so hard now, her chest was heaving.

"Let me get you some water," soothed Rohini.

"To hell with water — get her a drink! She needs one." Cynthia was wiping at her own eyes. "God knows I need one."

"No. Thank you, no. I just need to be by myself for a while." With a deep breath, Angela stood up, her face swollen and her eyes puffy. "Sorry for the meltdown, but I guess it's better that you know, anyway." And with that, she fled.

Cynthia and Rohini sat in silence as they took it all in.

Finally Cynthia said, "Well, shit. That was a terrible story."

"Yes."

"You know, I'd have thought that the last place Jane would want to be was on the water now, considering."

"Perhaps it's the contrary," mused Rohini. "Perhaps being on the ship reminds her of her daughter and husband in happier days. Do you suppose she wants him to come back to her?"

"Oh, definitely." Cynthia walked over to the kitchenette and pulled out a bottle of single malt that she kept tucked there in the cabinet for just such emergencies. "Half of why she behaves as she does is because she misses him, I bet. And because she's just not ready to admit that." Pouring herself a shot glass full, she looked over at Rohini. "Want one?"

"As a rule, no, but today I don't mind at all if I do."

They were both lost in thought as they sipped. After a while, Cynthia slanted a glance at Rohini. "So, how about you — any deep, dark secrets?"

Rohini drained her glass, got up, and poured herself another shot. Her mouth twitched into a smile when she saw Cynthia's expression as she knocked back that second one too. "Ah, Cynthia. If only you knew."

Angela climbed up to the deck above the restaurant and was relieved beyond measure to see that she was alone. She looked around. On this side, there was nothing of interest for any tourists, apart from two empty deck chairs and a low, rickety table placed between them. A mop that had seen better days rested against a rusty iron balustrade, and a metal ashtray filled with cigarette butts was set out on the table. Most likely no one but the crew came up here for smoke breaks, so it seemed a safe hideout for now.

Breathing deeply, she leaned against the railing facing the water and tilted her head up to the sun. As the soothing warmth calmed her, she looked down at the deck below, past The Secret Spice. At this time of day there were only smatterings of tourists out on the Promenade, as most were inside the ship on guided tours, or at one of the exhibitions or shows, or in one of the shops, picking out souvenirs. Observing a few taking photos, she imagined what they might be saying: To the right, by the vintage Cunard poster, is where Cary Grant once posed for a still for the film, *Holiday*. There, towards the bow, where the first-class night-club and restaurant once was, Clark Gable and Elizabeth Taylor sat drinking champagne. And on every deck, she knew, Allied soldiers had stood, packed shoulder to shoulder, during the war.

She'd learned all this whether she'd wanted to or not, from Sarita the teenage history buff. The kid was crazy about this ship. Much to her mother's exasperation, she talked about it practically every night at dinner, almost as though it were alive. Angela could admit that much of what Sarita told them was fascinating. And yet, some of it struck her as sad.

The *Mary* was still magnificent. But if she *were* a person and she could talk, what would she say about having traveled all over the world, transporting so many celebrated people, surviving storms at sea and an epic war, only to become a shadow of what she'd been — a glorified fossil even, if one were giving in to melancholy thoughts — moored forever now, in one place?

Moored just as Angela herself had been for her entire life.

Switching from that gloomy contemplation to another, she wondered if she should check on Jane or leave her on her own for the day. She tried imagining what she would want Jane to do if their places were switched, if it were she who'd lost a child.

But in a way she had, hadn't she? Although of course, it was far different. She still had a chance to see her son, to tell him how much she loved him. To put things right, if she could only bring herself to do so.

Vincenzo, she thought. I miss you.

A cool breeze fluttered in off the water. She watched as it ruffled through the white sails of the boats in the harbor and then drifted over her, briefly raising bumps on her bare arms.

Geez. What a lousy morning. She needed a cigarette, was pining for one, in fact. It was just her bad luck that even after fifteen years of no smoking, she still craved tobacco so much that sometimes she could even smell it in her dreams.

She could smell it right now. In fact, she could see it: curls of smoke coming from behind her. She spun around and blinked in surprise. Sitting in one of the deck chairs that had just moments before been empty was a man — a rather attractive one — smoking a cigarette and watching her through a pair of the most amazing blue eyes.

No — wait. She was wrong. They weren't blue. They were more…gray. With just the suggestion of green.

"Oh, my God, I'm so sorry!" It was a habit of Angela's to burst into apology when she was flustered, even when she'd done nothing wrong. "I didn't know there was anyone else up here. I hope I didn't disturb your break."

The man stared back at her, glanced behind him and then turned to look at her again. He pointed to his chest with the hand holding the cigarette, "Are you talking to me?"

As off balance as she felt, she still had to smile. Boy, was he cute, or what? About ten years too young for her, to her mind, but she was a widow, not dead herself. She could still appreciate cute. "Who else would I be talking to?" She looked around the deck. "Unless there's somebody else up here I didn't notice when I came up?"

He studied her briefly, then shrugged. "It's usually me people don't notice."

"Oh, yeah?" She rested her back against the rail and looked at him drolly. "As much as I appreciate modesty in a man, I'm not convinced you believe that."

Now he gave her a full-blown smile. "Oh, trust me — I do. What brings you up here, then, beautiful? Hiding out from someone?"

Angela was embarrassed to find herself blushing. After years of her husband's indifference, followed by more years of almost sequestered widowhood, she was convinced he was just being charming. She didn't see herself as beautiful. Where others saw 'slender,' she saw 'scrawny.' She noticed only the lines around her eyes and not their soft, sloe-colored appeal. She thought her nose was too big and her mouth was too wide. Self-consciously, she touched the thick, sable ponytail that brushed past her shoulders. She couldn't think how else to wear it, and after all, she was a pastry chef. No one wanted to find a long, dark hair baked into their lemon mousse. Still, she should do something with it — get it cut, maybe cover the gray that had started coming in with a vengeance now. How long had it been since she'd put any effort into making herself look attractive? How long had it been since a man had flirted with her, like this one appeared to be doing?

Her discomposure had her speaking all in a rush. "I just needed a minute. It's a bad day for us today — my sister-in-law, Jane, and me. She's here on the ship too. We've taken over one of the restaurants below and we're renovating it. Well, I mean, we were. Now, it's about ready to open. We're happy about that. But today...well, today...is the anniversary of my niece's death. She died two years ago. She was only seven."

He'd been listening to her babbling with patient amusement up until that point. But as soon as she mentioned the death, his eyes became almost impossibly sad. "I'm very sorry to hear that. There's nothing worse than losing a child." He paused, and his mind seemed far away. "Nothing. No matter how bad."

Angela was about to apologize again. Clearly, she'd hit a nerve. But just as she started to speak —

"Ahoy up there, Mrs. Perotta!" came Cynthia's voice from the deck below. Something had put her in a playful mood.

Angela turned back to the rail again and called down. "Ahoy, yourself, Mrs. Taylor," she teased back. "How did you know I was up here?"

"We were looking for you and one of the crew saw you go up. Are you feeling better? Can you come back in? There's someone here I'd like you to meet." Cynthia shielded her eyes with her hands as she looked up.

"Is Jane still in her room?"

"No, she's in the restaurant now. She's just had some tea. She's fine." Cynthia drew a cross over her heart with her finger. "I promise."

Angela closed her eyes briefly in relief, then called over the railing again. "Okay — I'll be right down."

She watched with a touch of feminine wistfulness as Cynthia strutted back inside. Geez Lou*eeze*, the woman had a body. Next to Cynthia's, hers looked like a strand of limp spaghetti. With a sigh, she turned to say goodbye to her new friend. "I have to get back to work." Shyly, she added, "It was nice to meet you."

"Yes." He stubbed out his cigarette and watched as it smoldered in the ashtray. "I hope we see each other again." Those eyes singed back to hers and Angela felt his look jolt right through her. "I'd enjoy that very much."

Face flaming, she bobbed her head at him, and felt foolish again when she scuttled down the steps like an agitated goose.

Oh, my God. Geez. She hoped she didn't smell like cigarettes. If Jane thought she'd taken up smoking again, she'd never shut up about it. The last thing she wanted to do was explain that it was because she'd been talking to a man.

A very good-looking man, with a trace of Texas Sexy in his voice.

CHAPTER THREE

No matter how many times Angela had stepped inside The Secret Spice in the past month, she still felt a thrill. They'd done it. They'd built a restaurant. As she'd just blurted out to a stranger, they were set to open soon. Everything was ready except for the hiring of a few more workers, and the selection of a featured appetizer, entrée, and dessert that would be served at the grand opening. Naturally, these were challenging to decide upon, and naturally, the two making those choices most challenging were Cynthia and Jane.

Those two culprits sat at a table near the bar. A man sat she didn't know sat with them. As Angela walked closer, he looked her way, and when he did, she barely managed to keep walking casually toward them.

Whoa. Whoever he was, he was a dead ringer for Antonio Banderas. Of course, Antonio probably wouldn't be wearing chef's whites. Her mind made the leap when her sister-in-law cleared her throat noisily and gave her a quelling look.

Oh, of course. This would be Rohini's new assistant. Or, as Jane had referred to him earlier, "the criminal whom they were letting loose in their kitchen."

"And here's Angela, our pastry chef." Like a game show hostess, Cynthia stood up and extended her arm. "Angela, I'd like you to meet Cristiano de la Cueva."

He stood up to shake her hand. "Nice to meet you. Call me 'Cris.'"

He even sounded like Antonio Banderas. Angela smiled dreamily. She was having quite the day for meeting handsome men. "Hi, Cris."

Jane cleared her throat and frowned at them. "Before we go any further, there are a few things I'd like to ask Mr. de la Cueva —"

"Oh, Jane, for godssakes —"

"No, no, it's all right, Cynthia. Please. She has a right to ask." Cristiano sat back down after Angela and Cynthia were seated, and then smiled at Jane. "Call me 'Cris,' please."

Jane seemed impervious to that smile. "And so I will. Tell me — Cris — why is it I shouldn't be absolutely terrified to hire you?" She leaned back, used her forefinger to pull her reading glasses further down her nose and looked up over them at him, baldly, waiting for his response.

Cristiano's reply was equally blunt. "Any woman in her right mind would be." He wasn't smiling now. "Make no mistake — I did exactly what I was accused of doing. I killed a man and served ten years for it."

"It was because of his sister. The man he killed murdered his sister," Cynthia put in, looking at him with compassion.

"Raped her and then strangled her, to be precise." Cristiano's voice was harsh and Angela thought that she'd just seen that same look of hellish grief in another man's eyes. "So I hunted him down like the animal he was and I killed him. He didn't deserve to live, any more than my sister deserved to die. All of this is on record. I confessed to it. I spent ten years of my life in prison for it and every day of those years was an indescribable nightmare. I thought of killing myself too. Many times."

He paused as he saw he had the focused attention of the women. "But I will tell you this: As horrible as those ten years were, as much as killing him changed who I was and will impact the rest of my life, were the circumstances the same, I would kill him again. But I have never harmed anyone else." He leaned back in his chair and composed himself. "And that's as much of this subject as I care to discuss. If you don't want me to work in your kitchen, I understand."

The silence at the table stretched as Angela and Cynthia both looked at Jane. They knew what they wanted to do. But what would she do? She was still peering at him over her glasses.

At length, Jane spoke. "Well, that answers my first question," she said matter-of-factly. She pointed down at the sheet of paper in front of her on the table. "And I see here on your CV that you're able to do appliances and electrical repairs. Would you be willing to help in those endeavors if we ever needed you to? For additional pay, of course." She added that last without blinking an eye.

The megawatt smile was back on Cristiano's face. "Yes, I would be very happy to help with repairs." Solemnly he echoed Jane's postscript. "For additional pay, of course."

"Good." She turned to her two partners. "Well, I don't have any more questions. What about either of you?"

Angela and Cynthia's expressions were filled with naughty glee. They both shook their heads.

"Very well, then, Mr. de la Cueva — it looks like you're hired." Jane took off her reading glasses and stood up. "Now, if you'll all pardon me, I still have a lot of work to do today." She nodded to them and walked briskly off.

Cristiano watched her as she left. "A remarkable woman," he pronounced, as he rose too, and treated Angela and Cynthia to his smile again. "Well, ladies, it appears that's three down and one to go. So, I had better go on back to the kitchen and meet who I hope will be my new boss."

They waited until he was out of sight before they burst out laughing and gave each other a high five.

Cristiano exhaled a deep, slow breath as he stood in front of the closed doors to the kitchen and prepared himself to face another barrage of questions. He closed his eyes and pinched the bridge of his nose. For a man who'd once received a multitude of offers from some of the world's top restaurants, these days it was a challenge to get hired as a dishwasher, never mind as a cook. And then to keep a job, once he managed to obtain one.

Get over it, he told himself. Your glory days were over decades ago.

As he did each time before an interview, he brought up two images of Isabel: One of her at age six, with her front tooth missing as she beamed with victory from the top of the jungle gym in the school yard in their old neighborhood — "Mommy, look! I'm at the top! Cristiano helped me climb to the top!" — and the other of her at seventeen, laid out on a slab in the police morgue, ice cold and colorless except for her many bruises. With those visualizations at the forefront of his mind, he was as ready as he would ever be for this last confrontation. He pushed the doors open and stepped in.

It was anticlimactic to discover that the galley was empty, but he thought he heard music coming from the scullery to the back. He paused in the doorway for a moment, and looked around. Though renovated since he'd last been inside, the kitchen hummed with the same curious energy as it had when he'd worked here. He could never put his finger on what it was, but whatever it was, it was not unpleasant.

He listened as a female voice chimed in with the music. Indian music, he thought, as he followed the sounds to the scullery. A slender, petite woman with shining black hair that glided down to her waist had her back turned to him as she sang. She was washing and bagging pieces of chicken at a porcelain-covered, cast iron sink. With the music playing and the water running, he was sure she hadn't heard him come in. Afraid he would startle her, he said softly, "Excuse me."

Very deliberately, she turned as though she'd known he was there all along, and smiled. "Hello. You must be Cristiano."

"Uh..." Was that his name? He was so blindsided by the loveliness of the woman standing in front of him, that for a second he couldn't remember.

He'd already noted her size, but now he saw that her build was almost doll-like. Her hands and feet were delicate and graceful. That shiny black hair was natural, if the few streaks of white were anything to judge by, and it set off to perfection the velvety brown of her skin. The gene pool lottery that had awarded her such a flawless complexion complemented it with dark winged eyebrows and large, slightly up-tilted eyes. To a man who thought of fine foods and spirits with reverence, the color of her eyes reminded him of warm brandy, speckled with chocolate. Her nose, like the rest of her, was straight and elegant; her mouth full and luscious. Her face had an appealing maturity about it. He judged her to be in her early to mid-forties, and he was glad of it. He didn't find women who were much younger than himself appealing...in that way. He was unaware that his eyes had rolled over her form adoringly. For such a small woman, she had plenty of curves, just where he liked them. He itched to cup those beautiful breasts, and envisaged that he could span the full circumference of her waist with his two hands alone.

And weren't his thoughts much more eloquent than his speech at the moment?

"Uh...yes. Cristiano. And you...are Rohini, the...uh...head chef?"

Tonto del culo! He'd said 'uh.' *Three* times. And he was talking like Tarzan — 'Me, Cristiano, you, Rohini.'

She laughed. "Oh, no, I'm just the head cook." She pointed to him and smiled again. "You're the *cordon bleu.*"

That put him even more off balance. He was both puzzled and pleased that she knew. "And how did you learn about that? I don't think I put that on my application."

"I have my ways. After all, a woman has to know who'll be cooking in her kitchen." Was she being deliberately flirtatious, or was that just wishful thinking on his part?

"What about you? Where did you learn to cook?" He regretted the question the instant her face closed up. He'd seen that look on a number of inmates. It meant she was hiding something, and whatever it was, frightened her.

She waved a hand vaguely. "Oh, here and there." Instantly, she changed the subject back to the restaurant. "Come — let me show you how we've arranged things. You can tell me what you think."

He followed her back into the kitchen, as she pointed out the changes that had been made, the new, burnished stainless steel appliances and gas stoves, the station allocated for Angela to create her delectable confections, and the areas where she and he — Rohini and Cristiano — would be cooking together, side by side.

He was going to have to work with this woman every day, without touching her? That made the ten years of imposed celibacy he'd endured in prison seem easy. He became aware of his heartbeat. It had been drumming madly since he pulled into the parking lot in front of the *Mary,* and had continued to do so the entire time he'd sat with the stern-faced Jane Miceli. Now it pounded for an entirely different, and vastly unexpected reason. He wondered, briefly, if a heart was engineered to work so hard.

He forced himself to focus on business matters. "The upgrades are fantastic. This kitchen would be a joy to work in. You and your partners have done an amazing job. May I ask what made you decide to open a restaurant aboard a ship?"

That brought her smile back. "It's quite the story. We were all on the same food blogging site. Somehow, we started writing just to each other. At the beginning, it was solely about cooking. Jane is a fan of Indian food, and I was helping her try her hand at it. Cynthia has a sweet tooth, so she was always asking Angela for recipes. As for me, I loved reading what Cynthia wrote about the dishes they served at the posh restaurants attached to the casino where she worked. Some of them I'd never even heard of…" She'd become more animated as she talked, but then she stopped, dismayed by her volubility. "This must be boring you to tears."

"On the contrary." He was entranced. She could have been reciting multiplication tables, so fascinated was he by the way her face lit up as she relayed her happy memory to him. "Tell me the rest. Please."

"Well…if you're sure." She felt the blood rush to her cheeks as she heard herself say, "I never talk this much, usually. I don't know what's come over me."

At that, he grinned. The thought that she might possibly be as caught off balance by him as he was by her, delighted him. He was suffused, suddenly, with gladness. A carefree, youthful gladness he hadn't felt since long before he could remember. As for the anxiety he'd felt when he'd stepped back on the ship this morning, it was gone.

"Tell me the rest," he said again, his eyes fixed on her face. "I'm very interested."

It occurred to Rohini that, contrary to Jane's presentiment of catastrophe, she felt safe with Cristiano de la Cueva. Safe in a way she hadn't felt around a man in too long a time. Knowing Jane as she was coming to, she understood that before he'd been permitted to step into the galley to meet with her, he'd been interrogated, formidably. She didn't need to speculate on how that had felt to him; she understood what it was like to be the accused, to be trapped, desperate. Yet, even so, as she was telling her story, he'd looked at her in a way that made her feel…unnerved, for some reason. And that was just silly. After all, she was in charge here. For the first time in her life, she was in charge. That still felt strange, but remembering it put her more at ease. She straightened her shoulders. He'd asked to hear it, so why shouldn't she tell it?

"One day, Angela mentioned that she wished she could add a restaurant to her bakery. And then we all said how we'd love to have our own restaurant someday. At first, it was just something to talk about, something pleasant to dream about." She studied him for his reaction. "I suppose that sounds foolish."

"Not to me. I dream about restaurants all the time."

She charmed him by laughing again. "I suppose you do. In any event, it was Cynthia who first heard about this place becoming vacant. The price was so reasonable, it seemed too good an opportunity to pass up. Besides that, this is so much better than an ordinary restaurant. To me, there's nothing like an old ship. Especially when I think about all she's seen, all that's come to pass here." She hadn't put it together why she felt so at ease confiding in him. "I love her already. Love her, and all of her...mysteries."

"'Mysteries.' That's just the word, isn't it?" He glanced about. "I've cooked in many restaurants, all over the world. But there has always been something compelling about this particular kitchen." He pinned her with a look again. "There's nothing more appealing than a woman with secrets."

She blinked at that. Then she remembered he was talking about the *Mary*. At least, she hoped so.

Changing the subject, she put in, "We're all happy to be here, but with four of us, I expect there'll be some bumps along the way." She bit her lower lip. "Confidentially, there've already been a few… squabbles. I hope that doesn't put you off."

Cristiano shook his head. "Not at all. That's to be expected. It's no easy task to run a good restaurant. And with four partners, no less."

"Certainly, with your experience, you can tell us if we're steering too far off course." She added that in on impulse, because she wanted him to feel that he belonged here. To feel happy here, if that were possible. He was a lonely man, who'd not been happy in years, she knew. It wasn't because she was an empath that she knew this. It was because one lonely, unhappy person always recognized another.

She kept that to herself, and let him see only her admiration. "I'm so looking forward to working with you. And learning what you can teach me."

He stared at her. "You want me to…teach you?"

Her smile wavered as she looked at him in genuine puzzlement. He had that look on his face again — the look that had made her feel strange earlier. "Of course. It's not every day that I get to work with a master chef."

"Oh! Oh, I see. Well, thank you. It would be an honor to teach you. And I hope that you can…teach me too." Those last three words came out of him like a purr, and her beautiful eyes widened.

What the hell was wrong with him? Perhaps just seeing her for the first time had given him a brain hemorrhage. At his age, that was not impossible. He was risking the first good opportunity he'd had in years, just because he couldn't stop thinking about what it would be like to kiss her.

"*Ow*!" Out of nowhere, a copper pan hit him on the back of the head. He turned around swiftly as it fell to the floor behind him with a clang. "Where did that come from?" He looked down at the still vibrating pan incredulously as he rubbed his head.

"Oh, no!" Rohini clapped her hand against her mouth. She ran to the one of the refrigerators to get some ice. "Are you hurt?"

He could feel a lump forming, and checked to be sure he wasn't bleeding. "I'm fine," he lied. "But — how in hell? — "

"It...must have fallen from the overhead rack," she improvised.

Still holding his head, he looked up at the ceiling to the rack attached there. He frowned in bewilderment. Not one hook was empty. "But —?"

"Here." Hastily, she handed him the dish towel that she'd filled with ice. "Take this with you. Ask one of the others to show you where your cabin is, and go and lie down for a while. You should rest."

As delicate as she looked, she was strong enough to practically drag him across the kitchen. He looked down at her and held the ice she'd given him to his head as she frog-marched him out. "You should have Maintenance come and check that everything is secure. We wouldn't want pots to be tipping off loose shelves," he warned, as she swung the double doors open and pushed him through.

"An excellent idea. I'll do that. Goodbye, for now. I'll see you tomorrow." And before he could say another word, she pulled the doors shut and flipped across the latch.

"Dios mio." He leaned against the wall to catch his breath. His heart was still hammering, and the bruise on the back of his head sang.

What an interview. What a woman.

Well, he'd expected an ordeal, and he'd gotten one, hadn't he? Albeit not exactly the kind he'd anticipated. Frankly, he wasn't sure if he wouldn't be better off looking for work somewhere else.

He dismissed the thought as soon as it formed. People did not hire felons as a rule. He knew that very well. This was a job he needed, badly. He was fifty now, not thirty, and in the twenty years since he'd been convicted, he'd learned to control his impulses in and outside of prison. He could keep his desire for a woman in check — no matter how powerful it appeared to be. Perhaps a hit on the head was just what he'd needed to snap him to his senses.

He frowned again as he heard the subject of his thoughts talking in muffled tones behind the closed doors. "...should be ashamed of yourself. You could have hurt him."

Who was she talking to? He sighed and rubbed his head once more. Ah, well. If she was as crazy as she was beautiful, he would not be surprised at all. In fact, that would be just his kind of luck.

Straightening, he walked toward the office to find the others. It occurred to him that it might be tricky working for four bosses — four women who were, he'd already surmised, remarkably different from one another. However things turned out, he was grateful to them. They'd offered him their trust, as well as a paycheck and a place to sleep.

CHAPTER FOUR

"Mmmm. Lovely. It has to be this one. It's so creamy and lemony."

"Mmm-mmm. No — this one. Who can resist all this incredible chocolate?"

Rohini, whose forbearance was at this point celebrated by everyone who'd been hired to work at The Secret Spice Café, had visions of what Chocolate Hazelnut Mousse Pie and Ricotta Limoncello Cheesecake would look like if she squashed them together and then dumped them over Cynthia and Jane's heads. Without a word, she headed back to the kitchen, where the air was so thickened by the aromas of heated butter and cooked cream that she could feel it, settling on her skin and seeping through to congeal in her arteries.

Angela looked up from rolling out more dough for tart shells as Rohini came in. "Well?"

"Now it's between the pie and the cheesecake."

"For petessakes, Ro." Angela banged her fist on the pastry board in frustration and got a nose full of flour dust for her trouble. On her fingers, she counted, "They've tasted Raspberry Chocolate Truffle Tarts, Hazelnut Ganache-filled Cupcakes with Vanilla Bean Cream, Lemon Meringue Sponge Cake with Mango Liquor Sorbet, and only Jesus knows what else. I can't believe they're not sick to their stomachs, the two of them. I'm not doing this all day. They need to pick one to feature at the opening."

"So, tell them."

"I *did*. They didn't pay any attention to me. That's why I asked you to go out there."

Rohini looked over at Cristiano hopefully. He was bent over his work table, testing Rohini's exotic spices and jotting down recipe ideas, all while doing his best to pretend he was oblivious to what was going on. 'See no evil, hear no evil, speak no evil.' That had been his mantra since he'd started working with these women, and so far, it had served well. "Perhaps if you talked to them, Cristiano."

"What? Who, me?" He held his hands out in front of him, a gesture of panicked self-preservation. "No, no, no — don't get me involved. Nobody can talk to those two. It's like trying to herd cats."

Rohini's soft voice was entreating. "Please?"

Cristiano groaned. Why did she have to look at him like that, with those eyes? It wasn't fair. Scrambling for a way out, he turned to Angela. "Why must every decision be unanimous? *You* are the pastry chef. You know which dessert is your finest. You should be the one to choose."

It was as if he'd shined a light on a path Angela hadn't seen was there. "Oh, my God. Cris — you're absolutely right." She dusted her hands off on her apron. "And I pick my Raspberry Chocolate Truffle Tarts. And you know what else? I'm going into that office to tell them that right now."

Bowled over by her sudden nerve, they watched in silence as she marched out.

"Good luck with that," muttered Rohini, the minute Angela banged the doors shut behind her.

"You said it," Cristiano agreed. Then he looked at her beseechingly. "*Amada mia* — I would do anything for you, but I beg you — please don't put me in the middle of their quarrels. It's best for all of us if I stay out of them."

Surprised by the endearment, she stared up at him, considering. "Would you? Do anything for me, I mean?"

She couldn't believe she'd been brazen enough to say that out loud. Evidently, Angela wasn't the only one experiencing a burst of uncommon recklessness today. But she couldn't help herself. She'd been so disheartened — so *frustrated* — thinking she'd only imagined the elemental interest he'd shown in her when they'd first met. For a whole week since, they'd been working together every day, so close to each other that she could smell the soap he used on all that tantalizing male skin. And when he smiled at her, she got a quiver in her belly, a reaction that was as startling as it was exhilarating, because she'd never felt anything remotely like it before.

When she'd finally managed to flee to California, she told herself that her obligations as a dutiful daughter, a dutiful wife, were over. Zahir was dead. She'd escaped the fiendishness they'd both struggled against, but it was always at the back of her mind that her emancipation couldn't last; that one day, those demons would come looking for her here, and her life would essentially end. Until then, couldn't she be allowed to take one moment out of her time on this earth — just one — for herself, alone?

She'd hoped Cristiano might be that moment. She'd been drawn to him immediately, and judging by his behavior that day, she thought he'd felt the same way. But there hadn't been any evidence of that since. Not one word, not one glance, in seven whole days. She'd started to believe that perhaps she'd imagined his attraction to her, because she wanted it so badly.

Now here he was, making declarations and calling her sweet names in Spanish. It was confusing. She had no experience with this sort of thing, which was why she'd mustered up the nerve to jump in with both feet and ask, as soon as she saw an opening. And why shouldn't she? What was the point of being coy? Whether she was unmasked or wasn't, they weren't getting any younger either way, so she needed to know — did he, or didn't he, want her?

If only she could see the depth of it. He'd been so careful, scared to death he would do or say something that would reveal how much he felt for her. Maybe because he was older, maybe because he'd squandered so much of his life, he was in way too deep, way too fast, with this woman. He didn't want to lose this job. Not only because he needed it, but because he needed *her* — needed to see her every day, hear her voice, her laugh, watch her cook with such graceful skill, catch the scent of her hair when she turned — anything and everything about her, that made him thankful that all the hideous circumstances and events he'd endured, had somehow led him to her.

But now, she'd asked him a question, and if there was one thing he'd learned, it was that life was capricious, cruel, and too damn short. So he answered her honestly, his eyes caressing her face, his voice thick with love and nerves. "You know I would."

She looked like Calypso then, as she walked deliberately to him, and smiled. If he hadn't seen that her hands were clenched together in front of her, he'd have thought that only he was feeling vulnerable. He sucked in a deep breath. That she might want him as much as he wanted her, but feel just as uncertain as he did, gave him the courage to take those hands — those soft, small, yet competent hands — in his own, lean down and kiss her.

Reverently, he rubbed his lips back and forth across hers, and watched as her cheeks flushed and her amber eyes glowed. He meant to stop with just one soft kiss, but when she moaned a low sound of pleasure, stood up on her toes to lock her arms around his shoulders, and tremble against him, he was gone.

"Querida querida...poco princesa...bésame...bésame..." The embrace went wild. She caught her hands in his hair and whimpered as he trailed his lips up the side of her neck, then down her throat to the plump, satiny tops of her breasts. She smelled like ground cloves and sweet cream. He lifted her with a growl, and she wrapped her legs around his waist fiercely, their mouths and tongues clinging. He bent them both over the stainless steel table behind them, flinging out a hand for balance, shoving a sheet of paper and a pen to

the floor as he did so. He chuckled with the thought that they were about to make love on the same table he'd used to sample Rohini's spices. Now *that* was poetic. Smiling, he opened his eyes to tell her, and then went very still.

"Rohini?"

"Hmm... *Yes.*"

Whatever he was going to ask her, she already knew her answer was yes. She was lying beneath him with her eyes closed. Despite the cold metal at her back, she felt utterly divine, stirred as she'd never been, and yet completely at ease and secure. It was as though her body recognized by instinct what her mind had not yet grasped: that they'd traveled through tragedies and time zones, past birthplace and background, to get to where they belonged — only to each other, only in each other's arms, for always.

If she'd understood that, she would have been afraid. Instead, she only knew that she wanted his hands on her, yearned for the weight of him on her. She shivered as he traced her lips with his fingers.

"Rohini," he said again, and through her haze of longing, she was dimly aware that there was a tenor to his voice that sounded rather out of place. "*Corazon*, is it just your kisses that have made me dizzy, or is everything in this kitchen spinning?"

She tensed. Opening eyes that felt heavy with passion, she gasped as though she'd been splashed with ice water. Every pot and pan, every dish and utensil, was suspended in midair and circling silently around the edges of the room.

She sat up. "You...can see that?"

"I can," he said calmly, his arms still around her. "Does this happen often?"

Stalling, she straightened her blouse and brushed at her hair, before she spoke. "Yes." She kept her head down, her confession so faint, he had to lean even closer to hear it. "Just about every day. But until now, I've been the only one who was able to see it."

He looked around the room with interest. "Huh. Well, I guess that explains the sauté pan that hit me on the head. And a number of other dubious incidents, besides."

In surprise, she looked up. "You're being very casual. I'd have thought you'd be scared out of your wits."

He smiled cynically, his black eyes hard. "I've been to prison. There's nothing left that could possibly scare me after that. Not even pots doing a salsa by themselves." His eyes went from frost to anguished heat. "And that makes me think — though I feel sick to have to say it — it's you who should be frightened of me. I'm a convicted felon. I don't deserve to touch you."

"Please don't say those things." She couldn't manage to swallow, she felt so sad. And guilty. "I'm not afraid of you. If anything, you should be afraid of me."

"Afraid of *you*? Why, Rohini? No, *mi vida*, don't cry. Tell me."

"Isn't it obvious?" She gestured to the still spiraling cookware. "Things like this only happen around me. There's so much about me you don't know, Cristiano." Her voice sounded so bleak and fearful that his heart lurched. "And I know that when you hear it all, it will change everything."

His thumbs caressed her cheeks. He wiped away her tears and kept his eyes on hers so that she would see the truth in his. "You're wrong, *querida*. Nothing you could tell me would change the way I feel about you. And whatever this is —" he glanced up at the cookware dancing above their heads — "it doesn't frighten me at all. Whatever it is you have to tell me, *whenever* you're ready to tell me, I promise you, I'll be here and I will listen. In the meantime, let's start by learning to trust each other."

He might have said more, but just then, crockery and cookware all flew back into place and went still. The doors swung open and Angela was back, bubbling over with excitement.

"I did it. I actually did it. You should have heard me. I told them, 'Look, here's how it is — we don't tell you how to manage the dining room, and you don't tell us what to cook. All I had to do was tell them how I felt and they agreed to it." She snapped her fingers. "Just like that. Can you believe it?"

She was so pleased with herself that she chattered on, taking no notice at first that she'd walked in on quite the little scene. When it registered, she stopped dead. Rohini was sitting on the cooks' work table, her lipstick gone, her face tearstained, the top two buttons of her blouse undone, while Cristiano had his arms on either side of her hips. His thick, dark hair, which had been so neatly combed, was now standing up in clumps. They were looking at her the same way they'd looked at her yesterday when she'd caught them sneaking some of her freshly made profiteroles.

Thinking fast, she hurried over to her work station, seized a pastry cloth to cover the tart shells she'd been making, and then flashed them a big, bright smile. "In fact — you know what? I deserve to take a break now because of this. I'm going for…a walk. Yep. That's it. A walk on the decks will do me good." She slid the covered tray into the fridge, hastened to the double door, then stopped at the threshold.

"Um, I'll probably be gone for *at least* an hour," she emphasized without looking back at them. They watched her as she fled out, the doors flapping back and forth behind her.

With a grin, Cristiano turned back to Rohini and wiggled his eyebrows playfully. "Alone at last."

The behemoth freezer in the scullery lurched wide open and cold air bellowed out. Rohini tilted her head toward it. "Not quite."

Biting off an oath, Cristiano glared at the freezer. "Get lost. This is none of your business."

The freezer door thudded shut with insult, and the vague vibrations that were always present in the air ceased.

Cristiano dipped his head once. "Much better, Your Majesty. Thank you." And now that there were no longer any pesky spirits about, he'd make sure that the equally bothersome humans stayed away also. He walked to the kitchen doors and latched them, then turned to Rohini with a look of such intent that she felt her skin heat.

All that desire coming at her all at once was somewhat overwhelming, even if it was gratifying. "Cristiano," she said with sudden shyness, "we're supposed to be deciding on an appetizer and entrée for the opening, remember? Angela has already chosen her truffle tarts for the dessert. What are we planning to make?"

There was laughter in Cristiano's eyes and more happiness than Rohini had ever seen. "What shall we make? Hmmm...let's see." He peeled off his white apron and threw it across a chair, as he strode back to her to scoop her up and swing her around in one joyous circle. "First, we'll make love. And then, *mi amor,* we'll cook."

As soon as she escaped the kitchen, Angela sagged against the outside wall in disbelief. Ro and Cris. Wow. Boy, oh boy — she sure hadn't seen that coming. Rohini seemed so meek and guarded most of the time. Oh, well. *Acqua cheta* — 'still waters'— as her mother used to say. Through the doors, she heard them giggling like kids. Her face burned at the thought that she was eavesdropping. She pushed herself off the wall and, with an anxious glance at the closed office door, hurried out of the dining room. The last thing she needed was to run into those other two. She wasn't going to say

Word One to them about this, either. They'd find out soon enough on their own.

But now she had an hour to kill, didn't she? Walking past an excited, chattering group of Cub Scouts who were being escorted by their troop leader to the Engine Room for an educational tour, she headed for the sanctuary of the upper deck she'd discovered the week before, and then stopped, gnawing at her nails again. What if that man was up there, and thought she was stalking him? She straightened her shoulders. Well, that would be his problem, wouldn't it? After her successful rebellion today against the dessert tyrants, she was feeling feisty. It's not like it's his private deck, she argued with herself, as she held onto the wooden railing and climbed the steps.

Oh, my God. He was there — sitting in the same chair and smoking, just as he'd been last time. He watched her as she walked up. Her greeting was guarded. "Hello. Again."

This time he appeared more approachable. "Hey, there." He smiled. "I wasn't sure I was going to see you again."

"I hate to bother you. I get the impression you've claimed this as your particular spot to be alone. I feel like I'm disturbing your peace and quiet."

"You're not bothering me. Nor are you disturbing my peace and quiet. Believe me."

She gestured to the full ashtray. "Yet, you do sit up here a lot. I notice those are all your brand."

"That they are," he affirmed.

"I miss smoking," she told him, as she took her customary place against the rail. It felt good to come clean about that. To her family, she pretended differently, as she did about many other things she'd felt forced to sacrifice. "I gave it up because...you know..." her lips curved apologetically as she watched him blow out smoke, "bad for you and all that."

"Yes, so I've heard." He studied the cigarette he was holding. "I don't think I'm going to let myself worry much about that."

For the first time Angela noticed he was dressed in a military uniform. She hadn't known there were any troops on board. But, taking a closer look, she realized that it was a replica of a WWII infantry field uniform, just like the ones she'd seen in some of the old photos around the ship, complete with insignia, combat boots and cartridge belt. She smiled with comprehension. "Oh! I hadn't noticed your costume last time. You must be in one of the shows they have on board. No wonder you're up here so much during the day. What nights do you perform? Let me know, and I'll come and watch sometime."

He blinked at her, his expression puzzled. Then he burst out laughing. To Angela, the sound was rusty. Probably from all the cigarettes. "Very funny," he said dryly.

"No, I mean it. I *will* come and watch. And I'll bring the others. They'd enjoy it. Jane loves that kind of stuff. She even considered history for her major before she got hooked on chemistry. And then there's Sarita — Cynthia's daughter —" she put in for his clarification — "who pours over any information about the *Queen Mary* she can find. There's such a romantic past to this ship."

"'Romantic?' Is that how people see it?" His question was stated politely, but there was an undercurrent to it that Angela caught. "That's not how I'd describe it. I certainly agree she has a great deal of history, but some of it's quite horrible. That mightn't be in vain if folks would learn from it, but they don't seem to, do they?"

"You're talking about when she was a troopship, I assume?"

"Of course. She was a glorious ship before the war, but then they ripped the guts out of her, painted her navy grey and put in as many bunks as she would hold, so they could shuffle soldiers and prisoners back and forth, like cattle on their way to the butcher. More than ten thousand troops and five thousand prisoners of war at a time. Think of it — all those men on one ship — how cramped it must have been, how awful it must have smelled, with plenty of G.I.s getting sick on the rough seas. Weeks on end of travel, in the dead of night, so the U-boats couldn't see her or catch up with her. Did you know that Hitler put a bounty on her?"

Those gray eyes were mesmeric as they locked with hers. "Can you even begin to imagine what that was like? The threat of being torpedoed at any given moment, knowing that when it happened, there wouldn't be enough life boats or life jackets for everyone. The constant fear of being blown to bits, or worse — surviving only to freeze to death in the cold sea, or be eaten by sharks, as you prayed for a rescue that would never come. And if you weren't afraid, you were bored. With that many men on deck, all you could do was find a spot — just a spot — to stand. The chow line going twenty-four hours a day — most days, all there was to do was wait on that line for something to eat. Tell me, Angela, do you think it was 'romantic' for those men, or do you think that it was as hellish as it could possibly be?"

Angela watched him steadily as he spoke. He'd made his point. No wonder he didn't care to have her come see him perform. "I'm sorry you don't like the *Mary*. I'm sorry you don't like what you do."

"What I *do*?" he repeated. He flicked the ash from his cigarette. When he looked at her, his antipathy for himself was palpable. "That's a laugh. I do nothing. I know what I want to do, what I *must* do, but...I can't do it. I can't get it done."

She wasn't used to having such intimate conversations with men she barely knew. But he sounded so unhappy, that she felt it would be wrong not to ask. "What is it that you want to do?"

He didn't respond at first. It was as though he were debating whether or not to confide in her. Then at once, his face held such unholy agony, that Angela's breath stopped. "I want to see my son. He thinks I left him. He thinks I'm a coward." With passion, he asserted, "I'm not, Angela. I'm *not*. He needs to know that. He needs to know how much I love him. And if he doesn't find that out soon, it'll be too late."

The color drained from Angela's face. "That's not true. There's always time —"

"*No*." He voice became urgent, and he was looking at her as though he could see into her soul. "There isn't."

"I'm sorry!" Angela burst out. Then she whispered, "I'm so sorry. I don't know what to say. I —" she rubbed her hands along her arms — "it's cold up here now. I...I don't have a sweater. I have to go." She ran halfway down the stairs before she stopped. Feeling like the most spineless person ever, she turned to look back up at him, her fingernail between her teeth yet again.

He sat in a position of abject despair, his elbows on his knees and his head bent forward in his hands.

"I'm sorry," she whispered again.

But he didn't look at her, and he didn't reply.

She couldn't go back to the kitchen. She went to her stateroom and slammed the door, then flung herself across her bed, face down, murmuring to herself, "Oh, Vincenzo, what am I going to do? What am I going to do?"

She lay there, listlessly, until it neared dinner time. She had to make an appearance for that. She didn't want Rohini to think that she was avoiding her and Cris. As she washed her face, she mentally went over everything that had happened on the deck that afternoon. She hated herself for running off, but she'd felt so uncomfortable.

She knew what was stopping her from getting in touch with her own son, but what was stopping this guy, whoever he was, from getting in touch with his? Was there an ex-wife involved, did he maybe owe child support — what? She certainly didn't want to ask, and if he decided to tell her, she was definitely not the one to be handing out advice to anybody about their kids.

Besides, suppose he didn't like whatever she might say? That's why it was better that she'd left, she reasoned, as she brushed her hair and pulled it back into its usual tail. There was something about him that was so...eccentric. Who knew how he might react?

She should ask Michael, at the gift shop across from the restaurant, if he knew who the man was. Michael had been here the longest. He'd be able to tell her whether she should avoid him. The problem was she didn't know his name, so how would Michael know who she meant?

She paused, her lipstick halfway to her mouth. There'd been a name tag on the uniform, now that she thought about it. What had it said? L...something...Branson? L. Branson? That sounded right, but she couldn't remember for sure. Anyway, who knew if the name on that uniform was his? Assuming it was the real deal — that they weren't using replicas for the show — then it would have to be about sixty years old, wouldn't it? She was so lousy at math.

After she finished putting on lipstick, she pinched some color into her cheeks. There. She looked enough like her usual self now to not raise any flags with Jane. Boy, oh boy, could the woman sniff out when something wasn't right. She was like an English bloodhound. She glanced down at her nails. They looked terrible again, as bad as they had when she was a teenager.

God help her — this whole restaurant idea might have been a mistake. At first it had seemed like such a big adventure, but there was so much at risk. To herself at least, she could admit that she'd jumped in partly as a way to delay dealing with the mess she'd made with Vincenzo.

She looked at her reflection again. "You've got to fix this, Angela," she said to herself out loud.

Closing the door behind her, she'd just turned the key in the lock when it hit her: he'd called her Angela.

Here she was, trying to work out what his name tag said, because they'd never gotten around to introducing themselves. Cynthia had been fooling around the day Angela and the stranger first met. She hadn't called her "Angela." She'd called her "Mrs. Perotta."

And yet, today, he'd called her by her first name. How in the heck had he known it?

CHAPTER FIVE

Saturday, September 18, 2004

Michael Joseph McKenna was adored by all the women in his life, starting from the ninety-two-year-old grandmother who'd raised him, to the four-year-old Marisol, who came into his Queen Mary Memorabilia and Postcard Shop every Saturday to buy stickers. Stickers which, he'd never admit to anyone, he kept stocked for the sole purpose of seeing jubilation on the face of his favorite little customer, whenever she selected a new one. Marisol's mother, Inez, worked as a maid aboard the ship. On Saturdays, she brought her daughter with her to work, and kept her occupied with crayons and coloring books and the promise of a visit to Michael's shop if she was a good girl and let Mommy clean the big boat.

Inez guessed that Michael had a soft spot for Marisol. She knew of no other thirty-year-old, single, straight man who would keep a steady supply of Disney princess stickers in a shop that catered to tourists who wanted souvenirs from their visit to the *Queen*. It was one of the reasons that Inez adored Michael too, although she'd cut out her tongue before she ever revealed that to him. He was like a sultan with his harem. She'd be foolish to imagine he'd ever want a serious relationship.

She had that partly right. Michael did indeed take as much pleasure from women as they did from him. In fact, at the moment, he was reveling in his bachelor status by sitting in The Secret Spice Cafe, enjoying an amazing éclair and some light flirting with a foxy older woman who was one of the restaurant's owners.

"Cynthia, I hope you don't think I'm being forward if I say that this pastry is nearly as scrumptious as you are."

"You *are* being forward, Michael, but I forgive you because you used the word 'nearly.' I'd hate to think a man doesn't find me as appetizing as a bite of chocolate and whipped cream."

He howled with laughter. Michael's laugh was unforgettable once you got a taste of it. Frenetic, high pitched, yet throaty, it sounded like a teenage girl's giggle that had gone through an anabolism. "Hee, hee, hoo. You're so much fun, doll. And you're smokin' hot. I don't get why some man hasn't snatched you up. I mean that sincerely."

Michael and Cynthia had known each other since she'd flown out with Sarita four months before, to begin renovations on the restaurant. He spotted her one day shortly thereafter. She'd been standing on their shared deck, discussing exterior design with an obviously smitten carpenter, her full, voluptuous figure gloriously displayed in a clingy, white summer dress, her impressive height emphasized by mile-high heels, and her thick, chestnut curls piled up and spilling over from a haphazard bun at the top of her head. Her face was as pure sex as her body was — the full red lips setting off the milky skin, the narrow, slightly hooked nose, and the big, olive-black eyes. Liking everything he saw and imagining everything he couldn't, Michael introduced himself to her as the owner of the shop next door, and they fast became very friendly neighbors. For a while, he'd entertained the hope that they might become lovers, but when Cynthia took to treating him like a favored nephew, cosseting him with food and affectionate concern, he decided he liked that relationship too much to jeopardize it.

That morning, she'd invited him to stop by to join her for breakfast and have a peek at the new dining room before the grand opening the next day. She was having as much fun flirting with him as he was with her. Even so, her reply to his last comment was frosty.

"Did you actually just use the term, 'snatch me up?' Take a good look at me, Michael. There isn't a man alive who could manage it. Nor would I want one to." Then she punched his upper arm. "Jesus, you're an idiot. For someone so young, you talk like a sexist old man."

Michael rubbed his arm. "*Ow.* That hurt." Chuckling at her, he shrugged his shoulders. "What can I say? I'm a dinosaur when it comes to women. Blame my Irish Catholic grandmother. She's the one who raised me."

Cynthia had another retort at the tip of her tongue, but she cut it short when the kitchen doors swung open, and Cristiano strode into the dining room, holding a cloth-covered casserole dish. "I thought I heard voices out here." He beamed at them both. "Excellent! Not one, but *two* guinea pigs on hand to try my new recipe. This is the appetizer we're going to feature tomorrow night."

Cynthia watched as he practically bopped around their table. Wasn't he cheery this morning? He placed the warm dish down and uncovered it with a flourish. She narrowed her eyes suspiciously. "What's that?"

Cristiano looked at her in surprise. "Can't you tell? It's shrimp. With some special seasonings."

"I know shrimp when I see it. What I mean is — what's that on your neck? It looks like lipstick."

Cristiano's eyes widened, and damned if he didn't feel his face go red. "Lipstick?" Hastily, he rubbed at his neck with the cloth. "No, no. No lipstick. It must be...paprika. There's paprika in the shrimp. And other herbs and spices."

"Mmm hmm." Did he honestly expect her to believe that? He'd known exactly where to rub at his neck. And he was blushing like a virgin bride. She slanted a side glance at Michael, who was doing his best to keep a straight face.

Cristiano cleared his throat. "Er…please. Taste it. Tell me what you think."

"Unfortunately, I can't. I have a shellfish allergy."

"I'll be glad to give it a try, Cris." Michael reached for the platter with both hands.

Cynthia looked at him in disbelief. "How can you eat shrimp after you've just had an éclair and a cappuccino?"

"Believe me, doll, anything this guy cooks, I'll eat." Michael grabbed an unused plate and piled it with shrimp. "I almost broke down and cried when I heard they closed this place. I had some memorable lunches here thanks to Cris. I can't tell you how thrilled I am that you girls hired him back."

Cynthia's smile was guileless as she looked up at Cristiano. "Oh, we're certainly thrilled to have Cristiano here. One of us even more thrilled than the rest, apparently."

Cristiano was spared having to respond to that by Michael's moan of gastronomical bliss. "*Dude.* This is incredible. Absolutely incredible."

"You like it? It's not too spicy?"

"No. I mean — yeah, it's got some zing to it, but that's what makes it so tasty. What did you put in it?"

Cristiano wagged his finger playfully at Michael. "Ah-uh. That's my secret."

"Well, whatever — I've never tasted shrimp like this. It's amazing. You've got a winner here."

Cristiano nodded in satisfaction. "Well, good. Great. I'll go tell Rohini." And with one last flustered look at Cynthia, he made a hasty retreat back to the kitchen.

Observing Cynthia as he chewed, Michael commented, "You looked worried, doll. Don't be. He's a good guy and a fantastic chef. It's great that you gave him a chance to come back."

"All of that is true. But there's more being stirred up in that kitchen besides sauces and soups."

Michael winged one mocking brow, a mannerism she suspected he knew was effective, coupled as it was with his striking hazel eyes. "So...no fraternizing with the help — is that how you see it?"

Cynthia's chin came up. "Not at all. I just don't want my partner to get hurt. She's had it tougher than most."

"Yeah? Well, so has Cris. And I can tell you this, doll — I've never seen him treat a woman with anything but respect. If he and Rohini are...ah...let's see — how can I put this in a gentlemanly way?" He thought of Cris's pretext earlier and grinned. "Sharing spices, swapping recipes — whatever you want to call it — he cares about her. He wouldn't get involved with a woman on his work turf otherwise."

"I'm sure you're right. I'm not Rohini's babysitter, in any case. I've got more than enough runaway hormones to worry about living with a 'fifteen-and-three-quarters-going-on-thirty-year-old.' But I'm also thinking of my own investment, to be completely honest. You can't have a successful restaurant if your chefs will no longer work together."

She waved her hand dismissively. "Anyway, enough about them." With curiosity, she studied him. "So, the Irish Catholic granny, huh? That's probably a big part of what makes you tick."

Michael's eyes were wary now, as he swallowed. "What do you mean, 'makes me tick?'"

"Well, let's see." She smiled to soften her reproach, as she ran down the list. "You call grown women 'dolls' or 'girls,' which is kind of obnoxious, to tell you the truth. And yet, you notice whether or not Cristiano treats women with respect, because you treat them with respect yourself — when you're not trying to sound like Humphrey Bogart, that is. You say you're never going to settle down, and true to your word, I see you dating lots of women." She wrinkled her nose. "Lots of women who look like they're barely old enough to drink. But every Wednesday, you close your shop early, so you can pick your grandmother up at her assisted living condo — which I know you bought for her — and drive her to your sister's house, where you all have dinner together. *Every* Wednesday. In addition," she continued, ticking off on her fingers, "I, along with Sarita, Inez, and just about everybody else who lives or works on this ship, knows your niece's softball batting average, and that your nephew won first place in his school science fair, because you love talking about those kids. That doesn't sound to me like a man who doesn't want a family of his own."

She poked him in the chest. "You, my friend, are a fraud. I'm a lot older than you, and I'm not so easy to fool anymore. What have you got to say to that?"

Michael popped another shrimp into his mouth. "What have I got to say?" His tone was flip. "I'll tell you what I've got to say, Cynthia. You had me fooled, doll. I wouldn't have guessed you were more than a year or two older than I am."

Chuckling, she pinched his cheek. "Flatterer. But I wish you would answer my question seriously."

Without warning, Michael felt the room dim and recede. He looked at Cynthia, and the room came back. "What did you say?"

"I said, I want you to answer me seriously."

Her voice sounded weird to him, like it was echoing through his head. An inexplicable wave of melancholy washed over him. He felt a spontaneous desire to tell her the truth — the ugly, depressing truth — instead of throwing back one of his usual quips.

He leaned closer to her and kept his voice low. "You want me to answer you seriously? Okay — here goes. I got nothing going for me but my looks. When twenty-year-old girls see me, they see an older guy, who owns his own business on a 'cool boat.' They think, hey — he's cute and he dresses sharp. Know what they don't see about this particular fashion plate, Cynthia? It's got no silverware to go with it. No — I've got the tin flatware that comes from Target, and I had to buy it on layaway. I have a Chevy that's ten years old and needs a new muffler. I have a mortgage on a condo in a senior citizens' village, and a trinket shop that barely brings in enough to cover my expenses. Women my age? They're not naïve. They want nothing to do with me."

He studied her, waiting for a reaction. If she had one, she hid it well. She sat there silently, her eyes never leaving his face. He should shut up now, tell her it was joke, say anything to negate this embarrassing invective against himself that made him sound like a pathetic loser. But somehow he couldn't get himself to stop. "I date younger women because they're the only ones who'll have me. And I pretend I'm having a great time, when in reality, I'm bored out of my mind. Why do you think I like hanging out with you? Apart from being unbelievably sexy, you're the most interesting woman I get to hang out with, who's not my grandmother or my sister."

His eyes were clouded and bleak. "So, now you know the truth. Aren't you sorry you asked?"

Cynthia kept her expression neutral. She wasn't sorry she'd asked, but she was knocked for six that he'd answered so candidly. She'd only been — as Jane would say — "taking the mickey." As feigned as his arrogance was, it was sometimes hard to take, and every once in a while, she just had to call him on it. But as his eyes cleared, his complexion went pallid and she could tell that whatever had come over him that had made him pour out his heart, he was regretting it now, poor baby. Teasing him was one thing. Total humiliation he didn't deserve. She wanted to put her arms around him and tell him everything would work out, as she would with

Sarita, but that would only make things worse. So she did the next best thing.

She punched him in the arm. "You're an idiot! Do you think every woman over twenty-five is a gold digger?"

"Ow, again. Dammit. Why do you always *do* that?"

Now that she'd broken the tension, she went on. "There's a woman right under your nose who's perfect for you. And she likes you. *A lot*."

"Why, Cynthia, this is so sudden. I mean, there's that age difference you mentioned, but, hey, I don't mind if you don't. And I could get used to being a kept man."

She punched him again. "Inez, you moron."

"*Inez*?" He stopped rubbing his arm where she'd hit him, and stared at her. "You think Inez ...likes me?"

Cynthia swore at him in every language she knew, ending with English. "Horse's ass. You've never even noticed, have you?" She banged her fist on the table, rattling her empty coffee cup. "How is it possible that anyone can be so oblivious to what's right in front of them?" She glared at him. "*Parvo!* Just for once, I wish that you'd open your eyes."

Once more, the room went hazy. It felt like it was pulling back from the center. The sensation was dizzying. This time, Michael slapped his hand to his forehead. *Whoa*. What the hell was *this*?

"Michael! Are you all right?" Cynthia's voice came from far away. He felt her touch his arm, and he fumbled for her hand. The room brightened again, and her face swam back into focus.

"Yeah. Yeah, I'm fine. Just got woozy for a minute, that's all."

"It's all that shrimp. I told you not to eat it."

"You did." He counted to ten, and then tried standing up. He still felt foggy headed, but he was relieved when he realized that at least he wasn't going to hurl. Looking down at Cynthia, he kept his voice as natural as he could manage. "And you were right about… everything, I guess. I'd better go open my store. Thanks for the chow, doll."

She watched as he walked away, holding himself like a drunk trying to follow a straight line. *Puxa!* He looked so glassy-eyed and flushed. She hoped he wasn't getting a fever.

"Cynthia!" Jane came trotting in from the office, a look of awe on her face. "Guess whose office called and booked a table for the opening? Go on — *guess.*"

Cynthia smile was smug. "Sorry to spoil your fun, Jane, but I'm afraid I already know."

Jane scowled. "You already knew that Biff Hunt was coming here tomorrow night, and you didn't tell anyone?"

"*Biff Hunt*? Seriously? I thought you were talking about the governor and first lady. *Nossa* — Sarita will be over the moon when she hears." She bounced up and down in her chair. "Ooo. Ooo. Ooo — is he coming with his wife? I love her."

"Unfortunately, no. He's coming with his co-star, Evelina Janvier. They're filming an action flick or some such nearby." Jane raised her eyebrows. "The governor and his wife are coming as well? Oh, my."

"Uh-huh. She's organized a women's conference over at the Long Beach Convention Center. Lots of heavy hitters flying in to speak. All the hotels for miles are booked. Even the *Mary* has gotten some of the overflow, which bodes well for our first week's bookings. I sent her an invitation, but I didn't think the governor himself would come along too." Cynthia crinkled her brow. "Which one is Evelina Janvier?"

Jane waved a hand dismissively. "Oh, you know the one. Tall, long dark hair, looks a bit like Morticia, only thinner and with thicker lips. I'd have preferred it if his wife were coming with. I've seen everything she's ever done. There's nothing I enjoy more than a good comedy, and Jessica Green is brilliant at it. I think it has to be much harder to do than drama, but I'm a chemist, not an actress, so how would I know?" Jane sat in the chair Michael had recently vacated, and peeked into the silver coffee pot on the table. "Any more in here? I could use a cup. I've been taking reservations since eight o'clock this morning. You've done a marvelous job of advertising, Cynthia."

Cynthia shrugged self-consciously at the unexpected compliment. "Better than I'd hoped if we've got movie stars and politicians coming the first night." She knocked on the wooden table. "Let's hope things continue to go well."

"Good morning." Sarita trailed in, looking prettily drowsy-eyed, and carrying a large, thick book. She yawned and took the chair on the other side of her mother, kissed her on the cheek, and plopped the book on the table.

"Good morning, Sleeping Beauty." Cynthia moved the covered casserole dish out of Sarita's way.

Sarita sniffed and wrinkled her nose. "I smell Rohini's cinnamon waffles, but mixed with something else." With apprehension, she eyed the covered dish. "What's in there?"

"There are waffles and fresh éclairs, but Cris also made some shrimp he wanted us to taste. Would you like some? Michael tried it, and said it was very good."

Sarita shuddered. "No, thanks. Who can eat shrimp for breakfast?"

"I'd have to agree. I can barely choke down a piece of toast." Jane put milk in her coffee and twisted her head, as she tried to read the title of Sarita's book from across the table. "What have you got there?"

Sarita poured herself coffee, still not sure whether she wanted a waffle, or something else. "It's James Steele's picture book history of the *Queen Mary*. I just can't put it down."

Cynthia gave Jane a you'll-be-sorry look. "When you're still sitting here an hour from now, don't forget that you were the one who asked." She mimicked Sarita, "Did you know that the length of the *Queen Mary* is longer than the Eiffel Tower?"

Sarita scowled. "It *is* longer than the Eiffel Tower. And twice as powerful as the *Titanic*."

"*Ay*." Cynthia held her head in her hands. "Not this again, Sarita. Please."

"Oh, hush," Jane admonished. "I enjoy reading about times gone by, as it happens."

That was all Sarita needed to hear. Her morning grogginess vanished instantly. She stuck her tongue out at her mother, and crowed with triumph when Cynthia pouted. "Ha. Ha. Ha. See? I'm three for one." Playfully, she poked her. "Looks like you're the only one on the team who's not a ship geek, *Mamãe*."

She slid her chair closer to Jane's, pulling her book along with her. "Look at this, Jane. This is the section I started last night: *The Glory Years*. It's about all the famous people who sailed on the *Mary*."

Jane scooted closer to Sarita and leaned into the page. "Ah, there's Uncle Winnie," she said, tongue-in-cheek. She winked at Cynthia, who rolled her eyes.

"Winston Churchill, yes." Engrossed in the past, Sarita was oblivious to their antics. "During the war, the crew would list him on the passenger manifest as 'Colonel Warden.' He insisted that the lifeboat assigned to him had a machine gun fitted to it, so he could resist capture at all costs." She turned the page eagerly. "But here's the one I find the most fascinating — 'Dolores Simpson: The Notorious Brown-Haired Lady.'"

Jane peered down at the photo of a smartly dressed, but rather plain young woman. "She certainly doesn't look all that notorious."

"Looks can be deceiving." Sarita was thoroughly enjoying herself now. "She's wanted for manslaughter. In fact, guess what? She's still considered a fugitive, even though this was over fifty years ago."

"She killed someone? Who? And they never found her?" Cynthia was getting pulled into the tale in spite of herself. She dragged her chair around so she could see.

"Nope. Dolores fell in love with one of the crew, a man named Oliver Jenkins. They kept their affair a secret, because she was a nanny for one of the families who were aboard for a holiday cruise. She and Oliver sneaked off the ship together, when the *Mary* docked for supplies. Here — look." Sarita pointed to the page opposite the woman's photo. "There's a photograph of him too. And one of the letters he wrote her, and even a newspaper headline."

Jane was now sandwiched in between Cynthia and Sarita as all three of them examined the photos of the two lovers. "That's him? Yum. No wonder she left with him," declared Cynthia.

"I'm not so sure I'm with you on that." A tiny frown line formed on Jane's forehead as she examined Jenkins's photo. "It's true that he's very fit, but there's something about his eyes that's... unnerving."

Sarita sipped her coffee, and considered the photo again. "Maybe it's because this is a reproduction of an old sepia photo. They don't always come out as well as the original." She looked at the next reproduction — a newspaper headline — and read aloud. "*Manhunt for Dolores Simpson: Wanted in the Death of Jaclyn Torin.*"

"Go on — read the letter to us, Sarita," Jane urged. "You're the only one who doesn't need reading glasses."

Sarita was only too happy to oblige. She angled the book closer, and read:

My darling girl,

I see sadness in you, and I wonder if you see it in me, too. These bleak lives that you and I are forced to live, the deception we are forced to perpetuate, is driving me mad. I wanted to keep my feelings a secret from you, but I feel that I must tell you.

I saw you again at the pool today. We made eye contact, but I had my duties, and you were not alone. Were you thinking what I was thinking? I now know what it's like to hold you, and I can't wait until I can hold you again.

It's late. I'm alone in my quarters. The night sea air is cooling. That's a blessing, because my heart is beating fast, and I'm pining for the feel and taste of you. You're all I think about.

You. Just you.

Love,

Oliver

When Sarita put the book down, the three of them were lost in thought. And then Cynthia shook her head. "You might have a point about this fellow, Jane. I guess I'm a cynic, but I just couldn't see myself finding a letter like that romantic. It feels…how can I describe it? Too much."

Sarita nodded. "That's what I thought when I read it. But maybe that's the way men wrote to women back then?"

Jane inspected the photos, a thoughtful look on her face. "I don't doubt things were different half a century ago. Look at her clothing, for example. Quite stylish, for a nanny. The hat, the heels. Who could run after children in shoes like that? But I suppose everyone dressed like that back then."

"True. We can't expect nannies to have worn track suits and sneakers during the era. Especially on a luxury ocean liner." Cynthia pointed to the reproduction of the letter. "Where did they find this, Sarita? Does it say?"

"In her cabin, hidden among her things. According to the police reports, when she took off with Oliver, she left it behind, along with everything else she'd brought with her."

Jane picked up her cup and sipped. "Huh. You'd think she'd at least take the letter with her. I can see leaving the rest, if they needed to hurry off the ship. But a love letter from the man she loved, with whom she was leaving? That's something she could have tucked into her pocket, surely?"

"And so who was Jaclyn Torin, *filhinha*? And why did Dolores murder her?" Cynthia squinted at the page which showed the newspaper headline.

"It wasn't exactly like that, but that's the part of the story that's really awful," Sarita replied sadly. "Dolores was charged with..." she skimmed through the text and quoted from the article, "'reckless endangerment, bumped up to manslaughter because of her position and maritime law.' And there's a whole bunch of other stuff here that made those charges particular to just this case." She ran her finger down the page. "Basically, they hit her with every allegation they could, because Jaclyn — 'Jackie'— was the little girl in Dolores's charge."

"*Santa Maria*. She was killed by her own nanny?" Cynthia felt a chill run down her spine, thinking back to the days when, as a single parent, she had to rely on babysitters for Sarita.

"No, *Mamãe*. Let me finish. Jackie's parents slept in one of the staterooms, and Jackie slept in her nanny's room. What they think is that the little girl woke up in the middle of the night, saw her nanny was gone, and went to look for her. The police said that the nanny should have expected that to happen, should have known that Jackie was too young to be left on her own. That's why they charged her with reckless endangerment. What happened next was her fault." In an unconscious gesture, Sarita touched the cheek of the little girl in the photo. "They found Jackie in one of the swimming pools early the next morning. She'd drowned."

Jane lurched up so fast, her chair went crashing over. Sarita's head shot up in alarm. "What's wrong?" She looked over at her mother and saw that Cynthia had her eyes squeezed shut and her hands pressed against her mouth. "*Mãe,* what did I say wrong? Please tell me."

"Jane." Cynthia caught Jane's sleeve, then released it, as though it had scalded her. "She didn't know. I swear to you — she had no idea."

Hands gripped into fists, Jane forced herself to breathe. "I can see that. It's all right. I just wasn't expecting it." Sarita glanced back and forth between the two women anxiously. Jane patted her shoulder. "It's fine, truly, Sarita. Not to worry. I think I'll go up to my room for a bit. Pardon me."

Mother and daughter watched her as she walked off, their faces mirroring their dismay.

After his breakfast with Cynthia, Michael opened his shop, flicked on the lights, went to the cash register, and dropped his keys next to it.

Hands on hips, he walked from the front of his shop to the back, surveying every detail. For the first time, he noticed what a dreary place it was: Dusty shelves filled with tacky, uninspired souvenirs, guide books faded by the sun, cheap t-shirts he'd marked down to cost over a year before that still hadn't sold. The only thing that looked bright and fresh was the display where he'd hung Marisol's stickers.

He shook his head. He must have been blind not to see it before. The place was a mess. And he'd just bought random, stupid junk to fill it up — no thought, no plan whatsoever — the same way he handled everything else in his life. No wonder he was barely making ends meet.

Well, that was going to change, right now. He reached for the landline phone near the register, and pressed in a number. "It's Michael, sis. Good. You? Good. Hey, listen — can I stop by later tonight? Yeah, I know it's not Wednesday. No, I'm not bringing a date. It'll just be me. I've got an idea I want to run by you..."

After he hung up, he stood there, thinking.

"Inez," he murmured.

The corridor was lively with morning activity. Maids carrying linens and cleaning supplies bustled in and out of staterooms. Guests who were checking out herded their children and steered their luggage around cleaning carts, while chatting about flight schedules and what they'd seen while staying aboard the *Mary*.

Jane kept her cabin door open as a signal to the cleaners that it was fine for them to come through. She was usually down in the office by this time of day, and she had no intention of interfering with their schedule by staying in her room and brooding. She only needed a moment away from everyone, to collect herself. And looking at the ocean and the dock through the portholes, while munching M&Ms from her cache, was helping in that effort tremendously.

Was this who she wanted to be for the rest of her life — a woman who fell to pieces over any number of innocent triggers? Would the mere thought of the daughter and, if she was to be truthful with herself, the husband she missed, forever make her insides twist with that muddle of joy mangled by grief and regret?

She crumpled the candy wrapper, feeling slightly ill from sugar overload. Candy wasn't the solution, but neither was sitting in an analyst's office, as Angela had suggested time and again. Good lord, no. Her sister-in-law was well-meaning, but she was American, and Americans rushed headlong into therapy and took pharmaceuticals for "depression" at the slightest provocation. As a chemist, Jane knew better than most that it was healthier by a long ways to be addicted only to chocolate.

But perhaps it was time she let herself remember. Throwing away the wrapper, she pulled out a book of photographs she kept tucked in the bottom drawer of her dresser. She couldn't bear leaving her photos behind in England, but she hadn't been able to look through them since long before she'd arrived in California. She sat on her bed, and burrowed against the pillows. Propping the photo book against her knees, she took a deep breath, and opened it.

The photo right in front was from the final bunch she had of Gabriella, taken during the last holiday the three of them had shared. She'd left the photos loose at the front of the album with the intention of affixing them more permanently. And then she'd never opened the album again.

She blinked to keep her eyes from filling. Hand shaking, she held the photo up. They'd taken one of their fishing yachts down the Amalfi coast and docked it by a seaside fish tavern. Gabriella was hamming it up for the camera, grinning like a green-eyed imp, as she pretended to steal the last of the fried calamari — her favorite — from her father's plate. Her hair was bleached white gold by the sun, and, in defiance of the sunscreen with which her mother — having the Englishwoman's fear of sunburn — had coated her,

her skin was tanned brown as a monkey's. Gabriella had gotten her father's Mediterranean complexion, along with his thick, dark eyelashes. 'Miceli lashes,' Jane had dubbed them. Angela and Vincenzo had them too, and it had given Jane a secret delight that her daughter had inherited them, as her own lashes and brows were so pale they were almost colorless.

Antoni had played his part for the photo as well, pretending to be caught off guard as his food was pilfered; his palms held up, his warm brown eyes with those enviable lashes open wide and lit with humor. Although sorrow still clamped her throat, she managed a chuckle. She traced the image of her daughter's face, and, fingers wavering for just a moment, her husband's.

She wondered, not for the first time, where Antoni was now, although she had only to ask Angela, if she truly wanted to know. They never spoke of him. Or of Gabriella. Was he well? Had their daughter's death aged him as it had her?

Despite her sister-in-law's reassurances, she wasn't blind. She knew she looked at least ten years older than she had only two years before. Although admittedly, it still jolted her when she passed a mirror unexpectedly, always having the momentary, absurd thought that her mother had popped in for a visit.

She rifled through the loose photos, and found one of the three of them that the owner of the tavern had taken for them. Now *there* was the Jane she remembered — Antoni on her right, Gabriella on her left, and she with her arms around both, relaxed and smiling, in love with her family and her life. They looked marvelous together. They'd had such a fab time on that holiday.

Gabriella had her same silly sense of humor. They'd both guffaw over the puns that only made Antoni groan, "How can a woman with a doctorate degree collapse into laughter at a joke that starts with, 'a grasshopper walks into a bar'?"

It hit Jane then how much *fun* she used to be, and what an old fuddy-duddy she'd turned into. She was going to frame this photo straightaway, and put it on her desk in the office. It was stupid of her not to have photos out — what had she been thinking? Gabriella was still her daughter and Antoni, well, he was still Gabriella's father, if not her husband anymore, in any real sense of the world.

She propped their photo against the lamp on the night stand, put the rest of the holiday ones aside, and then picked up the album again. The photo that stared back at her from behind the worn plastic covering loosened something inside her, and this time her chuckle felt lighter. Taken on their annual trip to New York about ten years earlier, it was of the whole Miceli and Perotta clan, although certainly she and Vincenzo were the focus of the shot. It was the October trip when she was eight months pregnant, and Vincenzo had painted a pumpkin on her bulging belly. She stood there with her shirt lifted up to just below her bra, her huge, orange bump stuck right into the camera. She had crossed her eyes and stuck out her tongue, and Vincenzo and Antoni, on either side of her, had pointed to her belly and laughed like loons. Angela had her hand over her mouth, hiding her smile, because Marco, the old stick-in-the-mud, had scolded them that their behavior was "inappropriate."

She grunted with irritation as she remembered that. There Marco was, sitting next to his wife, looking displeased and constipated, as always. "Pickle Puss Perotta," as Antoni liked to call him. It was a pity that when he passed on so unexpectedly, neither she nor Antoni could muster up any genuine sense of loss. She'd always wondered if that might be true for Angela as well.

Meanwhile, at the far end of the photo, her parents-in-law were doing their best not to show how scandalized they were by her comportment. But they always had been, poor things. And when Gabriella was born, they'd had far too many provincial opinions about how to raise a girl. To Jane's mind, it had been a fortunate thing that they'd visited only intermittently. It had made it easier for her to bite her tongue and avoid serious rows.

"Of course they like you," Angela would insist time and again. "It's only that you're different from what they're used to."

And thank God for that, Jane had thought often enough, especially when she observed how beleaguered her sister-in-law was, her life spent doing headstands trying to please them, as well as her husband.

They were all gone now. Even with their imperfections, they'd been family: Marco, Mr. and Mrs. Miceli…Gabriella. Everything was changed. She and Angela had only each other, now. Vincenzo had been away for longer than Antoni had.

She touched the inside of her cheek with her tongue as she thought of her nephew. That business was utter nonsense. She preferred not to stick her nose in between people and their own children, but after all…

From the doorway came a childish giggle. Standing there was the same little girl who'd paid Jane a visit a few weeks before.

Jane sat up, both surprised and annoyed. "Still here, are you? I thought you'd be long gone by now."

"I'm always here. I never go home." She giggled again and sashayed right in. Once more, the scent of lavender filled the room. It was early enough that she was still in her nightclothes, just as she'd been the last time she'd barged in. But this time, she was wearing a pair of women's high heels that were far too big for her. As she walked, she dragged them along, trying to keep them from falling off.

"Make yerself ter home," Jane muttered. Then more loudly, she pointed to the shoes, "And where did we get those?"

The little girl stopped in the middle of room by the desk and pirouetted for Jane, the high heels digging into the plush carpeting and causing her to stumble here and there. "I'm allowed to wear them. Missy always lets me. Did you find her yet?"

"Find who, darling?" Was there *ever* an adult with this child? "Why don't you tell me your name, so we can get you back to... Missy, was it?"

"I want my doll." The little girl continued to circle, barely keeping her balance in her oversized footwear.

"Are you sure you should be wearing those? What if you fall?" Apart from the fact that it was unsafe for the child to be in them, something else about those shoes was niggling at Jane. Who allowed a child this age to traipse about unaccompanied, doing whatever took her little fancy? They deserved to be horsewhipped. "Where is your mummy?" She tried her best not to let her irritation show in her voice, but the little girl picked up on it all the same.

She stopped her spinning and gave Jane a sulky look. "You said you'd find my doll."

Uh-oh. Little Miss No Name was about to get stroppy. Gabriella hadn't been above a temper tantrum or two, that was for certain, especially when she was as young as this one. Time to divert. Tilting her head, Jane smiled at her. "Have you eaten? Should we go find mummy and see if she's waiting for you to have breakfast?"

Another pout. "I don't want breakfast." She banged her fists against her sides with each word. "I. Want. My. Doll." Then, quick as lightning, she snatched Jane's reading glasses off the desk and ran out the door with them, the borrowed heels slapping up and down with every step.

"Oh!" Jane gasped, and slid off the bed. "That little git!" She ran out the door, straight into a cleaning cart that was being pushed by one of the maids.

"Oh! I'm so sorry, *Señora* Jane —"

"No worries. It's my fault." Jane peered at the agitated maid. "We met when I first got here, I think. Inez, isn't it?"

Wringing her hands, Inez smiled nervously. "You remember me. Thank you. I'm so sorry," she said again. "Did you get hurt?"

Jane wasn't listening. She'd spied her reading glasses, flung down on the hall carpet. "*There* they are. Honestly, I can't believe it." She bent to retrieve them. Straightening, she turned to Inez. "Pardon me for jumping out at you like that. I was chasing a little girl who's been running around the corridors. She just marched into my room and snatched my glasses —"

"A little girl, *Señora*?" Inez was looking at her with dread. "About four years old?"

"Thereabouts. And she was wearing a pair of woman's high heels. Why? Have you seen her?"

"Oh, no." Inez was so distressed now, she felt ill. If her boss found out about this, she'd be fired. "I am so, *so* sorry. That is my daughter, Marisol. She comes with me here on Saturdays because my mother can't watch her. Oh, I can't believe she came into your suite! I left her alone for only one minute, just to go get some more towels."

Jane felt awful. "Oh, please. It's all right. It's fine, actually. I just thought she was up here on her own."

Inez stared at Jane in maternal fury as she remembered something else. "Did you say she was wearing a woman's high heels? *Dios mio,* she must have gone into one of the guest's wardrobes." She shoved the cleaning cart to the side of the hall, and slammed the lock on the brake. "Oh, I will spank her for this. She knows better, *Señora*."

As Inez turned to go, Jane caught her arm in alarm. "Good lord, no. Don't do that on my account. She's just a child. She meant no harm, I'm sure. Perhaps she was a bit bored, and felt like nosing around. Surely a telling off would do?"

Relief flooded through Inez. She had no intention of harming her daughter, but the *señora*'s concern for Marisol's welfare seemed like a lifeline. It meant that she wouldn't be reporting the incident. "*Ay*. It's so hard sometimes, being a working mother, *Señora* Jane. I *have* to bring her with me on Saturday. I have no choice."

Still holding Inez's arm, Jane patted the back of her hand. "Believe me, I know. I was a working mum as well. No one knows better than I how hard that can be. Talk to her, certainly, but I'd hate to think that she got a spanking because of me."

Inez smiled gratefully. "Thank you so much. I must go and speak to her about this right now. Please excuse me." Inez set off smartly down the hall to the room where she'd left her daughter, ready to give her a come-to-Jesus talk. It didn't matter how young Marisol was — she had to be made to understand that if Inez lost this job, they'd be in serious trouble. But when she got to the stateroom, she stopped short in uncertainty.

Marisol was sitting just where Inez had left her, still busily occupied with her crayons and coloring books. Nothing in the room was out of place, the wardrobe was closed, and her little pink Princess Jasmin sneakers were still on her feet, with the laces tied tight.

"Marisol? Did you leave this room at all while Mommy was gone?"

Marisol didn't even look up, she was so absorbed. She just shook her head. "Ah uh, Mommy. You told me to stay here."

A prickling sensation came over Inez. She sniffed the air and thought she detected a faint scent of lavender. "Did you see another little girl?"

That got Marisol's attention. She looked up. "What little girl, Mommy?"

Inez felt her whole body go cold. She hurried back to Jane's room and peeked in. Jane was at her desk, putting a photo in a frame, her reading glasses perched on the top of her head now, where they'd be safe.

"*Señora* Jane, sorry to bother you again, but…the little girl you saw…did she…have red hair?"

"Yes, indeed. Very pretty ginger hair." Jane glanced up with a smile, and then noticed Inez's expression. "Why? Was that not Marisol?"

"Marisol has black hair, like me." Inez spoke carefully. "I…have seen the little girl you saw too, *Señora*."

"You've seen her as well? Oh, for pity's sake. This is the second time I've seen her myself, and both times she was on her own." Jane spoke with passionate anger. "Honestly, some people don't deserve to be parents. Don't they understand how easily something could happen to a child that age, running about by herself on a ship this size, with all these tourists? I've a good mind to report it, I truly do."

The peculiar look on Inez's face made Jane realize she was reacting excessively yet again, when she'd only just promised herself that she wouldn't. Feeling awkward, she cleared her throat, straightening the photo in the frame to give her hands something to do. "Don't mind me, Inez. I have a tendency to dramatize these things. I'm trying my best to sort that out." She flipped the photo frame over, secured the back, and then forced herself to smile as she looked up again. "But at least now we know that Marisol wasn't being naughty. I expect that's put your mind to rest then, hasn't it?"

Inez continued to study Jane. Would it be a good idea to try to enlighten her? Probably not. She swallowed. "Yes. Yes, *Señora* Jane, that's put my mind to rest. Thank you. Have a good day."

She turned and hurried back to Marisol, crossing herself as she ran. Only God or the devil knew why that child walked these corridors, and there was no way she was leaving Marisol up here in a room by herself — not today, not for one minute longer.

"Marisol — put your crayons away. We're leaving right now."

"But Mommy, I was in the middle of my picture." Marisol held up her coloring book. "Look how pretty it is."

Her mother was frantically packing up the things they'd brought with them. "*Chiquita,* don't argue with me. You're going down to Michael's. I'm almost done, and I need you to wait for me there."

"I can go to Michael's *now*? I don't have to wait for you to finish?" Marisol started shoving her crayons back in the box, coloring forgotten, pleased by this unexpected change in routine.

Inez raised a finger in admonition. "Yes. But you stay out of his way, and you don't touch anything. If you do what I tell you, I will let you pick out two stickers today, instead of just one." She swept up their bags, grabbed her daughter's hand and made a run for it.

Marisol jumped up and down in elation as her mother skirted around her cleaning cart and pulled her along. "Thank you, Mommy, *thank* you. I won't touch anything. I promise."

Inez stopped short in the middle of the hall as the excitement in her daughter's voice registered. She looked down at her, and in the midst of her unease, all the joy that Marisol had brought to her in just four short years flooded back to her. The stress of single motherhood, the financial worries that were a permanent part of her life these days, were worth it, she realized, because she couldn't imagine life without her child. For the first time, she thought with pity, rather than fear, of another woman's little girl, trapped forever in the passageways of the ship, searching for something she would never find.

Dropping their bags, Inez kneeled down and hugged Marisol fiercely. "Oh, my baby, my precious girl. I'm so lucky to be your mommy, do you know that? I love you, Marisol. I *love* you."

Marisol wrinkled her nose in bewilderment, even as she hugged her mother back. "I love you too, Mommy."

"Let's stop by to see Cristiano also. Perhaps he and the nice ladies in the kitchen will give you a treat."

Marisol's eyes went wide. "Will the cake lady be there?"

"Let's go see."

"What a great day this is turning out to be!" Marisol and her mother trotted briskly down the hall, hand in hand, past the open door of Jane's cabin. Neither of them even glanced to where Jane sat silently at her desk, her newly framed photo clutched to her chest, a bittersweet smile on her face, as every word of their exchange in the hallway reached her, clear as a bell.

CHAPTER SIX

Sunday, September 19, 2004:
Opening Night

The dining room of The Secret Spice was packed with glittering guests, some famous, some simply foodies out for a new experience, but all from the socially elite. Every one of the anticipated A-listers had honored their reservations. Tony Chi had accepted Cynthia's invitation to see how his creation looked on opening night. He'd come with a party of six, and they were enjoying a bottle of Blanc des Millénaires, on the house. The Governor and First Lady, at the Governor's request, sat at a table where they were conspicuously visible to all other diners, while Biff Hunt and his co-star chose a more secluded spot, and then studiedly ignored those who were trying, discreetly, to celebrity-gaze.

One and all enjoyed the ambiance. Glowing white orchids arranged in cut crystal vases were at the center of every table. Champagne sparkled from glass flutes. Shining silverware was dipped into one-of-a-kind delicacies. And stainless steel platters, carried by waiters in starched white jackets, reflected the café lighting, and the gleaming smiles of the guests.

Cynthia, in her stoplight-red hostess dress, watched from the sidelines, and basked in all the glitter like a pirate gloating over newly plundered treasure. From disowned ranching heiress to single-mom cocktail waitress to *this,* she smiled to herself, and then hummed the refrain, *"If my friends could see me now."*

She stopped Emilio as he was going back into the kitchen with an empty tray, and murmured so only he could hear. "Don't look back, but in your section, table four, position three, is Eric Gladwell, top food critic. That whole check gets comped, and make sure you let Cristiano and Rohini know which order is his. Be your most courteous to him — you hear me? I sat him in your section because I know I can depend on you."

Before Emilio could recover from his surprise at that vote of confidence, she spoiled it by adding, "So don't let me down, or you'll be out on your ass tomorrow, I promise you. Now, go let the kitchen know he's here."

Flushed with nerves now, the boy bobbed his head once, and hurried off to do her bidding.

Oblivious to his discomfort, Cynthia continued her survey of the room. Table one, section two looked low on champagne. Before she could summon their waitress, Jane, chic in jade silk, stepped over smartly, and asked if they'd like another bottle.

Doesn't miss a trick, that one, Cynthia mused. None of them did. All four of the partners, and Cristiano too, had worked like dervishes to make this happen. It wouldn't have been possible otherwise. Although she did allow herself the private self-congratulation that it was her ingenuity and salesmanship that had gotten the ball rolling, above all. That, and the eight million dollars belonging to an old man who doubtless hadn't been in his right mind when he gave it to her. And in little more than a month, she'd have to find a way to return every penny, plus interest.

Sarita appeared at her mother's side. "What did you say to Emilio just now that got him looking so tense?"

Cynthia slanted her a glance. "Are you his lawyer now?" Then she turned to look at her daughter more fully. "Where'd you get that dress?"

"Do you like it? I ordered it online."

The dress in question was a deep mauve knit that clung to every one of Sarita's burgeoning curves, with a neckline scooped just low enough to reveal a hint of cleavage. The color emphasized the creaminess of her skin, set off her dark eyes, and the glossy, gilded-brown waves of her hair. There was nothing improper or flashy about it all, except that in it, Sarita, who was showing unambiguous signs that she'd inherited her mother's legendary figure, looked like a luscious, sweet plum just begging to be plucked. All Cynthia could do was stare at her and think, *God help me* — she's not even sixteen!

With a smug, female look in her eye that made Cynthia want to squirm, Sarita smiled at her.

She knew she looked good in the dress, just as she knew there was nothing about it to which Cynthia could object.

She was wrong about that. "I'm not sure that material is appropriate for this type of an event." Cynthia hated the stuffiness of her own words.

Sarita was incredulous. "It's knit. Same as yours."

"I'm older than you —" Cynthia began defensively.

"*Bollocks*," Sarita interjected, one of her newest exclamations, picked up from Jane.

Cynthia opened her mouth, then closed it again. Though they'd been whispering, she saw that some guests had turned to glance their way. So she pulled rank. Her voice low but resolute, she commanded, "Go in the kitchen. Help Angela fill the pastries. Isn't that what you promised you'd be doing for us tonight? And since I said I'd pay you for that, you'd better get to work."

Sarita may have looked like a budding movie starlet, but she was about to make her mother's point and prove just how young she still was. "That's not fair, *Mãe*. You promised you'd let me meet Biff Hunt first."

"You're not going anywhere near him in that dress," hissed Cynthia. "You look like jailbait in it. That woman he's with will want to suck out all your blood the minute she lays eyes on you. Get in that kitchen. *Now*. And for godssakes, put on an apron!"

Feeling as though she would burst into flames from anger and shame, Sarita glared at Cynthia. She wanted to stamp her feet, just as she had when she was a child. She *felt* like a child still — always, in fact — when she was around her mother. But she held on to her dignity. Spinning on her heels, she stalked away, a humiliated, but outraged Cinderella, exiled to drudgery, when all she'd wanted to do was enjoy the party in her cute new dress. Well, she'd still have her handsome prince — see if she didn't — and her mother could, as Jane would say, "go hang."

With a sinking heart, Cynthia watched her go, aware that she'd handled things horribly. There was so much she needed to explain to her daughter, but they had so little time together these days. Sighing, she promised herself she'd find a way to make it up to her. For the moment, though, she had work to do. The restaurant was an absolute mob scene by now. Even Michael had turned up, looking dashing, as always, and escorting an elegantly-dressed brunette.

"Can you squeeze another two in here, doll?" Michael winked at Cynthia.

Cynthia allowed herself a small pat on the back when she recognized the brunette. At least she'd gotten that right. "Well, well, Michael," she grinned as she kissed him on both cheeks, "Aren't you smart? And I'm not referring to your *GQ* outfit."

Michael got the message. "I am pretty smart, but sometimes… takes a while, you know?"

"I certainly do. Nice to see you, Inez. You look lovely."

Inez blushed prettily. "Thank you, *Señora* Cynthia. The restaurant looks fantastic."

"I hope you enjoy the food as much." Cynthia seated them at one of the nicest tables she had left, and told their waiter, "Comp the drinks for Mr. McKenna and his companion, please." She smiled at Michael again. "We've got three great specials tonight, although you've already tried the shrimp." With a wink at them both, she turned to greet new arrivals.

Meanwhile, Jane, who was sharing hostess duties with Cynthia, stopped back into the kitchen to report was what happening out front. "It's madness out there, but so far, everyone seems happy. The Shrimp Rohini appetizer is a smashing success."

Cristiano was so busy, he could barely glimpse at her. As hectic as it was in the dining room, the kitchen was a hive of activity, with dozens of worker bees buzzing about. "Tell me about it. We have to prep more. Rohini's in the back, cleaning them right now. We're pushing other appetizers in the meantime." He called over to one of the station chefs, "The mussels are done. Better check that calamari."

Jane turned to Angela. "And how's our 'cake lady' doing?"

The whole crew had adopted the title she'd been knighted with by Marisol, a fact that pleased Angela no end. Flushed from the heat of the kitchen, jittery with excitement and nerves over her debut, she looked up from the task of washing raspberries to give Jane a shaky smile. "We should be all set, but I've got some extra tart shells in the oven, just in case."

Sarita, on the other hand, looked positively morose as she worked beside Angela. Swallowed up in one of Cristiano's aprons, she stood with her head down and her shoulders stooped, as she zigzagged chocolate sauce onto dessert plates with little enthusiasm.

Observing this, Jane asked her, "I thought you were going to help us in the dining room for a while before you came back here."

Sarita keep her gaze downward. "Yeah, well, I guess my *mother* changed her mind."

The statement was uttered with such vitriol that Jane's eyebrows shot up. She slid a glance over to Angela for enlightenment, who just shrugged. No one in the galley had any idea what was going on.

Sarita hadn't said a word to anyone since she'd come in looking like thunder, and then set to work at the pastry station.

Wisely changing the subject, Jane went on lightly, "Well, I had a fascinating conversation with your Governor." She looked back at Cristiano. "He loved the shrimp, by the way. Didn't stop eating the whole time we talked."

Still working briskly, Cristiano just nodded.

Jane continued, "Anyway, it seems he and his wife are not of the same political persuasion. Did you know that?"

The entire kitchen, including the busboys who'd been rinsing plates, and the waiters who'd dashed in to pick up their orders, stopped what they were doing to gape at Jane. Even Sarita looked up from her sulks.

Angela voiced their incredulity. "For petessakes, Jane. Of course. Don't you know what family she's from?"

"As it happens, I do. I'm not an idiot. I was referring to the fact that *he's* a Republican. I'd no idea. How can one possibly make a marriage like that work? Not that I care much about your numbskull politics, anyway. Who in their right heads elects an actor to run a government?"

Rohini came in, carrying an enormous platter of cleaned shrimp. "Yes, indeed. You Brits did *so* much better when you elected a Thatcher." She set the platter down at Cristiano's station. "This should be enough, don't you think?"

Ignoring Rohini snideness, Jane went on. "That's what prompted the discussion, as a matter of fact. He remarked on my being English, asked about British society, and the next thing you know, we were debating healthcare. I said it was preposterous that there isn't a universal system in place here, and his wife agreed with me. I told him he should start a program in California."

"Hah. A Republican supporting government healthcare. That'll be the day." Cristiano dotted shrimp with butter, still working at the speed of light, but now actively listening to Jane at the same time. This was too good to miss.

"He seemed genuinely amenable to the idea. But I'd best get back out front. I don't want to leave Cynthia on her own for too long, although I must say, she's handling this like she was born to do it."

Everyone pretended not to hear Sarita's huff of disgust.

Jane's assessment was spot-on: Cynthia was a virtuoso. Her feet ached from walking in her signature heels. She was fretting over how to cut off Tony Chi's party without offending them. They were on their third bottle of champagne, and getting close to raucous. One of the waitresses spilled hot soup on herself. She wasn't badly burned, thank heaven, but still had to be sent home. Now they were understaffed. And every time she stepped into the kitchen, Sarita shot her a venomous look. Nevertheless, Cynthia soldiered on, looking for all the world as though she were having the time of her life.

Her next stop was Biff Hunt's table. Knowing he couldn't step outside his house to snatch his mail without it being front page news the next day, she'd given him space to settle in. But as hostess and owner, protocol dictated that she welcome him personally. In earnest conversation with his dinner companion, he didn't see Cynthia approaching. She got an unintentional earful, as a result.

"I'm married, Evelina. You know that."

"I don't care."

Oh, *shit*, Cynthia swore to herself. This is the last thing I need right now.

But her Vegas cocktail waitress training held. "And how are we doing here?" Feigning deafness, her smile slid across her face like honey over hot biscuits. "Ms. Javier, Mr. Hunt, I'm Cynthia Taylor, one of the owners. It's such an honor and a pleasure to have you both here at The Secret Spice Café tonight."

Hunt fixed Cynthia with his celebrated gaze. "Nice to meet you, Cynthia."

In a practiced, pleasant tone, she went into her spiel. "Our Grand Opening Specials this evening were specially chosen by our chefs. They are Arugula Salad with Citrus Vinaigrette, Shrimp Rohini Appetizer, Mushroom Pasta in Pink Gorgonzola Sauce, and for dessert, Raspberry Chocolate Truffle Tarts." Cynthia pulled her eyes away from Hunt's and looked down at his plate. "I see you've tried the shrimp."

"I'm enjoying it very much."

Oh my. He certainly was dazzling, wasn't he? Seeing those cheekbones up close, they could cut diamonds. And that voice, velvet over sand, was enough to melt the ice cubes in every glass in the dining room. Cynthia couldn't help but feel a spasm of awareness, even as she kept her tone professional. "The chefs will be so pleased to hear it."

Evelina must have been able to read her thoughts. She was practically glowering at her. Cynthia pretended not to notice. "And you, Ms. Janvier? Would you like to try the shrimp?"

Janvier gave a hand flick of disinterest. "No, thank you. It's swimming in butter."

"Oh, I'm so sorry. I hope you'll try something else. All our salads are organic and garden fresh." Years of waitressing kept Cynthia's tone resolutely obsequious. Celebrities, politicians and card sharks came in all shapes and sizes, from the spoiled brat to the downright humble. She'd learned to deal with them all. "Naturally this is our treat, and we'd love it if you'd order anything that strikes your fancy."

That coaxed a smile out of Evelina. "Thank you. That's very nice."

But the actress wasn't there to audition the menu. Her appetite was fixed on something else altogether. She'd barely taken her eyes off Hunt the whole time Cynthia had been standing at their table. Cynthia knew she was *de trop*. It was time to go.

"Well, I'm sure you have a lot to discuss with your new film coming out, so I'll leave you to it. Ah — here comes the waiter with your complimentary bottle of champagne. Please don't hesitate to call any one of us over if you need anything at all." Her smile was still cast in iron as she tilted her head at them and then turned away.

She'd barely walked three feet, when she heard Janvier get right back on topic. "You know she doesn't love you the way I do." She managed to make her whisper beguiling at the same time it was tenacious. "I just wish we could be together."

Cynthia's mask slipped just a tiny bit when she rolled her eyes. *That* was certainly not going to end well. Hunt seemed mesmerized by the woman. But, it was none of her business. She had her own problems.

By ten o'clock, there'd been a few minor calamities. Everyone in the Chi party was inebriated, and it took firm persuasion to get them to go home by taxi. A certain film idol left even before his main course was served. This was due to his experiencing a bizarre and somewhat missish attack of the vapors. And then there was the blister the size of Mars which had sprung up on Cynthia's heel.

But apart from these, opening night went much, much better than any of them could have hoped. Jane she blew out a breath of relief, and mentally went over all the fits and starts of the evening that they should discuss come tomorrow.

Most of the diners were gone by now, but a few lingered over a second cup of coffee and to savor one of Angela's desserts. Now that things had quieted, Angela, both ecstatic and unconvinced in regards to the reviews that had been coming back to her all night via the wait staff, stole a moment to come up front, so she could see what was happening for herself.

"I can't believe this," she whispered breathlessly, even as she stretched her shoulders and rubbed her stiff neck. "That's really Eric Gladwell over there, eating *my* Cinnamon Savarin." She stopped rubbing her neck to chew on one of her cuticles.

"What the devil's happened to your nails? I thought you'd stopped that," chided Jane. "There's no need to be so nervous. You're a smash hit. That's his second dessert."

"It isn't!"

"Is. I've kept a watch on him all evening. He had the Truffle Tart earlier, and ate every crumb."

"Oh, my God." Angela pressed her palms to her chest. "This... Jane...it's like I'm dreaming, you know? My whole life, I've never done anything right, but now, *this* happens. I feel like I'm going to be sick."

In a rare public display of affection, Jane patted Angela's shoulder. Then she snorted. "You surely wouldn't have believed it if you'd been out here to see Biff Hunt topple off his chair." She covered her mouth to hide her mirth. "I shouldn't be laughing at him. It's not right." She chuckled again. "But I can't seem to help myself. It was hilarious. And Emilio was absolutely gobsmacked, the poor lad. He'd just brought their champagne over to them when it happened."

"Yeah. We heard about Biff. The kid was as white as a ghost when he came back to tell us."

"He's had a rough night, what with that and Cynthia barking at him all evening."

"I noticed her doing that too. What that's about? Where is she, by the way? I thought she'd be out here."

"She limped off to see if Rohini has any herbs that will help her blister." Jane rolled her eyes. "Those heels are ridiculous, as I've said. Did you find out why she and Sarita quarreled earlier?"

"Nope. Apart from the one gripe we all heard, Sarita said nothing else about it. But she was mopey all night."

"Her mother infantilizes her."

"Oh, Jane. That's what you always think."

"What do you mean by *that*?"

Angela searched for words. Then she gave an irritated shrug. "Nothing. Never mind."

"Were you referring to someone in particular?" On the defensive, Jane's tone was icy now.

"No. Let's just change the subject, okay?" Angela tried to conciliate. She wanted to bite her own tongue. The remark had slipped out, and she knew she'd pay for it. "The last thing I want to do is have an argument with you, tonight of all nights."

Though far from placated, Jane dropped it. Angela was right. This wasn't the time or place. But sooner or later, they'd have to clear the air between them…over a number of things.

They stood silently, observing the remaining guests. Then Jane said, "Oh — I meant to tell you this earlier, and then it slipped my mind. When Hunt's agent called to confirm for tonight, he said, 'Tell Mrs. Taylor we saw her father. He sends his regards.'"

"'Mrs. Taylor?' That's Cynthia." Angela blinked at Jane. "Cynthia's father knows Biff Hunt?"

"So it would appear. And she still hasn't mentioned it. If you think about it, it was far too easy to get all these big names to come out this evening. There's more to Cynthia than we know. That bears scrutiny, don't you think?"

"*Shh,*" Angela hushed Jane. "She's back. She's coming over."

"What are you two whispering about?" Cynthia had surrendered to a more sensible pair of pumps. She was sporting a bandage on one heel.

"We were talking about Hunt," Jane answered, not untruthfully. "I wonder what the press is going to report tomorrow, regarding his little swoon this evening? Wasn't exactly in keeping with the manly image he strives to maintain, was it?"

Cynthia snickered. "Janvier almost had to use a fireman's hold to haul him out. It was all I could do not to burst out laughing."

"How'd she manage that? She's not much more than a bag of bones." Both were taken aback by Angela's disparagement, but her reason for it had nothing to do with malice, and everything to do with her being Italian. "It's not healthy for her to be that thin. She's even skinnier than I am. I bet she didn't have even *one* bite of my desserts."

Jane nudged Angela with her elbow. "Speaking of your desserts, look who's headed our way."

It was the food critic, Gladwell. "Excuse the interruption, ladies. I had to come over to congratulate you personally for such a fabulous meal." He'd already met Cynthia and Jane earlier. Now he positively beamed at Angela. "Am I right in assuming you're Angela Perotta, the woman responsible for those stunning truffle tarts?"

Angela was so bowled over by the description she could only nod. Did people actually describe chocolate tarts as 'stunning?' He astonished her further by picking up her hand and kissing it. "You, my dear, gave me some memorable moments this evening. I shall cherish them." Dumbstruck, Angela just stared at him.

From across the room, the sommelier was signaling madly to Cynthia. She turned to Gladwell and cooed, "We're thrilled that you enjoyed yourself, Eric. But it looks like we have some sort of vino crisis in the making. Perhaps California has run out of grapes. Will you excuse me for just one moment? I'll be back in a jiffy." Before she trotted off, she muttered to Angela so only she could hear, "Your mouth is hanging open. Close it."

Gladwell's smile encompassed both Angela and Jane now, his next words proving that his compliments were sincere. "My photographer is with me. I'd love to bring the chefs out and get some shots with you all for the magazine. Would that be possible?"

Unlike Angela, Jane rarely lost her self-possession, but this time she came close. Rohini would be so pleased. And what would it mean to Cristiano to have his name in a prestigious food journal again, after all these years? "Oh, *my*. I'm sure they'd be delighted, Mr. Gladwell."

"Call me Eric, please."

Angela didn't think she'd ever seen Jane's skin go that shade of pink. "Eric, then. I'll…I'll just go on back and get Rohini and Cristiano."

As she hurried off, Gladwell turned back to Angela. He still had her hand. "Now, you must tell me what that extra ingredient was in your chocolate sauce. It was a spice, I know, but not one I recognize. Wait, wait — the light bulb just went on." He grinned at her. "'The Secret Spice.' Clever, aren't you, you darling girl…"

Cristiano was jubilant when he heard the news, but neither Jane nor he expected Rohini's reaction.

"I'm not going out there. I can't."

"What do you mean, *corazon*? Of course you can." Cristiano pointed to himself and then to her. "We both did the cooking. This is a triumph we share."

"Cristiano, please. I don't want to go." Frantically, she waved him away. "You go. I'll...I'll clean up here."

Unaware of the true cause, Cristiano assumed that her reluctance was due to her shy nature. He spoke soothingly. "Nonsense. There's no need to be bashful, sweetheart."

Jane, also clueless, chimed in. "It'll be fine, Rohini. We'll all be together, and our photo will be in *Bon Appétit*. Won't that be lovely? Just think of all the publicity."

Cynthia was still with the sommelier, going over what wines and champagnes they needed to restock, when she looked up and saw Rohini being dragged from the kitchen by Cristiano and Jane. Then Jane left them to join Gladwell, where he appeared to be giving instructions to a woman setting up a camera. Rohini was wearing an expression of pure terror, and Cristiano was bent toward her, looking as though he was trying to reassure her. In a flash, Cynthia put it all together.

"Shit, shit, *shit*." Without a word to the startled steward, she hustled off, getting to them as quickly as her sore foot would allow. "Bring her back to the kitchen. She can't be out here for this, Cris." Cynthia's voice was soft, but frantic.

"What?" said Cristiano. "Why?"

"All right, everyone." Gladwell clapped his hands to get their attention. We're going to set up this shot by the bar. I want the entire crew. Cristiano and the ladies in front."

"Cynthia, help me." Rohini's whisper was desperate.

"Don't worry, I'll fix it." Cynthia murmured the promise, ignoring her own flutter of panic.

"Rohini, what's going on? Why are you afraid to have your picture taken?" As the photographer shuffled them all into place, Cristiano stayed protectively by her side and kept his voice low. But he was alarmed now, and frustrated, because he had no clue what was happening.

"I...I can't tell you."

"You can't tell *me* — the man who is in love with you — but you can tell Cynthia?"

At that startling declaration, Rohini's head shot up to see his face. He didn't look lover-like, though. He looked angry and hurt.

Just before the camera flashed, Cynthia — even without her heels, still seven inches taller than Rohini and wider by half — flashed a brilliant smile and stepped right in front of her. Before the photographer could set up the next shot, Cristiano snatched Rohini's hand and whisked her away.

It was after midnight now. Cynthia had more cramps in her muscles than a busload of pregnant women, and the blister on her heel was howling like a cat in heat. As exhausted as she was, she was still in the restaurant, closing up on her own.

Gladwell and his party were the last guests to leave, followed by the rest of the crew. As soon as they were gone, Angela ran into the ladies' room and vomited. The nervousness she'd been feeling all week over the opening, followed by the overwhelming abundance of accolades, had given her a whopper of a migraine. According to Jane, this was Angela's habitual reaction to accumulated anxiety. Cynthia insisted that Jane help Angela to bed.

But once Jane and Angela were upstairs for the night, she hadn't dared ask Rohini to lend a hand, either. Even though Cristiano had behaved like a true champion by stealing her away, and then coming back out alone to cover for her with Gladwell, the look on his face was anything but gallant as he stalked back into the kitchen to confront her afterward. Cynthia had straightened chairs, counted out receipts, closed up the register, and done everything else she could think of to stay out of their line of fire. She'd heard them in there, their voices more and more strident, as one had been hell-bent on getting an explanation, and the other had been equally determined not to give one. That little bout had ended with Cristiano stomping off, swearing in Spanish, and Rohini sniffling her way to her stateroom, alone.

She muttered to herself as she switched off lights. She *knew* this would happen. She'd said it to Michael. And now, unless her two chefs resolved their differences, they'd all have to deal with it. And wouldn't *that* be fun?

All in all, a physically and emotionally grueling day. Just as soon as she got the receipts and cash envelope into the office safe, she was going to head upstairs, fall face down onto her bed, and sleep until noon.

The sight that greeted her when she opened the office door had her wide awake in an instant. Emilio was sitting at her desk, in *her* chair, with Sarita sprawled on his lap. His hands were clamped to her hips, and they were kissing enthusiastically, so intent on each other that they didn't even hear her come in.

"*Santa Maria mãe de Deus!* What the hell is this?"

Emilio jumped up so fast, Sarita almost slid to the floor. Cynthia barked at him. "Is this what I hired you for — to neck with my daughter?"

While Emilio looked as though he would hotfoot it out the door the second Cynthia moved out of the way, Sarita appeared utterly composed, and even a little pleased. "Calm down, *Mãe*. We were just kissing. Surely you've seen kissing before. Maybe you've even done it yourself once or twice."

Cynthia's head whipped around to Sarita. "Seriously? You *seriously* think you're going to sass me now?"

"Yes, I do!" Sarita countered. "This is none of your business."

Emilio found the courage to interrupt, "Mrs. Taylor, I'm very sorry —"

"—Be quiet! No one was talking to *you*!"

"—Don't you dare apologize to her! What — are you sorry I let you kiss me?"

Cynthia and Sarita spat back at him in unison. Emilio looked from one to the other. Heedless of the fact that he was venturing into dangerous waters, he tried to reason with them. "Ladies, please, let's sit down and talk about this calmly."

"'Talk about this calmly'? You have the nerve to say that to me?" Cynthia could see the outline of the erection he still had in his pants, the little shit. "You're fired. Get your ass out of my restaurant." She pointed to the doorway. *"Now."*

Like a Pekingese trying to defend herself against a pit bull, Sarita stepped in front of him. "You can't fire him. He hasn't done anything wrong!"

"Oh, no? Just watch me."

All at once, Sarita's bravado deserted her. "Fine! Fine, *Mamãe* — play the dictator like you always do. Go ahead and fire him. It's not going to stop me from seeing him. He doesn't need your stupid job, anyway. You treat him like dirt, just like you treat me like dirt."

Cynthia was staggered. "What are you talking about, *filhinha*?"

"Don't call me that. I'm not your 'little' daughter." Crying with frustration now, she stuck two shaking fingers as close to her mother's face as she dared. "In less than two weeks, I'll be sixteen. But you still treat me like I'm ten. You don't want me to grow up, do you? That's why you made me stay in the kitchen tonight. God forbid I look good. God forbid I look better than you."

"That's not true at all. Sweetheart, please, listen to me —" Aghast, Cynthia tried to reach for her, but Sarita pulled back.

"No. I hate you. I *hate* you, *Mamãe*!"

Crying for all she was worth, she ran out of the room, while Cynthia stared after her, bulldozed and speechless.

Emilio squeezed his eyes shut and then opened them to look at Cynthia with remorse. "Mrs. Taylor, I'm sorry. Believe me — I'm so sorry."

And then, with all the courage he could muster in his young heart, he left her there to run after the girl he was sure he loved.

Cynthia stood motionless. What had just happened? She had no idea. But one thing she did know: she needed a drink, badly.

The moment that thought formed, she heard a 'pop' coming from the coffee cabinet, followed by the sound of falling broken glass. She walked over and opened it. In what appeared to be a case of spontaneous combustion, her bottle of Macallan had shattered. Vintage whisky was dripping everywhere.

Cynthia looked around the room. "Well, thank you. That was one of my best bottles of booze. But, good to know whose side you're on."

And with that, she finally went to bed.

CHAPTER SEVEN

September 27, 2004 – Sarita's sixteenth birthday

It was Monday morning, a week and a day after the opening. The women had decided that on Mondays the restaurant would be closed, giving everyone the opportunity to prepare for the rest of the week. For Jane and Cynthia, that meant corroborating receipts, handling the payroll, and doing the rest of the necessary book-keeping. For Angela and Rohini, Monday was market day, when they went into town to purchase the produce and other perishables they'd need for the week. Market day also meant that it was the only day out of seven they dared risk driving Cynthia's Porsche. That was a sight to behold.

If Cristiano went with them, all was well. He loved driving that car as much as Cynthia did, and he was far more mindful of his passengers' sensibilities than she had proven to be. But if it were just the two women, taking the Porsche was a trial for them. Angela shook at the mere thought of getting behind that wheel, so it was left to Rohini to drive. She'd pull the seat as far forward as it would go, and they'd both squeak like baby mice every time she turned the key and the powerful engine zipped and roared to life.

Today however, there was a variation in that routine, a crucial one, as far as Angela and Jane were concerned. They still had no idea what had happened after they'd gone up to bed the night of the opening, but clearly, things had — deep, dark, dreadful things.

For a start, to say that Rohini and Cristiano were not speaking would be an understatement. They'd managed to continue cook-ing side by side, so far, but the tension between them throbbed like a bad tooth. This made the galley environment unpleasant, to put it mildly, for everyone who worked there. In addition, Emilio was gone, and when questioned, Cynthia flat out refused to discuss it. It involved Sarita, though. That much was also obvious, as she spent most of her time in her cabin. If she did come downstairs, she avoided her mother whenever possible. Cynthia wasn't taking this well.

"She's been a tempest all week," Jane reported peevishly. "It's unbearable sitting in that office with her, honestly. I hope whatever this row is about, they resolve it soon."

"You think you have it bad? Try being in the kitchen with Ro and Cris. They don't talk to each other at all, and they say the bare minimum to everyone else. He always looks angry, her eyes are always red, and he keeps dropping things. Yesterday, in the middle of the rush, I hear this big clang, and when I turn around, a giant pot of tomato sauce is spilled across the floor and splattered all over him. Oh, my God — you should have heard the filthy swear words that came out of his mouth. Like it wasn't his own darn fault for being so clumsy."

Jane clucked her tongue. "This can't go on."

"I agree. We have to find out what happened. Let's start with Rohini. She'll be the easiest to crack."

That was how it came about that Jane went along with Angela and Rohini on their expedition. When she told Cynthia she was going, Cynthia just handed her the car keys, and said nothing about being left on her own for the day. She knew she'd been in a bitchy mood, and that Jane had been forced to bear the brunt of it.

Now, alone in the office, instead of tackling paperwork, she was squandering away the morning sitting listlessly in front of her computer, skimming through celebrity gossip, and playing *Spider Solitaire*.

She'd made a mess of things from the moment Sarita had stepped into the dining room looking so glorious and grown up in that dress. Put simply, it had scared her. Should she try again to talk to Sarita, explain her background, her fears? Or should she leave her be, for now? Should she hire Emilio back? Should she shift the jack of spades onto the queen of hearts?

Any of these moves could lead to trouble. Still, she had to take action of some kind, although what, she didn't know. Cards could be tricky — another thing she'd learned in Vegas — but now she was learning that teenagers could be ever so much trickier.

She dealt with it when she discovered that the parents she'd adored were criminals, and that all the money and education they'd lavished on her had come from the blood and tears of others. She dealt with it when Bobby Taylor took their rent money to play one last game of poker before deserting her and their baby girl. Hell, she'd even dealt singlehandedly with two muggers in the unlit back parking lot of a Vegas casino, in order to save a man's life. But she didn't know how to deal with her teenage daughter.

Bobby Taylor's mother had been a known Creole practitioner of voodoo in New Orleans. She and Bobby did not get on, so Cynthia had only set eyes on her once, when Bobby got a sudden wild hair to take his very pregnant wife to meet her. *Manman* Taylor took a long look at Cynthia, then placed her hands on her swollen belly, and smiled. "This one will be a girl. Marked by Erzulie Freda and Gran Ibo she'll be. She will be *trè* special. I know this as surely as I know my own name." She looked at her son darkly. "You take care of them, Bobby boy — you hear me? You take care of your *trè bèl* wife and baby girl."

Hah. That sure hadn't happened. But Sarita's Haitian *granmè* had been right about everything else. She'd given birth to a daughter who'd been unique from the start, incredibly warm-hearted and, even as a tiny child, sensing things she shouldn't have been able to, and feeling the wounds of others as though they were her own.

Like the night Cynthia brought poor Raul home. Still weak and dizzy from all that had happened to him, his clothing soiled, his wallet gone, he looked and smelled like a half-dead skunk. She'd been worried his appearance would frighten her twelve-year-old daughter. Instead, Sarita had unlocked the door to their shabby little apartment without even checking through the peephole first, as she'd been taught to do. She asked no questions, either. It was as though she'd known Cynthia would be bringing an injured man home. "Get him in, *Mamãe*. Hurry. He needs our help," was all she'd said, a stranger's pain reflected in her eyes far too much.

It was that trait especially that frightened Cynthia. That, and the fact that even at twelve, her face had already had strangers stopping in their tracks to stare. Cynthia didn't know about voodoo goddesses, or whether or not her daughter had been marked by their gifts. But she did know that Sarita was one of those rare beings who was as beautiful on the outside as she was on the inside. The combination was more of a curse than it was a gift. *How* could she explain to Sarita that this was why she felt such a compulsion to shield her — this unparalleled young woman — who, by some miracle or paradox of fate, was *her* daughter?

Damn. She'd had a feeling she shouldn't have played that jack. Now she was boxed in. Her card game screen flashed the message: *You have no more moves left. What do you want to do?*

God only knows, she sighed.

She closed the card game to restore *Yahoo! Celebrity News*. Her eyebrows shot up as the latest featured article popped up on screen:

Green and Hunt to Divorce

"Jessica Green officially filed for divorce from Biff Hunt in Los Angeles Superior Court on Friday. Green's

> court papers cite irreconcilable differences for the split. The two have been married for four and a half years and have no children. It was the first marriage for both. They released a joint statement to *People* magazine, saying, 'We would like to announce that after seven years together, we've decided to formally separate. Our separation is not the result of any of the speculation being reported by the tabloid media. This decision is the result of much thoughtful consideration.' Biff Hunt has been seen spending time alone with Evelina Janvier, his co-star in his latest film. They were recently together dining tête-à-tête aboard the *Queen Mary* in Long Beach at the opening of The Secret Spice Café, a new eatery hailed as "stunning" by top food critic, Eric Gladwell."

"Well, I'll be damned. Bless your hearts, Eric and *Yahoo!*," Cynthia said aloud. They'd just gotten a launch the likes of which the *Mary* hadn't seen since her maiden voyage.

Then she smirked. "'Thoughtful consideration.' Like hell."

She couldn't wait to show the others. They'd enjoy it on all the levels she did — from the business side to the catty. She'd suggest that they send Eric a case of their best wine. He'd done them a solid by giving them such a great write up in *Bon Appétit*. Here was proof that it was already being picked up by other news outlets.

She frowned, knowing Rohini would be troubled by that aspect. The digital version of the review was minimized on her screen. She chewed on the inside of her lip, as she clicked back to it and reread. Eric's review went into as much background as Jane had given him, including how the four of them had first communicated online, and then decided on working together even before they'd all met face to face. While an entertaining triviality for readers, it was information that could be dangerous for Rohini. Although she and Cristiano had done their best to keep her face out of the group shot, Eric had still mentioned her, naturally. Cynthia was privy to the fact that the surname Rohini was using was not her own, but her first name was her actual one. Would that first name, and the fact that she was missing from the shot raise any red flags to those who were looking for her? *Merde.* She sure hoped not. Of course, it was unlikely that the wrong eyes would be searching for information about her in *Bon Appétit.*

She was still contemplating this when she heard shouts coming from the kitchen.

Having the day off and the kitchen to himself felt like a reprieve to Cristiano. No Cyclone Cynthia, no sullen Sarita, no Angela looking at him like everything was *his* fault, and most of all, no Rohini with the big, sad eyes.

He shook his head as he carved a beef fillet into thin, precise slices and, with a staccato beat, chopped arugula, brown onions, and green bell peppers for the next day's special.

Dios mio. He was surrounded every minute of every day by... by...estrogenic dramatics. He just wanted some time alone to *think,* that was all. He needed to figure out how to handle this situation with Rohini. She had hurt him, dammit. Didn't she see that? He loved her so much, and she didn't trust him. Not to mention that he was...well...scared. What was she hiding? Could it — whatever it was — harm her?

He took his homemade sweet Italian sausage patties out of the refrigerator, and began shredding those up. Not too many, so as not to overpower the other flavors. The sausage was excellent. He was pleased that the women had trusted him enough to take his suggestion that they go for the higher priced meats. They'd only needed to charge a dollar more per dish to make up the cost, but the restaurant patrons would find it well worth it. This was going to be a superb "Arugula, Sausage, and Green Peppers Stuffed Fillet."

He should talk to Cynthia, that's what he should do. He set the shredded sausage into a glass bowl, and folded in Rohini's spiced breadcrumbs. He lifted a teaspoon of the mixture to his nose. With one sniff he determined that it needed a sprinkle more of imported, grated Pecorino, and perhaps just a pinch of fresh Italian parsley. He should *insist* that she tell him what was going on, so if necessary, he could help keep Rohini safe. In fact, today was his perfect opportunity, since they were the only two here. He covered the meat and the vegetables with plastic wrap and put them back in the refrigerator. He'd go to Cynthia's office right now.

A cast iron Dutch oven flew off a shelf, and suspended itself in midair, directly in front of his face.

Cristiano stopped short and glared at it. "Get out of my way, or I will melt you down for scrap metal, so help me God."

Undeterred by his threats, the pot remained steadfast. With a sound of impatience, Cristiano stepped around it. But this was a Dutch oven, and the Dutch are known for nothing if not their tenacity.

Cristiano only managed two steps before the pot soared up and around, and then clunked him on the forehead.

With a yell of outrage, Cristiano ran back to his station. Picking up the knife he'd been using to chop vegetables, he began swinging it. Specks of green parsley and sweet onion were flung everywhere as he defended himself against the pot, which was now rocketing around and around his head, trying to get in another hit.

"*¡Atrás! ¡Atrás! ¡Atrás!* I've had enough of this! Enough!" His knife clanged against the side of the pot, which swooped around for a rear attack. But Cristiano was too quick for it. He feinted left, pivoted smartly and batted the pot with a *klang!* It careened straight into a tray of stacked glassware. Only some managed to leap out of the way. The rest came crashing down. Broken glass scattered all over the countertop, and the Dutch oven fled back up to its shelf in shame.

"You *see* what you did?" In fury, Cristiano again lifted his knife and shook it, first at the pot in particular, then at the kitchen at large. "Last week, it was a bottle of our best olive oil; Sunday, it was my whole pot of Bolognese sauce, and today, this! All you do is cause trouble. You *never* leave me in peace. You're worse than a nagging mother-in-law. What do you want from me — eh? *Tell* me. Damn you, tell me what I'm supposed to do. I'm trying my best, but she won't talk to me!"

The only reply was the grinding hum of the ancient freezer. In frustration, Cristiano threw the knife in the sink and turned to leave. Then he stopped short. Standing right inside the doors, with her arms folded across her chest, was Cynthia.

Sighing heavily, Cristiano ran his hands through his hair. "How long have you been standing there?"

Cynthia's mouth twitched. "Long enough to see the duel." She held out a hand. "Come on, Errol Flynn, let's go to my office and have a drink. I should have at least one bottle in there that she hasn't broken."

He looked at her. "You too?"

Cynthia laughed. "Oh, hell yes."

"So, tell me why you're in such a snit." Cynthia poured him a shot.

When Cristiano was upset, his accent grew thicker. "A 'sneet?' I'm *not* in a 'sneet', Cynthia." He glowered at her. "It's much more serious than that. Rohini is in trouble. I want to help her, but she... she doesn't trust me."

That last was said with such despondency that Cynthia felt a rush of compassion. What else but love would make anyone so miserable? she thought. Wordlessly, she slid the glass toward him.

Cristiano rarely drank. Ever since his conviction, he'd wanted neither his emotions nor anything else to cloud his judgment or control his behavior. But today, with all that was going on, a drink or two couldn't hurt.

One hour later, his head was swimming, not only due to how cleverly she'd evaded responding his questions, but to the more than half a bottle of whisky between them consumed. As much as he thought of himself as a feminist, he'd felt compelled to match Cynthia shot for shot, his masculinity affronted by the fact that she wasn't affected by the alcohol as much as he was. Although she was relaxed in her chair, her feet up on her desk, she sounded far more sober than he himself felt. Resolutely, he forced himself to focus on what she was saying.

"There's something I've always wanted to ask about your conviction, if I may. Before hiring you, I read that your sentence was reduced by half, for good behavior. But you served ten years, which means you were given twenty. That's a long sentence for a case like this. Couldn't your lawyer do any better for you?"

Cristiano's smile was forbidding. "I wouldn't let him. I wanted the maximum sentence the law would impose for what I did."

Cynthia blinked as she stared at him. "Now *that's* something I hadn't expected you to say."

"To understand it, I would have to tell you it all, from the beginning. Ah, but I think I'll do it without any more alcohol for now," he added, as she reached to pour him another.

"You don't mind if I have more, do you? I have a feeling I'll need it."

"Help yourself." He shook his head to clear it, then smiled with admiration. "Though I have to say, I'm impressed with your constitution, Cynthia."

Cynthia laughed and lifted her glass. "And so you should be." She took a swallow. "All right, tell me. I'm ready for anything now."

His smile faded as he began, "My mother and father married when they were just out of high school. In those days, that's what a man did if he got a girl pregnant. At least, in the village where my parents came from."

"Which was?"

"Benaocaz, in the province of Cádiz, Spain. Even today, there are not even one thousand residents."

That was as far as he got. He stopped short when he caught the look that crossed her face. "What? What did I say?"

"Nothing." She hesitated. "It's just that…the phrasings you use, your inflections. If I didn't know better from your résumé, I'd have thought you were from Mexico. I've met a number of people from Spain. You sound nothing like them." Her smile was sheepish as she shrugged. "No offense meant."

He smirked. "None taken. You're observant. My speech patterns changed courtesy of my stay at a certain penitentiary in Santa Fe County, where I passed a lot of time talking with Mexicans. And with Blacks. The U.S slave trade is alive and well in its prisons, Cynthia. It's quite lucrative. And it's legal." His tone was somber as he watched her watching him. "Fortunately, they also have a library. I passed a lot of my time there too. And so, I became who you see before you: A Mexican-sounding, Spanish immigrant with a rather —" he grinned at her as he emphasized his point — "*capacious* English vocabulary."

She laughed as he'd hoped she would, then sighed and shook her head. "*Ay.* You've reminded me of a similar conversation I had with Angela and Rohini." She shook her head again as she mused, "The five of us are more alike than I'd have ever guessed. Misfits, every one of us. Each in our way."

At the mention of Rohini's name, Cristiano looked maudlin again. Leaning across her desk, Cynthia poked him. "Stop moping. Go on with what you were saying. Your mother got pregnant. Your parents married young."

He opened his mouth to continue, but she cut in again. "Oh! Of course. *You* were the baby your mother was carrying when she got married."

"Yes, and —"

"Huh. I bet your father wasn't happy about being forced to marry. Did he resent you?"

"Cynthia, am I telling this or are you?"

It was the whiskey that allowed a giggle to escape her, before she slapped her hand over her lips. "Sorry. I was getting caught up."

After one exasperated glare, he continued. "As it happens, my father did not resent having to marry. Nor did he resent me. He loved my mother all of his life. In fact, if either of the two felt confined by the arrangement, it might have been my mother. She loved my father too, but she'd always had dreams, you know?"

Cynthia snorted loudly. "Oh boy, *do* I."

He squinted at her. "Are you sure you haven't had too much to drink?"

"I'm fine." She waved at him to continue.

Still eyeing her doubtfully, he went on, "Because of their ages and their finances, they decided to wait to have another child. My father worked hard — on the vegetable farms, with the fisherman, in the tourist trade — whatever jobs he could find. My mother took in sewing. By the time I was ten, they'd saved enough money to come to the United States, to Albuquerque. They got their start there by cooking traditional village foods and selling the dishes as ready lunches at the open air markets. And then on my father's thirtieth birthday, they opened a restaurant."

"Your talent is an inherited one."

"Yes. I'd been helping my parents from the time I came to this country. I loved everything about it — picking the fresh ingredients, preparing the dishes, the smells, the tastes — all of it. My parents were so young, so excited about what they were doing, it didn't feel like I was working for my mother and father, but *with* them, you know?"

Sitting with her feet on her desk now, wrapped up in his story, Cynthia nodded. "That must have been a great feeling — working together as a family to build a life here."

"I remember how happy they were when we bought our first house." Cristiano smiled warmly as he thought back to that time.

But his expression grew pensive, and Cynthia tensed as he said, "Then my sister Isabel was born." Changing his mind, he picked up the bottle himself this time, poured, and took a sip. "I loved her from the moment I saw her." His eyes twinkled. "Not that she was very cute, at first. She had a head that looked just like a coconut— brown and hairy and very round — and enormous, expressive eyes that looked out of place on her tiny face. But she looked at everything with curiosity, from the beginning. Before she could talk, I could tell what she was feeling. Whether she was happy, scared, or sad, she could hide nothing from me. Until she was sixteen, when I stopped paying attention."

He paused for so long, frowning into his shot glass, swirling the liquid inside, that Cynthia couldn't help but prompt him. "What happened?"

He shifted his gaze to her, his tone brusque. "A whole shitload of things happened, Cynthia. The first of them was, when Isabel was only three and a half, my father had a heart attack."

"Oh, no! He was still so young."

Cristiano's nod was sardonic. "Precisely why he ignored the chest pains. That morning, he was on his feet, helping my mother prepare *Pollo al Ajillo*." He made a sound of repugnance. "I used to love that dish. Now, I hate to even smell it. By the time our dinner rush came, he was in the intensive care unit, oxygen mask, tubes, needles everywhere —"

He paused, seeing his young, handsome father in that bed, all over again. "It was a massive heart attack. He would never have been the same, had he survived it. But my mother couldn't accept that he would die. None of us could. It was…surreal. We begged the doctors to do everything they could. We were…naïve." He made a face, as though he tasted something that had gone sour. "The doctors listened to us, all right, even though they knew his case was hopeless. The pointless treatments cost us ten thousand dollars per day, and kept him alive — so to speak — for two weeks. At the end of that time, my mother had no husband, and shortly thereafter, no house."

Cynthia was appalled. "Ten thousand dollars a *day*? Didn't they have health insurance?"

Cristiano laughed with real amusement. "In this country? You know how much that would have cost. When my sister was born, we paid the hospital in cash. That's the way immigrants do it. The cost for insurance here is unthinkable to us. But even more unthinkable was that medical bill for my father's care. We had no choice but to sell our home. Even with that, we still owed money. My mother sold every valuable, right down to her wedding dress, which she'd made herself. She cried so much when she sold it. But she was offered five hundred dollars for it and…we needed that money."

Mutely, Cynthia watched him as he relived those days. "The only reason we didn't have to sell our restaurant was because the uncle who'd sponsored us to come to the States had advised my parents to open it in my name. I didn't know that. I didn't know until after my father died, that all along, I hadn't been working for my parents, they'd been working for me. At sixteen, I had a restaurant, a grieving mother, and a four-year-old sister to look after. My first order of business was to find us a place to sleep. And so, two of the waiters and I cleared out the small storage room next to the kitchen at the restaurant. That's where all three of us slept."

He paused to take a much needed swallow of whisky. "The next twelve years were both wonderful and terrible. First came some terrible. We let go most of the help to cut down expenses. My mother and I worked seven days a week, taking turns doing everything — cooking, waiting tables, paying bills. I wanted to quit school, but she wouldn't let me, so I took my GED instead. We put Isabel in day care, something my mother hated doing, so we could open the restaurant for lunch as well as dinner to bring in more revenue."

Glass in hand, he got up and walked over to the office window. He stopped talking, seemed far away in thought, as he looked out. She understood that it was hard for him to open himself up like this, so she waited patiently until, with his back to her, he went on.

"I saw my mother age right before my eyes, from grief and endless work. She would drop my sister off at seven a.m., hurry back to the restaurant until four, then rush to pick her up, feed her, bath her, spend an hour with her, then put her to sleep on her little cot in that back room." He shook his head. "How Isabel slept through the noise in that kitchen was beyond me, but she did, *niña buena* that she was. She never complained. Only once, when she was playing with her favorite doll. It was called 'Chatty Cathy.' I remember that doll well. She would sometimes fall asleep holding it."

Cynthia listened, blinking back tears, as with his back still to her, he described his little sister's doll, right down to the red headband in its blonde hair. "I heard Isabel tell her doll, '*Papi* had to go away and take our house. I know you miss *Papi*, and your room with the pink flowers on the walls, but don't be sad, Cathy."

"*Ay Dios mio*," was all Cynthia could say to that.

Her voice brought Cristiano back to the present. He turned to look at her. "Well. That was part of the terrible. But not long after that, finally came some good."

"Jesus, Cris. I sure hope so."

He laughed as he sat back down, but it was a harsh sound. "The first good thing was that everyone we knew frequented *Casa del Papi Chulo* much more often to help us out."

She held up a hand. "Wait. The name of your family's restaurant was…Hot Daddy's House?"

"My mother named it." Cristiano looked abashed. "Er, '*Papi Chulo*' was her nickname for my father."

Cynthia threw back her head and guffawed. When she managed to stop, she gulped in air, and wiped at her eyes. "Oh, thank you, Cris. I needed that."

"I'm glad I could help," he said, miffed. "Now, if you're finished making fun of my family, would you like me to continue this story — since you are the one who asked me to tell it — or should I go back to my kitchen?"

She nodded, still stifling a smile, and not at all sorry she'd put his nose out of joint. It had helped lighten the mood.

He went on, "It was always an active restaurant, but with the support of our friends, our clientele grew. We were able to hire back some help, which left my mother free for longer hours to be with Isabel. I did more of the menu planning and cooking on my own. I started to experiment with new dishes that I thought would be fun to make. My mother understood I was still only a teenager, getting restless with having to work all the time, so she pretended not to notice what I was doing, although I could have ruined the businessfor us."

"But of course, you didn't. You were a genius behind the stove even then, I bet."

That charmed him into a genuine smile. "I'm humbled that you feel that way about my cooking."

"Oh, bullshit. There's nothing humble about you when you put that apron on, Cris."

With a full grin now, he didn't contradict her. "As it happened, with only a few catastrophes, the new dishes were a hit. Before we knew it, the hottest restaurant in town was *Casa del Papi Chulo*."

Ignoring her smothered snigger, Cristiano persevered. "Now we could afford to rent a small two-bedroom. Isabel got back her pink flowered wallpaper. But with all the hours I was working, it was easier for me to still sleep at the restaurant. My mother worried about that, not realizing how much I enjoyed it. I was eighteen at that point, and felt like a big man. I got my family out of debt. I was virtually living on my own. I could come and go as I pleased. Everything I cooked turned to gold. And let me tell you, the girls really liked that." He lifted his hands and spread them wide. "In short, Cynthia, I was growing a head the size of a forty-pound Kabocha squash. It was too much, too fast."

She nodded again, remembering herself at that age, so cocky and hotheaded, yelling at her father, slamming out of the house, then not having a clue what to do next, yet refusing to go back, no matter what. Yes. Back then, she'd survived on nothing but her self-righteousness. Until she'd had a baby, who needed more than her mother's breast milk and imprudence.

He seemed to be reading her thoughts as his lip curled with his own regrets and self-disgust. "And then came even more. The local TV station did a segment on me. Something like, 'Teen Gastronomic Genius Saves Immigrant Family.' They spun it as a human interest story more than a culinary one, but they were an affiliate of a national channel. The exposure I received when it aired throughout the country got me interviews with a few food magazines."

He paused reflectively. "I can still remember how it felt to see my first recipes in those magazines. The best feeling in the world for me, Cynthia, the best thing that had happened to me up until then. If I had any hint of where it would lead, I wonder — would I have stopped it right then, or would I have taken my chances?"

Since the question was one neither of them could answer, she said nothing.

"One night, a man came into the restaurant alone, and ordered several of my special dishes. Hotshot that I thought I was by then, this annoyed me, as we'd been ready to close up. Instead, I had to start cooking all over again. It also made me suspicious. Why so much food for one man? What was he up to? It never occurred to me that he came in specifically to meet me and taste my recipes." Although many years had passed, Cristiano still marveled over the encounter. "It turned out that he was Raymond Thuilier."

Cynthia's eyes went wide. "Thuilier of L'Oustau de Baumanière? The one who trained Wolfgang Puck?"

Cristiano tipped his head once. "The very same."

"Wow, Cristiano. Just ...*wow*." In the way of a true culinary aficionado, Cynthia was more star-struck over this information than she'd been when she'd learned Biff Hunt would be at the opening. "What was he doing in Albuquerque, of all places?"

Cristiano pretended to be offended. "You don't imagine he could have flown from France just to meet an eighteen-year-old immigrant cook?"

"Not unless he's gay, saw your photo in the food article, and was looking for a boy toy. So, I'm going to guess *Celebrity Chef Tour*."

"You're partly right. He did see an article about me while he was on a chefs' tour in New Mexico, and that's what prompted him to come in and taste my food. But, rather than hit on me, Cynthia, he offered to train me at L'Oustau de Baumanière. He even helped get me a scholarship to pay for my trip and living expenses."

"I'm not only impressed, I'm jealous green. You lucky son of a gun."

Cristiano tapped the air with his finger. "You bet I was. He was the best mentor I could have asked for. For the next ten years, I had the time of my life. I trained with Raymond, I earned my *cordon bleu* status, I worked at top restaurants all throughout Europe. I dated a lot of beautiful women, and made more money than was good for me. I thought sending a great deal of it home to my mother was 'taking care of my family,' but the truth was, from the moment I left Albuquerque, I never wanted to look back. Yes, I saw them a few times a year and yes, I loved them, but I didn't want to be responsible for them any longer. I wanted to have fun. So I abandoned them and paid them off to ease my conscience."

"What absolute crap." With a crack, Cynthia slapped her glass down on the desk. "You'd been working since you were a kid. Your parents violated every child labor law that exists. You were the one who was solely responsible for keeping your mother and sister off the streets. For godssakes, were you supposed to pay for it forever, because your father couldn't keep his pants zipped when he was a teenager?"

Cristiano was so startled by her vehement defense of him that he disregarded her vituperation of his parents, and only felt compelled to make her understand. "It's not like that. I knew better than to leave my mother on her own with my sister. My mother was not..." he searched for the right word, "...worldly. She didn't know how to raise a female child in the United States. She only knew she didn't want Isabel to end up like her — pregnant and married at seventeen, with a life so difficult that she grew old before her time. So she became very strict with her, wouldn't let her do any of the normal things teenage girls do here. No sleepovers at friends' houses, no babysitting, no class trips — *nada*. As soon as she could afford it, she sent her to Catholic schools. The prettier and more womanly Isabel grew, the more my mother kept a tight rein on her, doing everything she could to suppress her budding sexuality. Although if you'd asked her, she would have said she was only trying to keep her safe. Without meaning to, our mother taught my sister to feel shame for being female, for having normal, human desires. And that's what got her killed."

Immediately, Cynthia's thoughts went to Sarita's crushed expression before she'd stomped away after being banished for her choice of dress. White-faced, she asked him, "What do you mean, 'got her killed'?"

Talking and laughter came from outside the closed office door. Inez's voice called out instructions to someone in Spanish. The afternoon cleaning crew had arrived in the dining room. Although Cristiano's head turned automatically toward the sounds, Cynthia doubted that, with blood and death on his mind, he was truly aware of them.

"When she was sixteen, my sister was seduced by one of the teachers from that 'safe' Catholic school my mother had insisted upon. He had her pegged for just what she was: A naïve virgin, insecure and discontent due to all the restrictions put upon her. He knew exactly how to manipulate her. Unsigned love notes, designed to flatter and make her feel desirable, slipped into her checked homework; small gifts left in her book bag, with no card attached, so they couldn't be traced back to him. She fell for it all, believed he loved her. We found out later he'd been shuffled around to different schools due to complaints about inappropriate behavior toward his female pupils. As I'm sure you've guessed, he was the man who eventually strangled her. The man I beat to death with my bare hands."

He paused again, once more staring into his glass, his dark eyes so bleak as he relived the tragedy, that Cynthia wanted to kick herself for ever bringing the subject up. "I'd thought of killing him right after I learned of her murder. I'd dreamed of it, even planned on how I would do it. Nevertheless, I could not have actually done it. Not if they hadn't acquitted him of murder and then reinstated him."

There was a sudden stillness in the air, as though even the walls could hear the unraveling of Cristiano's carefully contained rage. What he'd said was so atrocious, Cynthia thought she'd misunderstood. Then he looked at her, unspeakable torment reflected on his face as he repeated, "They gave him back his job as a teacher in a high school. Even after he'd murdered one of his pupils. My sister."

For a moment, she could only stutter. "How...*how* could something like that happen?"

He smiled then, in a way that made the hair on her arms stand on end. For the first time since she'd known him, his sarcasm was crude. "Oh, I don't know, Cynthia. Maybe it was because it was a Catholic school, and the church cares even less when one of their teachers kills a female than they do when one of their priests fucks a little boy?"

She felt pinned by his eyes. She hoped to God she'd never see the look in them on anyone else again.

He leaned back in his chair, and Cynthia realized she'd been holding her breath all the while he gazed at her. "Or maybe it was because the bastard's lawyer was as good a lawyer as I am a chef. I had to admire her for that — even as I wanted to jump at her in that courtroom. She painted a stirring picture of the lonely teacher and the Latina Lolita. That she was female herself, made her all the more believable. She convinced the jury that my sister had seduced *him,* and though he tried to rebuff her, she'd persisted until he couldn't fight his attraction to her anymore."

"And the fact that he strangled her? How did his *puta* of a lawyer explain that?"

He shifted in his chair. Talking about this, reliving it, made him want to smash everything in the room. He took a few calming breaths before he answered her.

"Simple. Hypoxyphilia."

"I don't know what that is."

It occurred to him that this conversation was remarkably intimate. "It's the intentional restriction of oxygen to the brain. Some people do it because it...enhances sexual arousal." He hesitated, trying to gauge her reaction. She said nothing, but her eyes narrowed as she waited for him to continue.

"He claimed that he pressed on her carotid arteries, as he always did. According to him, this was the rough sex that my sister preferred, and one night, it got a little too rough. Killing her was a terrible accident, one which he deeply regretted. Isabel was too dead to dispute that, wasn't she? The only thing the jury had to go on were his lies and her letters. Letters that she'd written in reply to his, of course."

Cynthia clamped her lips together so the litany of curses she was thinking wouldn't spew forth. "Wasn't there anyone she'd confided in who could speak up for her?"

He ran his hands through his hair, his gesture of frustration with which she was becoming familiar. "Yes. Her best friend, Amanda. She…she was brave at first. She testified that in the last month of her life, Isabel tried to break things off with him, but he'd threatened her. He said he'd tell my mother that she'd come on to him, if she did. The thought of my mother finding out that she'd been having sex with her teacher terrified Isabel, as he knew it would. Amanda said she tried to convince her to go to another adult, perhaps a guidance counselor, but Isabel was too ashamed."

"The jury didn't believe her?" The question was rhetorical.

"Not after his lawyer got through with her cross-examination. Hadn't Amanda herself slept with any number of boys? Didn't she also have a crush on this same teacher? Wasn't she so jealous that he'd chosen Isabel instead of her that she was trying to destroy an innocent man with these accusations? The poor girl was a wreck by the time she left the stand. Isabel's death was ruled nothing more than an unfortunate accident. As soon as the school board reinstated him, Amanda and her family moved away."

Cynthia considered pouring another drink, but decided against it. All the booze in the world wouldn't wash away what was coming next.

"I might have been able to live with it if it hadn't been for that — for the fact that he'd annihilated not one, but two young girls I knew, one completely and the other psychologically — and that he was now in the position to get to even more. I knew where he lived. The evening before he was set to return to Isabel's high school, I paid him a visit. I asked him if we could talk."

"He let you in? He didn't call the police?" Cynthia asked in some astonishment.

"He had no reason to fear me." He shrugged. "After all, I was just a cook. I'd shown no violent tendencies all throughout the court proceedings. I think he might have even been arrogant enough to believe he'd convinced my mother and me that my sister was a whore." Cristiano took another sip. But this time, the expensive whisky felt gritty and hot in his throat. "I never thought that I was capable of beating a man to death. Never. It's one thing to *want* to do it. It's another thing entirely to know for sure that it's in you to do it."

He looked down to study his hands. The more brutal his words became, the softer his voice grew, as though to counteract the monstrosity of what he'd done. "He begged me to stop, and I almost did. Then I thought of Isabel, and how she must have begged also. Do you know what he looked like when I was done with him, Cynthia? I hit him mostly in the face. There's a copious amount of blood in the human head, more than I ever would've assumed. The entire thing took less than five minutes from start to finish. Can you imagine that? I had no idea it would be so quick. But by the end of that time, his blood was on everything in that room, all over me. I could feel it in my hair. I could even taste it. I went straight from his house to the police, and turned myself in. I knew that if they saw me like that, they'd want to lock me away for a long time. I wanted them to, after that. I wanted them to. She tried to call me, you know."

"Who did?" Cynthia asked quietly.

"Isabel. About a week before it happened. I was in the *Vanity Fair* Feast and Fashion photo shoot. I had one hand holding up my Charlotte Russe for the camera, and the other around supermodel Paulina Porizkova, when my assistant told me she was on the phone. I was not about to let go of either of those gorgeous ladies to chat with my little sister. I told my assistant to tell her I'd call back. Of course I forgot."

He eyes teared up and his voice grew husky with self-reproach. "*Jesús mío.* For the rest of my life I'll wonder if she'd be alive today if I'd taken her call."

Cynthia leaned forward on her elbows. "And in penance for that, you were willing to give up twenty years of your life and your entire career?"

"Yes, for that. And for the fact that I'd killed a man in cold blood. He deserved to die, but I deserved to go to prison for making it happen. I should have been charged with first degree murder, just as he should have been. I suppose it's ironic that neither of us was. They charged me with voluntary manslaughter. I pleaded guilty because I *was* guilty. My lawyer said that under the circumstances, he could probably negotiate my sentence, but I wouldn't let him. You know the rest."

"Not quite. What happened to your mother?"

"All of this was too much for her. She died of cancer, less than two years after I went to prison. So you see, I didn't save either of them, after all."

He pressed his palms against his eyes for a moment, and then forced himself to look at her, waiting to see the condemnation on her face. But she was looking back at him impassively.

She was no babe in the woods. She had firsthand knowledge of what evil was. And what it most definitely was not. And she knew men. Just as when Michael had bared his soul to her unexpectedly, she wouldn't show the pity she felt. Men hated that, even more than they hating shopping for shoes.

They stared at each other silently for a while. Finally he cleared his throat, shook his head. "I should have stuck to coffee." But he couldn't resist asking. "So, what do you think of your cook now?"

She poured the last of the bottle into her glass. "I think that if it had been Sarita, I would have done the same as my cook. But they'd have definitely charged me with first degree murder, because unlike him, I wouldn't have had one iota of remorse. And I would have cut off his balls for good measure." And with that, she knocked back her drink.

That snapped Cristiano out of his melancholy. He laughed soundly, looking at her with such male appreciation, she felt a fleeting regret that he was already spoken for. Thinking of that, she had one last question to ask. "Tell me something, Cris. Does Rohini know all of this — just as you've described it to me?"

"Certainly she does." He pouted again as he thought back to his original conundrum. "Unlike her, I don't keep big secrets."

Cynthia stood up, picked up their empty glasses and sashayed them over to the coffee bar with nary a stumble. Once again, he could only marvel at her fortitude. And, since he was a man who appreciated women, her legs in those heels. "Then I can tell you this much, at least. If she knows this and still wants you, she trusts you much more than you think. When she's ready to tell you her story, you'll understand why I say that."

"How did you get her to confide in you, by the way?"

"I got her drunk." She tilted her head toward their empty glasses. "Works every time."

He laughed again. "You're an exceptional woman, aren't you, Cynthia?"

"I have my moments. Will you be all right now? You've got the busboys and line chefs terrified of coming to work, and according to Angela, this isn't the first disagreement you've had with one of the pots."

As he got up to leave, Cristiano's eyebrows rose in surprise. "Angela said that? I thought for sure she was —"

"Clueless about this ship? She sure is. So's Jane, for that matter." She shook her head. "People only see what they want to see, that's for damn sure."

Later that same Monday, several decks below the office where Cristiano and Cynthia had been sitting, the pretty 'professional paranormal guide' was winding down her three p.m. Haunted Encounters Tour, a tour in which guests aboard hoped to perceive evidence of the paranormal activity for which the *Queen Mary* was famous.

"Here we are in Shaft Alley, where the notorious Door Number Thirteen is located. Jonathan Pedder, an eighteen-year-old crewman, was unluckily crushed to death when, as legend has it, he and other crewmen were playing a game of 'chicken,' trying to squeeze through the narrow watertight door before it slammed shut. Let's all close our eyes and concentrate. Jonathan, are you here with us now?"

As the excited tourists played along, the guide winked at Sarita and Emilio as they snuck away from the back of the group and hurried on by, down through the old boiler room ahead.

"Where are we going?" Emilio whispered.

"You'll see," Sarita whispered back with a beguiling smile.

Everyone under the age of twenty-five who worked on the ship knew that Sarita and Emilio were seeing each other behind her mother's back. Some who were friends with the couple, such as the young tour guide, actively abetted their relationship, while others, particularly those who knew Cynthia and feared her wrath, simply pretended not to notice. When Sarita was being honest with herself, she acknowledged that part of the spice of her romance was that it was a secret she held from her mother.

But this afternoon was not the time for such introspections. She'd allocated it for something else, entirely. It was her sixteenth birthday today, and Emilio said they could do whatever she wanted. He didn't know what he was in for. In her backpack, she was loaded for bear with a flashlight, a blanket, a bottle of cooking wine smuggled from the kitchen, two scented candles she usually kept in her cabin, and the condom she'd swiped from Michael's newly renovated shop. They were going to do *it*. She was determined to lose her virginity today, and she knew just the place to proceed with that intention where they wouldn't be interrupted.

That is, if she could convince Emilio to go along with her plan. She held his hand, gently tugging him along through the tomb-like underbelly of the ship. Their steps made clanging sounds that echoed across the metal platforms of the old, abandoned engine room with its massive steam turbine engines and their gigantic propellers, turning gears the size of flying saucers, and water tube boilers that looked like aerial bombs. They passed through a dim, dank sector, which had once housed the marine propulsion equipment. Nothing was left there except for rusty old bilge pumps which now lay idle. She continued ahead with confidence, and he followed compliantly, as they descended cold, iron stairways with chain link railings, down and then down again, to the entryway of her destination, where he stopped dead.

"The old cargo hold? You want to go down *there*? But…what if there are rats?"

"Oh, don't be such a baby. You know the exterminator comes though the ship regularly."

Emilio still looked doubtful. "Have you been down there before?"

"Of course," she lied, as she pulled open the door.

Emilio knew she was lying, but why kid himself? If she were leading him down into hell, he knew he'd be right behind her. He'd already lost his job because he'd been stupid enough to follow her into her mother's office when she'd beckoned, and he knew damn well he was going to follow along with this reckless whim too. All she had to do was look at him, and the blood rushed from his brain straight to…other body parts. He couldn't think when they were together. He considered himself lucky he managed to breathe.

"Okay. I guess. But let me go down first to make sure it's safe."

"Here — take this." She pulled the flashlight out of her pack and handed it to him.

They sure needed it. It was as dark as tar in that hold. He flicked it on and then, poking his head though the doorway, he looked down, ran the light around the perimeter and down the center of the space below. The hold, originally used for carrying mail, was curved in the middle like the rest of the ship, and narrowed in toward the bow. Bulky, horizontal wooden beams lined its lower sides, braced by more thick wood cut into curved, perpendicular angles, and spaced evenly between them. The heavy plank flooring was grungy but bare, apart from some scattered old pieces of rope and wire. And on the riveted iron sheeting of the upper walls, graffiti had been written in grime, maybe by some of the crew. All in all, not a welcoming space. Emilio had no clue what would make Sarita want to venture down into it.

"It's bigger than I expected. You're right, though — there's nothing down there but dust."

Instead of steps, there was a worn-looking, flat wooden ladder nailed to the base of the entrance opening. He took a cautious step onto it. "It seems sturdy." He went down two more rungs, then held out his hand to her. "Come on, baby."

Together, they climbed down.

"Wow. It's super dark."

"Yeah. And it smells kinda musty."

He propped the flashlight straight up against the corner beam, so that it shined off the dome of the hold, and then turned to Sarita. Silently, she held her arms out to him. There were no words to describe how he felt when she did that. To him, she was a precious jewel he'd somehow had the incredible luck to discover. He took great care to show her how much he valued her. Yet today, she was looking at him with such unusual scrutiny, that he felt the pulse in his throat and loins throb almost painfully. He wished he were older and more experienced, that he might know what she was thinking. He wished they were someplace else, somewhere more...girly and romantic that might please her.

"Sarita." Tamping down on his own desires, he walked to her, and kissed her on the lips. He forced himself to be a gentleman about it — to keep it soft and closemouthed.

Sarita was having none of that today. She smoothed her hands over his cheeks and down to his shoulders, then pulled him closer and deepened the kiss, swirling her tongue around his in the way the *Cosmopolitan* article she'd read the day before had counseled. He groaned with pleasure. It seemed the writer had offered competent advice.

Stepping back from him, she opened her backpack and shook out the blanket. Kneeling on it with her back to him, she pulled out the wine and corkscrew, lit the two candles and set them near the edge of the blanket. Then, with an expression a siren could aspire to, she looked back up at him over her shoulder.

He stared at her, bug-eyed with both hope and uncertainty. Could he be reading this right?

Obviously he needed another hint. She patted the blanket. "Come sit next to me."

When her message was finally clear, he couldn't move fast enough. Kicking off his tennis shoes, he plunked down beside her. This time when he pulled her to him, he wasn't nearly as circumspect. He kissed her deeply and with surprising expertise, then ran his lips softly along the line of her jaw and up across the back of her ear.

"You're beautiful," he murmured against her neck, as he combed his fingers through her hair. "Everything about you is so, so beautiful."

Sarita felt several very nice tingles. That boded well. She placed her hands on either side of his waist, then slid her hands up under his t-shirt, so she could stroke his bare skin. Her touch was tentative at first, but when she reached his chest and could feel the rapid beats of his heart under the light sprinkling of hair, she grew bolder, brushing her thumbs back and forth over his nipples. He clenched his fists and groaned her name.

The change in his demeanor was surprisingly speedy after that, to Sarita's mind. He was gazing at her with a hot-eyed sensuality she'd never perceived in him before. "Would you like me to do the same to you?" he asked.

His intensity caught her off guard. She was the one who'd engineered this escapade. When had *he* taken over the reins?

Seeing her falter, his face softened. "Only if you want it, *chica*." Tenderly, he brushed back her hair again. "I love being here with you like this, but we do nothing you don't want to do. You only have to tell me once to stop, and I will. Okay?"

Still tense, she nodded. That he'd promised her control over how far they'd go, restored her confidence. Enough to take on the next task, anyway. Biting on her lower lip, she unbuttoned her blouse, bit by bit, pulled out of the sleeves, and then, like Botticelli's Venus, she covered her breasts with her arm.

Emilio sucked in a breath. To his absolute delight, she wasn't wearing a bra. That made things much less awkward. If he fumbled with the clasp, he'd feel like an idiot, but if he unhooked it with ease, knowing Sarita, she'd demand to know where he'd gotten the practice.

He smiled at her reassuringly. "Why are you hiding yourself?"

"I…just need a minute."

"Of course. Sure." His tone was soothing, in the way of a man endeavoring to tame a wild mare. It was all based on mutual faith. The mare had to trust that the man wouldn't break her spirit, and the man had to trust that the mare wouldn't throw him over and stomp him to death, once she allowed him to mount her.

She lowered her arm, watching him anxiously as his eyes took her in.

No matter how long he lived, he didn't think he'd ever see anything as glorious as Sarita Taylor's breasts in his lifetime again. In fact, if he could, he'd have them declared two of the Seven Wonders of the Modern World.

"You're exquisite." He didn't dare touch her yet. She still looked like she might bolt any second. More than he wanted to touch her, he wanted the wariness to leave her expression. He wanted — desperately — for this first experience to be wonderful for her. "Would it make you feel more comfortable if I took off my top too?"

Sarita tried not to sound as frantic as she felt at that. "No! Not yet."

He held his hands up at his sides as though she held him at gunpoint. "The t-shirt stays on." Quirking a smile, he teased, "I wouldn't look as good without my shirt as you do without yours, anyway."

That got a nervous laugh out of her, but a laugh nonetheless. He searched for something to put her at ease, and noticed a mark on her shoulder. "Hey, look at that — you have a tattoo right above your clavicle. An unusual place for one."

She stiffened. "It's not a tattoo. It's a birthmark."

"Really? It's fantastic. It's in the perfect shape of a star." He swallowed. "And the color reminds me of maraschino cherries." Just like her nipples, he'd noticed.

"I don't like it. Who has a birthmark in the shape of a star? It's weird."

Well, *that* line of conversation hadn't gone the way he'd hoped, had it? He smiled in exasperation. "Why do girls do that? Say negative stuff about themselves that's not even true? There's nothing 'weird' about you. You're perfect."

And unable to resist her naked loveliness any longer, he leaned across and placed his lips on that rosy little star. Then licked it. Then, he traced his tongue from that sexy birthmark down to the tip of her silky cream breast. He closed his mouth over it, and suckled.

Oh, my God, Sarita thought. She tilted her head back and reveled in this new sensation. It felt miraculous. It felt delicious.

But it didn't feel exactly *right*. Not now, and not with Emilio. He was great, but it was as though a light had just snapped on in her head, making her realize that he wasn't 'the one.' Shivering with sudden cold, she started to tell him to stop. "Emilio, wait..."

She got no further than that. He pulled away from her — brusquely, it felt to Sarita — and sprang to his feet. "What the *fuck*...?"

At first she thought he was angry with her for her change of heart; then she saw that he wasn't looking at her at all, but, with horror on his face, behind her. She glanced back, then she too jumped up, and choked in a scream.

The cargo hold was filled with men — so many that they scarcely had room to move. They wore different, tattered uniforms and identical expressions of misery. Their feet and hands were chained. Sitting huddled together on makeshift cots with threadbare linens, or slumped against the hold's sides, they stunk of sour sweat, stale urine, festering wounds, and hopelessness.

Her bareness forgotten, Sarita cringed against Emilio and held her hand up to her nose against the stench. She could hear some of them murmuring to each other in German or Italian. It was some time before she could accept what she was seeing and say it out loud. "Emilio — they're war prisoners!" Her whisper was incredulous. "This is where they were held when the *Mary* was converted into a troopship."

"You mean, they're...?" Emilio let the question trail off. He didn't have to ask it, when the evidence was right in front of him. The sight was so staggering, so wildly terrifying, he held fast to Sarita in as much an attempt to protect her as to keep himself from falling to his knees.

There was a rush of wind. The candles Sarita had set beside their blanket blew out. Though she knew without a doubt that the modern day *Mary* where she slept every night was permanently docked and secured in its slip, the ship now appeared to tip violently, and the cargo hold began filling with water.

"It's not real. It can't be real!" She shook her head in denial, even as her shoes were soaked and the sting of damp salt air hit her nostrils. The ship pitched again, and the young couple watched as the shouting, screaming prisoners tumbled to the floor or scrambled to stay upright. The entryway through which they'd climbed down was now closed, secured tightly from the outside. Several men at once, hampered by their manacled hands and feet, struggled to climb up the ladder and pound on the door.

Just then, it burst open. More water and wind came rushing down into the hold. Shouting voices could be heard coming from the deck above, and two men were arguing.

"You're crazy to do this, Lee. Our orders are to leave them. There are thousands of us who need to get secure. There's a gale out there. The waves are high as mountains. She's on her beam ends. She's going to roll!"

"They're men too, Steve. I can't leave them down there to drown like rats."

"Do what you gotta do, but I'm not violating orders! I'm getting out of here. You're on your own."

Presently, a pair of arms and hands came into sight, and began pulling the prisoners up the ladder. "Take it easy. One at a time. I'll get you all out."

Emilio and Sarita sank to their knees, and leaned knotted together against the curved side of the hull, as the ferocious wind bellowed and the battered ship lurched. The unseen man hauled each clamoring prisoner up, one by one. At last, only one remained. He looked younger than the rest, and frightened to death. He started toward the ladder, but then inexplicably changed his mind and dropped back, lurching, shuffling in reverse to the far end of the hold, as swiftly as his leg shackles and the rocking of the ship would allow.

"What the hell are you doing? You'll drown down there. Come toward the ladder, dammit!"

The prisoner shook his head vehemently and cowered against one of the beams, muttering in German, looking as though he would bawl like a baby at any moment.

The still-concealed man gentled his voice. "You're afraid? Is that it?" He hesitated. They heard him swear with frustration, over the roar of sea and wind. "All right, I'm coming down."

He came backward down the ladder, barely able to hold on to it himself. When he reached the planked flooring of the hold, he swayed to steady himself, then turned toward the German POW. It was then noticeable that he also wore a military uniform, only his was that of an American soldier. He shook his head, his expression one of amused irony, and Sarita couldn't help but notice that his eyes were even prettier than Emilio's. Except they weren't brown. In the dim light of the hull, they glinted like silver.

"I can't believe I'm doing this. You're gonna get me in so much trouble, buddy." He walked toward the prisoner and held out one arm. "Come on — let's get out of here. This hellhole is no place for anybody to die."

What happened next was swift and vicious. Sarita and Emilio both shouted and jumped back as the prisoner swung his arms toward the American, hitting him in the face with his chains. Blood spurted from the soldier's nose. As he reeled from that, in a flash, the prisoner positioned himself behind him, and used the same chains to garrote him. The soldier clawed instinctively at the vice around his neck to no avail, as his legs kicked and his body jerked. After what seemed an agonizing, endless time to the young couple who'd been compelled to watch by a force beyond their control, his hands fell, his body slumped, and his movements stilled. The eyes Sarita had admired were still open, wide with shock, but now sightless. Sobbing, she dug her hand into Emilio's, pressing his fingers together painfully, as the prisoner released his hold, and the dead soldier crumpled to the sodden floor.

Every rasping breath the German took seemed impossibly loud, as he kneeled down and searched his victim's pockets, dumping out the contents as he went: a wallet, a pocket watch, a small leather-bound book and, at last, the keys he needed. He found the one that fit his shackles and unfastened them. Riveted with revulsion, they continued to watch as the prisoner stripped the soldier and himself. He pulled on the American uniform and cap, checked the wallet for cash, and then stuffed it into the stolen jacket, along with the pocket watch.

The *Mary* tipped again, this time the opposite way. Though she was still sobbing, Sarita caught the motion of the little leather book as it slid across the water, and down between two of the perpendicular ribbings of the curved hull. The prisoner's expression was pitiless as he clamped his foot on the body to secure it. When the ship stopped swaying momentarily, he dragged the dead man to the metal heating shaft at the back of the hold, and Sarita felt Emilio shudder.

"*Dios mio.* Close your eyes, *chica,* close your eyes." Knowing what would happen next, he felt a burning sickness travel up to his throat. "You don't want to see this. You don't."

But neither of them could look away. They felt every wrench, heard every bone crack, as the prisoner used all his strength to twist and force the body down into the shaft. At last, it fell with a thud into the underpinning of the hull below the hold. The discarded German uniform was shoved in after it. With a grisly sneer of triumph, the prisoner ran toward the ladder.

But for the second time, he stopped before he climbed. Swiveling back around, precariously balanced as the ship still tried to right itself, his gaze fixed on Sarita and Emilio.

"He can't see us. It's not possible!" Sarita cried.

Somehow, it appeared that he could. He sprang at them with a snarl, and Sarita finally closed her eyes, and screamed.

When she opened them, the water in the hold was gone. Her shoes were dry, and their things were just as they'd been before the wind had blown through. Emilio had his arms clamped around her, holding her to him tightly.

And standing before them was not a long-dead POW, but Cristiano. The look on his face as he stared at Emilio was equally as terrifying as anything they'd just experienced.

"You son of a bitch. What did you do to her?"

CHAPTER EIGHT

Meanwhile, somewhere over the Pacific

He could feel the Gulfstream begin its descent. Yawning, he'd refastened his seatbelt even before his pilot announced, "Please prepare for landing in Haneda Airport, in approximately twenty-nine minutes, sir."

To pass the remaining time, he unfolded the letter and read the pertinent sections again:

You should have seen her. She rescued me with no thought at all to her own safety. She's an exceptional woman. Here's what I want you to do…

As his jet dipped, he slid the letter back into the folder with all the other relevant papers. Picking up the issue of *Bon Appétit*, he flipped through to where his secretary had bookmarked it with a yellow Post-It. After skimming through the article one more time, he put the magazine on top of the folder and closed them both safely away in his briefcase. They touched down seamlessly, and he leaned back as they glided along the runway, rolling to a stop.

His pilot spoke over the speaker system once again, "Welcome to Tokyo, sir."

Smiling to himself, he thought, Last stop, and then on to California. In just a few short weeks, we will all meet, face to face.

PART II: THE MEN RETURN

A Sailor, Three Sons, and One More Killer

CHAPTER NINE

Same Monday again, a few hours prior...

Not long after Cristiano left Cynthia's office, there was a knock at the door. "*Señora* Cynthia?"

Cynthia called back, "Yes, come on in, Inez."

Inez peeped in and looked about the room. "Oh. I thought I heard *Señor* Cris in here."

"He was, but he's just gone back to the kitchen, I think."

"No, he's not in the kitchen, *Señora.* I didn't want to disturb you while you were in a meeting, but it is one o'clock. The ladies are just back from the market and are preparing something to eat. I thought I should clean the office before they needed to use it."

Cynthia waved her in, and then huffed with friendly impatience. "Inez, I thought I told you to call us by our first names. This '*Señor* and *Señora*' stuff — it makes us feel ancient."

Inez colored self-consciously as she pulled in her vacuum and bucket of cleaning supplies. "I know. I can't seem to stop myself." Picking up a rag, she began polishing the other three work stations, moving papers and folders carefully aside as she did so, hoping silently that Jane wouldn't complain about anything being put back "in the wrong place," when she was done. "It's an old habit from when my mother used to work here as a maid too. She taught me that it shows respect, but Michael says that it smacks of classism."

"Michael said that? Good for him," Cynthia declared. "So, are you two an item now? You looked pretty cozy on opening night."

Inez's blush deepened. Carefully, she adjusted the position of the new photo frame on Jane's desk, and then looked at Cynthia with deliberation. She wanted to confide in her. Michael and Cynthia were good friends, and she might have some insight about him to share. But, as they'd just been discussing, she was also one of Inez's employers.

With a reassuring smile, Cynthia added, "You don't have to answer if you don't want to. But I'm very good at keeping secrets."

In fact, she added grimly to herself, you'd be amazed if you knew how many of them I've been stockpiling around here.

That was all the prompting Inez needed. "It's so hard to know, *Señora*. I mean …Cynthia. One week, he's dating every twenty-year-old *chichona* in Long Beach" — still clutching the rag, she pressed her hands to her chest and then extended her arms to indicate big breasts — "and the next, he has eyes only on me, a single mother. And let me tell you, at way past twenty, and after a baby, my body has seen better days."

"Whose hasn't?" Cynthia was surprised but pleased by how openly Inez was now speaking to her. But as she watched the younger woman put down the dust rag and polish, and pick up a spray cleaner, her thoughts were racing. "Maybe he's ready for a real woman, at last," she ventured. "Maybe he's finally gotten tired of playing around with girls."

"Hah. I don't buy it." Inez moved to the coffee cabinet, spritzing and wiping all around the sink as she unburdened herself. "I've been under his nose forever. What — he opened his eyes and noticed me there, after all this time? " She tut-tutted dubiously as she rinsed out the coffee pot. "No, no. *Something* is up with him. He's like a different man. Take his shop, for example."

"What about it?"

Inez turned. "You haven't seen it? Sarita was in there yesterday. He got all new stock. He hired me and two other maids to clean the whole place, top to bottom."

Cynthia's brow puckered. "I was in there two days before the opening here. It was in its usual chaos. He's done all that in less than two weeks?"

"Yes, *and* he has even more plans for it. It's like...he...all of a sudden, has this passion for something he never cared anything about." She turned back to the sink to scrub vigorously. "He's so cute when he's talking about all his new ideas. I've always found him sweet. Now, even more so, especially since we..." she trailed off, and sighed. "Ah, well. It won't be the first time I've set myself up for a broken heart," she finished with philosophic certainty.

Cynthia hoped the twinge of guilt she was feeling didn't show on her face. "Must we be so fatalistic about this? I mean, even if he's just rolling with some new whim and it all changes back to the way it was, couldn't you just enjoy it for as long as it lasts?"

With a caustic chuckle, Inez hung a fresh dish cloth on the hook by the cabinet. "That's what my mother says. 'Embrace it for the moment.' She forgets that's how I ended up with Marisol."

Before Cynthia could say more, Jane strode in, looking pleased with herself, an open copy of the *Long Beach Gazette* in her hand. "Have a look at this. I was right. I should have bet you all five quid. Oh, pardon me, Inez."

"We don't have 'quid' in this country, Jane," Cynthia told her dryly. "Just like we don't have lifts, car boots, or biscuits with tea."

"Rubbish. You're just jealous because we invented the language and you lot mucked it up. In any event, thanks to me, you do have universal healthcare. Or at least, you might. Go on, then. Read it." Setting the paper down on Cynthia's desk, she tapped her finger on one of the articles. Cynthia put on her glasses and leaned in.

"'The Governor of California becomes the first Republican governor in the nation to announce his support for federal health care reform efforts.'" Cynthia pulled her reading glasses off and stared at Jane. "This is a fake newspaper, right? You've had it printed as a joke?"

"Hah!" Jane smacked her hand on the desk. "I *told* you he was listening to me that night. Where's Cristiano? He didn't believe me, either. I want to rub his nose in it as well."

"I thought for sure he was going back to the kitchen." Comprehension struck Cynthia. "Although, he did have a few dr — er, that is…he did say something about not feeling well. Maybe he's in his cabin."

Jane eyed her thoughtfully. Then she slanted her head toward the door. "Have you got a moment? I wanted a private word."

Standing up, Cynthia smiled at Inez. "Let's talk again soon, okay? In the meantime, you have the office to yourself for a while, so you can finish up in peace."

Inez smiled back. "Thank you, Cynthia. I'll use the chance to vacuum. This thing is so powerful, it sounds like a jet engine."

The moment Cynthia closed the door behind them, Jane remarked, "Well, what do you know? She called you 'Cynthia.' That's a long overdue change."

"I agree. So, what did you want to talk to me about?"

Jane kept her voice low. "Rohini. While we were driving home from the market, she told us everything." With some indignation, she added, "She also said you knew. Why on earth didn't you say anything?"

Cynthia leaned against the wall, watching Jane carefully. "It wasn't my secret to tell."

That mollified Jane. "I suppose that's true." Then she shook her head. "The poor thing. To be living in such fear. Isn't there anything we can do to help?"

"Nothing that I've come up with so far, unfortunately. But does this mean she's finally going to tell Cristiano? If this strain between them goes on much longer, the kitchen staff's going to need trauma counseling."

"So we told her this morning, although not in those precise words. She's been looking for him since we got back. Hopefully he'll turn up soon. There's an electrical short in the scullery I wanted him to investigate."

"Well, if he's not in the kitchen, tell her to check his room." Lifting a brow, Cynthia gave her a half smile. "So, I take it the task force you and Angela formed this morning was a success?"

"That depends. Are you and Sarita on speaking terms yet?"

Cynthia's expression changed. "She barely looked at me when she left for school this morning, except to say she'd be staying late to work on a project with some classmates. It's her sixteenth birthday today, you know." She sounded almost as hopeless as Inez had, when she'd spoken of her destined-for-doom relationship with Michael. "I asked Angela to make her a vanilla mousse cake. Sarita loves that, but now, who knows if she'll even want to sit with us and have some?"

It wasn't often that Cynthia showed her vulnerable side. The last thing she'd appreciate was being pitied, so Jane did her best to hide the unexpected empathy she felt. "Oh, now — don't be silly. She's just wanting to sneak in a bit of birthday fun and mischief with her friends, more than likely. What could be the harm in that?"

"Well, call me a cynic, Jane, but you know that five quid you wanted that I don't have? I'll bet you double that or nothing that she's somewhere with Emilio right at this moment. And if he has his way, I know what her birthday present's going to be."

Jane debated with herself on whether or not she should speak. At length she said, "Look, it's not my place to say, but don't you suppose that if you just left her alone, she'd figure things out for herself?"

"Of course she'll figure things out. We all do, eventually." Behind the office door they heard Inez's vacuum roar to life, and Cynthia jerked a thumb in that direction. "Inez did — *after* she got pregnant. I did, after my *pinche gringo culero* of a husband left me with a baby and a bunch of bounced checks."

"You don't know that that's what's going to happen with Sarita." Jane tried to press home her point on raising children, although she suspected she was wasting her breath, just as she had been with Antoni over Gabriella. "She needs the autonomy to learn these things for herself. She needs to know you trust her and that you're her friend."

Cynthia could literally feel her back go up. Cristiano's perspective on how his mother had had some culpability in Isabel's murder was still too fresh in her mind for her to remain cool about Jane's little homily, however well-intended. "She's sixteen and I'm forty-five. At her age, she needs me to be her *mother*, Jane, not her friend."

Though she tried her best to hide it, her voice shook. "Those years between us have taught me a lot. In the hardest ways possible, I learned from my mistakes. Some days, I look in the mirror, and all I see is how much of my life I lost to my foolishness. No lipstick or makeup can disguise that, Jane. On those days I have so many regrets I can taste them. Do you think I want the same for Sarita?"

Jane started to interject, but clearly she'd hit a nerve. Cynthia was off and running. "I don't want her to waste her youth, carrying a baby on one hip everywhere she goes. Or working minimum wage jobs in order to feed them both, worried sick the whole time, because she has no choice but to trust strangers to look after her little girl."

Jane watched the mask of invincibility that Cynthia habitually wore plunge to the ground and shatter. Behind it was another woman entirely. A woman, Jane saw all at once, that she'd judged too severely.

"Who's going to try to stop her from making those life-altering mistakes if not me, Jane? Her friends? Of course not — they'll encourage her to make them, because they're sixteen too. We were *all* naïve at that age. We all —" she uttered the next phrase with outright self-loathing — "believed in 'love.' So I think I'd prefer she see me as her enemy rather than her friend, if that's the way it has to be for now."

"I see." Jane studied her business partner with a tenderness she'd never expected to feel for her. Well. This tirade explained rather a lot.

"I'm not sure you do." Cynthia was too busy with her rant to notice the softening of Jane's features. "Perhaps if you had a teenage daughter — oh, shit, shit, *shit*. I'm such an idiot. I'm sorry, Jane. I didn't mean —"

"Let's not have any more of that." Though her gut twisted at what Cynthia had been about to say, Jane cut off her apology. "I'm sick to death of everyone feeling as though they have to walk on eggshells around me in regards to...this subject." Matter-of-factly, she added, "Although I suppose I've no one to blame for that but myself."

With a nod at Cynthia's expression, she continued. "Shocked you into silence, I see. Good. Perhaps now you'll listen to me for a moment."

She paused to gather her thoughts. "I do understand what you're feeling, truly. As her mother, you want to protect her. You want her to have the best life she can have." She swallowed. "There's no guarantee you can always do the first, and the second is entirely up to her. Entirely. That reality is the hardest thing to accept about being a parent, Cynthia."

Her eyes shadowed as she thought of her own daughter, and of how she'd wrongfully accused Antoni. The residual resentment was gone, she realized, replaced by acceptance. "We never really have any actual control over what happens to our children, or over what choices they make. Right or otherwise, whether she decides to fall in with Emilio or not, is up to her. You can only advise, not demand. Because — just think — if she were to do what you wanted her to do, for the sole reason that you told her to do it, you wouldn't haven't raised her at all well, would you have?"

Cynthia sighed and admitted grudgingly, "I guess not." Her shoulders sagged with sudden weariness. "It's terrifying, though — you know?"

"I do, indeed," Jane replied sadly. She changed the subject briskly. "We were about to have some lunch. Join us, why don't you?"

Coming from Jane, that invitation meant a lot. Cynthia felt her mood lighten. Nonetheless, with her thoughts switching from Sarita to another young woman — the one who was currently cleaning their office — she still sounded dour when she replied, "I'd like nothing better. Unfortunately, I have unexpected business to discuss with our next door neighbor."

Cristiano wasn't sure if the knocking he heard was coming from inside his aching skull or if, as he suspected, from outside his cabin. Damn Cynthia and her whisky. Damn whoever it was who was drumming on his door. He tried to ignore it and go back to sleep. The knocking continued.

Chingalo! he swore to himself. "Just a moment."

Naked, he got out of bed. Wrapping the sheet around his waist, he made his way groggily across the room. "Who is it?"

"It's…me."

That soft, uncertain voice had him instantly alert. Tugging the sheet around himself more securely, he opened the door. There stood Rohini, looking delectable in her go-to-market clothes. He was certainly wide awake now. Shifting so that the lower half of his body was hidden behind the door, he cleared his throat and said gruffly, "Is there something I can help you with, *señorita*?"

"As of matter of fact, there is." Rohini tried to sound assertive, even as she twisted her hands together. At last she blurted, "I'm sorry. I'm sorry, Cristiano. I should have talked to you."

Though he wanted to crow joyfully, he kept his expression neutral and his tone as firm as he could manage. It wouldn't do to give in too easily.

"You're sorry. I see." He paused. "And you think that after putting me through one whole week of hell — both you and that…that invisible virago in the kitchen — that's all you have to say to me, and I will forgive and forget?"

"No, I suppose not. You're right." Rohini's heart sang. Though he was trying to appear stern, his eyes told her she was already forgiven. They looked just as they did when he sampled a new recipe for the first time and deemed it a success. Oh, he was just adorable.

She pretended to think. "What if I say, I'm sorry, Cristiano and…I love you very much. Would that do it?"

"Absolutely." Letting go of the sheet, he caught her up with both hands, lifting her off her feet as he pulled her into his room. Slamming the door shut with his foot, he crushed his lips to hers.

She lay curled against his side, sated, happy and…*smug*, was the only word that suited. In her experience, coupling with a man had never been nearly this delicious. She'd had to wait so long to feel like this, but now she knew that the books she'd read covertly as a teenager hadn't overstated the gloriousness of this activity. When she was in her twenties, married to the sweet but ailing Zahir, she was sure they had. During those years, she'd felt more alone than she had when she'd lived under her parents' and brothers' rule.

But things were so different with Cristiano.

The renowned Spanish chef and the obscure girl from India. What had made them take just one look at each other and immediately feel that they were so alike, when in fact they were from such worlds apart?

He was sleeping on his stomach, his profile toward her. Shifting carefully so as not to wake him, she leaned up on her elbow, relishing the view of him as he slept. He had the body of a man twenty years younger. Sighing, she remembered what he'd told her when she asked why he worked so hard to stay in shape. Habit, he'd said. In prison, only the strongest survived. He'd lifted weights every day in prison. Now that he was free, he still lifted weights. And he took long walks along the ocean with the same precision and mindfulness that he brought to his cooking. As a result, his shoulders, back, and legs were sculpted with muscle, and his backside was as firm and glossy smooth as the apples she'd just brought home from the market. She found herself hankering for apples a lot, lately.

A wicked little smile curled her lips as she imagined what her business partners would think if they knew that sex was on her mind quite often these days. Cynthia would guess that. She gave them sly glances all the time. Jane suspected also, more than likely, although she'd be the last person who'd care to reflect on such things when it came to other people. But poor Angela might as well have been a virgin, with all her blushes and girlishness. Perhaps they didn't have much in common, she and Angela, but they'd both lived through unsatisfactory marriages, and knew how empty that made one feel.

For once in her life, however, she wasn't overly concerned about what others thought. Not of her, not of her relationship with Cristiano. Part of the reason for that, she suspected, was that she was changing and growing. Being on the *Mary*, owning a restaurant, were making her much more independent and sure of herself. Notwithstanding everything she had hanging over her head, she was content. She loved The Secret Spice, she loved the ship, and she loved Cristiano. Heaven help her, how she loved him. She hadn't planned for that, and now, what a bane she'd brought upon them both because of it.

He was her best friend, her lover, her work teammate. She felt a bone-deep joy when she was cooking beside him, observing his concentration, listening to that voice, as he mumbled to himself in Spanish, watching those wide, strong hands as they sliced and stirred, those long, skilled fingers as they sprinkled herbs, spices, or cheeses on one of his glorious dishes. When he was in that mode, just watching him made her skin flush and her body go liquid in a way that had nothing to do with the heat of the kitchen. A man who cooked as well as Cristiano and looked the way he did to boot, well, that combination was as irresistible as the raspberries and chocolate pairing in Angela's most revered dessert.

He turned over in his sleep. As exquisite as the view had been from his other side, she appreciated this side most. Because when he was on his back, she could rest her head on his chest, just below his broad shoulder, turn ever so slightly, and flick his nipple with her tongue. Much to her delight, even at his age, he got hard instantly when she did that. And that was another thing that was perfect about him: He was just the right height that she could reach down without too much trouble and cup him at the same time. It was as though they were built to fit each other. Oh, it felt so good to lie next to him like this...so soothing, and yet so incredibly arousing...to breathe in his warm, enthralling scent while caressing him. She felt so powerfully female when she made him smile, made him groan.

Like he was doing now. "Mmmm. Stop that, will you? I'm worn out. I've still got a hangover. Besides, I was trying to be all romantic when I carried you over here, and I think I hurt my back. You're harder to lift these days. You've gained weight." With a lusty grin, he reached around and squeezed her backside. "I bet you must be at least ninety-five pounds by now."

"You'd better stop feeding me, then."

His smile was lazy. "No can do, *corazon*. You are my best taste-tester."

"You're my best taste-tester too." She licked at him again. "See?"

"Hey," he laughed. "Didn't you hear what I said?" With a fake sigh he complained, "I'm old, Rohini. I need time to recover."

Giggling, she held him in her hand. "Are you sure? Because that's not what it feels like."

He play-pinched her bare buttock again. "You're a greedy girl. Who knew when I met you that you would be so naughty?"

She stopped touching him, and went still. Slanting her a look, he saw that she was eyeing him with uncertainty. "Is that...does that bother you, Cristiano?"

And there it is, he thought. That is what happens when a woman is taught to be ashamed of her sexuality.

"Certainly not." He pulled her on top of him and kissed her everywhere he could reach, until she relaxed again and splayed herself wantonly across him. "I am a thankful, thankful man." He ran his hand soothingly up and down her bare back. "So, are you ready to talk to me?"

She went rigid all over again. "I suppose I must. Though I have to warn you, Cristiano — you'll hate what I'm going to tell you."

"Oh, come on, *mi vida*. What could be so bad?" He tilted her face toward his, and saw that her eyes were huge and frightened. Trying to lighten her mood, he teased her again, "What — were you once a man? Because I could get used to that. I find you more appealing than some of the other men who tried to have sex with me in prison." When that got a chuckle out of her, he smiled. "You see? Nothing is so terrible that we can't laugh at it."

With a shaky breath, she plunged in. "Well, then. Let's see how 'funny' you think this is: I ran away. I ran away from my husband's family in India."

A husband. He hadn't expected that. Trying not to sound as devastated as he felt, he said softly, "So that's it, then? I'm in love with a married woman?"

Her eyes filled. "No. No, Cristiano, I'm not an adulterer. My poor husband is dead. As I would be, if he hadn't taken steps to get me away from his brother before he died. But I'm still not safe. His brother is trying to find me, and when he does, he'll kill me."

She was crying now, and her skin had gone cold. "If you stay with me, you're not safe, either. That's why I didn't tell you. The less you know, the better. I didn't think this would happen — that we would fall in love. I didn't think ahead. And now, I'm so frightened that he'll find me, and when he understands what you mean to me, he'll kill us both."

He pulled them up into a sitting position against the pillows. Reaching across to the nightstand, he handed her the cup of water he kept there. "Here, now — drink some of this." Though his mind was reeling, he spoke soothingly. "Does he know where you are?"

She shivered and sniffled. "I don't think so. Not at the moment. But he'll never let this rest. He always has people looking for me. It's only a matter of time before he finds me."

Caressing her arms to warm her, he forced himself to keep his tone even and calm. Some sort of family vendetta, he supposed. They were not unknown within certain segments of society in his country, either. "Which was why you didn't want your photo in the magazine." He shook his head as he thought back to that night. "I'm a jackass. You looked scared out of your wits, but I thought you were just being shy. Then I made things worse by getting angry. I'm so sorry, baby. "

"You didn't know. I should have said."

"We both made a mistake." Taking the cup from her, he put it back and handed her a tissue. As casually as he could manage, he asked, "So, since your husband wanted to save you from his brother, I can assume it wasn't you who killed him?"

She looked at him in horror. "Of course I didn't kill him! It was my healing herbs that kept him alive, far longer than his doctors had anticipated." With misery she added, "I didn't want him to die."

That stopped his breath. He couldn't tell what he was feeling most — relief that she wasn't a killer on the run, or despair that she might still be in love with a dead man. "Do you miss him?"

"It's not like that. I didn't want him to die, but I wasn't in love with him. I'd been promised to him by my parents. My brothers knew Zahir's family. They thought that a match between us would bring us admiration in our community."

He held up a hand. "Wait. What? Your parents and your brothers picked out your husband for you? You mean…you had no say in it?"

"It wasn't my place to choose my own husband," she explained matter-of-factly. "Although, I did ask them if I could meet him first." She lifted a shoulder. "That didn't go over well. They said, 'What for? You'll marry him, no matter what.' But Zahir was kinder to me than I'd dared hope. I was fortunate. I had friends who'd been given to husbands who were cruel to them."

Cristiano was having a hard time wrapping his mind around all this. He worked with this woman, slept with her, loved her with all his heart, and never knew, never dreamed, that she'd had such a fundamentalist upbringing. While he was still speechless, she dropped another bombshell.

"The doctors never could figure out what illness he had that caused him to die. If it *was* an illness. Something wasn't right there… not at all right." One of her tears plopped down onto his wrist. "But my herbs were helping him. I know they were. Until Naag went to his parents and accused me of being a witch. "

Watching her eyes go dark as she dredged up the memory, he asked, "Naag? Would that be the brother-in-law?"

Blowing her nose, she nodded. "He's a year younger than Zahir. He inherited everything when Zahir died. Including me."

Cristiano was stunned. "What do you mean, 'including you'?"

She described for him something that was commonplace to her. "If Zahir died, I was to be given to Naag. It's customary."

That revelation did nothing to help his hangover. Nausea churned again. He swore to himself that he'd stay out of Cynthia's office and far away from her liquor cabinet from now on, so help him, God. He took one deep breath, willing himself to stay calm, hoping like hell his face didn't give away his distaste for this 'custom.'

"If I'm to be honest, part of the reason I was so desperate to keep Zahir alive, was because I didn't want to go to Naag. I knew he wouldn't be as kind to me." She shuddered. "The way he'd look at me when no one else was around — it made my flesh crawl."

Cristiano said nothing, although he was appalled. How could his vibrant, intelligent Rohini speak of her slavery as though it were nothing other than what she'd been taught to expect? He'd *killed* for his sister. Yet Rohini's brothers had sold her off to be used and bartered over by two strange men. And she called this subjugation her 'marriage.' No, this was definitely not helping his stomach.

"Naag convinced his parents that there was something bad in the medicinal herbs I was giving to Zahir. I'll never know if they favored Naag and wanted him to inherit, or if they actually believed I was evil. Either way, they forced me to stop making potions for my husband. And then…" he felt her fingers flex compulsively around his arm, "they began guarding me. I wasn't allowed to leave the house by myself. They thought I'd find a way to procure more herbs and sneak them into Zahir. I couldn't even visit him in his sick room without a servant or a family member coming with me."

"This is unimaginable." The words burst out of him at last. "That you went through this is…is…"

Rohini smiled sadly. "You think so? You need to meet more women from my country."

Cristiano shook his head in disbelief. "My God, Rohini. How did you keep this inside you for so long?"

But it was all coming out now. He could feel his body and spirit drain of vitality, as he absorbed it all for her, like poison.

"Zahir was afraid for me too, I could tell. He no longer trusted his brother. Why should he? My herbs had been helping him — we both knew it. But he was so ill by that time, he couldn't even leave his bed. There was nothing he could do to change what Naag had in store for either one of us."

Her throat felt dry, even though she'd just had water. She tried to swallow. "At least, that's what I thought. Then one evening, when I was by his bedside with Vanu, Zahir's closest servant, Zahir motioned for me to move closer to him. He whispered, 'Tomorrow night, Vanu will come for you. Do what he tells you. This is the last thing I'll ask of you. Promise me, Rohini.'"

"He helped you escape." Cristiano felt lighter just saying that out loud.

"Yes. I promised I would do what he asked. I took some of my things, only what I could carry without raising suspicion. Everything else, I had to leave behind. But Zahir had it all arranged: Money for me to live, passage on the Central Railway from Kolhapur to Mumbai, even a passport. He'd done all this right beneath his family's eyes. All the time he lay there, sick and in pain, he was thinking of me, planning with Vanu how to help me get away. For as long as I live, I'll remember that." Her voice cracked. "I'll remember that he saved me. And that I could do nothing to save him."

Wordlessly, he wrapped his arms more tightly around her. It was agonizing to relive every long-ago regret. He'd been through it today himself. Hopefully it had helped her. It hadn't done a damn thing for him, certainly, other than to make him feel heartsick and powerless. Releasing her, he brought her hands to his lips and kissed them. She still felt so cold. He spoke quietly, trying to contain his emotions for her sake.

"There wasn't anything you could do. You know that. He was dying. Despite that, he found the strength he needed to help you. I will always be grateful to him for getting you away from…that."

She did her best to stop crying. She'd shed enough tears. "My family didn't see it that way. They disowned me when I wrote and told them I'd left. They believed they could never hold their heads up in Kolhapur again, where my husband's family was so powerful. So they also left. As for Naag, he felt he'd been dishonored. Luckily, he never found out that Vanu helped me, because Vanu still works for Naag's family. Vanu kept in touch, as he'd promised Zahir, visiting me whenever possible while I was in Mumbai. It was Vanu who warned me that Naag began a search for me again, after his parents died."

"Rohini —"

"No, please let me get the rest of this out, now that I've worked up the courage. That's when I finally left India altogether, and came here. Naag became first son after Zahir passed, inheriting all when his parents died. He obtained a very young wife from a prominent family. And yet, he's never forgiven me for shaming him by running away. A short while ago, his wife died too. He told everyone she died from a miscarriage, but," her look was vehement, "I don't believe that at all. In any event, according to Vanu, the fact that Naag is now a widower has given him a renewed impetus to seek revenge. He's been looking for me for more than ten years."

Cristiano's eyes went wide. "Are you serious? You've let this hang over you for *ten* years?" As though a giant weight had been lifted from him, he sat up straight and started laughing.

She jerked away from him immediately. "Stop that, Cristiano! Don't make fun of me." She whipped the sheet around her and scrambled off the bed, glaring down at him furiously. "You know nothing about my culture or that family. If I tell you there's a danger, you have to believe me. It's nothing at all to laugh at!"

"All right, all right. I'm sorry, Rohini. I believe you." He held his hands up, and sobered immediately. "But I also believe that allowing yourself to live in fear for the past decade means that he has already gotten his so-called revenge." He leaned back against the headboard again. There was so much he could say, so much he shouldn't and wouldn't say. He chose his next words with more care.

"Rohini. Love of my life, listen to me, please. Those people were your jailors. Your former in-laws and — though I hope you forgive me for saying this about your family — your parents and your brothers. And you've let yourself remain in their prison, even after your husband and his friend went through so much trouble to unlock you from it. Don't you see? Living like this, you might as well be back in India under your family's rule, or wasting away in your dying husband's house, where every move you made was monitored."

Watching her face to see if his words were getting though, he went on. "I lived under the thumb of others for ten years myself. It can drive you mad. Your husband loved you, Rohini. However you felt about him, I'm telling you — he loved you. He died with the one hope that he'd managed to set you free, so you could be happy. It's long past the time to face whatever might be out there, for his sake, as well as your own."

"I'm afraid."

Sighing, he climbed off the bed, and put his arms around her once more. "I know. But when you feel that way, remember that you are here with me, not there with them." He cradled her face with his hands. "I've shared my past with you, and now you've shared yours. We're in this together. Whatever comes — whether it's your ex-brother-in-law or anything else — we'll face it together."

She pushed away from him. "No. That's just what I don't want. I don't want you involved." She held her hands out in front of her as she pleaded, "Don't you understand? With your background, this could bring you terrible trouble. It's my problem, Cristiano, not yours."

"Someone is trying to kill you, and you expect me to stay out of it?" He chuckled softly at that, much too softly, and something about the sound made her go still. She took a step back from him, caught by the lethal expression on his face. For the first time she comprehended, fully, that the man she loved — the *only* man she'd ever loved — the man she'd trusted with her secrets and her life, had beaten someone to death with the same hands that touched her with such tenderness, the same hands that cooked with such elegance in her kitchen. The irony of it washed through her, not only that he was capable of both violence and beauty, but that she'd left her home and her family to escape one murderer, only to run into the arms of another.

He seemed to know just what she was thinking. In an instant, his eyes changed. They were sad now, and resigned. "You've known who I am, Rohini, all along. And now, I know who you are. Is this an idyllic romance for either one of us?" The smile that tugged at his lips was sardonic. "Hardly. But I still feel the same way about you as I did before you told me all this." He pulled her toward him again. "*Nothing* has changed for me. I love you. You've taken me with my past. Now I do the same."

She stared up at him, as what he was saying began to sink in. He spoke the truth. Nothing had changed. Revelations and realizations aside, they were exactly who they'd been when they'd first set eyes on each other. If their love was genuine, they would deal with all that entailed, she supposed. "You're quite right, of course."

His relief showed in his smile. For a moment, he'd been afraid that he'd lost her. "I'm glad you think so."

The cabin phone rang. Releasing her, he answered it.

"Hello? Oh, hi, Jane. Yes, she's here. What? Where? The back of the kitchen, again?" He made a sound of frustration. "I said it last time that those wires have to be replaced." He glanced with reproach at Rohini. "I know she did. I will talk to her about it now. Okay. I'll check it out and get back to you."

Hanging up, he turned to Rohini. "This is the second time the wiring near that freezer of yours has shorted since we opened. We have to upgrade the electrical system in there."

The change of subject was a welcome respite for them both. Hiking up the sheet she'd wrapped around herself, Rohini tilted her chin. "You know perfectly well why I don't want anyone to go near that freezer."

He nodded as he dressed. "To my eternal damnation, I do know perfectly well, yes. However, the freezer has nothing to do with the electrical system. There's going to be a fire in there one of these days, I'm telling you."

When she said nothing, he huffed in exasperation. "*Dios*, you are stubborn. Jane wants me to try to fix it. Do you know what that means? It means I have to go to the junction box, which, for some ridiculous reason, somebody years ago decided to put all the way down in the boiler room in the lowest deck. I hate going down there," he complained, as he found his tool box and opened it. "It's dark and creepy."

Rohini lifted a brow. "I didn't know you were such a scaredy-cat."

"I'm the scaredy-cat? Which one of us has been hiding out for ten years, *Señorita* Whatever-Your-Name-Is?" His brow knit as he thought of it. "What *is* your name? I assume you've been using a false one?"

She bit her lower lip. "It's only my surname that's false. It's borrowed from Deepa Mehta, my favorite Indian film director."

He hesitated in the middle of checking that he had all his tools."-Does anyone else know who your favorite director is?"

"I'd hardly think so. Why?"

"No reason. Just asking." He closed up the tool box, and walked back to her. Smoothing his hands over her bare shoulders, he gazed down at her solemnly. After some time, he said, "You know, I've thought of another last name you might like to borrow." He smiled what appeared to Rohini to be an unusually shy smile. "In fact, if you wanted to —" he bent down to whisper in her ear — "I'd let you keep it forever."

When her mouth popped open in surprise, he put his thumb over it and pressed his lips to her forehead. "Don't say anything yet." Looking down at her, his expression was satiric. "With all you've been through, I can guess what your first instinct would be. But, if it were you and me in it, 'marriage' would have a different definition than the one you learned as a child. That I can swear to you. Just think about it." He kissed her, picked up his tool box, and left.

She stood staring at the cabin door he'd closed behind him, the taste of him on her lips, his scent clinging to her skin.

CHAPTER TEN

In wild fury, Cristiano charged toward Emilio and seized him by the neck of his t-shirt. "You have three seconds before I kill you to tell me why she screamed."

"No! *No*, Cristiano — he hasn't done anything to hurt me. Let him go — please let him go!"

Sarita's words came at him through a red haze, but come through they did. Cristiano's rage faded, replaced by confusion as he took in the fact that Emilio was doing his best to shield Sarita from his view. Even though he was the stronger of the two of them, and had his hands dangerously near Emilio's neck, the boy held his ground, keeping Sarita positioned behind him as she, Cristiano now realized, was scrambling to get her shirt back on.

"Stop being an asshole," Emilio said to him in Spanish. "Let go of me, and turn your back. You're embarrassing her." Though he'd managed to speak calmly, there was a shadow of panic on his face, although apparently it wasn't Cristiano's threats of his death that had frightened him.

With a curse, Cristiano released him and turned swiftly around. Running his fingers through his hair, he continued to swear as he took in the candles and blanket, and came to grips with what he'd walked in on. Now what was he supposed to do? Play the outraged adult? He'd feel like the biggest hypocrite this side of hell, if he did.

Sarita solved his dilemma for him. Voice quavering, she asked, "Emilio, would you please go up with Cristiano, and give me five minutes down here alone?"

"Are you kidding me?" Cristiano's presence momentarily dismissed, Emilio stared at Sarita with disbelief. "You want me to leave you here by yourself?"

"I need five minutes."

"Sarita —"

"*Five* minutes. Please, Emilio," she insisted tearfully. "I'll be all right for five minutes. You can wait for me up top."

Once again, Emilio gave in to her. "Okay. But —" he glanced to where Cristiano stood with his back still to them — "if anything happens, we're right up there." Still overwhelmed by all that had transpired, he implored her, "Please, Sarita, please — *please* don't take too long."

With one last anxious look at her, he turned to the ladder and climbed up. Without a word, Cristiano followed. He couldn't get out of there fast enough.

Once they were gone, Sarita hastily tucked her shirt into her jeans. Stupid, stupid, *stupid*. You're *so* stupid, Sarita, she scolded herself. Who in their right mind tries to lose their virginity just to spite their mother? And, *ah, God* — Cristiano finding them — could anything be more humiliating?

She used the blanket to wipe at her eyes before she folded it and stuffed it into the backpack. If she hadn't come up with this lame-brained idea, they wouldn't have been down here, wouldn't have seen those terrible, horrible things. Tugging her fingers through her hair to get out some of the tangles, she wondered why stuff like this only happened to her.

She was a freak — that's why. She always had been. She never dared tell anyone about the strange things she felt and saw. They'd probably lock her up. But Emilio had been with her this time, so now what?

It's a gift. Learn to embrace it.

A gift. Yeah, right. Some gift. And on top of everything else, now she was hearing voices. Great.

She was about to blow out the candles, when she realized that would leave her in total darkness. Glancing about for the flashlight, she saw that it had fallen from where Emilio had propped it and rolled to the opposite side of the hold.

Right near where she'd seen the soldier's little book slide down into the gap between the horizontal wall beams and the flooring of the hull.

Staring across at the spot, she stood where she was, gnawing on her thumbnail.

Embrace it. Don't be afraid.

Warily, she inched her way toward that side. Retrieving the flashlight, she held her breath and, aiming the light behind the curved edge, she peered down.

Something *was* there, but she couldn't see it clearly.

Please don't let it be a dead rat, please don't let it be a dead rat, she prayed, as she reached down gingerly and pulled whatever it was up.

It wasn't a rat. It was the book.

Shining the flashlight on it, she saw that it was wrapped in a clear plastic covering that had provided some protection from the elements. Even so, it was damaged, spotty with mold. With her shirt sleeve, she wiped off some of the debris, and opened it. The ink was water-splotched in places, but much of the writing was still legible. She flipped through and saw that each entry was dated: July 16, 1944, August 10, 1944. It was a diary. She turned another page, and saw that a photo, faded with age, was wedged into the fold of the binding. Loosening it gently, she tipped the flashlight toward it, and then sucked in a breath.

It was him — the same man, dressed in a WWII soldier's uniform, just as he'd been when she and Emilio had watched him die.

Whoever he was, whatever divinity or demon had revealed him to them, he was as real as the book she was holding.

Cristiano and Emilio's voices drifted down to her faintly, snapping her out of her reverie. They were waiting for her as promised, like death and taxes. Returning the photo to its place, she closed the diary and placed it with care deep in her backpack, between the folds of the blanket. Zipping up the pack, she shrugged it onto her shoulders. With the flashlight as her talisman, she blew out the candles and left them.

When she reached the base of the ladder, she turned for one last look at the heating shaft at the back of the hold.

"I'll come back," she whispered. "I promise."

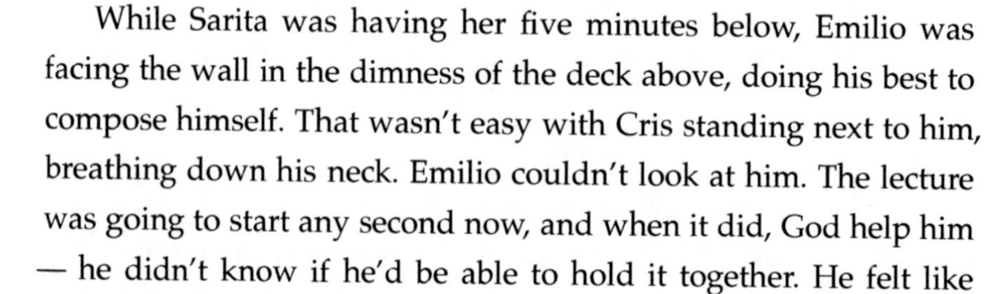

While Sarita was having her five minutes below, Emilio was facing the wall in the dimness of the deck above, doing his best to compose himself. That wasn't easy with Cris standing next to him, breathing down his neck. Emilio couldn't look at him. The lecture was going to start any second now, and when it did, God help him — he didn't know if he'd be able to hold it together. He felt like punching something. He felt like throwing up. But mostly, he felt like his heart was being squeezed tightly from within, and would burst at any moment.

Cris's voice when it came was a lot softer than he'd expected. "What happened down there? What did you see that made her scream?"

Risking a glance at him, Emilio saw that his expression was kind rather than fierce. He shook his head and looked away. "Man, if I told you, you wouldn't believe me."

Cristiano let out a half laugh. "You think not? Try me."

"I know you know. Everybody who's worked on this boat knows there's some weird shit that goes on. I mean…the kitchen. I'd hear you in there sometimes, when you were alone…supposedly. And then Inez and the other cleaners have some stories. But, nothing like this." He swallowed. "Nothing at all like this."

"Hmmm." Cristiano cleared his throat and ran his hand across his jaw. He had to say something. He sure as hell didn't want to, but he had to try. "Look — I'm not your father —"

Emilio tensed. *Here it comes.*

"— but, man, what the hell are you thinking?" He kept his voice as gentle as he could. "It's her sixteenth birthday only *today*. I was in the kitchen while Angela was making her birthday cake. She put little pink flowers on it and sixteen pink candles. Sixteen," he emphasized again. "She's not much more than a girl. You're lucky it was me and not her mother who caught you down there. She'd already be using your *cojones* as a change purse."

"I know how old she is, okay? I know!" Just as he'd known he would, Emilio exploded. He swore, and then slammed his fist against the wall once, twice, three times, until his knuckles began to bleed. He looked at Cristiano with tears in his eyes, as much from the pain in his hand as in his heart. "I love her. I *love* her, Cris. She's everything to me."

He kept his voice low so Sarita wouldn't hear. If she came up and saw him crying over her, he'd simply die where he stood, because now he knew for sure that she didn't feel about him the way he felt about her. That was hard enough to deal with, without also having to deal with her pity. Even the pity in Cris's eyes was making him furious. He balled his hands into fists, just spoiling for a fight. "You think that's stupid, right? You think I'm just a kid? Isn't that what you're going to say next?"

"No. If I did say that, I'd be lying." The statement rang with such frank sincerity that it silenced Emilio at once. He studied Cristiano again, and realized that it was understanding, not pity, that he saw on his face. "My father was your age when he fell in love with my mother. You could be him, fifty years ago." He put his hand on Emilio's shoulder. "I know what you're feeling is real, *amigo*."

Those shoulders fell as Emilio whispered over the lump in his throat, "Yeah, but there's nothing I can do about it, if she doesn't love me back."

"That's true. Sucks, doesn't it?" Cristiano responded almost pleasantly, as though they were discussing nothing more traumatic than inclement weather.

That approach was just what Emilio needed. "Yeah. It sucks." Considerably calmer, he rubbed his forearm across his eyes. "Do me a favor, will you? Would you look out for her? She...well...you know she doesn't have a father. Cynthia loves her more than anything, but she can be kind of overwhelming, you know?"

"I do, yes. And I will, of course."

"Thank you. Thank you, Cris, for everything." He put his hand out to shake Cristiano's, realized that his knuckles were still bleeding, and wiped them on his jeans before extending his hand again.

Cristiano took it. "You're not going to wait for her?"

"She won't want to see me." His expression one of pained resignation, he added, "Give her another minute, but don't leave her down there too long. I don't think it's safe."

And with that, he left.

Shortly thereafter, Sarita came back up. Cristiano turned red as a beet the moment she looked at him. He simply was no good at this.

Jesú Cristo, what a day this had turned out to be. This was all Rohini's fault. He wouldn't even be down here in the Tenth Circle of Hell, if it weren't for her and that godforsaken freezer. Having no idea the young couple was in the hold right below where he'd been patching frayed wires, he'd dropped a screwdriver and nearly had a heart attack when he heard Sarita scream. Then he twisted his ankle when he jumped down into the hull instead of using the ladder, so he could get to her faster. This, only a few hours after he'd sprained his back carrying Rohini around his cabin, and then making love with her. Twice. Not that he was complaining about that part. At least they'd gotten to enjoy themselves a little before that mind-blowing revelation about her background and her batshit crazy in-laws. *Dios mio* — he was still even now trying to recover from Cynthia having goaded him into drinking with her — before noon no less. Last but not least, *this* now, with Sarita. And he still needed to finish prepping the stuffed filets for tomorrow night's special. He was not that young a man anymore — didn't they see this? Four of the five of them had done their best to aggravate him on his one day off. The only one who ever left him alone was Angela.

But he kept this litany of vexations to himself, and smiled at Sarita. "Are you ready to go, sweetheart?"

She glanced around. "Where's Emilio?"

"He...had to leave."

She kept her eyes downcast. "Are you going to tell my mother?"

Oh, sure. That's exactly what he needed on top of everything else. If he had to choose to go back to prison, or to face Cynthia with this, he'd choose prison, gladly.

He didn't tell Sarita that, either. Instead, he looked at her unhappy face, and recognized that he was being given a second chance to be for her what he hadn't been able to be for Isabel. "You know, when you're ready, I think that should be up to you."

CHAPTER ELEVEN

Two weeks later, Tuesday, October 12, 2004,
1:30 in the morning, in the village of Kambalwadi,
outside of Kolhapur, India...

He should have learned by now to have faith in no one. Yet he'd been foolishly sure he could trust a servant who'd worked in his family home for more than thirty years. That betrayal stabbed as deeply as the blade he'd thrust into that same servant's heart.

Looking down at the bloodied body, he felt neither remorse nor gratification. He would never be at peace, never be restored to his former self, until he gained retribution for the humiliation he'd suffered at the hands of one woman and those who'd conspired with her in her plot to disgrace him.

He pulled out the knife, wiped it clean on the dead man's shirt, and slid it back into his trousers pocket. Quietly and swiftly, he searched the tiny home, looking for clues to her whereabouts.

He found what he was looking for in a battered-looking cardboard box that had been pushed to the back of a free-standing pantry in the kitchen area and hidden behind a sack of rice. Rifling through the contents, he grunted with satisfaction when he found two letters written by her. One was probably useless to him. It was nine years old, and had been sent from Mumbai. But the other was far more recent.

He ran his finger over its stamps. They were from the United States. He frowned when he saw that the envelope bore no return address. Squinting at the postmark, he could make out that it had been mailed from Los Angeles. He stuffed both letters into the same pocket with the knife, and put back the box.

Getting to his feet, he peeked out the makeshift door of the house. At this hour, no one would be out on the dark and dusty tar road. He gritted his teeth as he thought of this so-called "enlightened" village. He detested it — all its squawking about environmentalism and women's property rights, its biogas and gobar gas, its medicinal herb gardens, and its female *sarpanch*. That last was the most revolting to him. A female in charge, telling the *panchayat* — the men in the village government — what to do. It was because of these western ideas that women were out of control, and a man could no longer be sure about his servants' loyalty.

His outrage renewed, he turned back inside, and picked up the paraffin lamp that was set on the cheap, pocket-sized dining table. After splashing the oil all over Vanu's body and around the kitchen, he swiped the dishrag off the hook by the sink, and pulled out his lighter. He waited for the flame to catch, and then dropped the burning rag on top of the body. As fire ate at the dead man's cotton shirt, he hurried out, slipped back into his car, and drove away. It was thirty-five kilometers back to Kolhapur. Before the sleeping villagers were alerted to the blaze, he'd be safely home. By sunrise he'd be on his way to California.

CHAPTER TWELVE

At the same time, with a 13 and 1/2 hour time difference from Kolhapur, it is noon on Monday, October 11, back on the RMS Queen Mary.

"Oh, my God. Our first wedding. My first wedding cake."

Angela sat in the dining room, all geared up for their planning summit. She was surrounded by recipe books: *Wedding Cakes: Romantic Yet Elegant, Fun and Frisky Wedding Cakes, Your Very Own Fairytale Wedding Cakes, Wedding Cakes: Religious Themed Chic,* and last, but certainly not least, *Martha Stewart's Impeccably Perfect Wedding Cakes.*

"I'm so excited. Aren't you excited, Cynthia?"

"Mmhmm."

"Do you think she already has a theme in mind, or do you think she'd be open to suggestions?"

"It's hard to say."

"I mean, she's always seemed pretty easygoing, and she *is* more excited about the actual marriage than the wedding, God bless her."

"One would hope."

Cynthia's answers were absentminded. Although she was thrilled about the extra income and publicity that would be generated for The Secret Spice by the wedding, and would do her utmost to make it a success, she was far too worried about her daughter to be fully in the moment. In actual fact, she was so worried, she couldn't sleep.

In the two weeks since Sarita's birthday had come and gone, she was transformed, going from defiant to docile all within the first twenty-four hours of turning sixteen. And that was what had Cynthia terrified. Like magic, she now had the daughter she'd thought she wanted — one who was obedient and who hovered by her side. On the night of her birthday, she'd slammed Cynthia for six when she'd knocked on the door of her mother's stateroom and asked if she could sleep in with her. As gently as possible, keeping all accusation from her voice, Cynthia asked, "Is anything wrong? Did you have a fight with Emilio?" hoping that her little girl would confide in her, as she used to.

But all Sarita said was, "No, nothing's wrong. I just want to stay in here with you."

Trouble was evident from the moment she got home from school late that same day. Just as Cynthia suspected, wherever Sarita had spent the afternoon, she hadn't spent it working on a class project, because it was plain that she'd been crying. When questioned, she avoided giving an explanation. But instead of getting testy, which was her usual diversionary tactic, she'd thrown her arms around Cynthia, hugged her fiercely, and said, "I'm fine, *Mamãe*. I'm sorry we fought."

That shocked Cynthia into silence. And after dinner, when Angela brought out the vanilla mousse cake, and they all sang "Happy Birthday," Sarita, who'd been silent through the entire meal, burst into tears. She'd followed that up by circling around the table, hugging everyone else in the group. The uncharacteristic gesture only startled the others, but it made Cristiano very uncomfortable.

He knew something. Cynthia was sure of it. She'd watched him for the last two weeks, as he noted Sarita's moping and looked just as worried as Cynthia was herself. What was *that* about? God help her — she didn't want to think the worst. Especially after all he'd confided to her. Surely he hadn't hurt her baby — surely, surely not — but no one could be trusted completely. She'd trusted her parents and her husband without a single doubt, hadn't she, and where had that gotten her?

In short, something was terribly wrong, and Cynthia was hell-bent on finding out what.

Today being Columbus Day, Sarita was off from school, and currently in the kitchen preparing lunch for them. In keeping with her newfound, unflinching spirit of cooperation, it was just one more thing she'd insisted on doing for them, so that they could eat while they discussed the reception, she'd said.

Cynthia squinted as a thought occurred: In the kitchen. Sarita was in the kitchen.

"Where's Cristiano?" She was unaware that she'd interrupted Angela mid-sentence.

Not that Angela was surprised. Cynthia had been preoccupied for weeks, and everyone knew the reason why. "Ah…I'm pretty sure he went to the market with Rohini."

"Oh." She frowned. "You mean, they won't be here for this?"

"No, Cynthia. Remember? They told us last night that the three of us should go ahead and make whatever plans we thought best."

Cynthia blinked in confusion. "But, surely…I mean, you'd think Rohini, at least, would want to have some input."

"Yeah, I would've thought so too, but you know Ro." Angela responded patiently, even as she made a mental note to tell the others that until this temporary madness passed, they should put any information they needed Cynthia to retain in writing.

Unless it wasn't temporary. Maybe it had nothing to do with Sarita, and was just a symptom of the onset of menopause. Who among the four of them couldn't relate to that?

"Sorry I'm late." Jane looked frazzled as she hurried over. "I had to deal with a delivery that got here earlier than expected. There were piles of things that needed refrigeration. Fortunately, Sarita offered to help me put everything away."

Cynthia grunted as Jane settled into her chair. "Sarita is nothing if not helpful these days."

"Speak of the devil," Angela exclaimed brightly to alert Cynthia that Sarita had come in behind her from the kitchen, carrying their lunch tray. "We were just saying how nice it is of you to help us today. *Oooh.* Whatever that is sure smells good."

Sarita set the tray down. "It's mostly shrimp. Rohini told me that Cristiano's feelings are hurt that none of us have tried it yet."

"Oh, well, we can't have that." Cynthia words were drenched with sarcasm. "I'll just have mine with a side of epinephrine, if you don't mind, in case I go into cardiac arrest. But it'll be worth it if it makes our chef happy."

Sarita looked at her mother with amusement. "Don't worry. I've got chicken salad for you. I'll share it with you so you won't feel lonely."

Share it with you so you won't feel lonely? "Sarita, I don't need company to eat chicken salad."

"Don't be silly, *Mãe.* I want to share it with you."

Cynthia barely managed to stop herself from jerking her hand away when her daughter patted it soothingly, as if she were some poor old granny suffering a bout of crankiness. Her eyes narrowed with sudden skepticism as Sarita slid into the chair next to hers, and began filling both their plates.

Could she be pretending — trying to demonstrate how irksome it was to have an offspring fawning over her every minute of the day? If so, she'd proven her point well.

No, that couldn't be it. She'd have given herself away long before now. Like her father, she was short on patience. And her face still held too much unhappiness whenever she thought no one was looking for her to be up to that kind of mischief. Cynthia sucked in a breath as something else came to mind. Oh, *shit, shit, shit* — could she be pregnant? Was that it?

"Wow. This is delicious." Always first in the attempt to lessen any collective friction, Angela jumped in, waving around her fork with its half eaten shrimp. "My God. No wonder everybody's raving about it."

"Oh, my. I have to agree," Jane seconded with her mouth full. "Shame you can't try any, Cynthia."

When Sarita patted her hand again, Cynthia felt like snarling. This was too damn much.

"Mmm. Yum, yum, yum." Jane swallowed, and dived right in to the purpose of their gathering, "So, I've talked with the bride. She has her heart set on a Day of the Dead theme."

"For a wedding? Eww. That sounds creepy."

Jane's hackles went up immediately. It was so like Angela to straight off disparage anything with which she wasn't familiar. Her provinciality brought back bad memories of the entire Miceli-Perotta clan.

But her tone was light as she responded, "It's not at all 'creepy,' if you happen to be Mexican, Angela. Which our bride is."

"But her future husband is Irish-Catholic," Angela pointed out, and downed another mouthful of shrimp.

Jane put down her fork, kept her eyes and voice steady. "Do you know anything at all about Day of the Dead celebrations, Angela?"

"Not really, no."

Proving that Sarita hadn't inherited her impatience only from her paternal side, Cynthia cut in. She wasn't in the mood for silly bickering when there was work to be done and she had other things on her mind, besides. "I'm familiar with the holiday. It's very big in Mexico, but in my country it's celebrated as well." She gave Angela a brief overview. "It focuses on gatherings to remember friends and family who have died. It's a three-day celebration that starts on October 31 and goes until November 2. That would be All Hallow's Eve, All Saints Day, and All Souls Day, to Catholics. Very holy days, suitable for wedding celebrations. Halloween, with evil goblins and vampires, is something American corporations thought up." Turning back to Jane, she asked, "So, what does this entail, from our side?"

"Well, Inez wants the reception to be on November first. Her father has passed, and that's the day her mother honors him. She says it will make the whole family feel like he's there celebrating with them." Her tone was distinctly snooty as she added, "Her Irish-Catholic groom is fine with that."

Angela blushed, recognizing that she'd just been put neatly in her place.

Cynthia ignored all that too, as she was getting into the discussion now. She addressed both Angela and Jane. "Well, that works perfectly for us, being that it's a Monday. We won't have to close to regular customers, as we would have on any other day of the week. And it gives us all day to set up."

Jane nodded her agreement as she picked up her fork again. "I found some decorations online that would be delightful, I think."

"I still don't get it." Angela was very much out of her element. Not only that, Jane's highhandedness had annoyed her. If she was such an expert on this stuff, why couldn't she just explain it as Cynthia had, instead of getting all huffy? "I still don't get why anyone would want to think of dead people on the day they're getting married. And what kind of a cake do I make?"

Even though Jane bit down on her tongue, she couldn't resist rolling her eyes. Angela's jaw clenched when she caught her at it. She loved her sister-in-law, but sometimes she just wanted to smack her for being so patronizing.

This time it was Sarita who interjected. Like her mother, she didn't miss the undercurrents, but she felt sorry for Angela, who'd been talking about the cake ever since Michael and Inez had announced their engagement. "Well, one thing you could consider for cake decoration would be marigolds, Angela. Marigolds have special meaning in all Day of the Dead celebrations. They have a strong scent that's believed to attract souls into coming back and visiting the living. And they're a very long-lasting flower." She smiled encouragingly. "To symbolize life after death — get it?" Becoming more inspired by the moment, she added, "Oh! And *calavera*. They're big on *Dia de Los Muertos*. Maybe you can decorate the cake with marigolds and *calavera*?"

"Okay, I guess." Angela pushed her recipe books aside, realizing with disappointment that she wouldn't be needing them. "What's *calavera*?"

Jane knew what was coming the moment Sarita answered the question.

"Tiny skulls. They're made from sugar paste and decorated with edible glitter and flowers. The sugar represents the sweetness of life, and the skull represents the departed loved one."

Angela's eyes popped wide open, and she spoke without thinking. "Oh my God. Skulls on a wedding cake? It's like something Tim Burton would think up."

Everyone at the table went silent. Without malice or intent, Angela had attacked a custom that was an integral part of all of Latin America, and parts of Europe and Africa, to boot.

Cynthia spread her hands, and smiled drolly. "By all means, don't hold back. Tell us exactly what you think."

As soon as those words were hanging in the air, it was as though a switch inside both Jane and Angela flipped from off to on.

"Sometimes you embarrass yourself, Angela." Jane was smiling, but the smile made Cynthia and Sarita wince.

The dining room pulsed with silence as Angela stared stony-faced at Jane.

At last, she spoke, astonishing herself and everyone else, by countering, "I embarrass myself or I embarrass you? Let's face it — we both know you think I'm beneath you. You think my whole family was beneath you."

Jane shook her head. "I don't think that. It's just that sometimes your family was maddening because they could be so ..." she searched for a word that wouldn't sting too much, "... constrained."

And then her face went pinched and tight as she realized that she was bloody tired of being careful of what she said to Angela, and how she said it. "Actually, that's not the word I'd use. 'Inflexible' is more like it, isn't it? 'Rigid,' 'blinkered' — call it what you will, but if something or someone didn't fit into their precise world view, that thing or that person was dismissed, immediately. I should think if you were honest you'd admit that, surely. Their ways have stuck to you quite a lot, wouldn't you agree? Even though your parents and your husband are long gone, aren't they still affecting your opinions and decisions, in particular about Vincenzo?"

In all the years they'd known one another, Jane had never spoken to Angela so bluntly. She felt both relieved and sickened that it was now all coming out in a rush.

"I can't believe you would bring Vincenzo up, here and now, like this." Angela's eyes were already wet, her breathing ragged. "It's just cruel, is what it is. You're cruel, Jane — do you know that?" She was looking at Jane almost as though she hated her.

Neither Cynthia nor Sarita had eaten a bite of their chicken salad, staring at the sisters-in-law in stunned silence. Cynthia had handled a lot in her career, yet for the first time she found herself floundering. "Uh...ladies, I think —"

At the sound of her voice, both women turned their heads, and she stopped mid-sentence. There was a similarity to their expressions, a sameness that was eerie. Their eyes looked so...wrong. Yet somehow, familiar. Where had she seen that look before?

When she said nothing more, they went straight back to their argument as though they hadn't been interrupted, like a car careening down a hill with no brakes, unable to stop itself from crashing at the bottom.

"I'm cruel to bring up Vincenzo, you say? Well, someone has to shake some sense into you. He's *gay*, Angela, that's all. He's not a serial killer. He's not carrying a contagious, fatal disease. But when he finally gathered the courage to come out to you, poor lad, you sent him away."

Angela stood up unsteadily, her face ashen as she stared, horrified, at Jane. "Oh, my God. That is *not true*. I did not send him away, Jane. He left."

"Sarita, let's you and I go eat our lunch in the kitchen —"

And then Jane was up too, slapping her napkin down on the table like the gauntlet it was. "Oh, no — you stay right there, Cynthia. We're supposed to be having a meeting and we're bloody well going to have it. This will only take a moment."

Cynthia's sound of protest went unheeded, as Jane turned back to Angela and snapped, "He left because you told him you had to *think*. He didn't even attend Gabriella's funeral, because he thought he wouldn't be welcome." Now her eyes were as wet as Angela's. "That was more than two years ago. Have you spoken to him even once since then? No?" She tilted her head at her sister-in-law and crossed her arms over her chest, "So, tell me, what have you had to think about, for *two* bloody years?"

"Shut up, Jane!" Demolished by her sister-in-law's accusations, Angela leaned across the table and shouted the words in her face. "Just shut up! You have no idea. No concept at all of what kind of world I come from, no matter how many times I've tried to explain it to you. Day after day after day, my parents repeating how much they loved me — their good little girl — and in the next sentence, the sermon on how sad I would make them, how sad I would make 'Our Heavenly Father,' if I didn't obey them on everything from how many disgusting vegetables they forced me to eat, to how many boring, endless Rosaries they forced me to say!"

Angela's face contorted as the first undiluted confession of her true feelings about her upbringing came hurtling out of her, like a demon being exorcised. "They brainwashed me young. I really believed them. I believed it was my personal responsibility to keep them *and* God happy." She smacked the side of her own head, and said through gritted teeth, "That's what they put in here, Jane. Try getting that out with no help — just *try* it — and see if it's as easy as you think, if you were the one who'd been hearing it since the first time you could talk."

Sarita was listening to Angela, openmouthed. She glanced at her mother, who looked equally dumbfounded. How sad and terrible it must have been for Angela, as a little girl, to have her own love for her parents be used by them against her, to blackmail her into obedience. It occurred to Sarita in that instant that Cynthia would never do that to her. Never. The thought made her see her mother in a whole new light.

Angela was bawling now, and though she stood up straight again, she was holding onto the back of her chair to keep herself steady. "Did you know that at night, I'd pray — trying to get God to step in for me? 'Please God, let them understand how much I want to go to cooking school.' And then it was, 'Okay, God, I won't go. I'll stay home like a good girl, if you'll only give me the strength to not let them force me into getting married. Please, *please* — I don't want to marry Marco Perotta.' Those are the kind of bargains I would try to make with God, Jane." She laughed unexpectedly, and the sound was bitter, the taste of wine turned to vinegar. "He never negotiated back. And even now, I can still hear my parents arguing with me in my head. Isn't it amazing that they managed to pull that off? They've been stone cold dead for years, yet they can still make me feel like shit."

Angela never swore, yet she didn't even notice that she had. Her face was a mess, swollen, covered in snot and tears. Sarita and Cynthia both listened to her with stunned, silent compassion, but Jane's voice was still cold.

"So what? What does any of that have to do with Vincenzo?"

Angela absently rubbed her dripping nose on her sleeve. "When Vincenzo finally said it to me, God in heaven — I knew all his life. He's my son. Of course I knew. Do you really think I cared that he was gay, Jane? But then he said it out loud to everybody and it… scared me. I was just *so* scared of what people would think of me as a mother, scared that they'd think it was my 'fault.' I wanted to tell Vincenzo that I supported him, I *wanted* to."

She put her head in her hands for a minute, and when she looked back up, the naked suffering on her face was heartbreaking. "But you're right. I didn't. You know why? Because I fell for it. I bought into the idea that my son's coming out was God's way of punishing me for being ungrateful for my life, for my parents, for Marco. I let them convince me of it, Jane — all those church people who'd come to my house, force me to make coffee and sit with them, after Marco died. They weren't there because they liked me. It was their 'Christian duty.'" She was sneering, her contempt as much for herself as for those she was describing. "They'd put their hands together and pray for me and my sweet son, because he 'was living in sin, beyond God's grace.' And *that* was more revolting to me than if they'd taken a dump right there on my kitchen floor."

Cynthia and Sarita jumped and grasped each other's hands in reflex, as Angela banged her fist on the table. "But I let them break me. Since then, I've been trying *so* hard to glue myself back together, to make things right. I *am* going to make things right. I just needed time. That's all."

Finger wobbling, she pointed at Jane. "And you have no right to judge me, because you're the same neurotic mess I am. My brother was the only person besides Vincenzo who ever truly loved me, and you sent him away. You've convinced yourself that he got his own daughter killed, because he didn't adhere to your perfect methods of raising children. You thought you were smarter than your own husband, smarter than all of us. You laughed at us. You laughed at *me*." It was heartache, not fury, through which she heaved that indictment, but even so, there was enough acid in it to burn through steel, as she leaned toward Jane again. "And you know what, Ms. Perfect? I'm goddamn sick of your smug, superior attitude!"

Jane was staring at Angela with both horror and hurt. "You're mad, you are. Do you honestly believe that — that I sent your sainted brother away? *Bollocks*." She spat the word. Her tone was different, slipping, in the depth of her feelings, into the cadence of her native northern England. "Now who's judging whom? My child drowned, Angela — my happy, loving, beautiful girl. She's *dead*. It took me so long to have her, and then...she was only mine for seven years." Jane's hands clenched into fists. She kept them pinned to her sides as she leaned toward Angela, willing herself, even in this, to maintain some restraint and control. "You needed time? So did I. Seven years is no time at all."

But try as she might, she couldn't stop herself from crying, except that her tears were soundless, streaming down her face as she stated her accusations and sorrows quietly, rather than shouting them.

"You have guilt and confessions? Here are mine. Have you any idea how many times I thought I'd have been better off if I hadn't tried so hard to conceive, if I'd never become her mother at all?" Her throat closed up completely as she admitted this. She paused, trying to pull herself together enough to continue. "Since Gabriella's death, I'm not the same woman I was, not by a long ways. You're trying to put yourself to rights? So am I. But I already know that what I want mended about myself can never be mended." Her eyes swam with the torment of that truth. Even so, she smiled then, a small, bitter smile. "I never got an answer from God when I tried bargaining with him, either."

Cynthia squeezed Sarita's hand, as they watched Jane tremble. It was hard to say which was more harrowing for mother and daughter to hear: Angela's wails of agony, or Jane's whispered despair. They sat huddled together in their chairs, pinned there by the two who were so wrapped up in their anguish, they were no longer aware that they were being observed.

"Yes, I screamed at Antoni and told him to leave. I was out of my mind that day. We'd just *buried* our little girl, and there was nothing left of her for me but dirt, and wilted flowers, and a stone with her name on it." Her eyes stayed fixed as she went back in her mind to that point in time, the day after both her daughter and her husband were gone. "But he didn't have to go, Angela. He's left me alone, all this time, to mourn for our daughter by myself."

Fury filled her voice, replacing the boundless hurt. "He was always there for you when you needed him." Her face revealed the resentment and envy she'd always felt for Angela, resentment that she was only now exposing, not only to her sister-in-law, but to herself. "He was such a good brother, such a good son and father, insofar as you and your parents were concerned, wasn't he? But he was useless as a husband. *Useless.*"

Angela heard only the bitterness in the allegation, but to the two other women sitting there, the segregation Jane had felt all through her marriage was apparent. "He didn't have the backbone to be there for me through the worst days of my life. Now I'm entirely alone, Angela. Can you not see that? Your son is only a phone call away. My daughter is beyond my reach forever." Now it was her turn to jab a finger in front of Angela's face. "Don't you ever, *ever* again, say that your situation is the same as mine. If you do, I'll slap you, see if I don't."

And just as unpredictably as it had begun, it stopped. They'd said everything they'd held inside for years, and never dared express. Now, as though they'd been snapped from a trance, they stood frozen, staring at one another in dismay.

Angela was the first to flee. Still wild-eyed, she ran out of the restaurant. With a heart rubbed raw, Jane nearly called her back. But if she did, what was there possibly left to say?

It was only when she turned to leave too, that she noticed Sarita and Cynthia still sitting at the table. They stared up at her with tear-stained faces, clinging to each other, looking as though they'd just survived an earthquake, and the damage surrounding them was enormous and unfathomable.

Jane was mortified. She'd completely forgotten they were there. Luckily, she did remember that she was English. "I beg your pardon. That was terribly rude. I hope we haven't spoiled your lunch. Please go ahead and finish without us." With as much dignity as she could gather under the circumstances, she made her escape.

After she'd gone, Sarita turned wide, wet eyes to Cynthia. "Oh, *Mãe.* All those things they said to each other — were they true?"

Wiping under her own eyes with her fingers, Cynthia waited until she had herself under control to answer as earnestly as she knew how. "All of them were true. And none of them."

Unlike her mother, Sarita wasn't finished crying. Throwing herself on Cynthia in a heap, she blubbered, "Oh, *Mamãe*, I'm so, so sorry. I had no idea it was so hard being a mother." She buried her face in her mother's shoulder. "I'm never having children, ever."

Cynthia clasped her reflexively. "What on earth are you talking about?"

"Didn't you hear Jane? She said it would have been better if she'd never had Gabriella."

"No, she said she felt like that *sometimes*," Cynthia corrected.

"Yes, but then Angela said —"

"Hang on a minute." Cynthia stopped her. "Look at me." When she did, Cynthia placed her hand on Sarita's cheek and smoothed away tears. "I wouldn't draw conclusions based on this incident. They'd bottled this up for a long time. They said what they were thinking in the heat of the moment. Besides that, being a mother is a profoundly emotional experience for most of us. Our feelings shift drastically depending on the circumstances."

"Jane and Angela's circumstances seem awful at the moment."

"I'm aware of that every day I work with them. A prison of the mind can be harder to escape than an actual prison, Sarita. Every human being has had their heart broken, in one way or another. Every person you'll ever meet lives on a daily basis with a private pain they work hard to conceal. Every one of us. But for some, the past *is* the present. And because they can't forget the past, whatever sorrows they experienced in it can never die."

Sarita sat back in her chair. "And you? When you think about your past, does it make you feel sad?" She knew some of her mother's story, though not all.

"Unless I believe I can learn from it, I force myself not to think about the bad parts. The way this world works, to even have a shot at happiness, it takes self-discipline more than anything else, *filha doce*."

The endearment gave Sarita the courage to ask, "Does being a mother make you happy?"

"Of course." Cynthia lifted a brow. "Did you have any doubt?"

"Yes, because I've been a horrible daughter lately." Sarita's voice was tremulous again.

Leaning across to hug her once more, Cynthia asserted, "No, you haven't. You've been a perfectly normal daughter. And we've had perfectly normal mother-daughter disagreements. That's all."

Sarita studied her mother's face, searching for truth. When she found it, she grinned. "But we still love each other."

"That's for sure." Cynthia's smile felt like a balm to Sarita after the trauma of the last half hour. Until she looked serious again. "So, tell me — are you pregnant?"

"*Mamãe*!" Sarita was floored. "Where did you get an idea like that?"

"This discussion about motherhood, for one. The fact that you've been moping around for two weeks and —" Cynthia shrugged apologetically "— being rather clingy, which I must admit is annoying. And the most significant thing that made me think it is, well...I don't hear a certain young man's name anymore." She waited to see if her daughter would finally confide in her.

Sarita mulled over how much, if anything, she could tell her mother. Finally she spoke.

"Emilio and I broke up on my birthday. He wanted…a more serious relationship, and I realized that isn't what I want right now. In fact," she bowed her head in tremendous discomfiture, "Cristiano heard us and thought Emilio was hurting me." She looked up again.

"He wasn't, *Mãe,* I swear. I was afraid Cristiano was going to tell you, but he said that it was up to me to tell you myself when I was ready."

"I see." Cynthia nodded. She did see, quite well, and all she could think was, *Thank God.* Gazing at Sarita, with her breathtaking face, her beautiful spirit, Cynthia felt some compassion for poor Emilio, and even a pang of regret for the way she'd abused him the entire time he'd worked for her. Ah, well. Unrequited love was just one more agony of the human condition. He'd get over it eventually. At least she was learning not to express thoughts like these out loud to her daughter.

Observing her mother's uncharacteristic restraint, Sarita grinned. "Well, how about that? Our first real discussion, woman to woman, with no arguing involved."

Nonetheless, she didn't divulge the rest of what took place on that occasion. It felt great being able to talk with her mother like this, but she still wasn't ready to tell her about her so-called "gift." She didn't want the next pleasant conversation they had to be held during visiting hours at the local psychiatric ward.

"Yeah, how about that?" Cynthia laughed with relief that things with Sarita appeared to be taking a better turn. But her mood was dampened by the episode that had just taken place. "It's a shame Jane and Angela couldn't achieve the same."

Thinking about them again, Sarita frowned. "Why did it start? It came out of nowhere. One minute they were exclaiming over the shrimp, and then you said something to Angela, like, 'tell us how you feel,' and the next thing you know, they were fighting."

As Sarita voiced her replay of the scene, it was as though a combination lock began turning in Cynthia's head — click, click, *click.*

Sarita broke off when her mother jumped up to stare across the dining room at the closed kitchen doors. "*Mãe*? Is everything all right?"

"What? Oh." Turning back to Sarita, she offered a wide, distracted smile. "Yes, yes. Everything's fine. It's just...I...have to get back to work. Lots of things left to do today."

"Oh-kaay. Well, that was an interesting segue. But I've got some homework to do for tomorrow, anyway, so I'll see you at dinner." Sarita snatched up her plate of chicken salad. "I'll take this up with me. I didn't get a chance to eat any of it."

With her bright smile still in place, Cynthia watched her daughter leave. The moment Sarita was out of sight, her smile vanished, and she dashed for the kitchen.

When the doors from the dining room flung open, Cristiano jumped and nearly sliced off the tip of his finger with the knife he'd been using to turn a block of Manchego cheese into meticulous slivers for his Puff Pastry Pinwheels with Quince Paste. It only took one glance at the alarm on Cynthia's face for his shoulders to sag. "Oh, no. What now?"

"Where's Rohini? Where is that *bruja blanca*?"

"Hey! Take it easy." Cristiano threw down the knife. Wiping his hands on his apron, his jaw set, he strode over to Cynthia, and held up his finger in warning. He spoke calmly and quietly, but it was clear that he was angry. "Don't call her that. She doesn't like it. She is not a witch. She is..." He searched for a word, "...a healer. You're my boss, and I like and respect you, but if I hear you say that again, you can get yourself another cook."

Acknowledging that she'd opened her big mouth once again, Cynthia slapped her palm to her forehead. "*Ay*. Fine. I'm sorry. Just tell me where she is."

"She left here about a half an hour ago. Ran, at the first excuse, is what she did, Cynthia. And I don't blame her." Still scowling, he gestured toward the dining room. "We could hear all the carrying on in there from the minute we got back from the market. If I didn't have things to do in here today, I would have gone with her." He flung his hands in the air. "*Dios mio*. There's drama in this place every damn day."

Cynthia pointed to herself. "You're telling *me*? I hate it too." She held up her index finger and whirled it around like a helicopter blade. "And I have not caused it, not even once." In contradiction to that statement, she raised her arms to the heavens and beseeched, "*Nossa!* All I wanted was a quiet little restaurant, so I could put some money aside for my daughter to go to college. Is that too much to ask?" Dropping her arms, she looked back at Cristiano and demanded again, "Now, where is she? Please? I need to find out what the ingredients are in that shrimp."

He looked at her in surprise. "Rohini doesn't make the shrimp. That's my dish. You know that."

Cynthia shook her head as if to clear it. "Oh, that's right. I must be losing my mind. But then why is it called, 'Shrimp Rohini?'"

"I named it after her because I seasoned it with some of the spices she brought from India."

"Spices?" On full alert now, she fixed on him like a sniper's beam. "What spices?"

When he hesitated, reluctant to reveal his recipe, she grabbed his shirtfront. "Oh, no, no, no, Cris. Don't you dare get all 'Secret Master Chef' on me. This is a potential disaster." A drill sergeant in four-inch heels, she leaned in to him and barked, "Tell me, right now — what *the fuck* did you put in the shrimp?

CHAPTER 13

"It's unlikely, but it's possible. I wish I could assure you that it's not. I've never used them in this combination before."

Rohini was now in the office with Cynthia and Cristiano. She was looking over the list of herbs and spices he'd written down, while Cynthia paced like a twitchy cat.

"Some of these are used for medicinal purposes as well as for flavorings. They do have properties that can be hypnotic or hallucinatory. They're harmless, but certainly potent, so I'm not going to say that used together, they wouldn't cause the kind of reaction you're describing."

"I knew it." Cynthia slapped her own thigh. "Well this is just terrific."

"I wouldn't worry until we speak to Jane. Being a chemist, she'd know for sure."

"Yes, well, she's not available at the moment, Rohini. She's just had a spontaneous nervous breakdown, due to what we fed her at lunch," Cynthia retorted.

"*Ay mi madre.*" Cristiano ran his hands through his hair, and looked from Cynthia to Rohini. "So, should I change the ingredients?"

"Yes."

"No."

Cynthia and Rohini answered simultaneously.

"I just don't think it's necessary. None of these plants or roots are dangerous in any combination. If they were, I wouldn't have left them out in the open. The recipe is delicious and healthy, Cynthia. No, don't make that face — it *is*. These spices are beneficial. Besides, the shrimp is a hit. People have been coming in solely to order it, because they've heard others rave about it. I don't think we should change it merely on the basis of the isolated incidents you've described." Rohini rarely voiced a preference on anything involving the business, but now that she had, her perspective made sense to Cristiano. Cynthia, on the other hand, was still unconvinced.

"You should have been there today. You should have seen them." She shivered. "It was very unsettling."

"Perhaps they just needed to say it," Rohini pointed out. A true homeopath, she added, "Keeping all of that bottled up is not at all good for the digestive system."

With fascination, Cristiano asked, "How did you learn so much about this?"

"Vanu, the friend I told you about, lives in an exceedingly progressive village back home. Among other advances they've made there, they grow medicinal herbs to treat illnesses. He taught me a lot."

She turned to Cynthia again. "Something else just occurred to me. You told us that your words were, 'Don't hold back. Tell us how you really feel.' You didn't say, 'Tell us how you feel about *each other*.' With a statement like the first, if they were hypnotized by the spices in the shrimp and the power of suggestion, as you're theorizing, well…they might have commented on any number of feelings they have, from 'I love cats' to 'P. Diddy is the worst musician I've ever heard, and yet he's at the top of the charts this year.'"

Cristiano grinned with pure appreciation. "Maybe, just for further experimentation, Rohini, we could feed you some shrimp to hear what other thoughts you have."

"I try to stick to a vegetarian diet." The smile she gave him was provocative. "Mostly."

Cynthia made gagging sounds and gave them an exasperated look. "Can the two of you please spare me the besotted banter for now, and get back to the business at hand? This is important." She continued her argument. "What about the other incidents — that business with Hunt and Janvier, for example? I was right there, as he was eating the shrimp. I heard her tell him she wanted him to leave his wife, and he *did*."

"Ah. Yes, that is a concern. After all, men never cheat on their wives. Especially not in Hollywood."

"But the Governor?" Pacing again, Cynthia reiterated what she'd told them earlier, "A Republican governor announcing that he's going to institute universal health care throughout the state, after just one chat with an Englishwoman while having dinner here — that doesn't strike you as a strange coincidence?"

Cristiano held out his hands. "Oh, come on, Cynthia. First of all, he's married to a Democrat." He stopped and shook his head. "And, boy — would I like to be a fly on the wall in their house sometime." He went back to his original point. "Second of all, he's a politician. A particularly cunning one, in my opinion. He could have made that announcement for another reason altogether. That man is not what he pretends to be." His face showed his dislike. "That will come out sooner or later, mark my words."

"I'll tell you what else might come out sooner or later, Cris — the fact that The Secret Spice Café is cooking up its own version of magic mushrooms. One call to the Health Department is all it would take to close us down." Cynthia was beside herself at this point. "I just can't believe neither one of you is taking this seriously." Like a high school principal dressing down two misbehaving teenagers, she lectured, "Cris, that sort of publicity won't do you any good at all, considering your background. Nor would you want it either, Rohini, not only for his sake, but for yours. A short while ago, you were ducking out of photos. Is this the way you want your former brother-in-law to find you — when the DEA throws all five of us in the slammer, and our booking photos show up on the front page of the *Long Beach Gazette*?"

"All right, Cynthia, dear. It's not going to help to get yourself so worked up. Let's stay calm and think this through." Even with the revelation that their restaurant could be an inadvertent drug front, Rohini responded with her usual equanimity. "I understand your concern. As I said, Jane would be the person to give us a better assessment of the mixture of spices and what their combined properties would be. We need the input of the other two partners on this, anyway. Even if I agreed with you, we can't make this decision on our own. As for the other, Cristiano and I have talked about that. He's right that I need to stop looking over my shoulder every minute of my life."

When his face softened with pride, she added a qualification to both of them, "I'm not going to say I'm not still afraid, but let's face it, I can't avoid publicity forever if we want our restaurant to do well."

Steering her comments at Cynthia once again, she continued, "And that's the other thing you haven't considered. This dish is popular, which means it's making us money. I've put all I have into this restaurant. I wouldn't want us to lose our business over one dish, certainly, but neither do I want to kill the sales if the dish is harmless, which it might very well be. If it's not affecting our patrons, we're removing a source of income for no reason."

Her practicality was having a visible effect. Seeing that Cynthia was beginning to lose her mutinous look, Rohini drove home her point. "We have to talk to Angela and Jane, but until we do, I honestly think that we can leave things as they are for now, and see if we have any more occurrences." She gestured to Cristiano's list.

"Given what I know about these ingredients, I'm just not buying into your theory. We need a bigger sample size before we panic."

Although her foot had been tapping the entire time Rohini had put forth her argument, the mention of money reminded Cynthia that she still had eight million dollars to return to its rightful owner, a fact she'd momentarily forgotten in her panic over potentially hallucinogenic prawns. There was no getting around it. She'd have to give in for now, but eight million or no eight million, if Jane thought that her theory was valid, that appetizer was coming off the menu. "You're the expert on this, so I'll concede for now. But I'm going to tell Michael what happened here today, and on opening night. He's not just a patron, he's my friend. He was the first to taste the dish, and I'm pretty sure he had a reaction right after I made the suggestion that he should date Inez. Now, they're getting *married*. In less than a month." Her face held real concern. "Michael the tomcat, who, if you recall, used to change girlfriends every time he changed his sheets. There's no time to wait for more proof. He needs to know about this."

After she charged out, Rohini looked at Cristiano, her vexation plain. "Michael's going to think she's lost her mind. Once she gets something into her head, it's stuck in there for good, but she's off the mark on this one."

"Then why didn't you tell her that?"

"Because, like I said, there's always the possibility. Hopefully Jane will agree with me that it's a remote one." She sighed in resignation. "Oh, well, at least it's finally quiet. With any luck we'll have some peace for the rest of the afternoon."

He wasn't convinced. "I think I'll go finish the cheese pinwheels while I can. Just in case."

When Angela ran from the restaurant, she headed for the deck above. She'd come to think of it as her refuge, a place on the ship where the other women never ventured; a secret hiding place like the one she'd always longed for.

The last few times she'd ventured up there, her gray-eyed mystery man had been absent, and she assumed he no longer worked on the ship. Today she was so unglued, she hardly gave his whereabouts a thought.

When she reached the deck, once again it was empty. Flinging herself down into one of the worn wooden deck chairs, she stretched her legs out in front of her, leaned forward, covered her head with her arms and wept with great, wracking sobs, until she'd cried herself out.

When she managed to straighten back up, she took several long, deep breaths, closed her eyes, and shifted back to rest against the chair. The moment the back of her head touched, a static jolt, strong enough to produce a crackling sound, ran through her.

"Ow!" Lurching upright, she got a second fright when she saw that her mystery man was leaning on the rail with his arms crossed against his chest, watching her.

"Oh, my God. You scared me to death. How long have you been standing there?" She was so hoarse and stuffed up, she didn't recognize her own voice.

He said nothing. He just kept looking at her with an inscrutable expression on his face.

Instantly self-conscious, she drew her knees up to her chest, adjusted her skirt, and tried to pull herself together. Dammit, why did he have to show up today, of all days, after not being around for so long? She knew she looked a total wreck, but did he have to stare at her like that?

Finally he spoke. "Why don't people do the right thing, Angela? It's not so hard."

Ignoring her fidgets and her state of dishevelment, he went on. "Take my buddy, Steve, for instance. If he'd done the right thing, everything would have worked out fine." Although his tone was light and conversational, she got the impression that he was actually fuming over something. "But he didn't, because he thought he had to 'follow orders.' And that's why I'm in this situation."

He shrugged and smiled, in a way that only managed to make him look bleak. "Even so, I'm still glad I did what I did. I didn't do myself or my wife and child one damned bit of good, but I saved them. Only one man died that day, not hundreds. And you know what I like to think, because it makes me feel a little better? I like to think that when those men finally got back to their families, in a way I never will, that they remembered me. They remembered that I did the right thing. That's what I would have taught my son to do, if I'd had the chance. Because that's what we're all supposed to do, no matter what the consequences."

What was he saying? What men? What consequences? Angela feared she was getting another migraine, this time from hysteria, dehydration, and the fact that she'd only managed to choke down a few pieces of shrimp. She wanted so badly to be up here alone. Instead, once again, she felt compelled by her Italian-Catholic upbringing to behave like a lady, and listen patiently to the ramblings of man she'd finally concluded was out of his frickin' mind. "I'm sorry," she told him. "I have no idea what you're talking about."

Those eyes, usually so splendid and clear, went darker and cloudier until they were the same color as the stormy steel waters that now surrounded the *Mary*. "I'm talking about you, Angela, of course."

The dismal look of the ocean should have warned her that the weather was about to change. She could feel the temperature drop, as he leaned forward from the rail and stared right down into her eyes. "Are you doing the right thing, or are you too, 'following orders'?"

The pulsing at her temples made it hard to think. "What do you mean?" She pressed back into the chair as far as she could, and hugged her knees tightly. He was beginning to make her nervous. He was good at that.

She jerked with alarm when his voice suddenly blazed with anger. "You let me down! I used to look forward to you coming up here. It was the one bright spot of my existence. But I was wrong about you, wasn't I?" She was startled again to realize that he was eyeing her with distaste. "You're just a foolish woman who's confined herself to a prison of her own making."

Her heart pumped in rapid thuds as her thoughts raced. He *was* out of his mind. Should she try to make a run for it? "You don't know anything about me."

He went on as though she hadn't spoken, becoming more outraged by the moment. "Why didn't you stand up for him, Angela? Why? Even if you couldn't manage to stand up for yourself?"

"Stand up for…who?" But her blood froze, because as impossible as it was, she guessed what he was going to say.

"Vincenzo, of course."

She was thunderstruck. "How —?"

"So, you thought God had 'punished' you by giving you a son like him? And why was that — because he wasn't the one you ordered?" he scoffed. "Or your sanctimonious husband ordered? Or did you listen to some phony evangelist on the radio, maybe?"

The electricity in the atmosphere around them seemed to be growing. She heard more static pops, as he pushed away from the rail to pace. She stared, both fascinated and repelled, as little frissons of light sparked along the handrail where he'd been leaning. As he continued to shout at her, the wind picked up, tossing debris around the deck. "Trust me, it doesn't work that way. Your son is a gift, not a punishment. But you have no idea how lucky you are to have him, do you?"

"Who are you?" she whispered. "How do you know these things about me?"

"I know everything that happens on this ship. I've been stuck here for decades, with nothing to do but roam around. Do you know how much I wish I were in your place? Do you? Shame on you, Angela. Shame on you for letting that boy go."

"How *dare* you?" Angela had finally had enough of everything and everybody. She stood up and stalked toward him. Still not getting it, still not seeing what he was or what he was trying to tell her, her next words vibrated with New York. "I don't know how you know what you know, but who the hell do you think you are, to come up here and talk to me like this?" With her fist on her hips, she glared at him. "Oh, yeah — you wish you were in my place? You don't know *jack* about my place, pal. Besides, when it comes to your kid, you *are* in the same place. You haven't talked to your son, either, so what's *your* problem?"

It was getting colder outside by the minute, but Angela wasn't about to use that as an excuse to slink away. Not this time. She swung her other arm out behind her and pointed toward the chairs. "What's stopping *you* from picking your ass up off your goddamn deck chair with all your goddamn cigarettes and your quirks and cryptic stories, and going to see *your* kid? You've got two arms, two legs —"

She jabbed her finger at him, and got the shock of her life — the literal shock of her life. The punch of energy that charged up her arm brought her to her knees. In a flash, it felt as though she were encased in ice.

"No!" The wind was so fierce now she could barely hear him. He was shouting, but his voice sounded far away, tinny and hollow, as though it were coming at her from the depths of a metal tunnel. "You're blind as well as foolish. You only see what you want to see. *Look* at me, Angela." His command was harsh, but his eyes were pleading. "I don't have anything! I'm nothing but a pile of bones."

As soon as he said it, she saw it. She staggered back as the uniform he was wearing changed, became grimy and moth-eaten. Around his neck, a band of patterned, rubicund contusions spontaneously appeared. He was deteriorating right before her eyes, more and more, until she saw exactly what the remains of a human being looked like after sixty years of exposure to heat, rodents, and the salty seepage of oceans and seas. She thought all the veins in her body would rupture, as she screamed and screamed. Then, she ran. She made it halfway down the steps when, in her panic, she missed a step and met only air. Her leg gave out beneath her. Before she could right herself, she went toppling forward.

Since Marisol's pre-school was also closed for Columbus Day, but Inez was scheduled to work, Michael volunteered to keep his soon-to-be stepdaughter with him. This arrangement suited both him and Marisol perfectly, as Cynthia was about to discover.

Opening the door to The Queen Mary Memorabilia and Postcard Shop, she saw the upgraded décor the moment she stepped in.

The walls had been faux-finished in silky ecru and fawn brown, and the baseboards and cornices freshened up with a soothing forest-green. New glass displays were arranged in a way that invited browsing, and the cheap novelties had been replaced with unique bric-a-bracs and clever keepsakes. The pile of toys behind the register was also new. But what hit her smack in the eye was what she saw at the back of the shop. Sitting spread-legged on a tasteful new area rug that was strewn with doll clothes, was Michael, being coached by Marisol in Doll Playing 101.

"Now, wait — which one is mine again?"

"You have Mary Kate. I have Ashley."

Cynthia couldn't have been more astounded than if she'd walked in and found that he'd shaved his head, gotten a Hell's Angel tattoo, and stocked all the shelves with guns.

"Michael, have you turned this place into a toy store?"

He stood up, and even though she'd caught him in the act of dressing dolls, he greeted her with an unabashed smile. "Oh, hey. We were just helping Mary Kate and Ashley try on some of their new clothes. Right, Marisol?"

As Marisol nodded, Cynthia winged a brow. He didn't seem at all uncomfortable to say that out loud. She'd rectify that first chance. But for now, she told him, "I'm sorry to interrupt your playtime, but —" she angled her head toward the little girl meaningfully — "I needed to speak with you for a moment."

Catching her drift, Michael handed the doll down to Marisol with a smile. "Cynthia and I have to go into my office and talk business for a little bit, okay, sweetie?"

He blushed bright red at Marisol's ingenuous response. "But you left Mary Kate with her blouse off."

Cynthia covered her mouth with her fist, but Michael still heard her snicker.

He whirled around. "Will you knock it off?" Turning to Marisol again, he managed to choke out, "You put her blouse on her for me, okay?"

"Which one should I pick?"

"Uh..." He looked at Cynthia helplessly, so she went in for the save.

"I think the red one with the white collar would match that pretty skirt she's wearing."

Marisol smiled at Cynthia, showing off her dimple. "That's a good idea. I like the red one too."

Leaving her to it, they moved to his miniscule office, where Michael left the door partially ajar so he could keep an ear out for the little girl, and be aware when a customer walked in. "What's up?"

She had important things to tell him, but she couldn't resist teasing him first. "Mary-Kate and Ashley, huh? Satisfying a secret yearning to undress blonde twins?"

He scowled. "Ha. Ha. You're real funny. You didn't come in here just to needle me, so what is it you wanted?"

Having no idea how to begin, she employed a delaying tactic. "What's with all the toys behind the register? You bought them for Marisol, didn't you? She's only four, Michael. Does she really need all that stuff?"

"Oh, not you too, Cynthia. That's what Inez said." Cynthia had to smile. He sounded like a kid being told he couldn't have ice cream before supper. "Can't you guys give her a break? She's never had anything nice. Inez has had to do it all on her own."

"I understand that, but you're going to spoil her."

"You bet I am." His declaration rang with satisfaction. "I'm going to spoil both of them. Now that I have more money coming in, I plan to spend it on Inez and Marisol. They deserve it."

She searched his face. "You seem very happy with the idea of a ready-made family."

"Are you kidding me? I'm thrilled. I feel like I should congratulate myself. I got a wife *and* a daughter, Cynthia." He grinned. "Two for the price of one."

The statement as presented made her chafe inwardly, as she found a sturdy box on which to sit. He believed he'd made his own choice. She hoped that was the case, but that's what she'd come in here to find out.

Still stalling, she changed the subject. "I'm glad the shop is doing so well now."

This was another happy topic. His eyes lit up as he talked about the changes he'd made and the plans he had for the future. "And look at this." With a touch, he flicked on his computer, and showed her the shop's new eBay account. "I've been selling *Queen Mary* relics online. Some of them go for a fortune."

She peered at the screen with interest. "Is that allowed?"

"Sure. Stuff like old menus, or photographs — any memorabilia that the museum has too many of or doesn't want — I pick up from them at a wholesale price and resell at a profit." He clicked on one of the items. "Check this out."

He showed her a photo of a plastic white box a foot long in length, about four inches wide, with two push buttons on it, one red, one green. "Oh. I have one of those on the wall next to the door in my stateroom. I wondered what it was."

"It's a cabin steward call box. They haven't been in use since the late 1940s. I'm guessing that's when they installed phone lines in the rooms. When they renovated the ship, some of them were left in place for the tour guides to point out. The rest were sent on to the museum." He looked at Cynthia with pride. "I picked up a few real cheap, and someone bid me three hundred bucks for one yesterday."

"Well, look at you." Cynthia smiled at him, impressed. Then it dawned on her that this new entrepreneurialism was just one more thing that was not the typical Michael. Could it be another result of his having ingested the mysterious spices?

Michael knew when Cynthia was brooding about something. He tapped her on the nose to jostle her out of her pensiveness. "Okay, doll. Spill. What's on your mind?"

After Jane fled the restaurant, she went straight to her stateroom, shut the door and turned the latch, but not before hanging the "Do Not Disturb" sign on the outer doorknob for good measure. She needed to have a stiff drink and a good cry, and to be left in peace while having them.

She poured two fingers of vodka and knocked it back in one fell swoop. Eyes stinging from the alcohol now, as much as everything else, she poured another, but with a modicum of sanity, remembered that it was still early afternoon, and none of them had eaten much of their lunch.

That didn't deter her from wanting a second glass. She diluted the drink's potency with some ice, and left the glass on the bedside table to allow the ice to melt. Still teary, she plopped down against her bed pillows and dabbed a tissue at her eyes.

It took a while for her to notice how quiet it was. Even with her door closed, at this time of day, she was always able to hear the bumps and squeaks of luggage carts as they rolled past her door, or the muffled chatter of the maids as they cleaned. But today it was dead hushed out there, for some reason. In her agitated state, the sound of the ice as it adjusted to the room temperature seemed unusually loud: *Crackle, hiss. Crackle, hiss.* Then it hit her that what she was hearing wasn't the ice in her glass at all.

She sat up to listen more carefully. What was that noise?

It sounded like some kind of transistor static. She had a nebulous thought that it reminded her of something...something from her childhood. Presently, it came back to her: It sounded just like the old ham radio that had been in her uncle's house in Newcastle. He claimed he'd used it during the war. Jane recalled feeling exhilarated that the static sounds they'd heard were interspersed with voices of people from all over the world who also had radios.

The hissing continued intermittently, coming from inside her room, to be sure. She couldn't pinpoint from where, but it sounded like it might be coming from above. She held her breath and concentrated, as she looked up at the ceiling and ran her eyes from corner to corner, waiting for the next burst of sound.

When the crackle and hiss blasted much louder this time, it made her jump. But that last burst had narrowed the sound field to above the door of her stateroom where, affixed to the top of the frame, was one of the old cabin steward call boxes.

Brow furrowed, she thought out loud, "What the devil? That thing hasn't been useable for ages."

Yet it appeared to be working now, sort of. Wondering if anyone on the ship was tinkering with them for any reason, she decided to ring reception to find out. Of course, when she connected through her mobile phone, the call dropped.

Blast. She was always forgetting that wireless reception was dismal, unless one stood near a porthole. But by unfortunate happenstance, the landline phone wasn't working, either. She flicked the button on the handset several times, and swore when she couldn't get a connection.

Well, this was frustrating. She'd have to go downstairs and sort it out. But not before she finished her drink. Picking it up from the side table, she turned to climb back on the bed again. Ice, vodka and glass went flying, as her whole body lurched and she squawked with fright.

Standing not six feet away, by the wardrobe, was the little ginger-haired girl.

"How the *devil* did you get in here?" All the finer points of how one should deal with a child fled from her mind. She simply didn't have the patience for this today. She'd come up here for some much needed peace, and the child had absolutely terrified her, for starters. By now Jane firmly believed that the girl's parents were criminally negligent for allowing her to wander about so freely.

"I know I locked that door, young lady, so you were hiding in here." She pointed to the wardrobe. "You were — weren't you? Well, that was naughty of you and *very* rude. I've truly had enough of this. I'm calling down to the reception — oh, bugger it." That last slipped out when she remembered that both phones weren't working. "Right, then. We'll just walk down there together, shall we?"

She marched over to the door and flipped the latch, but when she tried to pull it open, it was jammed. She huffed with frustration, and tugged at it again. "What is going on in here today?"

"You haven't looked for her."

Jane turned to look at the child again. "What are you talking about? I'm quite furious with you."

The little girl seemed unmoved by that statement. "I asked you to look for my Missy Doll. You haven't. I want my doll."

Jane squinted at her, wondering for the first time if perhaps the poor thing wasn't quite right in the head. Even the way she was staring at Jane now was…abnormal. She was expressionless, neither animated nor frightened in the least. With her coloring, she always looked a bit drawn, but today she was more pallid than usual. And here it was, gone two in the afternoon, and she was still in that nightdress of hers. It occurred to Jane just then that she'd never seen the child in a proper set of play clothes. And now that she was being so observant, something else caught her attention: the child didn't smell of her usual lavender soap. In fact…

Jane sniffed the air. There was another odor in the room. What was it?

She was just about to take a step closer to question her, when the crackling from the call box started up again, louder this time.

"May I help you, Madam?"

"Oh!" Jane spun around and looked up in disbelief. "Hello?" she called up to the box. "What's happening? Is this thing working now? Shall I press one of the buttons?"

More noise came from the box, and the same voice, a male voice with an English accent, said again, "May I help you, Madam?"

Jane opened her mouth to speak, when another voice came through, a woman's this time, indistinct at first and then clearer. She had an English accent as well, and sounded panicked and tearful. "Yes, please help me. I can't find Jackie. I can't find my little girl."

More static crackling. "Where should she be, Mrs. Torin?"

"Here. Right here, in her room, with her nanny. I came to take her down to breakfast, and they're both gone. I've searched everywhere. The nanny never takes her out without telling me first. Something's happened, I know it has. Help me, please."

"It can't be." Jane's words were barely a whisper. "It isn't possible."

The crackling fizzled, then stopped.

In the silence, Jane stared up at the call box, a vein beating at her throat. It all made sense now; a macabre and horrible sense.

Without moving her head, she slid a glance from the side of her eye to see if little Jaclyn Torin was still standing where she'd been.

She was. Jane turned back around to face her fully, as if she were meeting a firing squad instead of the small, desolate ghost of a child.

The moment she did, a metamorphosis set in motion. Water appeared from nowhere and drenched the little girl from head to toe — starting with her bare feet and the hem of her nightgown, then up to her shoulders, and finally, her head. The water seeped from her scalp down through her shiny red hair, saturating it, deepening the shade to the color of blood. The baby-fine skin became a clammy whitish-gray, throwing her sweet smattering of freckles into stark relief. Her bow-shaped lips flattened out and turned chalky blue. Shadows beneath her eyes sprang up, purple and vivid as bruises. More water dripped from her nightdress and onto the carpet. When her eyes began to shrink back into their sockets, she called out to Jane one last time, plaintively, "I want my doll. Please help me find my doll," and her appeal echoed loudly, resounding over and over, all throughout the cabin.

Jane was unaware that the entire time she watched the ethereal Jackie transform from plucky little girl into heartrending drowning victim, she was keening wildly, a feral sound of grief and terror. She wailed on and on, never stopping, not even when Sarita, who'd been tackling an essay while finally eating her lunch, and Inez, who'd been training a new maid, both ran to her stateroom upon hearing her cries, and banged on her door, shouting her name, begging her to let them in.

Both Mary-Kate and Ashley were now smartly dressed. Marisol was pleased with the results, but secretly she wished that they could have superhero costumes, like maybe Saturn Girl's. One time, Sarita had read to her about Saturn Girl from a *Legion of Super-Heroes* comic book. Saturn Girl had special powers, and Marisol loved hearing about how she used them to save people.

She was deliberating over hair ornaments, waiting patiently for Michael to finish his meeting and come play with her again, when, outside the shop, the wind began to squall.

She lifted her head at the sound of it. She knew what wind was, just as she knew what thunder and lightning were. Her mother had told her not to be afraid. Most of the time she wasn't, but today, the wind's shrill voice made her feel like it was about to whisper a secret to her, a terrible secret she didn't want to know, but was bound to learn, just the same.

Marisol put down her dolls and stood up. Something wasn't right. Something big and important.

With a soft whimper, she turned her head toward Michael's office. She could hear him talking with Cynthia in there. Would he be angry with her if she ran to him?

Come to the window, Marisol. Come see.

"No," she whispered, but somehow, her legs wouldn't listen. They went one in front of the other, until she was standing with her nose pressed to the glass, her heart beating wildly. She watched as the sky darkened, swiftly, as though the sun had run in fear to cower behind the clouds. The hanging shop sign swayed back and forth on its chains, as the wind squealed around the strangely empty deck.

Where were all the people? she wondered.

She could see the entrance to The Secret Spice Café, and the metal steps that led to the deck above.

Look up. Look way, way up.

She was trembling even before she raised her head and peeped up at that deck. She didn't see anything at first, but then, in the far right corner, she spotted the cake lady, sitting on a long chair with her feet up. The cake lady was alone, and she was crying.

No, wait — she wasn't alone — someone was with her. Or... something. Something against the railing. What was it? She couldn't tell. Then it moved, and Marisol recoiled in terror. Whatever it was, it both scared her and made her feel sad. She covered her eyes and started to cry. She didn't want to see it. She didn't understand what it was. All she understood was that she was afraid, so afraid. With a gasp of shame, she looked down and cried even harder. Her pants, socks, and sneakers were wet. She didn't mean to do it. Mommy would be upset with her.

Michael was treating Cynthia to a large helping of his signature laugh.

"Hee, hee, hoo. Hoo, boy — that's the funniest thing I ever heard."

"It wasn't a joke, Michael." She was offended that he didn't believe her.

"Oh, come on." He ticked off what she'd said on his fingers. "You're trying to tell me that I turned my business around, started adoption proceedings on a kid who was already the daughter of my heart, and am about to marry Inez, the woman I love, the woman I make love with every night — enjoying the hell out of it, I might add — all because I ate some shrimp?" He tittered and hooted again. "Boy, I knew Cris was a good cook, but I gotta tell ya, I didn't think he was *that* good."

Cynthia was persistent. "Just listen to me. Don't you remember feeling strange that day?"

"Yeah, because I ate like a pig."

"Michael, dammit. That isn't what happened. I just want to be sure you're doing all this for the right reasons. I just want you to be happy."

"Doll, you have a colorful imagination. I mean — look at me. Do you really need to ask if I'm happy?" He used the age-old male method of logic to try and sway her from what she felt intuitively. "Okay, sure, I did get the idea to date Inez from you." He shrugged self-deprecatingly. "To tell you the truth, I always thought she was hot and nice and a great mom, but I didn't think she'd be interested in me, until you pointed it out."

The moony, lovesick look on his face, so unlike his usual self when it came to women, was defeating his own argument. Cynthia was more convinced than ever that his infatuation with Inez had to be food-borne. "I never would have believed it, never would have thought I was good enough for her, otherwise. And when we started dating, we were having fun, but I still didn't think she'd want to take it up a notch, even though I certainly wanted to, until you told me what she said to you in your office."

Smiling he reiterated, "And now we're getting married. Both of us are very glad about that, Cynthia, 'Shrimp Rohini' or no 'Shrimp Rohini.' Marisol, as you can tell, is also happy. She gets a brand new Daddy to wrap around her finger — one who won't leave her mother in the lurch this time around — and as many toys as I can afford. Your matchmaking was successful. That makes you a candidate for best man. It doesn't make you a co-conspirator in distributing behavior-altering substances disguised as appetizers." He put his palms on his thighs and tapped his fingers, as though the matter was settled, and he was anxious to go back out to his shop and Marisol.

Cynthia tried one last time. "What if you're wrong? What if —" she searched for a visual that might convince him, "— you wake up one day and think that Inez is boring, or that Marisol is too much trouble, or that you hate your job?"

He waited a beat to respond. "You mean, like regular marriage, regular parenthood, and regular life?"

Cynthia saw it was time to throw in the towel. She held up her hands. "Fine. If you're happy, I'm happy. But don't say I didn't w—"

"Shh. Hang on a second." He held his hand up and angled his head, listening. "Does that sound like the wind out there to you, or is Marisol crying?"

After about ten seconds of beating on Jane's door, Sarita and Inez both recalled that Inez had a card key which fit all the rooms. "Use the master!" Sarita shouted, just as Inez was digging it out of her apron pocket and fumbling with the lock. Not a person came out into the corridor to investigate all the noise. It was as though the other rooms were empty, or that somehow, no one but Inez and Sarita could hear Jane's screams. Even when they heard the lock click, the door was stuck fast, so they slammed against it together until it swung open, and they burst into the room like Starsky and Hutch.

Looking about frantically, all that seemed amiss to Inez was a broken glass along with some melting ice on the carpet next to the rumpled bed. That couldn't be the reason that Jane was curled up on the floor, weeping. Inez ran to her and kneeled by her side. "Jane, what's wrong? Are you hurt?"

But Sarita knew immediately. For her, the smell of chlorinated pool water still clung to the air. Kneeling next to Jane too, she touched her shoulder tentatively, "It's Sarita, Jane. I know what you saw. She's gone now. You're here with me and Inez."

Inez's head shot back up to Sarita. "You mean…?"

When Sarita nodded, Inez clasped her hands together. "*Ay dios mio,* I was afraid this would happen. She's seen her more than once. She thought she was just a guest of the hotel. I should have told her the other day, but I was sure she wouldn't believe me."

Jane was finally able to speak, but she was rambling. "Poor little thing…poor little thing. How can it be? How can something like this be?"

"She's in shock." Inez put her arm around Jane's shoulders. "Help me get her on the bed. I'll stay with her while you go get help."

They lifted Jane up and dragged her to the bed. She fell back onto it, curled herself into a ball again and wept on. Inez was right. She needed attention immediately.

Sarita ran for the kitchen. Rohini might have some calming tea or something. But she also wanted her mother. Her mother would know what to do, for sure.

Marisol stood in her own urine, cringing against the shop window, staring at Cynthia and Michael as though they were monsters that had crawled out from under her bed. More familiar with little girls than Michael was, Cynthia could tell that something had frightened the living daylights out of her, whereas Michael assumed she was upset merely because she'd had an accident.

"It's okay, sweetie," he was saying. "We'll clean that right up. That's no big deal. It happens to me all the time."

Cynthia gave him a look that warned him he was clueless, and that he should let her handle it. She approached the little girl the way one would approach a frightened, stray kitten — with tender caution. When she got near enough, mindless of the puddle that was now spreading about their feet, she knelt in front of Marisol, until they were eye to eye. Marisol's little body was shaking. Cynthia could smell bubble gum each time the poor thing took a rapid, shallow breath.

"What wrong, *chiquita*?" she asked gently. "You can tell us. Nothing bad is going to happen to you."

Marisol knew Cynthia was Sarita's mommy. Sarita, who read Marisol stories and helped her pick out stickers in Michael's shop. Marisol was still scared, but she felt safer now that Sarita's mommy was holding her. She'd called her '*chiquita*' just like her own mommy did. Even so, she still hesitated. In her mind, what she knew was a secret she wasn't allowed to tell.

Michael finally got the picture and kneeled down next to Marisol too. "It's okay. Michael's here. Tell us what's wrong, sweetie."

Still trembling, Marisol turned her eyes to Michael. He loved her so much, she knew. He was going to be her real Daddy soon. Her breathing slowed, and her body lost some of its tenseness. She could tell him. Even though she couldn't precisely articulate what she knew, she did her best. She whispered, "The cake lady. The cake lady…has a boo-boo."

Michael's eyebrows drew together in confusion. "'The cake lady has a boo-boo?' What do you mean, sweetie?"

The moment the question was out of his mouth, they heard a scream come from outside unlike any they'd heard before. It scared Michael so much that, for a second, he really did think he might pee himself too. He pulled Marisol to him instinctively as his gaze shot to the window. "Holy shit," he pronounced, forgetting little ears, when they saw Angela standing on the top deck, screeching for all she was worth. She was only partly visible from where they were, so they had no inkling of what might have triggered her screams.

"Angela!" Cynthia sprang up, but Michael was already out the door. "Stay here with Marisol," he shouted, as he took off like a shot.

Marisol was crying again. Cynthia picked her up and held her close. "Don't cry, little one. It'll be all right." But even as she said it, she prayed that it was true.

Michael reached the steps just as Angela took her tumble. He caught her virtually midair, the force of her body slamming him back down onto the steps, with Angela sprawled on top of him.

"Please, God, please," he whispered as he reached out from under her to feel for her pulse. He breathed a sigh of relief when he felt one, strong and steady. He'd broken her fall, but somewhere on the way down, she'd fainted. Now, it was like trying to maneuver out from under a five foot sack of bricks.

"Jesus, Angela," he muttered to himself, "you're a hell of a lot heavier than you look." He twisted his head sideways to look around. The deck was completely deserted, which was weird. Where was a security guard, or even a tourist, when you needed one?

Cynthia pushed the shop door open with her hip, still holding Marisol, patting her back to soothe her as the child continued to cry. "Michael! Are you all right?"

"We're both fine. She fainted, that's all. I'm having just a little trouble lifting her." A little trouble? His ass, thighs and shoulders were on fire. He was going to have a shitload of bruises by tomorrow.

Cynthia's whole body sagged with relief. Nobody was dead. That was something, at least. A catfight between two of her partners, then funny shrimp, and now this. All in one fun-filled afternoon. "I'll go get help." Taking the soaked Marisol with her, she scurried back into The Secret Spice, shouting for Cristiano.

From the kitchen, Cristiano heaved a sigh, covered up the cheese pinwheels with a damp cloth, and looked at Rohini. "Did I tell you, or didn't I tell you?" Dusting his hands of flour, he went out into the dining room to see what the trouble was this time.

Just as he left, like a comedy of errors, Sarita came dashing in through the delivery entrance. "Rohini! Inez and I need your help. We need my mother too. Do you know where she is? I can't find her."

Backside, shoulders, knees, head. It was the throbbing soreness of them all that brought Angela around. When she came to, Sarita, Cynthia, and Cris were standing around her bed, peering down at her with varied expressions of alarm. Worse, they were talking about her like she was a mental case.

"She's waking up. Her eyes are open, but they don't look right." That was Sarita.

"Maybe she's concussed." That was Cris. "Should we get a doctor — some kind of doctor?"

'Some kind of a doctor?' Geez. Who did they think she was — Dorothy?

Then it was Cynthia's turn. She leaned in close and waved two fingers. "Yoo-hoo, Angela, can you hear me? How many fingers am I holding up?"

Angela wrinkled her nose. "Eww. Oh, my God, Cynthia, why do you smell like pee?"

Before Cynthia could answer, Angela tried to sit up, and realized that her leg was propped up on two pillows. An impressive sized bandage was wrapped around her calf. "Wow. I took a heck of a fall, huh?'

"You remember that? You remember what happened?" Cynthia had stepped back from Angela and the others. She really needed to change.

"Yep. I remember everything." She sucked in a breath. They'd really think she was nuts now. "I saw a ghost. I was talking to him."

She corrected herself. "No. Make that, I have talked to him. Several times. And I never realized what he was. The hype about this boat is true. And today, he just..." She shivered once, but fought it back. "He scared the heck out of me, is what he did. But I'm okay now, and I'm not crazy. That's what happened. I'm telling the truth."

She looked at all three of them, prepared for anything, more prepared than she'd felt in her life. No matter how wacko the Lion, the Tin Man, and the Scarecrow around her bed would think she sounded, she knew that what she'd experienced was real. And somehow, now that the initial terror was over, the event was working through her like an epiphany. She waited for them to do and say their worst.

But Cynthia just smiled sardonically. "I don't know an easy way to break this to you Angela, so I'll just come out and say it. This ship is lousy with ghosts."

Cristiano's full lips curved with relief and amusement. "That's what this is about? No offense, *amiga*, but what took you so long to notice? You really have to open your eyes."

His words echoed her gray-eyed soldier's. Angela bent her chin to her chest as she recalled some of the other things he'd said to her. And the terrible things she'd said, while the whole time, she'd been oblivious.

"Yeah, I guess you're right, Cris." She thought of Vincenzo, and then Jane and the fight they'd had at lunch. Loss and despair washed through her.

She needed to see Jane and apologize. At least that was something she could fix right away. The rest she'd deal with later. She lifted her head back up. "Where's Jane?"

Her stomach jumped when she saw the look they exchanged. "What's wrong? What's happened to Jane?"

Sarita figured she might as well be the one to pick up the short straw. "She's...fine. Rohini's in her stateroom with her now. But..."

she tried for a smile, "it's an interesting coincidence. Jane also had an…encounter today. With Jackie Torin."

Angela's eyes went wide. "Not that poor kid they talk about on the ghost tour? She's real? They didn't just make her up?"

All three of them looked at her helplessly.

"Oh, no. Not a drowned kid. Oh, my God, this is terrible. I've got to get up." Though her bruises objected vociferously, she swung her leg down off the bed and stood, tottering.

Cristiano cupped her elbow to help steady her. "You need more time to recover. Rest for a while first, Angela."

Angela didn't have time for her usual niceties. "Screw that. Jane needs me." Leaving them gawking, she limped out into the hall, calling Jane's name. Her sister-in-law's stateroom was only a few doors down.

Cynthia turned to Sarita. "Go with her, *filha,* hurry. I'll meet you there." She waved her hand under her own nose. "Oof. I've got to get this dress off."

Cristiano took that as his cue. God help him if he got dragged along. His testosterone levels wouldn't be able to handle the deluge of female sentiment that was bound to be unleashed during this reconciliation. He was beginning to think he should find a way to be off the ship every Monday. He ran straight out on Sarita's heels. "I've got work to do in the kitchen. As many ghosts as we have around here, they're not going to help me make tomorrow night's special."

Two hours later, the four partners and Sarita were gathered in Jane's stateroom, discussing the afternoon's chain of events. The room smelled wholly female, with a hint of sadness, wine, and freshly baked bread. Along with their apologizing, ruminating and commiserating, they were also eating and drinking. To make up for his absence, their chef had sent up an appetizing tray of snacks, including the cheese pinwheels he'd finally managed to get into the oven. There were no shrimp.

Angela and Jane were sitting next to each other on the bed, leaning against the headboard, Angela with her leg propped straight out in front of her. They each had a plate of food and a glass of pinot noir.

"I'm ashamed to admit this with everything that's happened, but I'm starving. I hardly ate anything all day. And no offense, Rohini, but this is having a better effect on my nerves than the chamomile tea you made." Angela saluted her with the wine.

Rohini had commandeered one of the throw pillows from the bed, and was leaning her elbows on it while lying on the floor on her stomach. "Herbal tea has its place, but today I think we all needed something with more of a kick."

"I won't argue with that." Cynthia sat lotus style next to Rohini, and she raised her own glass. Both had their mouths full of puff pastry.

Jane's eyes still felt swollen from all the crying she'd done. She didn't have to look in a mirror to know she looked like hell. "I couldn't drink enough to forget what I saw today." She shuddered. "But as dreadful as it was, it was sad more than anything else."

Angela nodded. "I thought that too. I mean…after. During, I was scared to…well, to death. But when I think about it, the part that stays with me was that the poor guy seemed so desperate."

Jane took a sip of wine. "That's how I felt as well. The child said the same thing over and over: 'Please find my doll.' It was just pitiful. But," she looked over at Sarita, "you said that her doll is here, in the museum on board, isn't that right?"

Sarita was sitting on the desk chair, swiveling it left and right with her foot, as she tasted a stuffed porcini mushroom and sipped some juice. "Uh-huh. A Raggedy Ann doll. They found it on one of the decks after she'd drowned. They think she went looking for it when she woke that morning to find her nanny gone. Apparently, the police kept it for a while. When they returned it, her mother couldn't bear looking at it, so she boxed it away. Somehow, it ended up in the museum, years later." She wiped her fingers on a napkin. "If Jackie's spirit is here still, she'd have to know that her doll is here, wouldn't you think?"

"Perhaps she had another that wasn't recovered?" Rohini licked quince paste off her lip.

"No." Sarita answered with certainty. She looked at Jane, unsure if she'd want to be reminded of the time she'd first learned who Jackie was. "Um...remember when you, my mom, and I read her story in the ship history book I have? Afterward, I looked up everything I could find on her. Jackie only brought that one doll on board. She carried it with her everywhere." She shrugged. "So, if it's not that, I can't think of what she meant, either."

Cynthia tried to imagine what would keep the ghost of a small child wandering around on a ship for so many years. "She was so young. She probably has trouble expressing what she knows." She thought of what had happened that day with Marisol, and added, "*Pobre menina.*"

"Yes, poor little thing," Sarita agreed with her mother. "And they've turned a tragedy into an attraction with that ghost tour stuff." She looked at the older women, wondering if they felt the way she did. "It just seems wrong, doesn't it?"

"I'm not sure they have much choice, darling," Rohini offered. "It's expensive to maintain this ship. It's essentially a floating museum, with many costly artifacts to preserve. And there's a lot of competition with the other hotels in the area."

Jane drew a long breath. Still focused on Jackie, she rested her head on Angela's shoulder. "I just wish I knew what she was trying to tell me."

Angela gave her a consoling hug. "I know exactly what you mean." She released Jane and leaned forward to encompass them all. "My soldier was a lot more articulate, but even so, I still couldn't make heads or tails of a lot of what he said. Something about how his son thinks he's a coward, but that he isn't. That he wishes he could tell him. I should have listened more closely, but every time he spoke to me I always felt so...ill at ease." She sighed. "I thought he was kind of an oddball, but at the same time, I thought of him as my secret friend. My secret, handsome friend." Her eyes got misty. "And when he told me how much he missed his son, I thought of Vincenzo right away, and...I didn't know what to say." She looked at Jane miserably. "Everything you accused me of today is true. My soldier thought the same. That's what we fought about, he and I: Vincenzo. I hate myself for some of the things I said." Her shoulders slumped. "I hate myself, period. I'm such an idiot. I hope my son can forgive me."

The others looked at her in silent sympathy. Jane patted her leg. "Of course he will. Don't be daft."

Angela shifted up on the bed and the movement jarred her leg. "*Ow*. But even before today, I wish I'd paid more attention." She looked over at Sarita. "You'd have, I bet, knowing how you feel about the *Mary*'s history. He knew so much about her— about the war, about the prisoners that used to be kept aboard. He said that parts of her past were downright terrible, and now I realize it's because he *lived* parts of that past." Frowning, she thought back, trying to remember. "But he lost me when he said something about saving some men."

Sarita felt as though she'd been dropped from a great height. The conversation had engrossed her because Jane and Angela, two of the most conventional women she knew, had seen and talked with two ghosts. That meant that she, Sarita, wasn't such a freak after all. But Angela's last sentences filled her with dawning dread.

"*Filha*! You just went white as a sheet. All of this hasn't frightened you, I hope?"

There was simply no way Sarita could remain silent. A man's life was infinitely more important than her discomfort. Her mother was going to have a fit, though. With a look of apology at Cynthia, she blurted, "It's not that. It's…something else, *Mãe*."

Biting her thumbnail, she turned to Angela. "He had gray eyes, didn't he?"

CHAPTER FOURTEEN

"Oh, my God. It's him." Angela stared down at the photo Sarita had handed her.

"Private First Class Lee Burwell Branson, United States Army. The last entry is dated 1945." Jane held the diary with care as she read from it aloud.

"That's the year he was killed. I looked him up online, same as I did Jackie Torin." Sarita had everyone's attention as she recited the information about Lee Branson from memory. It was impossible to forget. She'd been thinking about him non-stop for the past several weeks. "He was charged with 'Desertion during Time of War,' the most contemptible of crimes, according to the military. It can be punishable by death."

Angela was aghast. "But he didn't desert. He was murdered."

"They didn't know that at the time, right? All they knew was that during that storm, he disappeared. A week later, his uniform and empty wallet were found abandoned in a navy dockyard. They assumed he'd jumped ship during the mass confusion onboard, and managed to get away on one of the lifeboats. When the war was over, he was tried in absentia by a military tribunal and received a dishonorable discharge. His pay was forfeited. His wife had to sell their home and move in with her brother's family. Their son was less than a month old."

"Oh, Angela, *that's* what he meant when he told you his son thought he was a coward." Rohini looked down at her glass as she blinked back tears. "What a tragedy."

Angela felt a constriction in her chest as something else hit her. "That's why he said he was running out of time. My math sucks, but if this was 1945, that means his son is like — what? — around fifty-nine years old now? I wonder if his wife is even still alive. Oh, my God, can you imagine how he must feel if she died thinking he'd abandoned her and their baby?"

Jane squeezed Angela's hand. "Surely we can do something about this?" She looked at the others. "Report it to the authorities, certainly, but can we also locate his family, perhaps?"

"Oh, I plan to. You can bet on it." Without realizing it, Angela repeated the soldier's philosophy. "We have to do the right thing." She looked at Sarita. "I know this is awkward for you. But we'll find a way to leave you out of it, honey."

Sarita blushed. "I don't mind all that much, I guess." Sighing, she looked over at her mother. Cynthia hadn't said a word all throughout, but had been regarding her daughter with a probing look ever since she'd brought in the diary. Sarita couldn't stand it one more minute. "*Mãe*, I know you have something to say, so please just say it. Stop boring holes into my head with your eyes."

Cynthia's voice was composed, but precise, when she finally spoke. "I'm wondering how long you'd planned to leave that poor man down there. I have to say, Sarita, for the first time in your life, I'm disappointed in you."

Jane stepped in to defend Sarita. "Cynthia, is this necessary at the moment? Truly, how does it help?"

"No, my mother's right. I should have said something sooner." Sarita's voice was clogged with the tears she'd been holding back for weeks. "I just didn't know how. It wasn't because I was embarrassed, or worried about what you'd do when you found out that Emilio and I were down there. I was afraid you'd think I was crazy." She gestured to Jane and Angela. "Up until today, I thought I was the only one who saw ghosts."

"Hah! Spend some time in the kitchen, when the pots are displeased with Cristiano." Rohini scooted closer to Sarita and laid a hand over hers in comfort.

"Is that what's been going on in there?" Angela was amazed. "Geez. I must be totally out of it. This whole time, I just thought that for such a good chef, he was incredibly ham-fisted."

"Anyway," Sarita valiantly returned to the subject at hand, "I was going to tell you, *Mãe*, I swear. I was working up to it." *Oh, God.* She hated herself for sounding so stupid.

"Sarita, after seeing how we behaved today at lunch, you have nothing to be embarrassed about in front of us, believe me." Angela also tried to put Sarita at ease.

Jane added her voice. "I'd have to agree. We're beyond that in this little coterie by now."

Cynthia made one more point while Sarita was open to it. "For the last couple of weeks, you've looked as though you were being chased by all the hounds of hell. I was worried sick, trying to figure out what was wrong." She pushed past the lump in her own throat, not wanting to cry in front of her daughter, but her voice had a hoarseness to it when she continued. "I *know* I'm a pain in the ass, Sarita. But you should have told me. I'm on your side. Always. I never would've thought you were crazy, for one thing. You've been an intuitive since you were a baby. Your grandmother was a voodoo priestess, for godssakes."

Sarita was beginning to believe she could confide in her mother about the extent of her abilities, yet the words remained lodged in her throat. Watching the emotions flicker across her daughter's face, Cynthia knew her well enough to suspect that, even with the afternoon's admissions, she was still troubled, still hiding something. Her instincts told her to be patient — no matter how hard that was — and wait for her daughter to come to her. With wicked humor in her eye, she switched tactics. "And a dungeon? Of all places for you to let him take you for your first time. Didn't I teach you anything? No wonder he didn't succeed in popping your cherry."

"Oh, for pity's sake, Cynthia." Jane slapped her glass down in disgust. "Sometimes you can be so crude, honestly." But she was surprised to see relief, not humiliation on Sarita's features, and pleased when she picked up the ball.

"Yep, my mom can be a gutter brain, but that's why we love her." Sarita was impressed with herself that she could say that out loud. When everyone laughed, including Cynthia, she was heartened enough to divulge, "To be honest, it was my suggestion to go down there. I thought it was the one place we wouldn't run into any of you." She lifted her shoulders and smiled with self-deprecation. "Oops. Guess I was wrong about that."

Cynthia watched her daughter's self-effacement slip away with that comeback, and chuckled with relief. "No, that certainly didn't work out the way you planned it, did it? A *cordon bleu* chef and a room full of POWs as witnesses." She saluted Sarita with her glass. "That's my girl."

They all got it now. Even Jane put in her own gibe. "A room full of soldiers? Well, you know what they say, Cynthia. As the twig is bent."

"My first time was on silk sheets." Rohini grinned. She rarely drank and the alcohol was beginning to have its effect. "It was still blah."

Angela snorted. "At least your first time wasn't on a heart-shaped bed in The Poconos."

"Oh, good lord. A heart-shaped bed, Angela? What is wrong with you Americans?"

Angela grinned too. "That's why I didn't tell you, Jane." She emptied her glass. "But at least it added humor to the situation. And believe me, humor was definitely needed."

That got another laugh out of Sarita, who went from feeling self-conscious to enjoying the conversation tremendously.

"Pay no mind to this lot, Sarita." Jane finally felt compelled to weigh in. "They'll put you off the business altogether. The fact is that when you're in love — truly in love — and it's just you and him, there's nothing else like it in the world."

Angela looked at her sister-in-law. That last sentence had sounded dimly forlorn. "My brother is a jackass," she pronounced. "How, oh how, did I not realize that he's a jackass for leaving, and for staying away this long?" She took hold of Jane's hand. "Jane, I'm so sorry."

Jane knew she'd start crying again if she wasn't careful, and she was damned if she wanted to. But she managed to get out an apology of her own. "I'm sorry as well. I had no idea you were so unhappy. I knew you were frustrated, certainly, but, as you said this afternoon, I never understood the extent of how manipulated by everyone you felt."

"Let's face it, they got away with it because I let them," Angela acknowledged. "I was a wimp."

Cynthia saw the turn in conversation as an opportunity to bring up her concerns. "I think I know what caused your…shall we say, 'tiff' this afternoon."

"Oh, you're like a dog with a bone, honestly, Cynthia." Rohini felt emboldened to make that observation as she enjoyed sipping just a bit more wine. She liked wine, she realized. She should indulge more often.

Paying her no heed, Cynthia put forth her hypothesis. But she was disappointed when Jane repeated what Rohini had said. "We need a bigger sample size."

"I *knew* it." Rohini tipped her glass to Jane.

"Are you serious?"

"I am, actually. I'm sorry, Cynthia, we can't formulate a conclusion based on only two subjects. That's not scientific, that's anecdotal." Jane went on before Cynthia could argue, "Apart from that, I can't speak for Angela, but as for me, I felt nothing unusual after I'd eaten the shrimp." She looked at Angela contritely. "I think I just had an overpowering sense that certain things at long last had to be said."

"Yeah, and we behaved like two lunatics when we said them," Angela put in. "But…I don't know. Maybe I did feel a little funny, now that you mention it." She tried to think back. "Kind of like when I take my motion sickness pills before I get on an airplane." When she saw Cynthia's look of satisfaction, she held up a hand. "Maybe. I can't be sure."

"That should be enough for us to take this off the menu, ladies. For godssakes."

"I get what you mean, Cynthia." Angela tried diplomacy, as always. "But I know from personal experience how difficult it is to come up with a successful recipe. I'm not saying we shouldn't be on our guard about this, but Rohini and Jane are the ones who know best what the attributes of the spices are." She spoke kindly, but made it clear where she stood on the subject. "I guess you're outvoted here."

"Well, what can I say to that?" Cynthia wasn't happy, but it was three to one. She hoped they didn't live to regret it. They weren't taking her seriously, but she knew what she knew.

Jane rubbed her arms, and looked pensive again. "I just thought of something, Angela. If we hadn't argued, I wouldn't have run up here, and you wouldn't have gone up to that deck."

Angela thought about that. "Why do you think they picked us? Lee and Jackie, I mean?" She addressed the question generally, not just to Jane.

No one dared venture an answer except Cynthia. "I think I might know. It's that old 'unresolved issues' concept." She turned to Sarita. "Remember what I said to you at lunch, after Angela and Jane left?"

Sarita thought back. "You mean about heartbreak?"

"Exactly." Looking at Jane and Angela, Cynthia spoke candidly. "Both those spirits have heartbreak from the past that they've carried into the present. Though you might not like to hear it, you're kindred souls."

Angela pressed her lips together, thinking of what she'd left unsettled with her only child. "That makes sense, doesn't it?"

Jane blinked back a sudden welling of tears. "I don't know anything about this — how it works, I mean. But if people can come back as spirits, why hasn't my Gabriella ever come back to me?"

"But, Jane — Lee and Jaclyn didn't come back, did they? They've never left. Like *Mãe* says, they're discontent and...unsettled." Sarita didn't know where the knowledge was coming from, but she could feel the truth of it in every word. "If Gabriella was happy while she was alive, what would there be to stop her from going on after she died, right?"

Angela looked at Jane sadly. "We can't argue that, can we? She *was* happy, Jane. Some people know how to be happy." She sighed, and looked down at her glass. "Others only know how to make themselves miserable. Even in the afterlife."

After they left Jane to get some much needed rest, Angela hobbled back to her own room, her knee still sore. She switched on her computer, found a pen and some paper, and sat at her desk with resolve.

After her encounter with Lee, she finally saw that she'd been nothing more than a coward all her life, a hypocritical little mouse who patted herself on the back for being a good daughter, a good wife, a good Catholic, while at the same time seething with anger behind her own complaisance and self-righteousness. So she made herself a promise: From now on, she'd live only as she saw fit. To heck with what anyone else thought. Even so, it would take all her newfound nerve to get down in writing what needed to be said. She wrote the most difficult first, while her courage was at its peak:

My sweet, beloved son, the last two years of silence have been all about me, and nothing at all to do with you. You are a wonderful human being and I love you very much …

By the time she'd finished all, the sun had nearly set. She went up to Lee's deck by its waning rays, and waited in hope. But when night fell and she was still alone, Angela knew that she'd never see him again. Nevertheless, she stood in the moonlight, at her place by the rail, and whispered her plans and promises and prayers to him. Her only answer was the wind. It swirled once, gracefully around the deck, lifting some of his cigarette ashes from the ashtray on the table near his chair, and scattering them out into the ocean surrounding the *Queen.*

Over the next two weeks, all of the following took place:

A team comprised of the L.B.P.D., the Military Police Corps, and the Port Authorities pulled apart an old heating shaft to exhume from beneath the *Queen Mary*'s hull the bodily remains of Private First Class L. Branson, his dog tags, and the remnants of a German WWII uniform.

In Fort Lauderdale, Florida, a jogger just back from his morning run went through his mail and came across a letter with a name on the return address he hadn't seen in too long a time.

Off the coast of Mexico, a sea captain docked his trawler at Puerto de Ensenada where he was finally able to access his email. He discovered one among them that filled him with both elation and dread.

In Dallas, Texas, a widower received two extraordinary pieces of correspondence: one from the United States Army, and another from a woman he'd never heard of, in Long Beach, California.

In Tokyo, Japan, a businessman successfully concluded a deal over a dinner of snow crab and sake at Kozue, then checked out of the Park Hyatt to be chauffeured back to Haneda, where his pilot patiently waited to fly him to the west coast of the United States.

In Kambalwadi, India, the family of a dead man's loyal servant sent the tragic news of his passing to his friend of many years, a cook aboard the *RMS Queen Mary*.

And in the neighborhood of Watts, Los Angeles, in a grubby one-room apartment, a hacker, notorious for his skills, worked on his laptop cross-referencing names, dates, and the information in some personal belongings — a stamped envelope, a magazine, two letters — to successfully locate a woman living under a false name. The young hacker was unaware that the woman had been running from his new client across two continents and ten years; a new client who repaid him for his efforts by slicing his throat immediately thereafter.

CHAPTER FIFTEEN

Monday, October 25, 2004

It was seven days before Inez's and Michael's wedding, and everyone at The Secret Spice Café was determined to make it an event to remember. Cynthia was worn out from the planning of it. Not only that, she hoped she hadn't caught her own strain of whatever mammoth virus Sarita had. The girl had been complaining of stomachache for days, yet refused to take any time off from school because it was "exam review time."

If they didn't look so much alike, Cynthia would swear the hospital had made a mistake, and her real genetic issue was out there somewhere, getting into all kinds of mischief, and most especially not giving a fig about high school exams. She'd finally gotten Sarita to stay home and rest for the day by convincing her that she wouldn't do well on any tests if she were sick.

Before Rohini left that morning, she'd made up a soup using some of those numinous herbs and spices of hers, and left instructions for Sarita to drink a cup every few hours. It was almost lunchtime. Sarita should be down soon, and Cynthia thought she might join her, and have some soup too. Her head was aching with enough force to be the portent of apocalyptic doom, or a brewing sinus infection. Unhappily for her, she guessed it was the latter. Since Jane and Angela were in the office working on Inez's seating chart, and being damn noisy about it, she'd decided to go over the week's receipts in the more peaceful surroundings of the empty dining room.

"Good afternoon."

Cynthia looked up. A man had come in the main entrance of the restaurant and closed the door behind him. He was holding a pamphlet from one of the ship's tours. She smiled with courtesy, but her aching head made her sound dismissive. "I'm sorry, but we're closed today."

The change in his tone was barely perceptible, but Cynthia could tell she'd annoyed him. "I'm not here for the restaurant, madam." His accent was thick. "I'm looking for a friend of mine, Rohini Mehta. My name is Vanu Joshi."

Cynthia stood up immediately. She'd been mistaken. Her headache was the sign of impending disaster after all.

This man was not Rohini's friend, Vanu. Only last week, she'd received word that he'd died in a fire in his village, a fire which had burned his home to ash, along with several others, before they'd managed to get it under control. No, no, no. This was not Vanu.

Think, Cynthia, think. This time she made sure her smile was much warmer. "Vanu. Yes, of course. Rohini has spoken so highly of you." Walking toward him, her smile fixed in place, she held out her hand. "I'm Cynthia Taylor, one of Rohini's business partners."

He didn't take it well that he was forced to shake her hand, but he did his best to conceal that, playing it as cool as Cynthia was. "A pleasure to meet you, Mrs. Taylor." His eyes scanned the room, caught on the kitchen doors and then arrowed back to Cynthia. "Is Rohini here?"

"Not at the moment, unfortunately. But we expect her within the hour. Today is market day. It's a shame you didn't call ahead and let us know you were coming. But I'm sure you wanted to surprise her."

Something slithered across his face. "I do want to surprise her. Yes."

The blood pounded through her head rapidly, aggravating the pain. But she kept her voice friendly and smooth. "I was just about to have some lunch. Please, do me the honor of joining me while you wait for Rohini?" She gestured to one of the set tables. "I certainly hope you like shrimp."

Sarita had to admit she was glad her mother had talked her into staying home. She was feeling worse by the minute. If she had her druthers, she'd stay burrowed in her cabin for the whole afternoon. But when she'd gone down to the kitchen this morning for some tea, Rohini was there, looking particularly pretty for her trip to the market with Cristiano, and cooking soup just for her. She made Sarita promise she'd have some for lunch. Dragging herself out of bed, she went down to The Secret Spice.

As she got to the entranceway, nausea hit her like a blow. *Damn.* She hoped she wasn't getting the flu. She had too much studying to do. When she was able to, she walked into the café where she spotted her mother, sitting with a man. His back was to Sarita, but she could see he had straight, jet black hair and dark skin. The moment he turned and his eyes met hers, she knew why she felt so sick.

Evil. He reeked of it, a miasma in the air surrounding him, so putrid, so potent, she nearly collapsed from it. She thought that it would stop her heart.

"There you are, Sarita! Come here, *filha*, there's someone I'd like you to meet." There was cheer in her mother's voice, but it was forced. That meant she was on to him, thank God.

Yet, it was impossible for Cynthia to know what Sarita knew — what she saw. Every murder he'd committed slammed into her like a tidal wave. She saw his brother sweating in his own bed, heard his groans, as a younger and even more beautiful Rohini tried to soothe him. She felt his parents' confusion, disbelief and twisting agony, as they were felled by the same poisons, fed to them by the son they'd adored. She wanted to cry out to the girl too impossibly young to be a wife, who writhed on the cold, marble floor of his luxuriously-appointed bath, begging for her mother, for her father, as the man who was now in their restaurant, sat in the adjacent bedroom and read a book to pass the time while she finished dying. She knew the gentle, older man with iron gray hair was Rohini's dear friend. He strummed a strange-looking guitar, and lived in a teeny house that had a vegetable garden he loved. She had to tighten all her muscles, so she wouldn't shiver at the brutality of his death. She could *smell* it — the coppery tang of his blood as he was viciously stabbed, the musky, candle wax smoke of the fire. She ached with a visceral pain for the eccentric, lonely, twenty-something who stayed in all day playing video games, while out on his street, other young men played real war. In her mind, she could touch him where he lay still quaking in his death throes, while the man who was now with her mother stepped over him blithely, and left him to bleed out.

Everything inside her from her throat to her bowels quaked with a terror beyond imagining. She wanted to scream and scream, but she knew if she did, he'd slay them too, as he had so many others, right there and then. So she clamped her jaw shut to keep her teeth from chattering as she saw, heard, smelled, tasted and felt his depravity, in powerful blasts of sensation that made her want to curl up in a ball and die, only so that it would all just stop.

And yet, by some means she forced herself to walk closer, to get to the table, to get to her mother, to try — somehow — to save her.

Cynthia's smile was as edgy as a surgeon's scalpel as she introduced them. Now that her daughter's life was in danger too, she prayed harder than she ever had in her life that her plan would work. "This is Mr. Vanu Joshi, Rohini's very good friend from India. Mr. Joshi, this is my daughter, Sarita."

"How do you do, Mr. Joshi." Sarita couldn't believe she heard herself say the words calmly, or that she managed to stand, not shrink back in blind fear as the beast whose plan was to slaughter them nodded to her. *God help us, God help us, please, please, help us.*

Her mother had something up her sleeve. Sarita willed herself not to panic, to follow her lead.

"Your timing is perfect." Cynthia was still looking up at her with sham brightness. "We're going to have lunch. The shrimp is freshly made. Perhaps you wouldn't mind serving us."

Sarita was flabbergasted. *That* was her plan — to defuse a ticking time bomb by getting him high on spices? She spoke urgently in Portuguese. "*Mãe,* listen to me. That's not going to work."

"Ah. Ah." Cynthia kept her tone playful. "No Portuguese, please. That's rude in front of a guest who doesn't speak the language. "

"*Mãe…*"

"Sarita, please." The words sounded sharper and more desperate than she'd intended. "Mr. Joshi has come a long way. He's hungry." Cynthia smiled at a stony-faced Naag again. "Just wait until you taste it. It's our best dish."

Sarita said nothing more. Her mother's mind was made up. There was nothing she could do, except to go into the kitchen and get the shrimp.

While Cynthia and Sarita served shrimp to a psychopath, Rohini and Cristiano were running out of the town courthouse. When they made it back to Cynthia's Porsche, they turned to one another and beamed.

"That was quick. I didn't expect it to be over so fast."

At her words, Cristiano's face fell. "Do you regret it? Would you prefer to do it again, maybe with our friends present?"

Rohini touched his cheek tenderly. "Definitely not. It's stressful enough working with them on Inez's and Michael's wedding. I adore them all, but this was glorious, just the two of us."

Awash with love, all he could do was gaze back at her. Fifty years. It had taken him fifty years, and all he'd been through in that time, to meet her and fall for her, from the moment she turned and smiled at him. She'd been worth the wait. He lifted her hands and brought them to his lips. "Thank you, Rohini. Thank you for taking this chance. Thank you for being my wife."

"Thank you for being my husband." She leaned over the stick shift to kiss him, savoring the moment. "I suppose we'd better get back. We have things in those bags that need refrigeration."

"Including an outstanding bottle of Perrier-Jouët."

"You got us champagne?" Her smile widened with delight. "Oh, goody. That will be a new experience for me. I've tasted more wines since we've opened the restaurant than I had in all my years before. I confess I quite like it."

"Uh, oh." He made a *tsk-tsk* sound as he turned the key and the Porsche roared to life. "You see? Not ten minutes married and already we have a problem. This is one secret you didn't tell me. What are you drinking now — two, maybe even three glasses of booze a week? It's those others. They're a bad influence."

"Aren't you a bad influence on me too?" she tossed back at him gaily.

His grin was gleeful. "The worst, *mi vida.* You will see how bad I am when I get you alone."

She laughed as the car glided into the street. She was glad — *so* glad — that she'd found the courage to take this step. In that moment, she promised herself that for now, she'd put all her fears aside. She couldn't wait to get back and surprise their friends with the news. And then, they'd all drink champagne and celebrate.

Naag was getting impatient. He'd been obliged to eat with a woman who looked like a whore, and her insolent teenage daughter who sat silently staring at him in a way that made him want to slap her. If Rohini didn't get back soon, he'd kill these two anyway, just to get the whore to shut up. Her voice was grating on his nerves.

"No, I don't want any more shrimp," he replied in answer to her question. Cursing his brusqueness, he forced himself to add, "Thank you." He was minutes away from regaining his honor. He needed to contain himself until his betrayer arrived.

Drained from her headache and her efforts at charm, Cynthia prayed that he'd eaten enough for the spices in the shrimp to have their effect. "And how are you feeling? You must be tired from your long trip."

"I'm fine." He grit his teeth again. "Thank you." He glanced at his watch. "Shouldn't she be back by now?"

"Yes, she should be here any minute." She leaned toward him slightly, and the whiff he caught of her perfume infuriated him. His eyes narrowed as it occurred to him that she was watching him the way a cat watches a mouse hole. "When she arrives, I hope that you're happy to see her. I want you two to be friends."

Sarita felt the bottom drop out of her world as she saw his eyes go sharp and deadly. Poor *Mãe*. She'd honestly thought she could save them with shrimp. For a while, as he ate, Sarita had hoped that was true. But they were both wrong.

"Do you, now?" he said softly. The bitch. She'd known who he was all along.

Cynthia sucked in a scream when, in one swift move, he sprang to his feet, yanked Sarita by the hair and jerked her head back. At her neck, he held a knife. "Don't make a sound, either of you. If you do, this slices through her soft skin like butter." Angling his body so that only his back was visible to anyone who might pass by and peer in, he ran the edge of the blade delicately across Sarita's neck, and Cynthia felt her heart shatter as the shallow cut he made turned red with her daughter's blood.

"Listen to me carefully, Mrs. Taylor. You're going to lock both restaurant doors. Quickly and quietly." He spoke like a driving instructor giving lessons to a jittery student. "Once again, don't scream. Don't run, don't try to signal to anyone. If you do, I'll cut her open like a piece of fruit."

Tears streaming, Cynthia did what he commanded. Then she came back to the table, never looking away from Sarita, silently begging her forgiveness with her eyes.

Although her pulse beat turbulently, Sarita remained composed. She knew he would kill her, but she was going to be as brave about it as she could manage, for her mother's sake.

"Well done, Mrs. Taylor." Again, Naag spoke to her as though she were his pupil. "I assume Rohini will come in through the back?" At her nod, he smiled, and Cynthia knew she'd never seen anything more chilling. "Let's all go into the kitchen and wait for her, shall we?"

"Now, then, this next one is tricky. Two of Inez's aunts aren't speaking. One of the aunts says she's fine if they sit together, but the other refuses to do so."

"Oh, for petessakes, there's one in every family. Okay, let's think." Angela picked up the seating chart. The tables had been rearranged twice already. She rubbed her eyes. "And...I've got nothing. I need a break."

"I'll go along with that. I'm feeling peckish." Jane pulled off her reading glasses and stood up. "I'd love a cup of tea and one of your biscuits." She looked at Angela hopefully. "Oooh. Maybe something lemony?"

Angela put aside the seating charts and smiled. "I could do with a cookie myself."

As they walked through the dining room, Jane noticed the lunch dishes that had been abandoned after Cynthia's thwarted plan. "Who the devil left those there? Let's take them in with us."

But Angela made her giggle when she clamped her around the waist and steered her back toward the kitchen. "No. I want a chocolate chip cookie *now*. C'mon, Jane, help me keep my resolution to live a more daring life. Those dishes aren't going anywhere."

They were still laughing and holding onto one another as they pushed open the kitchen doors. They stopped dead and shrank together in reflex when they saw a man holding a stoic, bleeding Sarita at knifepoint, and Cynthia sitting on the floor in mute, helpless tears.

Naag seemed to have been expecting them. Though his voice was calm, the malice on his face made their veins freeze. "Come in, ladies. Sit down next to Mrs. Taylor. Silently, please. Do as I say, or she dies right here, on your kitchen floor. And then, you will be next."

Cristiano and Rohini came into the scullery through the delivery door, and dropped the bags they were carrying onto the stainless steel work station.

Rohini glanced at the wall clock. "It's later than I thought. I need to start the roux right away."

"I'll join you as soon as I get the rest of the packages out of the car."

As she went left and he went right, the delivery door slammed shut and the lock clicked soundly on its own. At the same time, the old freezer swung wide open in front of Rohini, blocking her way out of the room. Astonished, they looked back at each other.

"Do you think she's upset that we didn't invite her to the wedding?" Cristiano's tone was dry, until the freezer banged shut once more, and they heard glasses and plates crash to the floor in the kitchen. Instinctively, they ran toward the sounds, and then froze in their tracks at the sight in front of them. One finger snap of time, and then everything happened at once.

Unnerved by the crash and the sudden appearance of Rohini, Naag jerked the knife away from Sarita, who used the chance to dive to the floor and scramble toward her mother. Rohini turned to flee. Naag lunged for Rohini just as Cristiano lunged for Naag, but, out of nowhere, a chair went airborne and flew toward Cristiano. It clamped its steel legs around him, trapped his arms to his sides, and propelled him backward until he slammed against the far wall. Though he struggled mightily to get loose, he was pinned to the wall by the chair as though he'd been locked in irons.

"What are you doing?" he screamed at the kitchen. "He'll kill her. Let me go!"

Naag had gotten a tight hold on Rohini, pulling her by her hair, but he was distracted from his victory by the spectacle of a piece of furniture whizzing across the room on its own. He recovered himself as soon as he heard Rohini's voice, pleading with him. "Naag, please let them go. I'll come with you, I promise. Please."

His vision blurred. He felt sick with rage as he looked down at her. He shifted his knife to the one hand still clenched in her hair. With the other, he backhanded her across the face. "You left me." Cristiano bellowed like a madman and the other four women gasped and recoiled. Naag hit her again, snapping her head back. "You dishonored me."

"You son of a bitch!" Cristiano strained against the chair, but it held fast. Near tears, he screamed, "Let her go!"

Naag stopped. He stared at Cristiano intently, his face flushed, his pupils strangely dilated. "Who are you? Who is she to you?"

"No one. He's no one to me. Please, *please,* Naag. Leave him alone." Rohini's mouth was bleeding, but she was beyond hope or care for herself. Her only fear now was of what Naag would do to the one person in the world who'd made her life worth living.

Every fire of hell was in Cristiano's eyes. "She's my wife, you motherfucker. I'll kill you for this, I swear it."

Naag laughed, and the sound crawled along Cristiano's spine. "How? Look at you. The witch has you trapped like a fly in a web."

Although he'd laughed, the thought of Rohini being with another man when she belonged to him was doing horrendous things to Naag's insides. He couldn't breathe. He felt dizzy. The shame this woman brought on him was coiling through him like a viper. He would die from the shame. He would die.

He *was* dying. He didn't understand why or how, but all at once, he knew.

He gaped at Rohini in horrified fascination, as the light in the room dimmed and then became so bright it burned his eyes. "You *are* a witch, aren't you? All those years ago, I was right. What have you done to me?"

One hand twisting at his abdomen, the other shaking as he pointed the knife, he backed away from her, away from all of them. A bilious, blackish-red liquid began seeping from his nostrils. He dropped the knife, doubled over. Sarita squealed when the same liquid poured from his mouth in one great gush and splashed to the floor. "How are you doing this?" He screamed it at Rohini now, his speech slurred. "Stop it. Make it *stop*!"

Everyone in the room seemed petrified — Rohini rooted to the spot where he'd left her, the other women huddled together on the floor and Cristiano still trapped against the wall — as Naag began to convulse and seize. He made gurgling noises as he tried without success to breathe, until, with one final jerk of his heart, he tumbled backwards against the shelf near the sinks. It collapsed, and every dish, glass and cup that had been resting upon it rained down on him, whether by accident or design, as he sank to the floor.

In the silence that followed, still no one moved, until the chair that held Cristiano captive remembered gravity and dropped away. He ran to Rohini, and both of them wept as he crushed her to him. Sarita had been the one held hostage, but she did as much comforting as being comforted, when her mother burst into tears and apologies in her arms.

Angela remained remarkably cognizant in the face of what she'd just experienced. She dashed to her station, wet two of her pastry cloths, and brought one to Cris and one to Cynthia, so they could wipe the blood off Rohini and Sarita. It occurred to her that someone should take a closer look at Naag to see if he'd somehow survived whatever in hell it was that had happened to him. She only took two steps his way, when Jane's sharp cry stopped her.

"Don't touch him. Don't go anywhere near him. He's been poisoned."

Everyone snapped to attention at that. Cynthia spoke up first. "Poisoned? How is that possible? I gave him the shrimp, and he had no reaction to it." She choked up again as she thought of her folly that had almost cost Sarita her life.

Jane's eyes narrowed. "What do you mean, you 'gave him the shrimp?'"

After blowing her nose on the pastry cloth Angela had supplied, Cynthia explained. "It all happened so fast. One minute he was just *here,* asking questions about Rohini. I knew who he was right away, and I didn't know what to do. Giving him shrimp was all I could think of. I should have just given him an engraved invitation to kill us all," she finished miserably.

"It's not your fault, *Mãe.*" Sarita held her mother close as she defended her. "There was nothing you could do. He was going to kill us no matter what." Wide-eyed and anxious, she turned to Jane. "Are you sure he's been poisoned? You don't think the…you know… the kitchen killed him?"

Cynthia shook her head. "That doesn't happen, Sarita. I told you, those are just stories children like to tell around a campfire. Spirits can make appearances, they can be mischievous, they can do a lot of things to let us know they're here, but they can't really harm us."

Jane and Rohini exchanged a look. They both knew that something much more corporeal had killed Naag. Both of them feared the same thing: that they'd made a dreadful mistake in dismissing Cynthia's claims. Jane's voice sounded thin to her own ears as she asked Cynthia, "Who served him the shrimp — you or Sarita?"

"Sarita did."

"Was there anyone else in the kitchen today, anyone we don't know?"

"Not as far as I know."

Another thought came to Jane, one that might help solve the puzzle. "The soiled plates out in the dining room — are those from the lunch you served Naag?"

Cynthia sniffed and wiped at her nose. "Yes. Yes. My plate is the one with chicken on it, obviously. Sarita had shrimp too, but her plate is nearly full." She shuddered, remembering. "We could barely swallow anything, we were so terrified, but we made a show of it, of course. He wasn't stupid. He wouldn't have tasted anything if we hadn't pretended to join him."

Jane picked up a freshly laundered dishcloth and snapped on a pair of plastic dish gloves from the bussing station. "I'll be right back. I'm going to fetch his plate. Don't anyone go near him while I'm gone." Grimly, she pointed to Cristiano. "That goes especially for you. I trust you don't want to get nicked for this unless you fancy another stay in prison."

"Oh." Realization set in as Rohini watched Jane walk out. "Of course." She looked up at Cristiano. "That explains why she pinned you to the wall. She *knew*. She knew he'd been poisoned and that you would try to stop him from touching me. If this is a homicide, your DNA can't be anywhere on him. And she made sure no delivery people could get in from the back door, either. She didn't want any witnesses to his death besides us."

Cristiano gently touched her swollen lip. "That doesn't make me feel any better. He should never have been able to harm you." He frowned. "Besides, if that's true, why didn't she just stop you from getting in when we came back from the market?"

"She was probably afraid he would hurt everyone else if I didn't show up."

"You're all talking about the kitchen like it's a person." Angela was astounded and even a touch hurt. "How come it's never communicated with me? I've been in here every day, same as both of you."

Rohini's smile was gentle. "Perhaps you weren't open to it then. Perhaps things will be different now."

That calculation bore out when the lid from the fat porcelain jar on Angela's workstation lifted of its own volition and a chocolate chip cookie floated out. Angela's face lit up as she watched it glide through the air toward her and settled gracefully on her lap. "Wow," was all she managed as she stared down at it. She looked up and around the room. "Thank you!"

The kitchen doors swung open, and Jane came in, carrying Naag's plate on the dishcloth. "Our goose is well and truly cooked," she announced, as she set the plate with the dishcloth down, making sure none of the food in it touched the kitchen surface. "It seems there was an extra ingredient in Naag's shrimp. Nightshade."

Rohini looked confused. Cristiano, Angela, and Cynthia looked blank. None of them caught the look on Sarita's face. It was altogether different.

Cristiano spoke first. "What's that?"

"It's an herb that homeopaths use to treat nausea and headache," explained Rohini. "I use it very sparingly. In fact, I used a smidgen of it in the soup I made for Sarita this morning."

"Well, somehow it got into the shrimp, Rohini, and more than just a 'smidgen.'" Jane's voice all but palpitated with panic. "Do you understand what this means?"

Rohini blanched. "But, how? I put it away right after I made the soup. I know I did. It's too dangerous to leave out in the open. That's why I don't keep it with the other spices and herbs."

"Wait — are you saying that's what killed him? But I…I thought nightshade was just a barbiturate. You know, to put you to sleep isn't it?"

All eyes shifted to Sarita. Something in her voice told them she had more than just a casual interest in the answer.

"In a certain dosage, yes. But it contains an alkaloid — atropine — which in larger doses is fatal. And as your mum's been saying, that shrimp has other medicinal spices and herbs in it too. They might have increased the potency of the atropine, even if the amount wasn't enough to kill him." Jane described these details quietly, but no one else said a word. It was becoming clear to everyone why Sarita had asked.

Cynthia broke the silence, alarm in her voice. "Sarita — what did you do?"

CHAPTER SIXTEEN

"I didn't mean it. I just thought it would knock him out. He was going to kill us, *Mãe*. He was going to kill us all. He's killed so many people, already. His whole family."

On the edge of hysterics, Sarita turned her tearstained face to Rohini. "Rohini, he...he...poisoned your husband. And he killed your friend...and set fire to his little house —"

"He killed Vanu?" Rohini whispered. "It wasn't just an accidental fire?"

"I'm so sorry!" Sarita wailed. She looked at all of them now, cringing and trembling so badly, she struggled to get the words out. She sounded helpless and young and terrified, as she recalled the visions that had pummeled into her mind, into her nervous system, when she'd seen Naag face-to-face for the first time. "He even killed the boy who found Rohini. He said... he'd pay him to search for her on his computer. He told him Rohini was his sister. That he...wanted to find her, because he missed her. The boy was so proud when he figured out that she picked a new name from a movie magazine. And then," Sarita shook with horror and heartache, "Naag cut his throat right there, while he was still smiling."

"My God. My God, *filha* — how do you know all this?" Cynthia's face was dead white.

"She knows because she's a seer." Rohini kneeled down and pulled Sarita into her arms, stroking her hair as she sobbed. "There, there, darling, it's all right."

Cynthia was reeling. She stared at Rohini as she held Sarita. "You...you knew?"

Rohini glanced at Cynthia. "I didn't know the extent of it, but I guessed when I saw her birthmark opening night. She came into the scullery and changed out of her dress into Cristiano's apron. A mark like that — in the shape of a star — it's a very clear sign of power."

In a daze, Cynthia put her arm around her daughter too. "I can't believe I wasn't aware of this. I even worried about that mark. I kept checking it to see if it would change shape — like they say can be a sign of skin cancer. It's not even a true birthmark. It only showed up about four years ago."

Rohini looked at her knowingly. "When she got her first period. Of course."

Cynthia patted Sarita's back. Her voice was unusually gentle. "Sarita, come on, now. Stop crying, sweetheart."

"I killed a man, *Mamãe*." Tears continued to spill as she looked at her mother. Her eyes seemed different, changed by the knowledge of what she'd done. Cynthia's heart sank. Sarita would never completely go back to being the girl she'd been, after this.

"You killed one. But you saved six." Anxiously, she pressed home that point, as she took the glass of water Angela had silently brought over and handed it to her daughter. "God knows how many others he'd have killed in the future, besides."

Sarita could not be consoled. "But I didn't *mean* to do it. I knew the shrimp wouldn't work the way you thought, so I sprinkled some of Rohini's herb on top." She was hiccupping, wiping her eyes with the back of her hand as she looked at Rohini. "I was watching you make the soup this morning and...I saw where you put the bottle."

"How did you even know what it was?" Rohini seemed more impressed by that than she did over Sarita's gift of sight.

"I learned about it in biology class. *A-atropa belladonna*." She was so distraught, she stumbled over the botanical name. "I thought it was just a sleeping herb. I knew he was going to kill us. I just meant to put him to sleep," she repeated desperately, her hands shaking so badly she almost dropped the glass.

"You put him to sleep, all right." Cynthia pulled the water out of her hand and held it up to her Sarita's lips. "Drink some. Why didn't you tell me that you had this ability, Sarita? It must have been horrible for you to keep this all to yourself."

"I already *told* you why. I was afraid you'd think I was crazy. I didn't want you to send me to a psychiatrist, like Kathy Knight's mom did to her, in ninth grade."

"Kathy Knight? You're comparing yourself to a girl who tried to set fire to the English teacher because she didn't want to read *Macbeth*? That child needed a lobotomy, never mind a psychiatrist."

"Okay—enough. Everybody *stop*." Cristiano's voice had an edge to it none of them had heard before. "This has been an entertaining afternoon so far, but it ends now." He sliced his hand through the air for emphasis. "I will take care of this from here. Sarita cannot be involved in this." His voice softened when he looked at her. "I understand how upset you are, *menina*. But you were right — he would have tried to kill us all. Rohini first." He thought of how helpless he felt when Naag attacked her and fury rushed through him once again. Well, he wasn't helpless now. "So, here's what's going to happen. *I* will take responsibility. I'll go to the police and tell them —"

"Like hell you will." Cutting him off before anyone else had a chance to protest, Jane marched over to him, and poked him hard in the chest. "*You* are not going anywhere near a cop shop, mate. You're mental if you think you're going to 'macho' yourself into another ten years in gaol — not if I have anything to say about it. I'm not having you be the sacrificial lamb a second time. I'm not having it!"

His eyebrows rose at her fierce protectiveness, when she'd once been his biggest detractor. The others were simply astounded that she was shouting. Except for Angela. No one caught the tiny smile on her face. Whatever else might come from this day, Jane was back. The *real* Jane.

Jane fixed them all with her haughtiest gaze. "Now, then — I suggest we all stop being such pantywaists and *think*. Starting with you." She looked at Sarita with kindness. "We understand you're upset, but let's be sensible — you were in a troublesome situation."

Angela snorted. "'Sensible.' 'Troublesome.' You're the queen of understatement today, Jane."

Jane looked daggers at her, and Angela, still amused, raised her palms up in capitulation. "Sorry. Continue, please."

Jane turned back to Sarita. "Considering what you knew, which was patently a great deal more than your mother knew —" this time her glare was for Cynthia, who hung her head and looked duly chastised — "what you did was good, old-fashioned quick thinking, to my mind." She nodded once, as if to say 'well done,' and then conceded, "Granted, you might have been overly generous with the dose, but that's neither here nor there. What's done is done. The only thing we can do now, is figure out how to get rid of him."

Five faces gawked at her. Once again, Cristiano was the first to speak. "What did you just say?"

"You heard me very well, I'm sure."

"Wait a minute. Wait a minute." He was staring at her like he'd never seen her before. "You want us to…dump a body?"

"Oh, for pity's sake, Cris. Don't be such a big girl's blouse." Jane radiated annoyance.

"We can't do that." Rohini sounded unusually definite. "That's insane."

"If you have another suggestion, Rohini, I'd love to hear it. Seeing as how this is all your fault, isn't it? Leaving poisonous herbs out where people can get their hands on them, being on the run from homicidal relatives, without cautioning us about them beforehand?"

When Rohini's face fell, Angela risked the consequences and interrupted again. "Oh, Jane, that wasn't very nice. C'mon now, calm down. You know how you get when you're upset." She bit down on her tongue to stop herself from grinning. If only Antoni were here. He'd be delighted to see her in action again.

"Calm down?" Jane was pacing and glowering. "Let me tell you precisely how your press is going to cover this if it gets out." Still wearing the plastic gloves, she counted on her fingers. It struck Angela that old "Winnie" himself, as her sister-in-law sarcastically called him, could do no better job of addressing his troops. "Number one: An Indian and a Mexican — two foreigners from the countries that have been most accused of quote — stealing American jobs — end quote — decide to murder an innocent man by poisoning him. The Mexican has already been convicted of one murder."

"I'm from Spain, actually." Cristiano had the temerity to correct her, but when she pivoted and gazed at him stony-faced, he hastily added, "But I get your point. Go on."

Jane held up two fingers. "Number Two: The other partners who, need I remind you, put their life savings into this café, decide to go along with it, and in fact, put a teenage girl up to the particulars of the task. Have a look at her."

There was a hint of censure in her voice against poor Sarita, as they all turned their heads to where she sat, teary-eyed and trembling still. "She's a mess. The moment they ask her one question, she'll break. And what will she tell them? That she 'envisaged' that he'd murdered multiple people? That 'she only meant to put him to sleep?' Won't that go over well? We're looking dodgy to them already what with that ridiculous story about how we knew where to find that poor soldier."

She looked at Angela and sniffed in disapproval. "What were you thinking? Who goes looking for a lost earring down a heating shaft in the bowels of a giant boat, and 'just happens' to discover a corpse?"

"Well, it was the best excuse I could come up with at the time." Angela defended herself indignantly. "I don't have much experience in lying to the police, the Coast Guard, and the United States Army all at once, Jane. Besides, they certainly can't accuse us of that murder. That happened before any of us were even born."

Jane leaned down toward Angela. "And what about that one?" She flung her arm out, pointing to where Naag's body still lay. "That one's nice and fresh, Angela."

Picking up the chair that had imprisoned Cristiano, she sat down on it with a clunk. "We'll lose The Secret Spice, end up in prison, and Sarita will be shuttered up in a loony bin." She tilted her chin at Cristiano. "As for you, they'll throw away the key this time." She fell into her regional dialect again for the grand finish. "In short, if we don't figure a way out of this, we're buggered."

"She's right." Cynthia pushed herself from off the floor where she'd been sitting since Naag had forced them into the kitchen. "There's no way we can talk ourselves out of this one. And frankly, I'll do whatever it takes not to have my daughter's life ruined over this." She looked at Angela. "What about you? Are you in?"

Angela hesitated only a moment. "I can't believe I'm saying this, but…yeah. I guess I am."

Sarita was appalled. "You're all serious? You're really going to… to…?" she couldn't even finish the sentence.

"Honey, we just don't see that we have any other choice." Angela kneeled down next to Sarita and looked at her solemnly. "Think about it for a minute. Even if we leave your…shall we say…talents out of it, we'd have to prove that you didn't mean to kill him. There'll be an investigation and lawyers and reporters. All our lives will be pretty much destroyed." She picked up Sarita's hands and chaffed them. They were ice cold. She tipped her head in Naag's direction. "That man was a very bad man. You *know* that, probably even better than Rohini does. He's already caused so much suffering. Not just for us. For others. Should we allow him to make us suffer even more?"

Sarita looked down at her lap in misery. "I guess not."

Angela nodded sadly, and patted her back. She stood up and looked at Rohini, her expression compunctious. "It looks like it's three against one again. You must think we're horrible."

"No." Rohini bit her lip. "No, I don't." She let out a long breath. "I'm in too." Turning to Cristiano, she looked at him beseechingly. "I know you don't approve of this. But I couldn't bear it if anything happened to Sarita or you because of Naag. And I'd hate to lose The Secret Spice, after we've all worked so hard."

As always, Cristiano was defenseless against the look in her eyes. Shaking his head, he paced, muttering to himself, glancing over at Naag and then back to the women, rubbing his hands over his face and through his hair.

At last, he said, "Does anybody have any bright ideas on where we're going to keep a dead body until we figure out what to do with it?"

From behind them in the scullery, they heard a loud click and a sound of rushing cold air, as the ancient freezer door swung open again.

Cristiano closed his eyes and exhaled noisily. "I should have guessed she'd be up for this."

He slid a look at Sarita, who was still shell-shocked. "Take Sarita upstairs for now, Cynthia." His expression spoke volumes about what he and the others were going to do next. "She's...had a bad day."

"Don't forget to take some of the soup. You can heat it in the microwave in her room."

Cynthia gave Rohini a speaking glance. "I'll think we'll skip the soup for now, Rohini, thank you very much."

Once mother and daughter had gone, Jane took control again. She got three more pairs of plastic gloves and handed them around to her proselyte accomplices. "Right. Angela, Rohini, let's us three get him into the freezer. Cristiano, you can clean up that horrible mess he made." She walked over to where Naag lay, stepping gingerly over the bile and whatever other ghastly fluids and bits had spilled out of him.

"Hold on a minute, Jane. I should be the one to get him in there. It would be a lot easier for me to lift him than for you three."

"*No.*" Jane made a sound of impatience. "Have you forgotten one of the main purposes of this strategy? We don't want your DNA on him. We're going to stick to that for now, just in case we don't succeed in coming up with a way to get him out of here." She shooed at him with her gloved hand. "Go on, then. The bucket and bleach and other cleaning supplies are under the sinks."

Cristiano looked like a mutinous boy as he stared at her. "You're being such a bossy pants today."

She put her hand on her hip. "Are you going to fanny about all afternoon calling people childish names, or do you think we might be able to get to work?" She bent down to Naag, and sucked in a breath. "*Oh.* He smells dreadful. Rohini, you take one leg, and Angela, you take the other. I've got his shoulders. If he's too heavy to lift, we'll drag him." Unlike their hapless chef, both women had enough sense not to argue with her.

He grumbled as he walked away, "Some wedding day this is turning out to be."

"Oh, yeah, that's right — I thought I heard him say something about that when the chair had him." Angela beamed at Rohini as she lifted Naag's leg. "You guys got married today?"

"Yes, this morning at the courthouse." Rohini gave her a shy smile and picked up Naag's other leg.

"Oh, that's great. I wish you all the best. We should have some cake later to celebrate. Ooh — I have a fresh pan of tiramisu that I could put some pretty butter cream rosettes on — you know — just to make it look more like a wedding cake. Do you like tiramisu?"

"Angela." Jane was ready to spit. "Will you shut your gob, please, and lift your end?"

"Oh, I'm sorry. I got carried away. Okay, tell you what — let's lift him on three. Ready? One. Two. Three."

The moment they lifted him, they exposed more noxious smelling liquids and other nasty things pooled beneath him, that the poison had caused to discharge from his body. The back of his trousers and even his suit jacket were soaked with them.

"Eww. Oh, my God."

"Oh, this is terrible."

"Don't lose your bottle, ladies. That's for Cris to deal with, fortunately for us." Jane was doing her best to breathe through her mouth. "We haven't got far to move him. Just focus on getting him to the back room and into that freezer."

"Wait. Jane, could…could you…take care of his eyes first? I can't bear it." As dusky as Rohini's complexion was ordinarily, her face looked colorless at the moment. When Jane had lifted Naag's shoulders, his head had tipped sideways and lolled forward. Now it appeared that his cold, bloodshot eyes were staring directly at Rohini, as though even in death, he still condemned her.

Jane swallowed hard. With a look of revulsion, she reached over and used her gloved index finger to push each lid down. "There. Let's keep moving."

They made it to the scullery entrance, and were just about to heave Naag into the freezer, when the delivery door clicked wide open and a man stepped in.

He stopped dead at the tableau he'd stumbled upon. "What the hell is going on in here?"

All three women froze with fright. They let go of Naag, and he bounced to the floor.

Jane slapped both gloved hands over her mouth, but Angela was more vocal.

"Oh, my God. Antoni!"

CHAPTER SEVENTEEN

"So, let me see if I have this straight. A ghost who might or might not be a former Queen of England unlocked the back door for me. This ghost also helped save your lives earlier today when the dead man I just helped you haul into a freezer for safekeeping — God help me — tried to kill you. And that man was accidentally poisoned by a teenage girl with the gift of sight, who happens to be your partner's daughter."

"That's it in a nutshell." Cristiano eyed the newcomer guardedly, hoping against hope that he'd believe them and that he could be trusted. If not, they were in even deeper shit than they'd been in before.

"I see." Antoni pressed his thumb and forefinger to the bridge of his nose. "Jesus Christ."

He'd been sitting with them all for more than an hour, listening to a tale that was so farfetched, there were only two possibilities: they'd all gone mad, or the story was true. Besides, it could take nothing less than a shipful of ghosts for his sister to risk incurring Jane's wrath by writing to him. Up to now, he'd directed his questions and comments solely to Angela and the handsome couple to whom he'd just been introduced, since his wife had done nothing except watch him in silence, so far.

Now he turned specifically to her. As unconceivable as the story would seem to most, as a sea captain, he'd seen a lot in his travels, and had heard tales even more incredible than this one. Jane was a pragmatic woman. If she validated what they were saying, he'd believe it.

Apart from that, he desperately needed to know if she would speak to him. It had taken all his nerve and then some to sail here after he'd gotten Angela's email. He was beginning to wonder if she'd made a mistake about Jane's feelings. Even more frightening to him than the account he'd just been told was the thought that she had, in fact, been speaking the truth two years before, when she'd said she never wanted to see him again. Asking her a question about the situation at hand was the only way he could think of to feel her out. "And you? Do you agree with all this?"

Jane needed to clear her throat before she managed to respond. She couldn't believe he was here. Good lord, he was a sight for sore eyes. Grayer and a bit more lined, yes, but tanned and fit. The bugger.

She kept her voice neutral. "I do, yes. In fact, it was my suggestion that we…dispose of him."

His eyebrows shot up. "*Your* suggestion? Is that so?"

She nodded, folding her arms at her waist and touching her elbows self-consciously, as he continued to study her. At length, she asked, "So will you help us get rid of the body, or not?"

All at once, he started laughing. She lifted her chin. "What's so funny?"

Antoni couldn't stop smiling. She'd tilted her pert nose in the air, in her classic "I'm-in-a-snit" mode that he remembered and loved so well. "Ah, Jane, Jane. I thought of all the things you might possibly say to me when I showed up after all this time. 'Help me get rid of a body' didn't make the list."

The silence that passed between them as they gazed at each other was so charged, that the other three did their best to look anywhere but at them.

Antoni broke contact first by turning his attention to his sister. "Angela, do you remember the story Pop used to tell about Mama's uncle?"

It took her a minute, but then she smiled slyly. "Uncle Nunzio. Yes, I do." Still smiling, she told everyone the tale, imitating her father so well that both Jane and Antoni had to smirk. "When my brother was a teenager and he misbehaved, my father would say to my mother, 'you better watch that kid of yours. If he doesn't change his ways, he's gonna be a hew-dalum and end up like your Uncle Nunzio.'"

Jane glanced back and forth between them. "What happened to your mother's Uncle Nunzio?"

She got her answer when Antoni stood up and exchanged a look with Cristiano. "Got any chipped ice around here?"

"Plenty."

"Good. We'll need it. I'm docked nearby, at the Shoreline Marina. Give me about a half an hour to get back to my boat and bring her around."

Michael had just come out to sweep the deck in front of his shop, when the delivery door of The Secret Spice Café opened. A tall, sinewy, dark-haired man stepped out, pulling an aluminum refrigerator box. He wore a fisherman's cap, and his complexion was suntanned and weather-beaten. The box was wheeled for easier transport, but even so, it looked heavy. The man noticed Michael watching him and nodded hello.

"Need some help with that?" Michael asked, as Antoni maneuvered the box onto the gangway that went down to the dock.

"I've got it, thanks. I'm just taking it back to my boat." He motioned down to the *Mary*'s loading zone, where an impressive-looking fishing yacht with the name *Gabriella* painted on its side was waiting.

Michael glanced down and whistled. "Nice."

"Thanks." Antoni stopped and tilted his cap back to get a better look at Michael. Friendly face, younger than he by at least a decade, likely a neighboring shop owner or manager, judging by the fact that he was holding a broom. Antoni held out his free hand. "I'm Tony Miceli." He tipped his head toward the restaurant. "I'm Angela's brother...and Jane's husband."

"Oh, no kiddin'?" Michael wiped his palm on his jeans as he came down the ramp, then shook Antoni's hand. "It's nice to meet you." He flushed when what Inez had told him about Jane losing a child and being estranged from her husband came back to him. "Yeah. Um...so...I'm Mike. Mike McKenna." He jerked his thumb at his shop behind them. "Jane and Angela are my neighbors, so to speak." When Antoni only nodded again, Michael looked down at the refrigerator box. "So, what have you got there?"

"Fish."

"Fish?"

"Yep. I brought them for the restaurant, you know?" Antoni shrugged casually. "The chef didn't want them. Said they weren't fresh enough." He grimaced. "How could they be any fresher, when I pulled them from the ocean only yesterday?"

Michael chuckled. "Don't take it to heart. I've known Cris for years. Even if you brought him fish that could still swim, he'd complain they weren't fresh enough." He rubbed his midsection. "One helluva chef, though."

"Antoni."

Both men turned at the sound of Jane's voice, but her eyes were only on one. She'd risked coming out after him at Angela's urging. "Are you coming back this time?"

Antoni looked across at her as she stood by the entranceway of the café. The sun hit his eyes. When he blinked, for just one brief moment, she looked exactly as she had when they'd met in Rome so many years before.

Love, desire, grief, regret: Everything he felt for her, everything they'd lived through together, swamped through him. It was all written on his face when he replied, "Do you want me to come back, Jane?"

She said nothing as she walked down to Antoni, trapping Michael there on the narrow gangway. Michael couldn't go back up without brushing up against her. He turned and pretended to be admiring the ocean, as she stopped in front of her husband and stared up at him.

Loving Inez had turned him into a romantic. He was hoping like hell Jane's answer would be what the poor guy standing behind him obviously wanted it to be. With no shame whatsoever, he strained to hear what was happening, but all he heard was a loud clatter. He risked a slight turn of his head, and from the corner of his eye he saw that Antoni had let go of the aluminum box to catch Jane, who'd launched herself at him and was now plastered to him, giving him a kiss that was so hot, Michael thought the hair on his own head would be singed.

Jane pulled away just when Antoni thought his knees would no longer hold him upright. Still without a word, she turned and walked up the ramp and back into the restaurant. He watched her go, convinced that all the ice in the cart had melted into boiling water, and he'd be left with one hell of a dripping mess right there in broad daylight. It took him a minute to remember he wasn't alone. His eyes slid to Michael.

"*Damn*, dude." Michael sounded just as bowled over as Antoni felt. "I…I think it's pretty safe for you to take that as a 'yes.'"

All in all, it was much too easy to 'disappear' a man, Antoni thought.

He knew the waters and currents. He knew how far out he should go. And he knew in what spot to anchor his trawler, so that he'd be secluded enough.

He set out that Monday afternoon and sailed all through the night, and on and off for the next two days. He stopped occasionally to snatch an hour or two of sleep, or to fish as he normally would, in case the Coast Guard or another private boat happened by. But he remained the lone vessel all day on Wednesday. On that night, the moon was full, bright enough to see what he needed to see, and do what he needed to do without the aid of the boat's lights.

It was short work for him to consign Naag's body to the ocean floor, but after it was done, he found that he was shaking. Hell and Sin were concepts he'd forsaken while watching them consume his parents and suffocate his sister. But now he couldn't help but cross himself; it was virtually a reflex. He closed his eyes, swallowing the taste of his own bile, as he braced his legs against a brief roll of waves that slapped the hull of his boat as though in reprimand.

Jane's face swam into his consciousness. The thought of her was like a cool breeze coming in off the water. In great gulps, he sucked it in, until the queasiness subsided.

When he was calm enough, he pulled up anchor, started the engine, and headed back to Long Beach. In less than three days, he'd be with her again.

At the very moment that Antoni cast Naag into the ocean, Sarita flinched as she stood on the uppermost deck of the *Mary*, looking out over the water in the direction his boat lay anchored, as if it were just in front of her, and not hundreds of miles away.

The changing tide filled the night air with the scent of the sea. She closed her eyes and tasted the salt of her own tears.

The ship seemed unusually quiet this evening, with a desolate air to it that matched her mood. For as far back as she could remember, she'd felt separate and isolated, and now she felt even more so, set apart by one rash act, an act that had completely and forever shattered any dreams she'd had for a normal life.

After the terrible thing she'd done, if there had been no one else to consider, she might have made another choice. But instead, for the sake of her mother, she'd made up her mind to pretend that nothing was different, to behave as though she were unchanged. It had taken her this long to recognize how much her mother loved her, how much she'd sacrificed for her. To end her own life would destroy Cynthia. Essentially, it would be a second murder. So, as hard at it might be, she would go on.

But standing alone, looking out at the full moon, she knew that the bright hopes of the past summer, of this new place, had faded as surely as fall was fading to winter. Brushing her finger over the star-shaped stain, she knew she was marked more than physically now, eternally affected, just as the moon she was staring at eternally affected the tides, pushing them forward, then back, in the same endless pattern.

She wondered if this all-consuming loss was what the *Mary* had felt when she understood that she'd be docked here forever, stagnant and withered, never to venture forth upon the seas again.

A warm, masculine arm wrapped around her shoulders, and Cristiano came up next to her, interrupting her impassioned reverie. Sighing, he looked out at the water also. She dried her cheeks and made an effort to calm herself.

A wry, watery chuckle escaped her. "You seem to be the designated spectator for all my life catastrophes."

"I don't mind if you don't." He was relieved to see the quip made her smile.

Leaning against the rail, he shifted sideways to face her, his expression grave. "What you did saved Rohini's life. I'm forever in your debt that she no longer has to live with that nightmare hanging over her. It was torture for us both."

She held her hand up, palm out, as though she could physically stop his words. "No. Please don't thank me, Cristiano. God, no. I never meant for things to happen this way." She whispered, her voice choking again, "I never, ever meant to be a killer."

He drew a deep breath and nodded, his voice reflecting her sorrow. "Yes. I know what you mean. Neither did I."

As Sarita and Cristiano looked out at the water from the deck above, the moonlight flowed in through the windows of The Secret Spice. The lights were off throughout the restaurant, save for one in the scullery. Its harsh fluorescence was stark against the bruises on Rohini's face, and the floor felt cold on her bare feet, as she stood gazing at the freezer, whispering every prayer of forgiveness and redemption she knew.

After walking Sarita back to her cabin, Cristiano looked for his wife, and found her there. He pressed his lips to her forehead. "Come upstairs, sweetheart. Let's go to sleep."

Switching off the light, she took his hand, the hand that now bore her ring, and held on to it tightly as they left.

In the darkness, the ancient freezer continued to hum.

CHAPTER EIGHTEEN

Sunday, October 31, 2004

Without a doubt, the place to be on Halloween, for Halloween enthusiasts, was the *Queen Mary.*

Capitalizing on its reputation as one of *Time* magazine's "Top Ten Most Haunted Places," the ship's marketing team went all out for the holiday every year. Their "Shipwreck Terror Fest," featuring attractions all throughout the ship, was a great success. Preparations had gone on the whole week prior with artists, actors, and set designers all being brought in. With all the extra people working on board, the restaurant was booked to capacity every night.

Angela came up with the idea that they should open temporarily in the afternoons, solely for the Terror Fest crew. Not for lunch, but for what she'd dubbed "Haunted Tea and Cakes." She was having a blast making fun recipes like Jack-o'-Lantern— Spice Cupcakes, Spider Web Cheesecakes, Devil's Chocolate Decadence, and Black Magic Lemon Tarts. The special effects people amidst her artist patrons were going mad trying to figure out how the café's "cookies floating out of the cookie jar" trick was achieved.

The opportunity for interaction with the many young people working aboard for the Terror Fest was doing wonders for Sarita. Every afternoon since Angela had started her Haunted Tea, Sarita had hurried home from school, dropped off her books, and gone in to help Angela serve. Today, she was even wearing a costume. When she hurried into the kitchen to pick up some extra licorice spiders for the desserts display Angela had set up in the dining room, Cristiano pronounced her "the prettiest witch" he'd ever seen.

Cynthia blessed Angela for coming up with the idea, not only because it was bringing in extra revenue, but because Sarita's buoyancy these last few days couldn't be missed; a welcome sight not only for her mother, but for everyone else on the team who'd come to love her like a favorite niece.

But with all these goings-on came added pressure. Today, being the official opening of The Shipwreck Terror Fest, The Secret Spice was a madhouse. They still had regular dinner service tonight, and Michael and Inez's wedding reception was the next day. Temporary added wait staff and two extra line cooks had been hired, but even so, Rohini, Angela, and Cristiano were pretty much chained to the kitchen for the next two days.

It was left to Jane and Cynthia to handle anything at all that didn't involved the actual preparation of foods. But Antoni had only just returned the night before, exhausted from the second long boat trip he'd taken within a day. He was also still recovering from the impact of consigning a man to Davy Jones' Locker; a man who more than likely would have protested the excursion had he been able to voice an opinion. Cynthia had taken one look at Antoni, and despite the crush, insisted that Jane have the day and evening off. Pulling Jane aside, she issued crisp instructions. "Lock your door and make him glad, Jane, not only that he came back to you, but that he committed a crime for you. I know you're out of practice, but do your best."

While Jane was happily following those directives, Cynthia double-checked liquor supply, place settings, and flower delivery times. She reallocated space for the wedding band when she discovered that there weren't enough electrical outlets where they'd been scheduled to set up the next day. This was being done as she smiled her way to and from tables currently occupied by bloodied zombies, green-fleshed ghouls and other assorted fiends, all enjoying their spiders and jack-o'-lanterns— made from frosting, cake and candy.

Then Sarita hurried over to her, her witch's cape swirling. "We're short two tablecloths for tomorrow."

"You're joking."

"I counted them twice. There were so many changes to the seating arrangements, and with everything that happened this week, I guess Jane and Angela forgot to do a recount." She held out a slip of paper. "This is the address of the place where Inez ordered them. I called. They're open on Sunday, but only until five. If you want to get them, you'd better go now."

"Damn, this is really going to cut into my afternoon." Cynthia took the paper. "Will you be able to manage here by yourself while I'm gone?"

Sarita looked around the dining room. "Sure. We're closing to set up for dinner in…" she looked at her watch, "about forty minutes, anyway."

"Well if you need any help, get Angela." She ran into the office to grab her handbag and keys.

Sarita was bussing dishes off a table, hoping that the stragglers would soon leave so they could start the dinner setup, when a man walked in who had such a presence, everyone left in the restaurant glanced his way.

He was in his forties, well over six feet tall, with toffee-brown hair and eyes the color of cinnamon. In a casual place like Long Beach, his tailored navy blue suit and gleaming Italian leather shoes seemed out of place, particularly on a Halloween afternoon. Yet on him they looked perfect, especially as he wore them without an ounce of self-consciousness. His expression enhanced his allure. It was intelligent and attentive. The grooves in his cheeks and the lines fanning the sides of his eyes added power to his face.

"Wow," a woman with a hatchet cleaved into her forehead murmured to her table companion. "Who let him out?"

The companion, a female zombie with flesh peeling off her face, preened. "Do you think I'm his type?"

The man's brows drew together as he honed in on Sarita. Her eyes went wide as he started toward her.

"Cradle snatcher," the zombie muttered to her friend.

Oblivious to the audience he'd gained, he approached Sarita and spoke softly to her, in the precise English of someone who was not a native speaker, but who'd studied it extensively. "Hello. By any chance, would you be Sarita Taylor?"

Sarita wondered why she couldn't get her so-called "ability" to work for her at will. Was it always going to be hit-or-miss — knocking her sideways when she least expected it, and no help at all when she wanted to make use of it? She had no bead on who this man was or how he knew her name. She only knew that he looked friendly and vaguely familiar. "Yes, that's me."

She shifted uncomfortably as he scrutinized her face. "I *knew* it. You're older now than in the photo I have of you, of course, but I recognized you." He held out his right hand. "Nice to meet you in person, *senhorita*."

Taking his hand, she smiled hesitantly. Well, how awkward was this? He spoke Portuguese, he knew her, and she was about to embarrass both herself and him by asking his name. She shook her head and lifted her shoulders in apology. "I'm so sorry, I don't remember you. Are you one of my mother's friends from back home?"

His eyes widened, and then he laughed out loud, a sound so enchanting that Girl Zombie and Hatchet Head turned to stare again. "I'm an idiot. Of course you don't know me. I'd entirely forgotten because I've known of you and your mother forever, it seems. I'm Raul Ferreira."

She was still puzzled. "The only Raul Ferreira I know is dead. Unfortunately."

With a patient smile, he tried again. "You refer to my father, Raul Silva Ferreira. I'm his son, Raul *Soares* Ferreira."

She sucked in a breath. "Of course. What was I thinking? Now who's being an idiot?" She smiled back at him, but inside she thought, *Oh, no*. Right before the wedding. Poor *Mãe*.

Remembering her manners, she put the bin of dirty dishes aside, and pulled out a chair for him at one of the clean tables. "Please sit down. I'm sure you want to... speak to my mother. She's not here, but she'll be back soon. Can I get you something to drink? Or, maybe you'd like —" she swiveled her head around to see what was left in the pastry display — "a Black Magic Lemon Tart?"

"No, don't trouble yourself. I do want to speak her. Of course. But to tell you the truth, I've just got off the plane. I wanted to come by and let her know I'm here, but it was a long flight, and I'm exhausted." He tipped his head toward the outside hall. "I've booked a suite. I'd like to go up and have a shower, maybe a short rest. Perhaps I could come back later this evening?"

"Sure. Great. I'll...I'll tell my mother to expect you." She gave him a nervous smile.

"Excellent." He smiled back at her, and Sarita couldn't decide what that smile meant. "I will see you both this evening. *Obrigado*, Sarita."

"You're welcome. See you later." She watched him go, biting down on her thumbnail so hard this time, she made it bleed.

It was gone four. After a glorious time spent reconciling with Antoni, Jane was famished and ready for a bite to eat. He, on the other hand, was still abed. They hadn't gotten much sleep. The boat trips, along with everything else, had physically and emotionally overwhelmed him. Her smile was self-satisfied. Apart from all that, she could take credit for some of his fatigue. Cynthia's concerns had been for naught. It was like getting back on a bicycle. Pleased with herself, she got dressed while he slept on.

And wasn't that strange — to see him sleeping in her bed again, on the same side he'd always slept — as though he'd never left? She looked down at him as she thought of that, savored that. At the same time, she found the flavor bittersweet. They still had a ways to go, but they were off to a good start.

She closed the door behind her as she stepped out into the corridor. And stopped short with a grin.

Standing across from her were seven children, who wheeled around in curiosity when they heard her door close. With varying shades of blonde hair, the same smattering of freckles, there was no doubt they were related. All of them were boys, except for one. She was the tallest and, as Jane got a good look at her, most likely the eldest, perhaps about ten. Jane guessed the others ranged in age from around eight to four, and the girl held the hand of the littlest boy, who couldn't have been more than two. The suite door behind them was open. A rather dowdy, middle-aged woman was still inside, gathering up cardigans and jumpers, and what all else she needed to cart around seven little ones.

"Don't stare, children," the woman admonished. "Say hello to the nice lady."

Jane smiled as she was treated to an echo of greetings from them all, with the exception of the littlest, who, too young yet to follow instructions, continued to stare. She leaned down to him. "And who have we here, then?"

"His name's Hayden." The girl had answered for him. "He doesn't talk yet. He's too little."

"I see. And what about you? Have you got a name?"

"I'm Amy." The girl knew what Jane would ask next, so she expedited matters, pointing to each of the others in turn. "He's Timothy, and next to him is Gregory, then Nicholas, and then Clint and Andrew. Those two are identical twins."

"I can see that, yes." Jane was enjoying herself. "And how are you all related?"

It didn't sound exactly like a long-suffering sigh when she responded, but it was close. "They're my brothers."

Jane looked at her conspiratorially. "Don't like that much, do you?

"I don't mind most of the time." Her eyes were unwavering in their candor as they fixed on Jane. "But sometimes they get smelly."

One of the twins took exception to that viewpoint. "You're the smelly one, doofus-face."

"Clint, apologize to your sister." The woman had come out into the corridor now. Although she was loaded down with the gear she deemed necessary for taking seven young children on an outing, she appeared as unruffled as anyone who was planning a casual stroll on her own. "Unless you'd rather stay behind with your parents and baby Charles."

"They're not yours?" Jane had to ask. She was astounded by their number and charmed by the lot of them.

"No, ma'am, I'm their nanny."

Jane's eyes went wide. "Isn't it difficult managing so many?"

"Not at all, ma'am. The Youngs are delightful children." With a twinkle in her eye, she added, "And their parents are very generous." She turned to the twin whom she just admonished, and reminded him kindly, "I'm still waiting, Clinton Young."

"Why do I have to apologize, Miss? She started it. She said we were 'smelly.'"

"No, she said 'sometimes.' And we both know that's true, while it's certainly *not* true that she is a 'doofus face.' So if you want to come down with us to see the submarine, we'll need to hear that apology."

"*Fine*. Sorry."

The little boy didn't sound sincerely repentant, but the nanny knew to quit while she was ahead. She nodded to him. "Good man." Looking back at Jane she said, "We'll be on our way, then. Everyone say goodbye."

Jane heard the same chorus of voices she had at the start. Still smiling, she watched after them as they chattered and chirped their way down the corridor, bombarding the nanny with questions, which she answered with patient affection.

"Missy, why is there a Russian submarine in California?"

"Miss, how come we can't go to the Terror Fest? I'm not afraid."

"Missy, can't I please hold Hayden's hand now? Why does Amy always get to do it?"

Missy. You said you'd find my Missy Doll. I want my Missy Doll.

Jane had stopped smiling. She was unaware of anything except the connection establishing itself in her mind.

Oh, no. Oh, dear God.

She ran, jogging past the startled nanny and abundance of tow-headed children, across the corridor and down the stairs. *Miss. Missy. Missy Doll.*

So focused was she on where she was headed, she didn't even notice the tour group of smartly-dressed Italians just coming out of the "Diana: Legacy of a Princess" exhibition. As they bandied about commentary regarding the late duchess's clothing and jewelry with exuberant hand gestures and exclamations of rhapsody such as, "*Come è bella*!" "*Splendida*!" "*Meravigliosa*," they also didn't notice Jane, whose aim straight into their midst was unintentional.

"Oh, I'm so terribly sorry —" She was pink-faced with humiliation when she collided with one of them — a dapper, elderly gentleman.

"Well, who have we here, eh?" The gentleman in question got hold of her arm, and held fast with a grip that was surprisingly strong for someone who had to be eighty years old, at least. When he looked her up and down with a leer, her face went slack with astonishment. "Is this the beautiful English *principessa* comeback to life?"

With compressed lips, she looked down to where his arthritic fingers were now caressing her elbow. Lifting his hand away from her with exactitude, her reply was tart. "Either you need spectacles, or you've seriously overestimated the power of your charms. Now, if you will please excuse me."

Nose in the air, she brushed past him and hurried on, muttering to herself, "Rheumy old lech," and reached the lounge entrance to The Secret Spice. Running into the restaurant, she looked around anxiously. The Haunted Tea crowd had cleared out, and the dinner shift wait staff were resetting the tables. Sarita sat behind the bar, folding name cards for tomorrow's wedding reception.

"Sarita!"

Sarita looked up as Jane came trotting over. "Your history book — the one you showed me about the ship — have you got it?"

She nodded, bemused by Jane's urgency. "It's on the coffee table in the office. Why?"

Jane took her hand, and pulled her out from behind the bar. "I just need five minutes. Come with me."

"Her name was Dolores. That's what Jackie meant when she said, 'Missy Dol." She didn't want me to help her find her doll, she wanted me to help her find her *nanny*." Jane pointed to the photograph of Dolores Simpson. "And look there — the heels she's wearing in this photo are the same ones Jackie was dragging on her feet when she appeared in my cabin one day. I know they were. It had been nagging at me even then that I'd seen them somewhere before."

Sarita gnawed on her sore thumbnail again. "That makes sense, but maybe all it means is that she was looking for her nanny when she drowned and she's still…looking for her?"

Jane mulled that over, then shook her head. "I just don't think so. I've thought there was something off about this nanny story from the beginning."

"Well, maybe you can try calling her? Since she's appeared to you before, she might respond."

"Call her?" Jane quailed at the thought of what she experienced the last time she'd had a visitation from the little girl. But putting a bald face on it, it paled in comparison to the incident on Monday with Naag. To paraphrase Scarlett O'Hara, she'd shoved a dead man into a freezer, so she could surely do this.

"Call her. Yes." She picked up the history book and looked at Sarita. "May I borrow this for a bit?"

"Sure, go ahead."

"Thanks much. I'll see you later." The office door opened from the outside just as Jane got to it, and Cynthia stood behind it.

"Oh! There you are." Cynthia studied Jane's face. Something was up. "Is everything all right with you and Antoni?"

Out of the blue, Jane stood on her toes to peck Cynthia on the cheek, a gesture so out of character that Cynthia froze in disbelief. "All's well so far. Thanks for the time off, pet. That was really big of you." Then she hurried out, the same way she'd hurried in.

Sarita looked at her mother. "'Pet?' I thought you said you weren't her favorite person?"

"I'm just as kicked in the teeth by that as you are. Still, it was nice."

Bracing herself, Sarita told her, "Well, I've got another kick in the teeth for you. You won't like this one as much."

Jane closed her door quietly, slipped off her shoes, and tiptoed into the stateroom. Antoni was still snoring, something she hadn't missed about him at all, now that she thought about it. She set Sarita's book on the desk, and looked about the room.

How did one summon a ghost?

She stood at attention, cleared her throat, and closed her eyes. "Jackie," she murmured. And waited.

Nothing.

She opened the wardrobe, stuck her head in, and whispered Jackie's name a second time. Still no little specter appeared.

Inspiration struck. Dragging her desk chair over to the wall next to the door where the cabin steward call box hung, she stood up on it, her nose almost touching the speaker, as she whispered into it, "Jackie — can you hear me? I know what you were looking for now, darling. Please come visit again, and I'll help you find it. I promise I will."

"Jane, what are you doing?"

She squeaked and whirled around when Antoni's sleepy voice came from the bed. "You scared the devil out of me." When he said nothing, she began to feel silly. "I was just…looking for a ghost. I'm sorry I woke you."

He studied her carefully. "You've taken up some new hobbies in the past two years."

She stepped down off the chair. "I know it's hard to take in, but there are ghosts everywhere on this ship. Truly there are."

He ran his hand over his face and yawned. "Were you looking for one in particular?"

"A little girl."

That got his attention. "Does she have red hair?"

Jane gasped. "You've seen her? When?"

He was wide awake now, leaning on his elbow, marveling at the fact that he'd actually seen a ghost. "Just after you left. I heard you click the door shut, and I opened my eyes for a minute. She was standing at the foot of the bed, looking at me. I thought I was dreaming. I just turned over and went back to sleep."

"Oh, no. I can't believe I only just missed her." She clenched her hands together. "What shall I do to get her back?"

Antoni sat up. The question was out of his range of expertise. "I've no idea. But I suppose that if she pops in and out like this, she'll come back eventually. What do you want with her, anyway?"

Jane sighed, and picked up Sarita's book again. "Let's go down for supper, shall we? I've got a story to tell you that you won't believe."

He barked out a laugh. "I doubt that's possible anymore."

The Secret Spice was a harmony of sounds. Conversations buzzed, silverware clinked, and intermittently came the popping sound of another wine or champagne bottle being uncorked. Every table was full, and there were patrons having drinks at the bar as they waited to be seated. The white jackets of the wait staff seemed a blur as they whisked to and from the kitchen. Cristiano and Rohini, along with the extra line cooks, worked like dervishes to get the dinner orders out. Angela fretted that she was running low on desserts.

For the first time, walk-ins had to be turned away by Sarita, who was subbing as hostess for Cynthia. But even as she was kept busy with reservations, she couldn't help but glance worriedly now and again to where her mother sat, having dinner with Raul.

Jane was still off the clock. However, after she and Antoni finished their meal while she'd filled him in on the details of her association with Jaclyn Torin, she dropped by the kitchen to say hello, and was commandeered by Angela to help fill tart shells. Antoni thought he'd best keep out of everyone's way, so he stood outside on the restaurant deck in the din and clamor of the Terror Fest, and waited for Jane.

"Who's the fit bloke Cynthia's with?" Jane asked as she spooned lemon curd. "Am I doing this right? I don't want to muck it up."

Angela glanced over. "One more dollop that size should do it. Figure five for each tart. What man?"

"Take a look. You can see them from the doors."

"Wow. You're not kidding. What a cute guy. And look at that suit. I bet it's Italian." Angela peered through the small windows in the kitchen doors for so long, one of the waitresses had to tap her on the shoulder so she could get past with her tray.

"I want to see too." The urgency of their pace aside, Rohini dropped what she was doing to hurry over and stand on her tiptoes next to Angela to check out Raul. "Oh, my. He *is* handsome, isn't he?"

"Ah, excuse me over there, *Señora* de la Cueva — the Wellingtons need sauce and garnish. I believe that's your task. And didn't you just get married, by the way?"

Rohini barely flicked her new husband a glance. "I got married. I didn't go blind." She peeked out again. "What are they talking about? They seem so absorbed."

Jane switched from lemon curd to chocolate mousse. "I couldn't say. They're speaking in Portuguese."

When she left the kitchen, Jane saw that Cynthia was still deep in conversation with her companion. Her curiosity was piqued too. But she expected they'd hear all about him straight from the horse's mouth in the morning. As for now, these were the last few hours of her busman's holiday, and she was going to spend them with Antoni. She spied him leaning along the rail, looking out at the water, unfazed by the mob of partygoers.

She weaved through the throng and edged her way in next to him. "One would think that all these people would have something better to do than spend their Sunday evening running about in fancy dress and having the dickens scared out of them at a 'Terror Fest.' Who thinks up these things? What a gruesome celebration."

Antoni looked down at her and grinned. "Two words: 'Guy Fawkes.'"

She laughed. "Touché."

They turned their backs to the rail, leaning against it so they could comfortably people-watch for a while. Some of the attire was fantastic, Jane had to admit. There was everything from the grisly to the whimsical. She spied a Nosferatu who was so convincing, she got an actual chill down her spine. She chuckled when Antoni pointed out the elderly, overweight couple dressed as Kermit the Frog and Miss Piggy. At the sight of the teenager painted head to toe copper and wearing an inventive getup that mimicked the profile of Lincoln on a penny, she smiled and decided that it was fun, after all. And when she turned her head left to watch the penny go by, all the way at the other end of the deck toward the bow, she spied a ginger-haired little girl wearing a nightdress, staring directly across at her.

"Antoni." She tugged his sleeve to get his attention. "It's Jackie!"

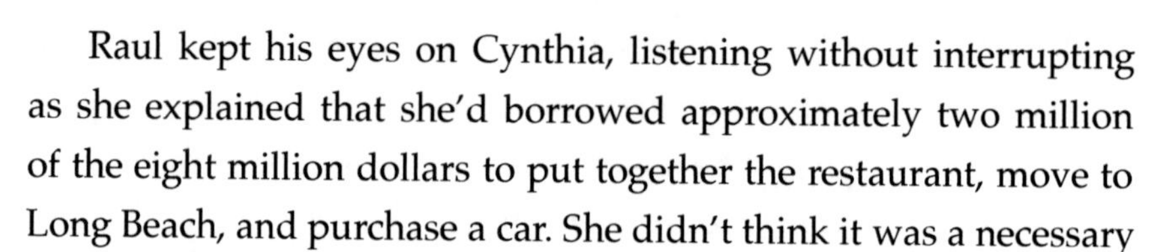

Raul kept his eyes on Cynthia, listening without interrupting as she explained that she'd borrowed approximately two million of the eight million dollars to put together the restaurant, move to Long Beach, and purchase a car. She didn't think it was a necessary detail to tell him that the car she'd bought was a Porsche.

She informed him that in the manila envelope she'd handed him, which he'd yet to open, were the bank details on the additional six million and the 25,658 dollars in accrued interest. She also didn't think it was a necessary detail to tell him that the 658 dollars of that 'interest' was all the money she and Sarita had in the world before his father's eight million was deposited into their account.

She went on to outline the payment schedule she had in mind for the two million, a schedule she assured him she could meet, based on the revenue The Secret Spice was already producing, and the loan agreements she had with her partners for fronting their share of capital. As a final point, she told him that if that payment schedule didn't suit him, he could, of course, take the restaurant, but naturally she hoped it wouldn't come to that.

After this valiant speech, she took a sip of wine. What she really wanted to do was chug the whole bottle.

Tapping the envelope against the edge of the table, Raul looked back at her steadily. When he finally spoke, his voice was soft, but even so, her heart jumped at the words. "I didn't come here so you could pay back my father's eight million dollars. Or to take over your restaurant. Is that what you thought?"

Panic squiggled in her belly and traveled up her chest into her throat. This was it. She was going to jail. She'd have to get a lawyer. She'd have to make arrangements for Sarita. Both their lives were ruined. The others would despise her for this. Oh, shit, shit, shit. She was going to collapse into a blubbering puddle on the floor, right here, right now. Even so, she strived to sound nonchalant. "I see."

He shook his head. "I don't think you do. My father wanted you to have that money. One million for every month he stayed with you."

Cynthia flushed. "I didn't expect payment for that. And it's understandable that as his son, you'd be upset that your father gave part of your inheritance to a stranger." She swallowed. "That's why, if you'll let me, I'd like the chance to pay it back."

"I don't want the money back. It's yours. It wasn't a payment for services rendered." He was affronted by the suggestion. "It was a gift." He placed the envelope back on the table between them. "I'm the one who transferred the money into your account in the first place."

"You?" Cynthia's brow knit. "But the paperwork had your father's name on it."

Raul gave her a short smile. "Sarita confused our two names this afternoon also. Check the papers again. The name on them is mine, not my father's."

Baffled, and still too suspicious of him to be relieved, she sat back in her chair. "Why would you do that?"

"Because my father asked me to. He wanted you and Sarita to have it, upon his death." He spoke with quiet gratitude. "You gave him eight very happy months. He loved you both."

Every muscle in Cynthia's body went rigid. Face taut, she held up her hand. "Just a moment, *Senhor*. There's something I want to make clear. There was nothing between your father and me in that way."

He looked at her, aghast. "Who said anything about that?"

"That's what you were implying —"

"No, *senhora*." He cut her off. "I implied no such thing. *You* assumed." Visibly offended, he leaned forward. "You saved my father's life. He would have died alone and nameless, if you hadn't happened along and had the courage to fight for him. Those hoodlums saw an easy target. They took everything he had on him while he was powerless to stop them."

His eyes heated to the color of dark honey, as he continued. "His only good fortune that night was that you were headed to your own car."

In a swift change of mood, his lip curved as his glance slid down to her leg. "I have to ask — do you still wear a Derringer strapped to your thigh?"

"Of course," she lied, without blinking an eye. Hah. Was he joking? This was California. They were lucky they were able to get the damn kitchen knives. "A woman on her own never knows when she might need it." She sent him a quelling look.

At that, he flung back his head and laughed, startling her. She was put completely off balance when his austere look softened into admiration. "Duly noted. Good for you."

Just that fast, he was over his annoyance with her. "You took a complete stranger into your own home that night, having no idea what kind of man he was."

"Oh, come on. I worked in the casinos, Raul. I could tell he wasn't a drunk. Before he fell, he was clean and well-dressed. He didn't smell of alcohol. Given his age, it was obvious the poor man had had some kind of a stroke, and those bastards took advantage of that." She shook her head as she thought back to how Raul Sr. had looked, lying there, unable to defend himself as they kicked at him, laughing, sneering. "Bastards," she repeated. "I regret I only shot at their kneecaps. It's too bad the one with his wallet got away. We could have located you much earlier."

Again Raul smiled, so tickled by her. "Instead you let him stay in your home, where you and your daughter tended to him as though he were family."

She lifted her hands, spread them. "Anyone would have done that. He was so lost and confused."

"No, not anyone. Not when money was as scarce for you as it was then. He was with you for eight months, and you never begrudged him a thing, having no idea when, if ever, he'd recover."

Cynthia fidgeted under his gaze. He was looking at her as though she were some kind of a hero. And there was an undercurrent of something else. "We knew it might take some time before his brain healed. The doctor told me it wasn't only the mini-stoke that caused the amnesia, it was the attack. That's why it took so long for him to regain his memory."

Now his eyes held chagrin. "Not exactly, I'm afraid." His lip twitched. "He lied to you. It took only two months, not eight. But he was so taken with you both, that he insisted he wanted to stay a while longer. He'd contacted me to let me know he was safe, but to you he pretended that he still didn't know who he was. After six months, I finally told him that if he didn't tell you the truth, I would tell you myself."

That surprised a genuine laugh out of her. "He didn't." She smiled as she thought back to those days. "Well, that's…charming. I'm pleased to know he enjoyed being with us as much as we enjoyed having him." Raul was basking in the first real smile Cynthia had given him since their conversation had begun. "Wait until I tell Sarita. That was four years ago, and she still talks about him." Her expression grew pensive again. "We were very sad when we heard he'd passed on."

"He had another stroke. This one was fatal, but at least it was quick. And he'd had a happy and interesting life." They both went silent, reflecting on that. Then he reached across the table and took her hand. "Now that you know this, surely you understand what you meant to him — what you mean to both of us — and why he left you the money."

She stiffened up immediately. "I do. And that's all the more reason not to take it." She moved her hand out from under his and slid the envelope back over to him. "I did something for your father and my reward was that we got to enjoy his company, that Sarita had a father figure in her life for the first time since she was a baby. That was the gift. Not this. I'm a grown woman, Raul. I don't believe in fairytales anymore."

"Fairytales?" He was genuinely perplexed.

"Yes." She gestured up and down at him, with a fleet and humorless smile. "The handsome Prince Charming comes to the rescue of a middle-aged woman and her teenage daughter. In the third act, no less. After I've been knocked on my ass for years, and met one rotten apple after another." She snorted. "Not likely."

He studied her curiously. "You're sneering at me. Why?"

"I'm not sneering. I'm being realistic. People with money use it to wield power." Another lesson she'd learned the hard way. "No one hands over eight million dollars without expecting something in return."

"I can well afford it." He was doing his best to hide his irritation, but it wasn't working. "Besides, you've already spent two million of it."

She colored at that. "I know that seems hypocritical." She hesitated, thinking about her indulgent choice of vehicle. "Fine. It *is* hypocritical. But the money was in the account and this opportunity came up. It's so much better for Sarita to be here in Long Beach, to have her mother be a restaurant owner, instead of a cocktail waitress."

He looked around. "You've done a wonderful job with it, and with your daughter." His gaze came back to her, direct, questioning. "You've put the money to good use. My father would be pleased and proud. So why not keep the rest?"

"*No*. Thank you."

He narrowed his eyes. "This isn't about me, is it?" He leaned back in his chair again, showing outward calm, when in actuality, he was more hurt than he was comfortable with. "This is about your father."

A chill danced over her skin. "What do you know about my father?"

"I know everything about you, Cynthia." He watched as wariness came over her face. "For all that you appear to think otherwise, I'm a good man. At least I try hard to be." Mouth set, his eyes were eagle sharp now. "But I'm not a stupid one. I had you investigated as soon as I got my father's call."

He crossed one leg over the other, as she digested this. "I was frantic about him. All our businesses came to a halt, as I spent two months searching for him. They found the hull of his car in downtown Las Vegas. Can you imagine how I felt?"

The look on his face changed again, making him appear surprisingly vulnerable. For the first time, Cynthia understood what his father had meant to him. She envied him that. "After I'd almost given up hope, I got a phone call from him." His voiced warmed and he chuckled at the memory. "One of the richest men in South America, calling his son collect. I didn't believe it was him, at first. He assured me he was well. Then he raved about you, told me he wanted to stay a while longer. I could hear in his voice how much he was enjoying playing father to the daughter he'd never had and grandfather to the grandchild I know he'd missed having when my wife left me for another man."

His smile was mocking when her eyebrows flew up in surprise, but it was himself he mocked. "Hard to believe, isn't it — that 'Prince Charming' doesn't always get to live happily ever after?"

He leaned across the table. "I hung up that phone, and within twenty-four hours, I knew everything there was to know about you. I wasn't going to leave my father with you until I did, Cintia Bianka de Azevedo Taylor."

He waited for her reaction. She appeared unruffled. Raul was impressed with her ability to pull that off. Only someone keenly observant would notice the tiny muscle on the side of her neck that had begun to tick at his use of her family surname.

Now his voice was as deceptively casual as her demeanor. "And here's what I learned: You were eighteen when you found out that what your father had told you he was doing to keep you and your mother in such luxury was entirely different from what he was actually doing. After you and he fought about that, you left home and haven't looked back since. You're to be commended for that and a great deal more, besides. Unfortunately, you then made a mistake. You married a fool who let both you and his lovely little daughter go. Neither one of these men, by the way, deserved you, nor have anything to do with the woman you've become."

Their noses almost touched now, as he leaned in further. "The men you've known disappointed you and squandered their lucky opportunity to have you in their lives. But allow me to tell you something you don't know, Cynthia — not every man would. Not every man is like your ex-husband, and not every rich man is like your father."

He stood up. The whole time he'd been speaking, he'd kept his voice low and even, but she could tell that inside, he was in turmoil. "I was so pleased when I got your letter. I moved heaven and earth to get here." He shook his head in disappointment. "But I guess *I'm* the real fool. I misunderstood that letter. And you. My father didn't tell me you were such a bitter woman."

When he looked down at her for the last time, she nearly winced at the disenchantment on his face. "I'm not taking the money back. Throw it in the ocean outside, if you're so offended by it." He picked up the manila envelope and ripped it in two.

"Goodbye, Cynthia." He turned and strode out.

Bemused and intrigued, Cynthia watched him go.

CHAPTER NINETEEN

Jane gripped her husband's elbow, dragging him along as she snaked her way down the crowded deck. They'd almost reached Jackie when she made an abrupt right turn behind the shops and restaurants that faced the port side of *Mary*'s Promenade Deck.

"I can't see her." Jane strained to look above and between the clusters of people.

Antoni was able to see over most of the mob. He unconsciously slipped into nautical terms. "She's there — starboard side of the bow. She's stopped to look back at us. Wait — now she's going astern. I think she wants us to follow her."

"Well, if that's her hope, she's not making it easy in this lairy lot." Jane had to shout to be heard over a group of werewolves who were howling with enthusiasm. One of them caught her off guard by leaping out in front of her with a roar. She made his night by screaming for all she was worth and then swearing at him.

Antoni had taken lead of the pursuit, holding onto Jane's hand as he kept eyes on Jackie, who was headed toward the stern of the ship. He stopped short. "Dammit."

"What's happened?" Jane craned her neck, frustrated by her inability to see.

"She went into one of the mazes."

Apart from live music, dance parties, and creatures springing out at thrill-seeking fright fans, the major draw of the Terror Fest was the assortment of mazes that had been set up. They had names like "Factory of Fears," "Decks of the Doomed," and "Corridors of Carnage." Those who'd paid to be spooked ventured through and were treated to special effects, dimmed lighting, and dubious performances by a cast of ghouls. For some reason, their ghostly little guide had led them to "Decks of the Doomed."

A red-eyed demon popped out at them near the entranceway, and addressed them in melodramatic tones. "Prepare to die, prepare to die-e-e-e-!"

This time Jane was unimpressed. She shouldered past him. "Sod off, you twit. I've seen you eating cheesecake in my restaurant every day this week."

They stepped into the standard issue haunted house with dark, narrow passageways, people popping up from coffins, and doomed prisoners rattling chains. Moans, screams and wicked laughter echoed off the walls as they passed through.

The maze forced them to veer left and then down a narrow set of stairs. They came to a larger room designed by someone with a grisly sense of humor. Suspended from the ceiling on invisible wire were dismembered body parts. Electronically operated knives hacked away at them merrily. In each corner of the room was an alcove in which a beastly carcass of some kind had been dangled on a butcher shop meat hook. In the far right corner, a little girl stood.

"She's there!" This time it was Jane who spotted her. But they were stymied when she turned and vanished straight through the solid wall behind her. "Blast. Now what do we do?"

Antoni walked over and examined the wall. It wasn't solid after all. He pushed at it until the back of the alcove gave way, revealing another passageway, possibly utilized as a hiding spot for cast members to leap out and do their work. They glanced behind them, but it appeared no one had noticed what they were up to, so they stepped through the opening, and closed it again behind them.

The noise from the maze ceased. The atmosphere inside was claustrophobic with quiet. Jane felt she could hear every beat of her heart and every breath, as if they were the only two sounds that existed. Although not as dim as it had been in the maze, the light had a peculiar quality, like the sky viewed from underwater. They stuck close to each other as they walked. Oddly, despite the silence, they couldn't hear their own footsteps. Jane couldn't place where they were, though it looked familiar. They kept walking, until they saw where Jackie had led them.

It was the old swimming pool.

Only yesterday the pool had been empty, no longer in use, save for being photographed by tourists intrigued by the notion that it was haunted by Jackie's spirit. Now, however, the pool was filled with water, sparkling and crystal clear. The area surrounding it — the aqua blue mosaics, the seafoam green sconces, the cream tile walls, the mother-of-pearl ceiling, and the white swan mural with its terracotta backdrop, all looked shiny-new and clean, ready to be enjoyed.

Jane tried to stay calm, to remember that this was only an apparition, that Jackie meant them no harm. Her husband was having more trouble implementing that attitude.

"My god. What the hell is this?"

"Antoni —"

"Shh." He was listening to something. "Do you hear that? That music?"

"I don't hear anything."

With a fixed expression on his face, he listened again. "I do. That's a swing band. Did you hear any swing bands playing at the Terror Fest?"

"Good lord, no. Just that awful thumping disco and some screamingly bad rock."

He took her hand, pulled her toward the pool exit door and pushed it open. "Stay close to me."

She heard the swing band then too, distinctly. Wherever they were playing, it had to be in one of the nearby ballrooms.

"Hang on — where's the souvenir shop?" She stopped dead and swiveled, trying to get her bearings. "It's supposed to be right there. And that's the entry that leads to our restaurant, but... where's our sign?"

Something about the way Antoni looked at her made her heart jump. "You haven't figured it out yet, have you? The sign isn't there, because the restaurant doesn't exist. *We* don't exist. We're on the same ship, Jane, but not in the same year. Look at the people."

He gestured toward the lounge, where the men were all wearing suits and ties, and the women were in dresses or skirts. A number of both sexes were wearing hats. Apart from that, some were smoking, a recreation no longer permitted on the modern-day *Mary.*

"Bloody hell."

"My sentiments exactly. And I'll bet if we go outside, we're going to see nothing around us but open water. Can you feel that slight movement beneath your feet? This ship is moving, Jane. I'm going to guess it's 1949, very likely the night Jackie drowned. So I hope we find your little friend soon, because frankly, I'd like to get the hell out of here as soon as possible."

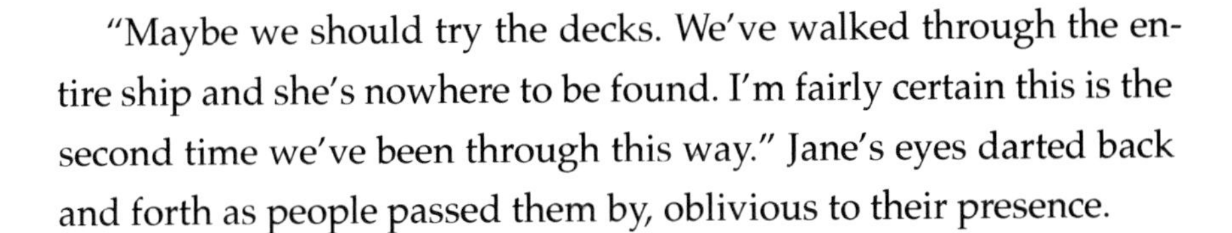

"Maybe we should try the decks. We've walked through the entire ship and she's nowhere to be found. I'm fairly certain this is the second time we've been through this way." Jane's eyes darted back and forth as people passed them by, oblivious to their presence.

"I did that purposely." Antoni stopped to survey the corridor. "If my guess is correct, this is the hall where your stateroom would be."

He pointed to the fourth one on the right. "Which means that Jackie and her nanny are probably in there, right now."

Jane looked intently at the closed cabin door. "It is, isn't it? Well spotted. But we certainly can't go in, introduce ourselves to Dolores, and ask her if she's planning to dash off with a man."

He sat on the corridor floor. "No, but we can wait to see if she comes out. If she does, we follow her."

"What if she doesn't?"

"Do you have a better idea?"

Jane settled down next to him, wrapping her arms around her knees. "No, I haven't." This latest encounter with the paranormal was going on far too long for her liking. What if they were stuck here? She did her best to quash her growing unease. "Well. This is what being a ghost feels like, I'd imagine. How long do you suppose we'll have to sit here?"

They heard a click, and the cabin door opened.

"Not long." Antoni whispered, even though he was certain he couldn't be heard.

Dolores Simpson stepped out.

"Oh." Jane was also whispering. "This is uncanny. She looks just as she did in that photo. She's even got on the same clothing."

A childish voice came from inside the cabin. Jane felt a lump in her throat when she realized she was hearing Jackie on the last night of her life.

"You promise you'll fetch her, Missy?"

Dolores poked her head back into the room and smiled. "Aye, I'll nip out and be back in a jiffy. But remember — you gave your word that you won't leave this room while I'm gone, there's a good lass."

Antoni murmured to Jane. "Her accent. She sounds a little like you."

Closing the door softly, Dolores moved off down the hall. Jane and Antoni got up to follow. They found themselves right back where they'd started when her first stop was the swimming pool. She glanced under the lounge chairs and behind the steps.

"What's she doing?"

"Looking for something, apparently."

Whatever it was, it wasn't in the pool area, and rather than exit by the main entrance the way she came, Dolores left by the side door which led out to the sports deck, securing the door stop to keep it open. When they followed, Jane was taken aback to see that the *Mary* was actually floating in the ocean. When the ship's horn sounded, she looked at Antoni in a daze. "I can't take it in. It's mind-boggling. We're passengers on *The Queen Mary* — the *Mary* she was."

"I told you. Look at the moon, Jane. It's barely visible. The one we left was three-quarters full. See there — those faint lights?" He pointed out into the distance over the water. "That's the port we're headed for. My estimation is we'll be there by early morning."

The threat of the situation broke through Jane's reverie. "Do you suppose we'll be sent back before then?"

Antoni tried his best to hide his growing alarm. "I was hoping you'd know the answer to that. This is my first experience with this sort of thing."

The music coming from the ballroom was more distinct out here than from the pool area. The sounds floated across the water, *"Some enchanted evening, you may meet a stranger…"*

Dolores walked toward the stern, stopping intermittently to peer under lounge chairs. They heard her soft exclamation when she found what she was looking for. "There you are."

"It's Jackie's doll. The one that's in the museum now. Oh, how sad." Jane leaned against Antoni, as they watched the nanny walk forward to retrieve it.

The *Mary*'s whistle blew again. Oliver Jenkins sprang from nowhere. Jane and Antoni jumped and cried out as he caught Dolores in a chokehold.

"He's killing her! We have to stop him!" It was a kneejerk reaction. Even as she shouted it, Jane knew it was impossible. All the same, she lunged for Oliver.

Antoni pulled her back. "There's nothing we can do. You know that."

She buried her face in his chest. "I can't watch this, Antoni. I can't!"

"I know, I know. But as sickening as it is, I think that's why we were brought here. We're witnesses, Jane. The only witnesses to what really happened that night."

They watched it all, powerless to stop any of it — her piteous struggle, his brutal, vicious strength, her heartbreaking, final acceptance, and his twisted triumph. The only sounds throughout were of Dolores's shoe striking the deck, the hammering of their own hearts, and the background music of Richard Rodgers. Jane knew she'd never be able to hear that song again. It would always dredge up how Jenkins looked as he spoke to the dead girl in his arms:

"Now you know. Nobody walks away from me."

When he callously pitched Dolores's body into the sea, Antoni thought he might boot. Then he wondered if that were even possible in his current state of disembodiment. He hoped not.

"Oh, it's horrible, horrible, horrible." Jane buried her face in his chest and Antoni pressed her to him, drawing as much strength from her nearness as she did from his.

Then Jane felt his body go tense. "Look what he's doing."

She forced herself to peek back over at Oliver. "Her shoe! He's stuffing her shoe into that…that whatchamacallit."

"The vent unit. Yeah."

Eyes wide with comprehension and hope, she looked up at Antoni. "Do you suppose it's still in there? That we can find it? I don't mean now. I mean —"

"I know what you mean. I'd say it's a good possibility." He scrutinized the vent and its location. "If we can get back, we'll look for it. At least then, the poor woman might be vindicated." His expression was cynical and sad as he looked back at his anguished wife. "Better late than never, I guess."

Oliver Jenkins stepped out from behind the stairwell, looking both portside and starboard before he turned and walked toward the bow. With loathing in her eyes, Jane spat at his retreating back. "You bleeding bastard! I hope you had a short, horrible life, and are rotting in the bowels of hell."

When Jenkins stopped in his tracks, Jane jumped back. "Oh, migod — he couldn't have heard me, could he?"

Next to her, Antoni sucked in a breath at something he'd seen that Jane hadn't. "No. He stopped for another reason." Blocking her view, he stepped in front of her and put his hands on her shoulders. "Jane, listen to me. The reason we're still here is because this isn't over yet." His eyes stayed on hers, his breathing uneven. "There's more. And it's going to be a hell of a lot worse."

"What do you mean?" She stepped sideways, so she could see past him to where Oliver still stood, and felt all the blood leach from her face. "Oh, no." She shook her head in denial of what she saw. "Please, no."

Jackie was crouched behind one of the deck chairs. Jenkins had spotted her and was looking down at her coldly, weighing his options, trying to decide how much she'd seen, and what he should do about it. She stared back up at him, white-faced and terrified, a tiny, trembling cottontail trapped in the mesmerizing gaze of a snake. Both of them remained perfectly still. To Jane, it was an image captured in time, a photograph in her mind she'd carry with her everywhere, for as long as she lived.

In a flash, the image changed, when Jackie darted out from behind the chair and ran.

Jenkins nearly snatched her as she bolted past, but she managed to zigzag out of his reach. Side by side, Jane and Antoni ran, tailing Jenkins as he went after her. The little girl dashed through the side entrance to the pool and Jenkins followed, releasing the door stop and closing the door behind him.

Antoni skidded to a stop and swung his arm out in front of Jane to halt her. "Wait, Jane." Once again, he blocked her way. "Don't go in there."

Jane was crying again, the night air making the tear tracks cold on her face. "Let me be, Antoni. I have to know what happened to her." She tried to move past him, but he put his hands on her shoulders and held tight.

"You do know, Jane. You *know*. We both do." The look on his face was familiar. She'd seen it, two years before. "Don't do it. Please don't go in."

"I have to," she whispered.

She pulled away and pushed past him, ran to the entrance and stopped, hesitated. When she opened the door and stepped through, Antoni squeezed his eyes shut for a moment, and then ran after her.

The door banged shut behind him.

Not long after, as the haze of the distant shoreline loomed, a night watchman walked by. Up ahead, under some flickering lights, he spied a Raggedy Ann doll.

After having borne witness to what had truly become of a little girl who hadn't kept her promise to wait for her nanny to return with her beloved doll, they'd closed their eyes in anguish. When they opened them, the movement of the ship had stilled. The swing music had faded away, to be replaced by the wild sounds coming from the Halloween Terror Fest. The empty, rusted swimming pool was their backdrop as they clung to one another.

Jane was sobbing. "She was running from him and she fell in. He just stood there and watched her drown."

Antoni's own eyes were wet as he held her to him tightly, stroking her hair. There was nothing he could say. She pulled back to look up at him.

"*Why*? Why would he do that? She was so young. She had no idea who he was. Even if she'd seen everything, he was leaving the ship the next morning. He could have gotten away without harming her."

"I don't know." Pity rolled through him for Jane, for Jackie. "I can only guess that if he killed Dolores in retaliation for her leaving him, then he also wanted everything she loved destroyed."

Jane hadn't loosened her hold on him as he spoke, nor taken her eyes off his face. He looked bleary with fatigue and emotion. Everything that had happened since his return had to be devastating for him. And yet here he was, holding her, comforting her. Without thinking, she let the words come.

"I was cruel to you two years ago. I blamed you when you weren't to blame." Her voice was strained with regret. "I never should have said the things I said." More tears fell as she lay herself bare. "I never should have sent you away."

His heart, already breaking, split in two. With shaking hands he cupped her face between his palms. "I never should have let you. You were grieving, in so much pain. I never should have left, no matter what you'd said. I never should have stayed away so long." Though he tried so hard to prevent it, his eyes filled and overflowed. "I missed you every day. I missed you so much, Jane. And I missed Gabriella."

The revelers in the "Decks of the Doomed" who'd found their way to the old swimming pool hardly gave them a glance as they held each other and cried. They cried for Jackie, they cried for Dolores. They cried for Gabriella and themselves; together, as they should have, two years before.

CHAPTER TWENTY

Monday, November 1, 2004

Angela's Day of the Dead wedding cake was a marvel. After her paranormal experiences, she'd put away the recipe books, along with all her other notions of how things "should" be, and allowed her repressed creativity to flow. The result was a cake that was unique and inventive.

It was traditional in that it was four tiers of graduated size, but it was covered by a chocolate fondant so rich and dark that it looked almost black. On this background she'd piped a Mexican folk art design of flowers, birds, and leaves, using royal icing in bright red, turquoise, lime green, and sunny yellow. She'd made marzipan roses in a deeper, richer red that she arranged at the top of the cake and around the edges of the bottom layers. That same marzipan was used to make red ribbon borders for the bottom of each tier. Deep pink hearts and yellow skulls, both made of hardened sugar and decorated with the traditional Day of the Dead flourishes piped in black, white, and turquoise, were attached on the sides of each layer.

Sarita uploaded a photo of it to their new Secret Spice Café website. For days after she posted it the phone rang off the hook with requests from other brides. Eric Gladwell phoned Angela personally to congratulate her when he spotted it there.

Inez was in raptures over it. She stopped by the kitchen with Marisol on the morning of her wedding day. She and Michael had taken two suites on the ship — one for themselves and one for Marisol and Inez's mother — so they could take their time getting ready for their afternoon wedding and evening reception. Now she held Marisol in her arms so the child could get a better look at the cake that sat on a wheeled serving table which was strewn with marigolds.

"Oh, Angela, it's glorious. I just love it."

"I'm so glad."

Inez's attention had been solely focused on it, but when she took a good look at Angela, she blinked. "*Ay, que linda!* You look just as pretty as the cake."

"You didn't think I'd show up at your wedding reception looking like a frump, did you?" A sassy haircut and makeover had taken about ten years off Angela's face. The new magenta dress she had on under her apron complimented her slim figure and dark Italian features. Her eyes danced as Inez admired her new look. The bride was making her day with all this appreciation. She hoped she could return the favor.

"I made these too, as a small gift." Slanting a look at Marisol, Angela saw her rapt face as she pulled out the tray of matching cupcakes. Winking at Inez, she looked at the little girl. "What do you think? Are cupcakes a good idea for Mommy and Daddy's party?"

Marisol flashed that dimple of hers and nodded. But she was studying Angela warily. She hadn't told anyone what she'd witnessed before Angela's fall, nor would she have been able to describe it if she tried. She still thought of it sometimes, still had the occasional nightmare which she also couldn't explain, when she woke up crying, and her mother or Michael came in to soothe her. But Angela's lighthearted attitude today was doing much to reassure the little girl that whatever had happened to her, the harm hadn't lasted.

As for Angela, she wasn't done with her plan to delight Marisol. After all, the kid had saved her from a fall that could've broken her neck. "I just need to top them with the little sugar skulls and hearts I made for them. I wonder if you might be able to help me with that?"

"Me?" Swept with reverence at the invitation, Marisol held her hands out for Angela to see. "My hands are small. I don't know if I can do it, *Señora* Angela."

But she looked as though she'd love to try. "Hmm. Your hands look just the right size to me. What do you say? Should we give Mommy some time to get ready for her party, and you stay here to help me?"

Stay in the kitchen — her favorite place on the ship next to Michael's shop — and help the cake lady make cupcakes. By herself. Angela had always been a person of significance to Marisol, even more so after the incident on the deck, but in that instant, she became her idol.

Seeing the reaction, Angela thought, You couldn't pay enough money to get a kid to look at you that way. "Let's get you an apron, honey."

Detective Betty Montalbano of the L.B.P.D. had been one of the first on scene when Angela had called in their discovery of Lee's body. Now, as she peered into the vent unit Antoni and Jane had directed her to, the morning sun bounced off her copper-colored hair. Using a pair of tongs, she pulled out Dolores's shoe.

"Very interesting." Placing the shoe in an evidence bag, she turned to Jane. "So, let me guess — you found this when you were looking for an earring."

Jane responded to that sarcasm head on. "Actually, no," she snapped. "It was a ghost who showed us where to look."

Antoni cast his eyes to the heavens. Here we go. "Jane —"

"Well, she was being cheeky, Antoni. I hardly think that's necessary."

Betty hid her amused smirk. The woman sure got her nose out of joint pretty quick. "I'd believe that version of events more readily than the other explanation, Mrs. Miceli. I'm a Long Beach native." She shook her head. "The things I've had people tell me about this ship." She looked at them. "If even half of them are true, it changes your whole perspective on life, you know?"

Perhaps this detective wasn't so bad after all, Jane thought.

Montalbano cemented that opinion when she told them, "I'm on your side about this. This case is a big deal around here because of the *Mary*. I even did a paper on it when I was at the Academy. I always thought they'd been too hasty in blaming the nanny."

Jane was listening intently. "What's your theory, then?"

"I think the cruise line was afraid they'd be held responsible for the little girl's death." She put the tongs back in her case as she spoke. "That swimming pool was unsafe. Why wasn't the door kept locked after hours? Jaclyn Torin's parents were high profile, first class passengers. The drowning was doubly tragic because she was a child. Accusing the nanny of taking off with a lover took the public's attention away from the accident itself." She looked back up at them. "But to me, it just never added up. Why would she leave without any of her possessions?"

"Quite the coincidence you having written a paper on this, and then being the one to show up here today." Jane gestured to the evidence bag.

The detective smiled tightly. "I don't think anything that happens involving the *Mary* is simple coincidence."

Antoni had been listening to Betty thoughtfully. "If you did a paper on the case, you had access to the evidence."

"That's right."

"Do you remember what possessions they took from Dolores's cabin?"

Montalbano smiled grimly. "I sure do. There weren't many. She was a nanny. She probably didn't own very much or bring more than she needed, since for her it was a working voyage. Two skirts, two tops, two sets of undergarments and stockings, the Agatha Christie novel she'd been reading, her suitcase and toiletries, her wallet, and her handbag."

"She left her wallet and handbag? And that didn't make them suspicious?" Antoni looked at her in disbelief. "Boy, was this case a screw up."

"Tell me about it." The detective grinned. "I got an 'A' on the paper, at least."

"Hang on." Jane interrupted their exchange. "If she left everything behind, why are there no shoes?" She looked back and forth between them. "Even if we assume she had more than one pair, why would she take her extra shoes with her when she left, but nothing else?"

"Bingo." Betty nodded at her with approval. Holding up the evidence bag, she waved it. "Here's the proof that the much maligned Dolores Simpson didn't leave the ship wearing both of them. This will be fingerprinted right away. You've turned this into a cold-case murder investigation, instead of a hunt for a missing person. You'd make a damn good detective, Mrs. Miceli." With somber-faced sincerity, she added, "This is the sort of discovery that makes my job so gratifying. To me, a death like this has long term effects. Sometimes in ways we can't even begin to imagine. I suppose it seems like a waste of time to think like that, to worry about a woman who lived so long ago."

Jane squeezed the detective's free hand. "It doesn't." She looked at Antoni. "Not to us, anyway."

Marisol was engrossed in decorating cupcakes. Angela was impressed by her concentration. They were on their second tray of twenty-four, when one of the waitresses setting up the reception swung open the kitchen doors, and popped her head in.

"Angela, there's a man out here to see you. I told him to wait at the bar."

Angela nodded her thanks. *Please let it be Vincenzo.*

Catching the look on her face, Rohini knew at once what Angela was hoping for, and prayed she wouldn't be disappointed. "Go. I can stay with Marisol. I'm caught up here for the moment."

"Thanks, Ro." Angela took off her apron, fluffed up her hair, and with a deep breath, stepped out into the dining room.

Her heart immediately sank. It wasn't her son sitting at the bar, but a man she didn't recognize. Until he looked up and her knees nearly buckled.

Lee.

The man looking at her was Lee. Older, grayer, but the same face, the same unforgettable eyes.

"Angela Perotta?"

Even the drawl in his voice was the same. "Yes. I'm Angela."

He stood up and walked to her, his hand extended. "I'm Jack Branson."

Briefly, Angela closed her eyes. Of course. This was his son. She took his hand. "Nice to meet you, Mr. Branson."

"Nice to meet you too. I hope I didn't come at a bad time. In your letter, you said Mondays were best since the café is closed." He tipped his head to where tables were being moved and the dais set up. "But it looks like you're getting ready for a party."

"Yes. There's a wedding reception later this evening."

"I see." He looked at her quizzically. "Are you all right, Ms. Perotta?"

"Of course," she said brightly. "Why do you ask?"

"You're staring at me very strangely, and you haven't let go of my hand."

"Oh! I'm so sorry." She released him as though she'd been burned. "It's just…you look so much like your father."

"So I've been told. You said you have his diary."

"That's right. I didn't want to risk sending it through the mail. God forbid if it got lost or damaged."

"I appreciate your concern for it." He smiled, and once again she was thrown by the remarkable resemblance between father and son. "That diary will mean a lot to my mother." Her whole face brightened at that, and he was startled by how pretty she suddenly looked.

"She's alive? Oh, that's wonderful. She must be so happy that your father's been exonerated."

He nodded. "She is. But she never once believed he'd deserted. She knew he was innocent. She told me that the Lee Branson she knew would always do —"

"— the right thing." She smiled and felt her eyes grow moist. "Of course. Of course she would know that, wouldn't she, if she was his wife, and understood him at all?"

She glanced over her shoulder and looked out the side window. He followed her gaze and saw nothing but an empty upper deck. Observing her reactions, Jack couldn't help but wonder if perhaps she wasn't a touch…off. But that didn't seem to be it, exactly.

"Ms. Perotta, by any strange chance —" He stopped himself. He was crazy for what he was thinking. But something made him blurt it out, anyway. "It's not possible that you knew my father, is it?" It was a preposterous thing to ask, but the moment he did, he knew he was right.

Impulsively, Angela took both his hands this time, squeezed them. "Mr. Branson, I know you'll think I'm out of my mind, but," she swallowed over the lump that had formed in her throat, "there's a lot I'd like to tell you. Unfortunately, I have to get back to my station soon because of this wedding tonight. Is there any chance you can stay, so we can talk later?" She glanced around the dining room. "Did you bring anyone with you? Your wife, maybe? You can both stay. There's a table reserved just for those of us on staff here. There's plenty of room for two more. The food will be terrific, I can promise you that. And I made the cake."

All of a sudden, he couldn't take his eyes off of her. "I'm here alone. I'm a widower."

"Oh, I'm so sorry. I know how hard that is. I lost my husband too."

Once again, she was holding onto his hands for far too long. This time he didn't mind it as much.

"Oh. My. God. Ma? Is that *you*?"

Jack watched Angela's eyes go wide as saucers at the voice. She released his hands and spun around to face two smiling young men. Then she let out a shriek that nearly sent him through the roof.

"Vincenzo!" With a laugh of wild joy, she sprinted across the restaurant to throw her arms around one of the young men, who grinned and hugged her right back. Even without the shout out, anyone would have guessed they were mother and son. Their dark eyes and thick lashes were identical. When she pulled the boy's face down to hers to kiss his cheeks again and again, all Jack could think was, *Wow*.

"Oh, Vincenzo, it's wonderful to see you!"

"It's great to see you too. You look fantastic. What the hell have you done to yourself?"

She waved a hand airily. "Oh, you know — makeup, some hair dye. No biggie."

Vincenzo gaped at her. "'No biggie?' What happened to Saint Angela?"

"She's dead and buried, kiddo. And good riddance. I couldn't stand her anymore." Her son chuckled, and then she turned her attention to the light-haired young man standing next to him. "And you must be Douglas."

"Douglas Rigby. Nice to meet you." When he held out his hand, Angela folded it between hers. From where Jack was watching, he could tell that Douglas wasn't getting his hand back any time soon, either.

Angela had to blink back tears. "Douglas. Thank you so much for coming."

He smiled at her warmly. "You invited me personally. How could I turn down such a thoughtful gesture?"

"Oh, my God, I hope I don't cry and smear all this stuff on my eyes." Angela sniffed. "Come on. Let me introduce you around."

"Let us get settled into our room first, and then we'll be back in."

"Okay. I'll just get Jack over there sorted out too, and then I'll be in the kitchen." Angela's eyes shone. "Wait until you see the cake I made. It's on the internet and everything."

Douglas observed her quizzically as she walked over to speak with Jack again. "Is that the same woman you've been telling me about for the last two years?"

Vincenzo shook his head in wonder. "Not at all."

Everyone had a grand time at the reception. There was simply no way not to, not with a bride and groom resplendent with love and thrilled to have their friends and family celebrating that love with them.

For his friends' wedding, Cristiano put even more heart than usual into his work, and the traditional Mexican dishes, done up with his distinctive flair, were unparalleled. Undeterred by Cynthia's theories, Michael insisted that his favorite, Shrimp Rohini, be on the menu also, teasing her with the comment, "Hey, doll, if it makes other people at my wedding fall in love like I did, I'm all for it."

The attention Angela got for her cake made her feel like a celebrity. Vincenzo was busting at the seams with pride in her, and Jack debated with himself forever whether or not she'd dance with him, before gathering the nerve to ask. Michael and Inez started everyone off with the dancing, of course, and then where Inez would have danced with her father, since he was only able to attend in spirit, Michael danced with Marisol. In between making sure all ran smoothly, everyone on the team made time to get up at least once. Cristiano did a first-rate tango with Rohini. Cynthia and Michael did a sexy cha-cha. Angela danced with Douglas, and Jane with Vincenzo.

Antoni was just happy to be dancing with his wife again. It had been far too long since they'd done something carefree and fun.

He smiled down at her as she snagged two marigolds from the cake display, put one in her hair and one in her husband's lapel. "You look beautiful. You *are* beautiful."

"Rubbish. I'm a wrinkled old prune. Let's be honest."

Antoni sighed. "I give you a compliment and you accuse me of dishonesty. I happen to prefer a woman with a few wrinkles. It means she's…" he grinned, "seaworthy."

Jane stuck her tongue in her cheek. "Is that so? That's what you were doing then, when you were gawking at the bride's bosom — thinking it needed more wrinkles?"

"Will you please keep your voice down?" He was appalled. "For christssakes, Jane — she's got dozens of male relatives here. What if one of them heard you? I was not gawking —" When he realized she was shaking with laughter, he made a sound of exasperation. "You're impossible. You really are."

"And you love it." After a moment, she asked, "So, where have you got the boat docked?"

"I was lucky. I got a slip right down next to the *Mary*. Got permission from the guard because of the wedding."

"Mmm. I haven't been on it in a while. I'd love to see it again."

"Maybe we can take her out tomorrow." But he missed one of the dance steps when she gave him The Look. "You mean...you want to go now?"

She kept her eyes on him and wiggled her brows playfully.

He looked around him. "Won't they wonder where we are?"

She leaned into him to nip the bottom of his chin. "We can be back before they even notice."

"I like the way you think."

Sarita came down a while later. She'd had some homework she'd deemed too critical to be left until after the party. Apart from that, she wanted to have the advantage of showing up late, wearing the damn dress she'd wanted to wear at the opening.

She spotted her mother standing at the edge of the room next to Angela and Rohini. The three of them were discussing what would be a good time to start cake service, when Sarita made her entrance. Cynthia's gaze zeroed in on her and her attire instantly.

"Lock and load," Sarita murmured to herself. Taking one deep breath, she sauntered over. "Hi, everyone." She kept her tone casual. "How's it going down here so far?"

Without speaking, Cynthia arched a brow and looked her up and down. In response, Sarita did the same. Profile to profile, they looked like bookends with their twin expressions. Rohini and Angela exchanged 'uh-oh' looks and stepped back.

Cynthia smirked. Her daughter had guts. It made her proud. "Where did you get that dress?"

Sarita put her hand on her hip. "I got it online. Do you like it?" Then she grinned.

Cynthia burst out laughing. "As a matter of fact, I do." With love softening her face, she added, "And you look beautiful in it."

"Thanks, *Mãe*." Sarita gave her a quick squeeze.

They stood arm in arm, surveying the room until Sarita tensed. "Oh, boy," she murmured. "That's Emilio over there. Did you know he was coming?"

"No, but I know he and Inez are family friends." Cynthia spoke *sotto voce*. "He's looking this way, *filha*."

Sarita smiled and waved. Then she sighed. "I should go say hello, I guess."

"Good for you. Classy move."

As Sarita walked toward Emilio, Angela and Rohini rejoined Cynthia, both wearing bemused smiles.

Nudging Rohini, Angela teased, "Cynthia, did I enter another dimension when I fell on my head? When did you start treating Sarita like she's older than five?"

"Yes, that's a new development, definitely," Rohini chimed in.

Cynthia gave them both a look. "When I realized she has more common sense than all four of us put together, that's when."

That answer shut them up at once, because it was too true. They gazed over to where the young woman under discussion was now chatting with the young man who was still so noticeably captivated by her.

"Look how he looks at her." Cynthia snatched a flute of champagne from the tray of a passing waiter. "It's pathetic."

Rohini breathed a sigh. "First love can be such a nuisance, can't it?"

"It was for me, that's for sure," Angela affirmed.

Cynthia grunted as she sipped. "Join the club." Behind Sarita and Emilio, through the glass entryway of the restaurant, her attention snapped to the tall man holding a suitcase and striding toward the main exit. "Excuse me, ladies, will you?" She set her glass down and hurried after him as quickly as her Blahniks would allow.

Angela shook her head as she watched Cynthia go. "She'll break an ankle one of these days, honest to God."

"Raul, wait." Cynthia called to him just as he'd reached the gangway to disembark.

Hearing her, he stopped and turned. His face was impassive as he watched her walk toward him.

"I owe you an apology. I shouldn't have said those things I said. You were right — they did make me sound like an embittered old witch."

She stopped to ease the tightness in her throat. Admitting she'd made a mistake was not something she did well, but when she saw he was listening, that he wasn't about to stomp off, she managed to continue. "I wanted you to know that in the short time I knew him, I loved your father. I saw from the first that he was a good man. Just as you say, whether he was rich or poor, he was…so good."

His eyes softened at that, she thought, so she went on. "It's silly, but while he was with us, I pretended to myself that he was my father, the father I never had." She gave an uncomfortable shrug, never one to relish bearing her soul. "That's why, when that money came and I thought it was from him, I could only imagine what people would think. What *you* would think." She held her hands out, palm up. "I didn't know you, you see. I expected the worst. ...I guess I have a biased view of wealthy men."

His mouth quirked. "You think?"

With a shaky laugh, she brushed back her hair. *God*. She hated this, hated feeling so exposed. "Anyway, I didn't want to leave things between us the way they were yesterday, so I hope we can be friends." She held out her hand.

"No."

She whipped her hand back. "We can't be friends?"

He put down his case. "Absolutely not." He cut off her sputters by leaning into her as he had during their dinner. "Let me tell you why. I've wondered about you, wondered what you might be like in person, on and off since my father told me about you. Naturally, I thought of you again when he died and I deposited your money. Then your letter came, and I said to myself, 'Why not go and find out, Raul?'"

His eyes smoldered with his feelings for her now. "I rearranged my schedule, flew for more than eleven hours, and when I got here, what did I discover? That you are just as...as...*perfect* as I'd hoped you would be. So, no, Cynthia Taylor, we cannot be friends."

With that, he picked up his case again and continued his walk across the gangway to the dock.

She stayed where she was, shaking her head with amazement. You would think a man of his age, of his position, would know better.

'Perfect?' There was nothing perfect about her. She was bossy, stubborn, and impetuous. She had a wicked temper. She was past her prime. From running around serving drinks in high heels, she had veins on her legs that made them look like a map of the New

York City subway system. In the war against gravity, her face and her boobs were losing. With all his money and connections, why wasn't he going after a fashion model, a starlet even, or a sweet young breeder who could give him lots of heirs? *Santa Maria* — first Cristiano, then Emilio, then Michael, and now Raul. What was wrong with the men on this ship that they all carried on like doleful-eyed puppies scrambling for affection...and milk? At least Emilio had the justification that he was only seventeen.

And yet, as her eyes followed Raul, she could feel her herself opening, relenting. Finally, she thought, *Oh, what the hell*. He was cute, he was smart, he was gainfully employed, he wasn't married, and for some reason, he was interested in her. Even if he didn't turn out to be the man he appeared to be, they could at least have some fun. She deserved a little fun.

"*Olá*, Raul!" she called.

He turned a second time, arched a brow.

"Why don't you come back in and enjoy the party with us? Come in and...have some cake." She angled her head toward her restaurant, and sent him a smile.

Raul simply squinted at her, as he felt something move in him that he hadn't felt in a long while. Something that shouldn't be there yet. That smile was already more than just captivating to him. He was afraid that, one day, he just might live or die on that smile. Whereas her heart, he knew, was solely with her daughter and her restaurant. At least, that's where she stood at the moment. Did he have the courage he needed with a woman like Cynthia, to try and change that?

Scents from the kitchen wafted out over to him on the breeze. Without a doubt, they were enticing.

He took a deep breath. Well, he was a businessman, after all. He should be up for the challenge. He smiled back at her, and just like her daughter, Cynthia couldn't decide what that smile meant.

They'd both find out.

She turned, and he followed her, back into The Secret Spice Café.

Emilio's heart wrenched in his chest. Sarita had been his unfinished business. If he hadn't had the courage to use Michael and Inez's wedding invitation as his excuse to come back and see her, he'd have always wondered. Now he could tell himself that at least he'd taken the shot, even if it had been a wide miss.

She wasn't in love with him. It was as simple as that. She was gracious, somewhat shy, due to their last encounter, most likely, and there was nothing else. As much as that hurt, he didn't blame her or himself. One of the things he loved about her was that even though she was so young, she wasn't a game player. She could have all the guys around her falling for her like dominoes, but she wouldn't do that. Not his Sarita. Correction — not Sarita.

Time to cut her a break and go quietly. He just wasn't the one for her. Since he wasn't the martyr type, he wouldn't settle for being a hand-me-down choice. He'd either be the preferred pick for the woman he loved, or nothing.

"So listen — it was great seeing you again. I'm going to head out. There are a few things I have to take care of. I'll be leaving Long Beach next month. I got a scholarship for U.C. Berkeley that starts in January."

Those gorgeous eyes widened. "You got a scholarship for Berkeley? Awesome. What in?"

Emilio grinned. At least he'd managed to impress her. "Business Administration." He shrugged. "I don't know what I'm going to do with it yet, but it seems like it'd be a pretty interesting degree."

"Well, that's great, Emilio. I wish you the best of luck."

"I wish you the best of luck too, Sarita."

They both meant it.

After they parted ways, he took a walk around the deck. It was such a magnificent ship. He would miss it.

When he went back in to say goodbye to the bride and groom, little Marisol, intent on eating a cupcake, walked right into him. "Whooaa — hey there." She looked up at him, her face covered with chocolate. He smiled down at her. "That looks good. Can I have a taste?"

She shrank back at once. With a vehement shake of her head, she ran off.

Chuckling to himself, he thought, You're batting a thousand with all the girls tonight, aren't you, dude?

It was clear, crisp night in Long Beach. The moon was headed into her last quarter. In the dark, the water was the color of aged cabernet, and the harbor lights reflected along its surface in misty blues and smoky pinks. The *Queen* looked especially regal draped in strands of tiny fairy lamps that winked in the darkness like yellow diamonds against black silk.

Jane and Antoni could see all this from the main deck of the *Gabriella* where they lay, wrapped in blankets and each other. It was a spectacular view, but on a November night, a chilly one.

"I'm freezing my arse off," Jane complained, as she snuggled closer to Antoni.

"Get dressed and go below."

"Not yet. If I get dressed, I'll feel that I have to go back. I want to stay here with you. Just a few moments longer."

He held her close, trying to warm her with his arms and legs. "There'll be fireworks soon. Right off the upper deck, compliments of the bride and groom. Good God, Jane — your feet are like block of ice."

"Fireworks now? I thought they were at midnight?"

He reached across to the deck chair where he'd piled his clothing, and picked up his watch. "It's ten to twelve."

"Oh, no. It can't be that late. I've got to get back. The party will be over soon. I've got to help them sort everything out for tomorrow." She'd only just started to fumble around for her clothes when all the lights in the harbor and on the *Mary* went black. "Blast. I can't see a thing."

She heard him shift into a sitting position. "Hold on. I'll get a flashlight."

A light beamed from the top deck of the *Mary*. "Oh, well done. They're starting them early. Now at least I can see where I left my damn knickers."

"Jane. Am I really seeing this?" His voice sounded odd.

"What?" She sat sideways on their lounger as she wiggled into her panties. "Where's my brassiere? Is it on your side?" She glanced back at him over her shoulder. He was crying, facing the *Mary*, the light shining off her reflecting in his tears. "What's —?" She swiveled around in that direction, looked up, and gasped.

A little girl was standing at the rail of the top deck. She appeared to be looking down and across…at them. Her hair was gold — or was that just the light reflecting? From such a distance, with so much brightness surrounding her, it was hard to tell. Her features were barely discernible. And yet…

Jane was staring up at her incredulously. "No. It can't be. Antoni, it can't be." Jane kept her eyes fixed on the little girl, who stood above her radiantly. The light shifted, and for a split second her smile was visible, an eager, mischievous, happy smile. Jane was sure she'd seen that smile before — the last time she'd kissed her daughter goodbye to go off on a boat trip with her father.

"Oh, dear God!" Jane felt her whole being quake. Yet, even as she sprang up, she still wasn't sure. "Is it her? Can this possibly be true?"

"I don't know. I can't see her face clearly. But it looks so much like her. This is unbelievable. Just unbelievable." He was so choked up he could barely get the words out.

Jane made up her mind. "It is her, Antoni, it's *her*! Oh, *look* at her. She looks beautiful. It has to be her." Jane began waving wildly, crying, sniffling, smiling, and at the same time, pulling the blankets up around them more securely. "We're nearly naked. What a way for her to see us."

Antoni hadn't taken his eyes off the top deck. "But, how? How would she be here — from across two oceans? It doesn't make sense." Nonetheless, he too, was hoping against hope. "Are you sure it's her?"

"Look — there's someone else with her now." Jane had moved to the very edge of the hull, her husband's arm around her the only thing preventing her from falling overboard. Oh, she *wished* she were closer and could get a better view.

"It's Jackie! I know her by her hair and her nightdress. Oh! Antoni — do you see? Do you see what Gabriella's doing?"

Transfixed, they watched as the taller girl leaned down and held out her hand to the smaller girl, who was finally free. Hesitantly, Jackie took it, and became encircled by the same light as Gabriella.

In a flash, Jane understood. "Of course." Her voice was filled with wonder. "I've just realized — it makes sense why she's here, why she's the one who'd come for Jackie. It's the Day of the Dead." Jane looked up at him. "This is *her* boat, Antoni. The thing she loved in life most of all. And the two people she loved most are on it together, for the first time in two years." Looking back to the top deck of the *Mary*, Jane decided she would accept that as true. "We've called her to us."

Antoni couldn't speak. He could only squeeze Jane's hand. He still wasn't sure, but like Jane, he wanted so much to believe. And as he watched the scene above, it came to him that, whether the child they were seeing was truly Gabriella or wasn't, his daughter was at peace. Not cold, not frightened, not calling out for her daddy to come rescue her from the waves, but at peace. He hadn't cried as much as he had in the last two days since he was a small boy. No — since Gabriella's death. This time the tears brought him comfort and closure.

In adoration, Jane kept her eyes on the spirit she was sure was Gabriella's. Both she and Antoni exclaimed when, with her arm around Jaclyn, she waved. In a flash, the two little girls vanished. The brightness disappeared, Jane and Antoni blinked, and then, with another sudden burst of light, the fireworks aboard the *Mary* commenced.

Shouts of laughter and cheers came from the Promenade Deck. They saw that all the wedding guests had poured out of The Secret Spice Café to observe the orchestra of colors and lights as they splashed across the sky with pops and booms. Sheltered from sight in the shadows of the *Gabriella*, Jane picked up the marigolds she'd taken from Angela's cake and tossed them into the sea: one for her darling daughter, and one for Jackie Torin. Then she put her arms around Antoni. They held each other as they stood in the cool night air, watching the celebration, rejoicing in what they'd seen.

And on this evening that was truly enchanted with luminosity and love, the *Queen* could rest peacefully in her berth. For now, all was well.

AUTHOR'S NOTE

(Warning: If you're one of those who likes to read this part first, you should know that it contains spoilers)

The fun thing about writing a novel, which is by its very name a work of fiction, is that you can weave actual events into it, yet at the same time, tweak those events or add your own details to them in order to serve your story.

All the facts mentioned about the *RMS Queen Mary* were researched thoroughly and are historically accurate, as far as I know, with a few exceptions. One example is that the *Queen Mary* did almost capsize while operating as a troopship, but the year and location of where this happened was changed. The actual event took place in 1942, "608 nautical miles from Scotland." Approximately 16,000 United States Army troops were aboard when she nearly capsized, "broadsided during a gale by a 92-foot wave." There may or may not have been prisoners of war aboard when it happened, and it's never been reported than any murders took place during this occurrence at sea.

Here are a few other things about the story you might like to know:

» Although not aboard the *Queen Mary*, the body of a real WWII soldier was found more than sixty years after the soldier went missing in action. This has happened more than once. One of the most heartbreaking stories, most similar to the soldier's story in the novel, is live-linked in the *Cooking for Ghosts* Reader's Guide, which follows this note, if you're reading this on an e-reader. If you're reading a printed version, you can download the Reader's Guide for free at: www.CookingForGhosts.com, or scan it using the QR on page 331.

» Little Jaclyn Torin did exist and, sadly, did drown in a swimming pool aboard the *RMS Queen Mary*. To this day, tourists visit the ship to see if they can catch a glimpse of her spirit, which is believed to haunt that now abandoned pool. I didn't know about Jackie when I first stayed aboard the *Mary*, nor did I know that the ship is considered to be one of the most haunted places in the world. What I experienced during my stay...well, let's just say it put me on to paranormal activity and inspired this entire trilogy of novels. (Again, in the Reader's Guide, there's a link to a video where you can hear me talking about that incident, but after this, I won't reference the guide again, since you've probably guessed that there are various links in it about everything discussed here.)

» There do exist spices that may cause hallucinations and/or a hypnotic state. And the forward-thinking village of Kambalwadi, India, where Rohini learned about healing herbs, also exists as described in the story. You can learn more in — Oops. I said I wasn't going to mention the you-know-what again.

» "Terror Fest" is an actual event that was held aboard the ship in 2004, the year the story is set. As of this writing, this fun-scary event is renamed "Dark Harbor," and takes place every October.

» Tony Chi is a real designer. To see his beautiful designs which inspired my descriptions of The Secret Spice Café, visit his website at www.tonychi.com. In fact, there are a number of famous people mentioned, some by name, some not, such as the unidentified former Republican governor of California who actually was married to a Democrat, and who actually did champion a universal health care plan. I doubt this was because of any shrimp he ate, but who knows? That's the point: The celebrities written into the story are included for fun only. I know nothing about their personal lives nor am I making any judgements about them. Perez Hilton has that market covered.

» The names of every character, even the ones mentioned only in passing, have personal, derivative, or historical significance. Oliver Jenkins is named for the gym friend who demonstrated strangulation techniques. In the same villainous vein, "Naag" means "serpent." In contrast, "Zahir" means "light" and "helper." I named Lee after a real-life minister friend in Texas, who supported the right for gays to marry. But his surname is in honor of another friend, who told me a story about his father that I'll never forget. I used the name with his permission, and it's probably too much to hope that Lee's tale gives him some closure. Lee's son, Jack, is named for my deceased father-in-law, a very good man who loved to talk books with me. I wish he were here to read this one. And Rohini's assumed surname, "Mehta" is to honor Deepa Mehta, an Indian filmmaker whose brilliant films champion women's rights. All other names also have special meaning to me.

» The mention of Deepa Mehta reminds me to point out that although *Cooking for Ghosts* is written in a lighthearted manner, the theme of the oppression of women is a serious one to me. The plight of the Indian widow — Rohini's plight — is real and tragic. No one illustrates that more vividly than Deepa Mehta in her films, and I felt I had to pay tribute to her in my story. A great article to read on the subject is, "Women Under Siege: The Ongoing Plight of India's Widows," by Sara Barrera and Eva Corbacho. But even some Western women feel suffocated under the weight of chauvinistic convention. The character Angela carries the emotional baggage of her upbringing too. Even though she resents her lack of independence, she allows negative habits and tradition to affect every decision she makes, a tug-of-war for many women, no matter where we're from.

» The main characters are diverse in birthplace, background, socio-economic status, and life experience. I tried to present their distinct voices with authenticity. Some of the idioms they use you might not recognize. One work-in-progress reader thought Jane's tendency to say "you lot" (meaning "you people") was a typo. It's my hope that their varied ethnicities only make the discovery of their hidden similarities more poignant as the story unfolds.

» The book, *Queen Mary,* is a beautiful photo history book by James Steele. But you won't find the "facts" Sarita reads from it about Dolores Simpson anywhere on its pages, because that tragic figure exists only in my imagination, I'm happy to report. Speaking of tragic figures, Sarita is all grown up, and back as the main protagonist in Book II, A SORCERER IN THE GALLEY. Her story has a much happier ending than Dolores's. If you'd like to read a chapter of Book II, you'll find it on my website. And for those who thought Emilio deserved more than unrequited love, he gets his chance at happiness, but not before some pretty scary stuff happens, in Book III, The FIENDISH HAUNTING OF THE RASPBERRY CHOCOLATE TRUFFLE TARTS.

That's all I have room for, but if you enjoyed reading the information here, you can find out more about the book series, and again, a live link version of the Reader's Guide at: www.CookingForGhosts.com. Or, as I also mentioned earlier, if you have a smart phone, you can also scan the QR code on the next page to take you there. If you liked the novel itself, I'd be so thankful if you could bring yourself to write a review about it on Amazon. In fact, even if you hated it, go ahead and write a review there. I'll certainly try to learn from my mistakes, but in addition to that, the more reviews the better, even if they're terrible, so please feel free to express yourself. If you have any questions not answered in the guide, or if you'd just like to say hello, I'd love to hear from you. Like most everyone else, I have a Facebook page, or you can send me an email at: patricia@patricia-Vdavis.com (mind the "V" in the suffix.) There's also a Secret Spice Book Series Facebook page, where you'll find updates on the second and third books in the series, photos, contests, giveaways, and even bonus epilogues. The Reader's Guide offers live links to that page and many other fun and informative sites.

Thank you so much for reading! Hope to see you back for A SORCERER IN THE GALLEY: Book II of "The Secret Spice Café Trilogy." To read an excerpt, visit: www.TheSecretSpice.com .

AUTHOR BIO

Patricia V. Davis is the author of ***Harlot's Sauce: A Memoir of Food, Family, Love, Loss, and Greece***, and ***The Diva Doctrine: 16 Universal Principles Every Woman Needs to Know***. COOKING FOR GHOSTS is her latest work, and the first book in "The Secret Spice Cafe Trilogy." For a number of years, she was a high school English teacher, teaching in Athens, Greece, and Queens, New York. She's an advocate for human rights, and all of her work encourages female dynamism. To that end, she also founded The Women's PowerStrategy™ Conference. Patricia lives with her poker player husband, and so divides her time between southern Nevada and Northern California. For news on the upcoming books, contests and giveaways, join The Secret Spice Book Series page on Facebook, or visit www.TheSecretSpice.com

CPSIA information can be obtained
at www.ICGtesting.com
Printed in the USA
LVOW12s2207121217
559534LV00015B/1998/P